The Whispering Mummy and Others

The Hippocampus Press Classics of Gothic Horror Series

CLASSICS
OF
GOTHIC
HORROR

Edited by S. T. Joshi

The Whispering Mummy and Others

By Sax Rohmer

Edited by S. T. Joshi

Hippocampus Press

New York

Contents

Introduction

The work of British writer Sax Rohmer (1883–1959) was once immensely popular, and even now his name conjures up images of bygone bestsellerdom, something on the order of Edgar Wallace or Dennis Wheatley. While a relatively modest proportion of his bountiful work could be said to enter the domain of the weird or supernatural, enough of it does to make all readers and scholars of the genre take account of his writings, whether in the short story or the novel.

Born Arthur Henry Ward in Birmingham, England, on February 15, 1883 (at the age of eighteen he replaced his middle name, Henry, with Sarsfield), Rohmer was the son of Irish parents. His family moved to London in 1885, although he did not begin formal schooling until the age of nine. Rather than attending college, Rohmer decided to take the Civil Service examination, but he failed; he later became a bank clerk, but the drudgery of the work compelled him to resign. It was at this point that he first attempted fiction writing—but his work was uniformly rejected. A brief stint on the staff of a newspaper, the *Commercial Intelligence,* was also unsuccessful. Rohmer then returned more determinedly to the task of fiction writing, and by 1903 he achieved success with the simultaneous acceptance of two stories by leading periodicals of the day. "The Mysterious Mummy" appeared in *Pearson's Weekly Christmas Extra* (November 26, 1903), and "The Leopard-Couch" appeared in *Chambers's Journal* on January 30, 1904.

Rohmer did not restrict himself to writing fiction. For a number of years, even after his initial breakthrough into print, he was attracted to the theatre and other performance arts. He wrote much material for a comedian, but the act failed when the comedian developed extreme stage fright. Over the years Rohmer also produced a number of performances in music halls and theatres.

7

He adopted the pseudonym Sax Rohmer early in his career, but did not apply it to his works of fiction until 1912. He later explained the origin and meaning of the pseudonym as follows: "In ancient Saxon 'sax' means 'blade'; 'rohmer' equals 'roamer.' I substituted an 'h' for the 'a' as a gesture in the direction of phonetics—pretty obscure gesture, I guess."[1] Strangely enough, even his wife, Elizabeth, whom he married in 1909, adopted the pseudonym, becoming Elizabeth Sax Rohmer.

A year after his marriage, Rohmer's first book, *Pause!* (1910), appeared. It was an anonymous collection of essays and sketches, and his second book, *Little Tich* (1911), about a popular comedian of the period, was similarly unrepresentative of the bulk of his published work. But in 1911 Rohmer wrote a series of sketches about the Limehouse district of London, then populated chiefly by Chinese immigrants, and it was in part from this work that he derived the idea of his celebrated villain, Dr. Fu Manchu. Rohmer began writing stories about this evil Oriental, and they were collected in *The Mystery of Dr. Fu-Manchu* (1913). (The hyphen in Fu Manchu was later dropped.) Rohmer attempted to deflect accusations of racism in his portrayal of Fu Manchu and his cohorts by declaring that his depictions were not intended to be as broad-based as they appeared to be:

> Nowadays, I like to think that a Chinese and a Chinaman are not the same thing. When I began writing, "Chinaman" was no more than the accepted term for a native of China. The fact that it has since taken on a derogatory meaning is due mostly to the behavior of those Chinamen who lived in such places as Limehouse.
>
> Of course, not the whole Chinese population of Limehouse was criminal. But it contained a large number of persons who had left their own country for the most urgent of reasons. These people knew no way of making a living other than by the criminal activities which had made China too hot for them. They brought their crimes with them. Naturally, it took our police some time to get their measure. They were dealing with enemies who did nothing in the expected way, who

---

1. Cited in Cay Van Ash and Elizabeth Sax Rohmer, *Master of Villainy: A Biography of Sax Rohmer* (London: Tom Stacey, 1972), 39.

thought differently, who communicated with one another in a language that few Englishmen could speak and fewer still could read.[2]

Whether this account sufficiently exculpates Rohmer from charges of racism and stereotyping is highly debatable. The irony, however, as far as his own writing career is concerned is that the popularity of the Fu Manchu stories and novels—they would fill a total of fourteen books, out of the more than fifty that he published in a long lifetime—became a kind of albatross around his neck. Over the next thirty or forty years, there were many occasions when Rohmer wished to write other work but was compelled by economic necessity to churn out more Fu Manchu tales in order to bring in an income.

For our present purposes, we need not take much account of the Fu Manchu volumes, because they are by and large adventure or crime tales without any hint of the supernatural aside from the vague patina of exoticism engendered by the Oriental atmosphere. But Rohmer was always attracted to the supernatural. Although he had renounced belief in religion at an early age, throughout his life he exhibited an interest in spiritualism and occultism; indeed, he believed that one of the houses in which he resided, shortly after World War I, was haunted. Rohmer also briefly joined the Order of the Golden Dawn and a Rosicrucian society. These interests led him to write the nonfiction volume *The Romance of Sorcery* (1914).

What is more, Orientalism was not his chief interest, either in literature or in life; instead, it was Egypt. Rohmer and his wife had first visited Egypt in 1913, and their exploration of the Pyramid of Meydûm on that trip led directly to the writing of *Brood of the Witch-Queen,* serialized in the *Premier* in 1914 but not appearing in book form until 1918. He wrote numerous stories about that ancient land of pyramids and Pharaohs, some of them collected in *Tales of Secret Egypt* (1918) and the much later volume *Egyptian Nights* (1944; published in the U.S. as *Bimbâshi Barûk of Egypt*). If he had had his preference, Rohmer would have written much more about Egypt and much less about the mustachioed Fu Manchu.

---

2. Cited in *Master of Villainy* 73.

Rohmer's literary and personal life underwent some turmoil in the aftermath of World War I. Toward the end of the war he worked in the office of military intelligence, although it is not clear what his actual responsibilities in this capacity were. After the war, on a book tour to the United States, Rohmer engaged in an affair with a young Englishwoman. This affair continued desultorily for years, even after his wife discovered it. Some years later, going alone to the island of Madeira to rest after a bout of overwork, he became involved with an eighteen-year-old Frenchwoman. Elizabeth found out about this affair also and demanded that he spend some time alone in the United States to decide whether he wished to remain with her or not. There was an ultimate reconciliation, and the couple continued in their marriage. In the later 1920s they took frequent trips to the Riviera, as well as another trip to Egypt. On this occasion Rohmer spent a night alone inside the Great Pyramid. Nothing untoward happened—except that he was pelted by large quantities of bat dung.

Although Rohmer was by this time one of the most popular and highly paid writers in the English-speaking world, he was constantly in need of money, thanks in large part to a somewhat extravagant lifestyle. The American magazine *Collier's* was continually dunning him to write more Fu Manchu stories, and he ultimately complied; *Daughter of Fu Manchu* appeared in 1931, the first original book of Fu Manchu (not counting the reprint omnibus *The Book of Fu Manchu,* 1929) since 1917. Five more Fu Manchu books appeared in the 1930s. Meanwhile, Rohmer continued his wide travels, visiting Panama and Haiti among other places.

During World War II Rohmer again worked in military intelligence. After the war, he and his wife moved to the United States, chiefly to avoid the high taxation on wealthy individuals instituted by the new Labour government; moreover, most of Rohmer's markets were now on this side of the water. He continued writing into the 1950s, but his work was chiefly in the mystery or adventure field. He was stricken with Asiatic flu in early 1959. Returning to England, he died on June 1, 1959.

Of Rohmer's prolific output of novels and tales, only a relatively small proportion is of interest to devotees of the weird and supernatural.

The Dream Detective (1920) features the psychic detective Morris Klaw, who solves his cases by his ability to visualize the last images seen by a dead person. But aside from this supernatural premise, the tales in this volume are orthodox mysteries.

The story collections *Tales of Secret Egypt* (1918), *The Haunting of Low Fennel* (1920), and *Tales of Chinatown* (1922) contain a certain proportion of weirdness, and all the short stories in this volume are taken from these collections. In many cases, Rohmer engages in either the "explained supernatural" (where supernaturalism is suggested, only to be explained away by natural means) or the "ambiguously supernatural" (where doubt remains to the end as to whether the supernatural has come into play or not). In "Breath of Allah," for example, a man thinks he can *see* words coming out of a person's mouth—but this is explained as a hallucination induced by hashish fumes. In "The Whispering Mummy" the mummy's whispers are explained as the result of trickery. But in "The Death-Ring of Sneferu" and "Lord of the Jackals," supernaturalism *may* come into play; indeed, in the latter story it is difficult to account for the sudden appearance of thousands of jackals in any other fashion. Less convincing is "The Haunting of Low Fennel," where the ghostly phenomena are unconvincingly accounted for by an emanation of vapor from the ground.

"Tchériapin" is without question Rohmer's finest weird tale, and it is authentically supernatural—or perhaps pseudo-science-fictional might be a better term. Here the premise is the discovery by a chemist of a formula that allows for rendering any vegetable or organic substance as hard as diamonds. One wonders whether Rohmer was influenced by Robert W. Chambers's tale "The Mask," in *The King in Yellow* (1895), where a somewhat similar petrifying formula is postulated. In any event, the story becomes grimly effective. "The Curse of a Thousand Kisses" fuses horror and poignancy in its suggestion that a hideous old woman is the centuries-old Scheherazade, the victim of a curse.

Brood of the Witch-Queen is Rohmer's most extensive exploration of the supernatural. This account of Antony Ferrara, a seductive young man who turns out to be the son of a "witch-queen" of ancient Egypt, follows the tradition of Egyptian horror set by Richard Marsh's *The Beetle* (1897) and Bram Stoker's *The Jewel of Seven Stars* (1903). Although there are scattered mentions of elementals and vampires, the most effective supernatural manifestations—chiefly hallucinations induced by Ferrara upon those who are seeking to eliminate him—are accounted for as a kind of elaborate hypnotism. The novel could have been somewhat more effective if Rohmer had not portrayed Ferrara as purely evil and his antagonists as purely good; and the romance element he includes—Ferrara is seeking to dominate the fetching Myra Duquesne, chiefly to gain control of her fortune—is contrived and conventional. But the novel does succeed in gaining cumulative power as Ferrara's opponents seem repeatedly unable to curtail his supernatural depredations.

Subsequent work by Rohmer in the novel form also featured the supernatural in somewhat lesser degrees. *The Quest of the Sacred Slipper* (1919) implausibly focuses on a slipper of Mohammed whose theft impels its Islamic owners to engage in various supernatural shenanigans to regain it. *The Green Eyes of Bast* (1920) returns us to Egypt, although it is really a mystery novel with supernatural interludes; and its account of a female child born with certain catlike features is unconvincing. Also with an Egyptian substratum is *She Who Sleeps: A Romance of New York and the Nile* (1928), where it is suggested that an ancient Egyptian priestess has awoken from a state of suspended animation, although in the end the supernatural manifestation is dispelled as trickery. Finally, there is *The Bat Flies Low* (1935), a weak occultist novel about a quest for a lamp of perpetual light.

Rohmer was a prodigious plot-weaver and tale-spinner, but there are times when his very facility seems to work against him: there is a distinct sense of the "slick" and the mechanical in much of his work, right down to the level of diction and characterization. The influence of H. Rider Haggard, Rudyard Kipling, and other writers of mystery and exotic adventure tales is patent, and all too often it seems as if Rohmer is just going through the motions to churn out another tale or serial for the popular magazines. But his authentic enthusiasm for ancient Egypt and his admirable ability to portray landscape, whether in far-flung climes or in his native England, as well as his unfailing skill at compelling narrative, render his work as readable now as it was when it was first written. No one will ever mistake Sax Rohmer for a writer of profound depth or meaning, but as one who can grasp readers' attention and keep them turning the pages he has few equals.

—S. T. JOSHI

A Note on This Edition

The stories included in this edition are derived from Sax Rohmer's early collections. Dates of original magazine publication are provided where known:

Tales of Secret Egypt (London: Methuen, 1918; New York: McBride, 1919): "The Death-Ring of Sneferu" (*Premier Magazine,* November 1917); "Breath of Allah" (*Premier Magazine,* February 1918); "The Whispering Mummy" (*Premier Magazine,* March 1918); "Lord of the Jackals"; "Harun Pasha" (*Storyteller,* July 1915); "In the Valley of the Sorceress" (*Premier Magazine,* January 1916).

The Haunting of Low Fennel (London: Pearson, 1920): "The Haunting of Low Fennel"; "The Valley of the Just"; "The Master of Hollow Grange" (*New Magazine,* June 1918); "The Curse of a Thousand Kisses" (*Premier Magazine,* November 1918).

Tales of Chinatown (London: Cassell, 1922; New York: Doubleday, Page, 1922): "The White Hat" (*Storyteller,* June 1920); "Tchériapin" (*Sovereign Magazine,* April 1920); "The Hand of the Mandarin Quong" (*Munsey's Magazine,* February 1922 [as "The Mystery of the Shriveled Hand"]); "The Key of the Temple of Heaven."

The Death-Ring of Sneferu

I

The orchestra had just ceased playing; and, taking advantage of the lull in the music, my companion leaned confidentially forward, shooting suspicious glances all around him, although there was nothing about the well-dressed after-dinner throng filling Shepheard's that night to have aroused misgiving in the mind of a cinema anarchist.

"I have a very big thing in view," he said, speaking in a husky whisper. "I shall be one up on you, Kernaby, if I pull it off."

He glanced sideways, in the manner of a pantomime brigand, at a party of New York tourists, our immediate neighbors, and from them to an elderly peer with whom I was slightly acquainted and who, in addition to his being stone deaf, had never noticed anything in his life, much less attempted so fatiguing an operation as intrigue.

"Indeed," I commented; and rang the bell with the purpose in view of ordering another cooling beverage.

True, I might be the Egyptian representative of a Birmingham commercial enterprise, but I did not gladly suffer the society of this individual, whose only claim to my acquaintance lay in the fact that he was in the employ of a rival house. My lack of interest palpably disappointed him; but I thought little of the man's qualities as a connoisseur and less of his company. His name was Theo Bishop and I fancy that his family was associated with the tanning industry. I have since thought more kindly of poor Bishop, but at the time of which I write nothing could have pleased me better than his sudden dissolution.

Perhaps unconsciously I had allowed my boredom to become rudely apparent; for Bishop slightly turned his head aside, and—

"Right-o, Kernaby," he said; "I know you think I am an ass, so we will say no more about it. Another cocktail?"

And now I became conscience-stricken; for mingled with the disappointment in Bishop's tone and manner was another note. Vaguely it occurred to me that the man was yearning for sympathy of some kind, that he was bursting to unbosom himself, and that the vanity of a successful rival was by no means wholly responsible. I have since placed that ambiguous note and recognized it for a note of tragedy. But at the time I was deaf to its pleading.

We chatted then for some while longer on indifferent topics, Bishop being, as I have indicated, a man difficult to offend; when, having correspondence to deal with, I retired to my own room. I suppose I had been writing for about an hour, when a servant came to announce a caller. Taking an ordinary visiting-card from the brass salver, I read—

Abû Tabâh.

No title preceded the name, no address followed, but I became aware of something very like a nervous thrill as I stared at the name of my visitor. Personality is one of the profoundest mysteries of our being. Of the person whose card I held in my hand I knew little, practically nothing; his actions, if at times irregular, had never been wantonly violent; his manner was gentle as that of a mother to a baby and his singular reputation among the natives I thought I could afford to ignore; for the Egyptian, like the Celt, with all his natural endowments, is yet a child at heart. Therefore I cannot explain why, sitting there in my room in Shepheard's Hotel, I knew and recognized, at the name of Abû Tabâh, the touch of fear.

"I will see him downstairs," I said.

Then, as the servant was about to depart, recognizing that I had made a concession to that strange sentiment which the Imám Abû Tabâh had somehow inspired in me—

"No," I added; "show him up here to my room."

A few moments later the man returned again, carrying the brass salver, upon which lay a sealed envelope. I took it up in surprise, noting that it was one belonging to the hotel, and, ere opening it—

"Where is my visitor?" I said in Arabic.

"He regrets that he cannot stay," replied the man; "but he sends you this letter."

Greatly mystified, I dismissed the servant and tore open the envelope. Inside, upon a sheet of hotel notepaper I found this remarkable message—

KERNABY PASHA—
There are reasons why I cannot stay to see you personally, but I would have you believe that this warning is dictated by nothing but friendship. Grave peril threatens. It is associated with the hieroglyphic—

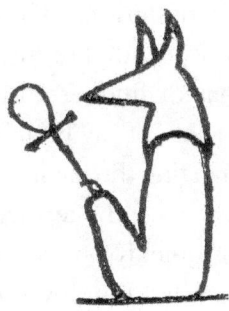

If you would avert it, and if you value your life, avoid all contact with anything bearing this figure.

Abû Tabâh.

The mystery deepened. There had been something incongruous about the modern European visiting-card used by this representative of Islam, this living illustration of the *Arabian Nights;* now, his incomprehensible "warning" plunged me back again into the mediæval Orient to which he properly belonged. Yet I knew Abû Tabâh, for all his romantic aspect, to be eminently practical, and I could not credit him with descending to the methods of melodrama.

As I studied the precise wording of the note, I seemed to see the slim figure of its author before me, black-robed, white-turbaned, and urbane, his delicate ivory hands crossed and resting upon the head of the ebony cane without which I had never seen him. Almost, I succumbed to a sort of subjective hallucination; Abû Tabâh became a veritable presence, and the poetic beauty of his face struck me anew, as, fixing upon me his eyes, which were like the eyes of a gazelle, he spoke the strange words cited above, in the pure and polished English which he held at command, and described in the air, with a long nervous forefinger, the queer device which symbolized the Ancient Egyptian god, Set, the Destroyer.

Of course, it was the aura of a powerful personality, clinging even to the written message; but there was something about the impression made upon me which argued for the writer's sincerity.

That Abû Tabâh was some kind of agent, recognized—at any rate unofficially—by the authorities, I knew or shrewdly surmised; but the exact nature of his activities, and how he reconciled them with his religious duties, remained profoundly mysterious. The episode had rendered further work impossible, and I descended to the terrace, with no more definite object in view than that of finding a quiet corner where I might meditate in the congenial society of my briar, and at the same time seek inspiration from the ever-changing throng in the Shâria Kâmel Pasha.

I had scarcely set my foot upon the terrace, however, ere a hand was laid upon my arm. Turning quickly I recognized, in the dusk, Hassan es-Sugra, for many years a trusted employee of the British Archæological Society.

His demeanor was at once excited and furtive, and I recognized with something akin to amazement that he, also, had a story to unfold. I mentally catalogued this eventful evening "the night of strange confidences."

Seated at a little table on the deserted balcony (for the evening was very chilly) and directly facing the shop of Philip, the dealer in Arab woodwork, Hassan es-Sugra told his wonder tale; and as he told it I knew that Fate had cast me, willy-nilly, for a part in some comedy upon which the curtain had already risen here in Cairo, and whereof the second act should be played in perhaps the most ancient setting which the hand of man has builded. As the narrative unrolled itself before me, I perceived wheels within wheels; I was wholly absorbed, yet half incredulous.

". . . When the professor abandoned work on the pyramid, Kernaby Pasha," he said, bending eagerly forward and laying his muscular brown hand upon my sleeve, "it was not because there was no more to learn there."

"I am aware of this, O Hassan," I interrupted, "it was in order that they might carry on the work at the Pyramid of Illahûn, which resulted in a find of jewelry almost unique in the annals of Egyptology."

"Do I not know all this!" exclaimed Hassan impatiently; "and was not mine the hand that uncovered the golden uræus? But the work projected at the Pyramid of Méydûm was never completed, and I can tell you why."

I stared at him through the gloom; for I had already some idea respecting the truth of this matter.

"It was that the men, over two hundred of them, refused to enter the passage again," he whispered dramatically, "it was because misfortune and disaster visited more than one who had penetrated to a certain place therein." He bent further forward. "The Pyramid of Méydûm is the home of a powerful *Efreet,* Kernaby Pasha! But I who was the last to leave it, know what is concealed there. In a certain place, low down in the corner of the King's Chamber, is a ring of gold, bearing a cartouche. It is the royal ring of the Pharaoh who built the pyramid."

He ceased, watching me intently. I did not doubt Hassan's word, for I had always counted him a man of integrity; but there was much that was obscure and much that was mysterious in his story.

"Why did you not bring it away?" I asked.

"I feared to touch it, Kernaby Pasha; it is an evil talisman. Until to-day I have feared to speak of it."

"And to-day?"

Hassan extended his hands, palms upward.

"I am threatened with the loss of my house," he said simply, "if I do not find a certain sum of money within a period of twelve days."

I sat resting my chin on my hand and staring into the face of Hassan es-Sugra. Could it be that from superstitious motives such a treasure had indeed been abandoned? Could it be that Fate had delivered into my hands a relic so priceless as the signet-ring of Sneferu, one of the earliest Memphite Pharaohs? Since I had recently incurred the displeasure of my principals, Messrs. Moses, Murphy & Co., of Birmingham, the mere anticipation of such a "find" was sufficient to raise my professional enthusiasm to white heat, and in those few moments of silence I had decided upon instant action.

"Meet me at Rikka Station, to-morrow morning at nine o'clock," I said, "and arrange for donkeys to carry us to the pyramid."

II

On my arrival at Rikka, and therefore at the very outset of my inquiry, I met with what one slightly prone to superstition might have regarded as an unfortunate omen. A native funeral was passing out of the
town amid the wailing of women and the chanting by the *Yemeneeyeh,*
of the Profession of the Faith, with its queer monotonous cadences, a
performance which despite its familiarity in the Near East never failed
to affect me unpleasantly. By the token of the *tarbûsh* upon the bier, I
knew that this was a man who was being hurried to his lonely resting-
place on the fringe of the desert.

As the procession wound its way out across the sands, I saw to the
removal of my baggage and joined Hassan es-Sugra, who awaited me by
the wooden barrier. I perceived immediately that something was wrong
with the man; he was palpably laboring under the influence of some
strong excitement, and his dark eyes regarded me almost fearfully. He
was muttering to himself like one suffering from an over-indulgence in
Hashish, and I detected the words *"Allahu akbar!"* (God is most great)
several times repeated.

"What ails you, Hassan, my friend?" I said; and noting how his gaze
persistently returned to the melancholy procession wending its way towards the little Moslem cemetery:—"Was the dead man some relation
of yours?"

"No, no, Kernaby Pasha," he muttered gutturally, and moistened
his lips with his tongue, "I was but slightly acquainted with him."

"Yet you are much disturbed."

"Not at all, Kernaby Pasha," he assured me; "not in the slightest."

By which familiar formula I knew that Hassan es-Sugra would conceal from me the cause of his distress, and therefore, since I had no ap-
petite for further mysteries, I determined to learn it from another
source.

"See to the loading of the donkey," I directed him—for three sleek
little animals were standing beside him, patiently awaiting the toil of the
day.

Hassan setting about the task with a cheerful alacrity obviously artificial, I approached the native station master, with whom I was acquaint-

ed, and put to him a number of questions respecting his important functions—in which I was not even mildly interested. But to the Oriental mind a direct inquiry is an affront, almost an insult; and to have inquired bluntly the name of the deceased and the manner of his death would have been the best way to have learned nothing whatever about the matter. Therefore having discussed in detail the slothful incompetence of Arab ticket collectors and the lazy condition and innate viciousness of Egyptian porters as a class, I mentioned incidentally that I had observed a funeral leaving Rikka.

The station master (who was bursting to talk about this very matter, but who would have declined on principle to do so had I definitely questioned him) now unfolded to me the strange particulars respecting the death of one, Ahmed Abdulla, who had been a retired dragoman though some time employed as an excavator.

"He rode out one night upon his white donkey," said my informant, "and no man knows whither he went. But it is believed, Kernaby Pasha, that it was to the Haram el-Kaddâb" (the False Pyramid)—extending his hand to where, beyond the belt of fertility, the tomb of Sneferu upreared its three platforms from the fringe of the desert. "To enter the pyramid even in day time is to court misfortune; to enter at night is to fall into the hands of the powerful *Efreet* who dwells there. His donkey returned without him, and therefore search was made for Ahmed Abdulla. He was found the next day"—again the long arm shot out towards the desert—"dead upon the sands, near the foot of the pyramid."

I looked into the face of the speaker; beyond doubt he was in deadly earnest.

"Why should Ahmed Abdulla have wanted to visit such a place at night?" I asked.

My acquaintance lowered his voice, muttered *"Sahâm Allah fee 'adoo ed—dîn!"* (May God transfix the enemies of the religion) and touched his forehead, his mouth, and his breast with the iron ring which he wore.

"There is a great treasure concealed there, Kernaby Pasha," he replied; "a treasure hidden from the world in the days of Suleyman the Great, sealed with his seal, and guarded by the servants of Gánn Ibn-Gánn."

"So you think the guardian *ginn* killed Ahmed Abdulla?"

The station master muttered invocations, and—

"There are things which may not be spoken of," he said; "but those who saw him dead say that he was terrible to look upon. A great *Welee,* a man of wisdom famed throughout Egypt, has been summoned to avert the evil; for if the anger of the *ginn* is aroused they may visit the most painful and unfortunate penalties upon all Rikka. . . ."

Half an hour later I set out, having confidentially informed the station master that I sought to obtain a fine turquoise necklet which I knew to be in the possession of the Sheikh of Méydûm. Little did I suspect how it was written that I should indeed visit the house of the venerable Sheikh. Out through the fields of young green corn, the palm groves and the sycamore orchards I rode, Hassan plodding silently behind me and leading the donkey who bore the baggage. Curious eyes watched our passage, from field, doorway, and *shadûf;* but nothing of note marked our journey save the tremendous heat of the sun at noon, beneath which I knew myself a fool to travel.

I camped on the western side of the pyramid, but well clear of the marshes, which are the home of countless wild-fowl. I had no idea how long it would take me to extract the coveted ring from its hiding-place (which Hassan had closely described to me); and, remembering the speculative glances of the villagers, I had no intention of exposing myself against the face of the pyramid until dusk should have come to cloak my operations.

Hassan es-Sugra, whose new taciturnity was remarkable and whose behavior was distinguished by an odd disquiet, set out with his gun to procure our dinner, and I mounted the sandy slope on the southwest of the pyramid, where from my cover behind a mound of rubbish, I studied through my field-glasses the belt of vegetation marking the course of the Nile. I could detect no sign of surveillance, but in view of the fact that the smuggling of relics out of Egypt is a punishable offence my caution was dictated by wisdom.

We dined excellently, Hassan the Silent and I, upon quail, tinned tomatoes, fresh dates, bread, and Vichy-water (to which in my own case was added a stiff three fingers of whisky).

When the newly risen moon cast an ebon shadow of the Pyramid of Sneferu upon the carpet of the sands, I made my way around the angle of the ancient building towards the mound on the northern side whereby one approaches the entrance. Three paces from the shadow's edge, I paused, transfixed, because of that which confronted me.

Outlined against the moon-bright sky upon a ridge of the desert behind and to the north of the great structure, stood the motionless figure of a man!

For a moment I thought that my mind had conjured up this phantasmal watcher, that he was a thing of moon-magic and not of flesh and blood. But as I stood regarding him, he moved, seemed to raise his head, then turned and disappeared beyond the crest.

How long I remained staring at the spot where lie had been I know not; but I was aroused from my useless contemplation by the jingling of camel bells. The sound came from behind me, stealing sweetly through the stillness from a great distance. I turned in a flash, whipped out my glasses and searched the remote fringe of the Fáyûm. Stately across the jeweled curtain of the night moved a caravan, blackly marked against that wondrous background. Three walking figures I counted, three laden donkeys, and two camels. Upon the first of the camels a man was mounted, upon the second was a *shibreeyeh,* a sort of covered litter, which I knew must conceal a woman. The caravan passed out of sight into the palm grove which conceals the village of Méydûm.

I returned my glasses to their case, and stood for some moments deep in reflection; then I descended the slope, to the tiny encampment where I had left Hassan es-Sugra. He was nowhere to be seen; and having waited some ten minutes I grew impatient, and raising my voice:

"Hassan!" I cried; "Hassan es-Sugra!"

No answer greeted me, although in the desert stillness the call must have been audible for miles. A second and a third time I called his name . . . and the only reply was the shrill note of a pyramid bat that swooped low above my head; the vast solitude of the sands swallowed up my voice and the walls of the Tomb of Sneferu mocked me with their echo, crying eerily:

"Hassan! Hassan es-Sugra. . . . Hassan! . . ."

III

This mysterious episode affected me unpleasantly, but did not divert me from my purpose: I succeeded in casting out certain demons of superstition who had sought to lay hold upon me; and a prolonged scrutiny of the surrounding desert somewhat allayed my fears of human surveillance. For my visit to the chamber in the heart of the ancient building I had arrayed myself in rubber-soled shoes, an old pair of drill trousers, and a pyjama jacket. A Colt repeater was in my hip pocket, and, in addition to several instruments which I thought might be useful in extracting the ring from its setting, I carried a powerful electric torch.

Seated on the threshold of the entrance, fifty feet above the desert level, I cast a final glance backward towards the Nile valley, then, the lighted torch carried in my jacket pocket, I commenced the descent of the narrow, sloping passage. Periodically, when some cranny between the blocks offered a foothold, I checked my progress, and inspected the steep path below for snake tracks.

Some two hundred and forty feet of labored descent discovered me in a sort of shallow cavern little more than a yard high and partly hewn out of the living rock which formed the foundation of the pyramid. In this place I found the heat to be almost insufferable, and the smell of remote mortality which assailed my nostrils from the sand-strewn floor threatened to choke me. For five minutes or more I lay there, bathed in perspiration, my nerves at high tension, listening for the slightest sound within or without. I cannot pretend that I was entirely master of myself. The stuff that fear is made of seemed to rise from the ancient dust; and I had little relish for the second part of my journey, which lay through a long horizontal passage rarely exceeding fourteen inches in height. The mere memory of that final crawl of forty feet or so is sufficient to cause me to perspire profusely; therefore let it suffice that I reached the end of the second passage, and breathing with difficulty the deathful, poisonous atmosphere of the place, found myself at the foot of the rugged shaft which gives access to the King's Chamber. Resting my torch upon a convenient ledge, I climbed up, and knew myself to be in one of the oldest chambers fashioned by human handiwork.

The journey had been most exhausting, but, allowing myself only a few moments' rest, I crossed to the eastern corner of the place and directed a ray of light upon the crevice which, from Hassan's description, I believed to conceal the ring. His account having been detailed, I experienced little difficulty in finding the cavity; but in the very moment of success the light of the torch grew dim . . . and I recognized with a mingling of chagrin and fear that it was burnt out and that I had no means of recharging it.

Ere the light expired, I had time to realize two things: that the cavity was empty . . . and that someone or something was approaching the foot of the shaft along the horizontal passage below!

Strictly though I have schooled my emotions, my heart was beating in a most uncomfortable fashion as, crouching near the edge of the shaft, I watched the red glow fade from the delicate :filament of the lamp. Retreat was impossible; there is but one entrance to the pyramid; and the darkness which now descended upon me was indescribable; it possessed horrific qualities; it seemed palpably to enfold me like the wings of some monstrous bat. The air of the King's Chamber I found to be almost unbearable, and it was no steady hand with which I gripped my pistol.

The sounds of approach continued. The suspense was becoming intolerable—when, into the Memphian gloom below me, there suddenly intruded a faint but ever-growing light. Between excitement and insufficient air, I regarded suffocation as imminent. Then, out into view beneath me, was thrust a slim ivory hand which held an electric pocket lamp. Fascinatedly I watched it, saw it joined by its fellow, then observed a white-turbaned head and a pair of black-robed shoulders follow. In my surprise I almost dropped the weapon which I held. The new arrival now standing upright and raising his head, I found myself looking into the face of *Abû Tabâh!*

"To Allah, the Great, the Compassionate, be all praise that I have found you alive," he said simply.

He exhibited little evidence of the journey which I had found so fatiguing, but an expression strongly like that of real anxiety rested upon his ascetic face.

"If life is dear to you," he continued, "answer me this, Kernaby Pasha; have you found the ring?"

"I have not," I replied; "my lamp failed me; but I think the ring is gone."

And now, as I spoke the words, the strangeness of his question came home to me, bringing with it an acute suspicion.

"What do you know of this ring, O my friend?" I asked.

Abû Tabâh shrugged his shoulders.

"I know much that is evil," he replied; "and because you doubt the purity of my motives, all that I have learned you shall learn also; for Allah the Great, the Merciful, this night has protected you from danger and spared you a frightful death. Follow me, Kernaby Pasha, in order that these things may be made manifest to you."

IV

A pair of fleet camels were kneeling at the foot of the slope below the entrance to the pyramid, and having recovered somewhat from the effect of the fatiguing climb out from the King's Chamber—

"It might be desirable," I said, "that I adopt a more suitable raiment for camel riding?"

Abû Tabâh slowly shook his head in that dignified manner which never deserted him. He had again taken up his ebony walking-stick and was now resting his crossed hands upon it and regarding me with his strange, melancholy eyes.

"To delay would be unwise," he replied. "You have mercifully been spared a painful and unfortunate end (all praise to Him who averted the peril); but the ring, which bears an ancient curse, is gone: for me there is no rest until I have found and destroyed it."

He spoke with a solemn conviction which bore the seal of verity.

"Your destructive theory may be perfectly sound," I said; "but as one professionally interested in relics of the past, I feel called upon to protest. Perhaps before we proceed any further you will enlighten me respecting this most obscure matter. Can you inform me, for example, what became of Hassan es- Sugra?"

"He observed my approach from a distance, and fled, being a man of little virtue. Respecting the other matters you shall be fully enlightened, to-night. The white camel is for you."

There was a gentle finality in his manner to which I succumbed. My feelings towards this mysterious being had undergone a slight change; and whilst I cannot truthfully say that I loved him as a brother, a certain respect for Abû Tabâh was taking possession of my mind. I began to understand his reputation with the natives; beyond doubt his uncanny wisdom was impressive; his lofty dignity awed. And no man is at his best arrayed in canvas shoes, very dirty drill trousers, and a pyjama jacket.

As I had anticipated, the village of Méydûm proved to be our destination, and the gait of the magnificent creatures upon which we were mounted was exhausting. I shall always remember that moonlight ride across the desert to the palm groves of Méydûm. I entered the house of the Sheikh with misgivings; for my attire fell short of the ideal to which every representative of protective Britain looks up, but often fails to realize.

In a *mandarah,* part of it inlaid with fine mosaic and boasting a pretty fountain, I was presented to the imposing old man who was evidently the host of Abû Tabâh. Ere taking my seat upon the *dîwan,* I shed my canvas shoes, in accordance with custom, accepted a pipe and a cup of excellent coffee, and awaited with much curiosity the next development. A brief colloquy between Abû Tabâh and the Sheikh, at the further end of the apartment resulted in the disappearance of the Sheikh and the approach of my mysterious friend.

"Because, although you are not a Moslem, you are a man of culture and understanding," said Abû Tabâh, "I have ordered that my sister shall be brought into your presence."

"That is exceedingly good of you," I said, but indeed I knew it to be an honor which spoke volumes at once for Abû Tabâh's enlightenment and good opinion of myself.

"She is a virgin of great beauty," he continued; "and the excellence of her mind exceeds the perfection of her person."

"I congratulate you," I answered politely, "upon the possession of a sister in every way so desirable."

Abû Tabâh inclined his head in a characteristic gesture of gentle courtesy.

"Allah has indeed blessed my house," he admitted; "and because your mind is filled with conjectures respecting the source of certain information which you know me to possess, I desire that the matter shall be made clear to you."

How I should have answered this singular man I know not; but as he spoke the words, into the *mandarah* came the Sheikh, followed by a girl robed and veiled entirely in white. With gait slow and graceful she approached the *dîwan*. She wore a white *yelek* so closely wrapped about her that it concealed the rest of her attire, and a white *tarbar,* or head-veil, decorated with gold embroidery, almost entirely concealed her hair, save for one jet-black plait in which little gold ornaments were entwined and which hung down on the left of her forehead. A white *yashmak* reached nearly to her feet, which were clad in little red leather slippers.

As she approached me I was impressed, not so much with the details of her white attire, nor with the fine lines of a graceful figure which the gossamer robe quite failed to conceal, but with her wonderful gazelle-like eyes, which were uncannily like those of her brother, save that their bordering of *kohl* lent them an appearance of being larger and more luminous.

No form of introduction was observed; with modestly lowered eyes the girl saluted me and took her seat upon a heap of cushions before a small coffee table set at one end of the *dîwan.* The Sheikh seated himself beside me, and Abû Tabâh, with a reed pen, wrote something rapidly on a narrow strip of paper. The' Sheikh clapped his hands, a man entered bearing a brazier containing live charcoal, and, having placed it upon the floor, immediately withdrew. The *dîwan* was lighted by a lantern swung from the ceiling, and its light, pouring fully down upon the white figure of the girl, and leaving the other persons and objects in comparative shadow, produced a picture which I am unlikely to forget.

Amid a tense silence, Abû Tabâh took from a box upon the table some resinous substance. This he sprinkled upon the fire in the brazier; and the girl extending a small hand and round soft arm across the table, he again dipped his pen in the ink and drew upon the upturned palm a rough square which he divided into nine parts, writing in each an Arabic figure. Finally, in the centre he poured a small drop of ink, upon which, in response to words rapidly spoken, the girl fixed an intent gaze.

Into the brazier Abû Tabâh dropped one by one fragments of the paper upon which he had written what I presumed to be a form of invocation. Immediately, standing between the smoking brazier and the girl, he commenced a subdued muttering. I recognized that I was about to be treated to an exhibition of *darb el-mendel,* Abû Tabâh being evidently a *sahhar,* or adept in the art called *er-roohânee.* Save for this indistinct muttering, no other sound disturbed the silence of the apartment, until suddenly the girl began to speak Arabic and in a sweet but monotonous voice.

"Again I see the ring," she said, "a hand is holding it before me. The ring bears a green scarab, upon which is written the name of a king of Egypt. . . . The ring is gone. I can see it no more."

"Seek it," directed Abû Tabâh in a low voice, and threw more incense upon the fire. "Are you seeking it?"

"Yes," replied the girl, who now began to tremble violently, "I am in a low passage which slopes downwards so steeply that I am afraid."

"Fear nothing," said Abâ Tabâh; "follow the passage."

With marvelous fidelity the girl described the passage and the shaft leading to the King's Chamber in the Pyramid of Méydûm. She described the cavity in the wall where once (if Hassan es-Sugra was worthy of credence) the ring had been concealed.

"There is a freshly made hole in the stonework," she said. "The picture has gone; I am standing in some dark place and the same hand again holds the ring before me."

"Is it the hand of an Oriental," asked Abû Tabâh, "or of a European?"

"It is the hand of a European. It has disappeared; I see a funeral procession winding out from Rikka into the desert."

"Follow the ring," directed Abû Tabâh, a queer, compelling note in his voice.

Again he sprinkled perfume upon the fire and—

"I see a Pharaoh upon his throne," continued the monotonous voice, "upon the first finger of his left hand he wears the ring with the green scarab. A prisoner stands before him in chains; a woman pleads

with the king, but he is deaf to her. He draws the ring from his finger
and hands it to one standing behind the throne—one who has a very evil
face. Ah! . . ."

The girl's voice died away in a low wail of fear or horror. But—

"What do you see?" demanded Abû Tabâh.

"The death-ring of Pharaoh!" whispered the soft voice tremulously;
"it is the death-ring!"

"Return from the past to the present," ordered Abû Tabâh. "Where
is the ring now?"

He continued his weird muttering, whilst the girl, who still shuddered violently, peered again into the pool of ink. Suddenly—

"I see a long line of dead men," she whispered, speaking in a kind
of chant; "they are of all the races of the East, and some are swathed in
mummy wrappings; the wrappings are sealed with the death-ring of
Pharaoh. They are passing me slowly, on their way across the desert
from the Pyramid of Méydûm to a narrow ravine where a tent is erected. They go to summon one who is about to join their company . . . ."

I suppose the suffocating perfume of the burning incense was chiefly responsible, but at this point I realized that I was becoming dizzy and
that immediate departure into a cooler atmosphere was imperative.
Quietly, in order to avoid disturbing the séance, I left the *mandarah.* So
absorbed were the three in their weird performance that my departure
was apparently unnoticed. Out in the coolness of the palm grove I soon
recovered. I doubt if I possess the temperament which enables one to
contemplate with equanimity a number of dead men promenading in
their shrouds.

V

"The truth is now wholly made manifest," said Abû Tabâh; "the
revelation is complete."

Once more I was mounted upon the white camel and the mysterious *imám* rose beside me upon its fellow, which was of less remarkable
color.

"I hear your words," I replied.

"The poor Ahmed Abdulla," he continued, "who was of little wisdom, knew, as Hassan es-Sugra knew, of the hidden ring; for he was

one of those who fled from the pyramid refusing to enter it again. Greed spoke to him, however, and he revealed the secret to a certain Englishman, called Bishop, contracting to aid him in recovering the ring."

At last enlightenment was mine . . . and it brought in its train a dreadful premonition.

"Something I knew of the peril," said Abû Tabâh, "but not, at first, all. The Englishman I warned, but he neglected my warning. Already Ahmed Abdulla was dead, having been despatched by his employer to the pyramid; and the people of Rikka had sent for me. Now, by means known to you, I learned that evil powers threatened your life also, in what form I knew not at that time save that the sign of Set had been revealed to me in conjunction with your death."

I shuddered.

"That the secret of the pyramid was a Pharaoh's ring I did not learn until later; but now it is made manifest that the thing of power is the death-ring of Sneferu. . . ."

The huge bulk of the Pyramid of Méydûm loomed above us as he spoke the words, for we were nearly come to our destination; and its proximity occasioned within me a physical chill. I do not think an open check for a thousand pounds would have tempted me to enter the place again. The death-ring of Sneferu possessed uncomfortable and supernatural properties. So far as I was aware, no example of such a ring (the *lettre de cachet* of the period) was included in any known collection. One dating much after Sneferu, and bearing the cartouche of Apepi II (one of the Hyksos, or Shepherd Kings) came to light late in the nineteenth century; it was reported to be the ring which, traditionally, Joseph wore as emblematical of the power vested in him by Pharaoh. Sir Gaston Maspero and other authorities considered it to be a forgery and it vanished from the ken of connoisseurs. I never learned by what firm it was manufactured.

A mile to the west of the pyramid we found Theo Bishop's encampment. I thought it to be deserted—until I entered the little tent. . . .

An oil-lamp stood upon a wooden box; and its rays made yellow the face of the man stretched upon the camp-bed. My premonition was realized; Bishop must have entered the pyramid less than an hour ahead of me; he it was who had stood upon the mound, silhouetted against the sky, when I had first approached the slope. He had met with the fate of Ahmed Abdulla.

He had been dead for at least two hours, and by the token of certain hideous glandular swellings, I knew that he had met his end by the bite of an Egyptian viper.

"Abû Tabâh!" I cried, my voice hoarsely unnatural—"the recess in the King's Chamber is a viper's nest!"

"You speak wisdom, Kernaby Pasha; the viper is the servant of the *ginn.*"

Upon the third finger of his swollen right hand Bishop wore the ring of ghastly history; and the mysterious significance of the Sign of Set became apparent. For added to the usual cartouche of the Pharaoh was the symbol of the god of destruction, thus:

We buried him deeply, piling stones upon the grave, that the jackals of the desert might never disturb the last holder of the death-ring of Sneferu.

Breath of Allah

I

For close upon a week I had been haunting the purlieus of the Mûski, attired as a respectable dragoman, my face and hands reduced to a deeper shade of brown by means of a water-color paint (I had to use something that could be washed off and grease-paint is useless for purposes of actual disguise) and a neat black moustache fixed to my lip with spirit-gum. In his story *Beyond the Pale,* Rudyard Kipling has trounced the man who inquires too deeply into native life; but if everybody thought with Kipling we should never have had a Lane or a Burton and I should have continued in unbroken scepticism regarding the reality of magic. Whereas, because of the matters which I am about to set forth, for ten minutes of my life I found myself a trembling slave of the unknown.

Let me explain at once that my undignified masquerade was not prompted by mere curiosity or the quest of the pomegranate, it was undertaken as the natural sequel to a letter received from Messrs. Moses, Murphy and Co., the firm which I represented in Egypt, containing curious matters affording much food for reflection. "We would ask you," ran the communication, "to renew your inquiries into the particular composition of the perfume 'Breath of Allah,' of which you obtained us a sample at a cost which we regarded as excessive. It appears to consist in the blending of certain obscure essential oils and gum-resins; and the nature of some of these has defied analysis to date. Over a hundred experiments have been made to discover substitutes for the missing essences, but without success; and as we are now in a position to arrange for the manufacture of Oriental perfume on an extensive scale we should be prepared to make it *well worth your while* (the last four words

33

characteristically underlined in red ink) if you could obtain for us a correct copy of the original prescription."

The letter went on to say that it was proposed to establish a separate company for the exploitation of the new perfume, with a registered address in Cairo and a "manufactory" in some suitably inaccessible spot in the Near East.

I pondered deeply over these matters. The scheme was a good one and could not fail to reap considerable profits; for, given extensive advertising, there is always a large and monied public for a new smell. The particular blend of liquid fragrance to which the letter referred was assured of a good sale at a high price, not alone in Egypt, but throughout the capitals of the world, provided it could be put upon the market; but the proposition of manufacture was beset with extraordinary difficulties.

The tiny vial which I had despatched to Birmingham nearly twelve months before had cost me close upon £100 to procure, for the reason that "Breath of Allah" was the secret property of an old and aristocratic Egyptian family whose great wealth and exclusiveness rendered them unapproachable. By dint of diligent inquiry I had discovered the *attár* to whom was entrusted certain final processes in the preparation of the perfume—only to learn that he was ignorant of its exact composition. But although he had assured me (and I did not doubt his word) that not one grain had hitherto passed out of the possession of the family, I had succeeded in procuring a small quantity of the precious fluid.

Messrs. Moses, Murphy and Co. had made all the necessary arrangements for placing it upon the market, only to learn, as this eventful letter advised me, that the most skilled chemists whose services were obtainable had failed to analyse it.

One morning, then, in my assumed character, I was proceeding along the Shâria el-Hamzâwi seeking for some scheme whereby I might win the confidence of Mohammed er-Rahmân the *attár*, or perfumer. I had quitted the house in the Darb el-Ahmar which was my base of operations but a few minutes earlier, and as I approached the corner of the street a voice called from a window directly above my head: "Saïd! Saïd!"

Without supposing that the call referred to myself, I glanced up, and met the gaze of an old Egyptian of respectable appearance who was regarding me from above. Shading his eyes with a gnarled hand—

"Surely," he cried, "it is none other than Saïd the nephew of Yûssuf Khalig! *Es-selâm 'aleykûm, Saïd!*"

"*Aleykûm, es-selâm,*" I replied, and stood there looking up at him.

"Would you perform a little service for me, Saïd?" he continued. "It will occupy you but an hour and you may earn five piastres."

"Willingly," I replied, not knowing to what the mistake of this evidently half-blind old man might lead me.

I entered the door and mounted the stairs to the room in which he was, to find that he lay upon a scantily covered diwan by the open window.

"Praise be to Allah (whose name be exalted)!" he exclaimed, "that I am thus fortunately enabled to fulfil my obligations. I sometimes suffer from an old serpent bite, my son, and this morning it has obliged me to abstain from all movement. I am called Abdul the Porter, of whom you will have heard your uncle speak; and although I have long retired from active labor myself, I contract for the supply of porters and carriers of all descriptions and for all purposes; conveying fair ladies to the *hammám,* youth to the bridal, and death to the grave. Now, it was written that you should arrive at this timely hour."

I considered it highly probable that it was also written how I should shortly depart if this garrulous old man continued to inflict upon me details of his absurd career. However—

"I have a contract with the merchant, Mohammed er-Rahmân of the Sûk el-Attârin," he continued, "which it has always been my custom personally to carry out."

The words almost caused me to catch my breath; and my opinion of Abdul the Porter changed extraordinary. Truly my lucky star had guided my footsteps that morning!

"Do not misunderstand me," he added. "I refer, not to the transport of his wares to Suez, to Zagazig, to Mecca, to Aleppo, to Baghdad, Damascus, Kandahar, and Pekin; although the whole of these vast enterprises is entrusted to none other than the only son of my father: I speak, now, of the bearing of a small though heavy box from the great magazine and manufactory of Mohammed er-Rahmân at Shubra, to his shop in the Sûk el-Attârin, a matter which I have arranged for him on the eve of the Molid en-Nebi (birthday of the Prophet) for the past five-and-thirty years. Every one of my porters to whom I might entrust this special charge is otherwise employed; hence my observation that it was written how none other than yourself should pass beneath this window at a certain fortunate hour."

Fortunate indeed had that hour been for me, and my pulse beat far from normally as I put the question: "Why, O Father Abdul, do you attach so much importance to this seemingly trivial matter?"

The face of Abdul the Porter, which resembled that of an intelligent mule, assumed an expression of low cunning.

"The question is well conceived," he said, raising a long forefinger and wagging it at me. "And who in all Cairo knows so much of the secrets of the great as Abdul the Know-all, Abdul the Taciturn! Ask we of the fabled wealth of Karafa Bey and I will name you every one of his possessions and entertain you with a calculation of his income, which I have worked out in *nûss-faddah!* Ask me of the amber mole upon the shoulder of the Princess Aziza and I will describe it to you in such a manner as to ravish your soul! Whisper, my son"—he bent towards me confidentially—"once a year the merchant Mohammed er-Rahmân prepares for the Lady Zuleyka a quantity of the perfume which impious tradition has called 'Breath of Allah.' The father of Mohammed er-Rahmân prepared it for the mother of the Lady Zuleyka and his father before him for the lady of that day who held the secret—the secret which has belonged to the women of this family since the reign of the Khalîf el-Hakîm from whose favorite wife they are descended. To her, the wife of the Khalîf, the first *dirhem* (drachm) ever distilled of the perfume was presented in a gold vase, together with the manner of its preparation, by the great wizard and physician Ibn Sina of Bokhara" (Avicenna).

"You are well called Abdul the Know-all!" I cried in admiration. "Then the secret is held by Mohammed er-Rahmân?"

"Not so, my son," replied Abdul. "Certain of the essences employed are brought, in sealed vessels, from the house of the Lady Zuleyka, as is also the brass coffer containing the writing of Ibn Sina; and throughout the measuring of the quantities, the secret writing never leaves her hand."

---

1. A *nûss-faddah* equals a quarter of a farthing.

"What, the Lady Zuelyka attends in person?"

Abdul the Porter inclined his head serenely.

"On the eve of the birthday of the Prophet, the Lady Zuelyka visits the shop of Mohammed er-Rahmân, accompanied by an *imâm* from one of the great mosques."

"Why by an *imâm,* Father Abdul?"

"There is a magical ritual which must be observed in the distillation of the perfume, and each essence is blessed in the name of one of the four archangels; and the whole operation must commence at the hour of midnight on the eve of the Molid en-Nebi."

He peered at me triumphantly.

"Surely," I protested, "an experienced *attár* such as Mohammed er-Rahmân would readily recognize these secret ingredients by their smell?"

"A great pan of burning charcoal," whispered Abdul dramatically, "is placed upon the floor of the room, and throughout the operation the attendant *imám* casts pungent spices upon it, whereby the nature of the secret essences is rendered unrecognizable. It is time you depart, my son, to the shop of Mohammed, and I will give you a writing making you known to him. Your task will be to carry the materials necessary for the secret operation (which takes place to-night) from the magazine of Mohammed er-Rahmân at Shubra, to his shop in the Sûk el-Attârin. My eyesight is far from good, Saïd. Do you write as I direct and I will place my name to the letter."

II

The words "well worth your while" had kept time to my steps, or I doubt if I should have survived the odious journey from Shubra. Never can I forget the shape, color, and especially the weight, of the locked chest which was my burden. Old Mohammed er-Rahmân had accepted my service on the strength of the letter signed by Abdul, and of course, had failed to recognize in "Saïd" that Hon. Neville Kernaby who had certain confidential dealings with him a year before. But exactly how I was to profit by the fortunate accident which had led Abdul to mistake me for someone called "Saïd" became more and more obscure as the box grew more and more heavy. So that by the time that I actually arrived with my burden at the entrance to the Street of the Perfumers, my heart had hardened towards Abdul the Know-all; and, setting my box upon the ground, I seated myself upon it to rest and to imprecate at leisure that silent cause of my present exhaustion.

After a time my troubled spirit grew calmer, as I sat there inhaling the insidious breath of Tonquin musk, the fragrance of attár of roses, the sweetness of Indian spikenard and the stinging pungency of myrrh, opoponax and ihlang-ylang. Faintly I could detect the perfume which I have always counted the most exquisite of all save one—that delightful preparation of Jasmine peculiarly Egyptian. But the mystic breath of frankincense and erotic fumes of ambergris alike left me unmoved; for amid these odors, through which.it has always seemed to me that that of cedar runs thematically, I sought in vain for any hint of "Breath of Allah."

Fashionable Europe and America were well represented as usual in the Sûk el-Attârin, but the little shop of Mohammed er-Rahmaân was quite deserted, although he dealt in the most rare essences of all. Mohammed, however, did not seek Western patronage, nor was there in the heart of the little white-bearded merchant any envy of his seemingly more prosperous neighbors in whose shops New York, London, and Paris smoked amber-scented cigarettes, and whose wares were carried to the uttermost corners of the earth. There is nothing more illusory than the outward seeming of the Eastern merchant. The wealthiest man with whom I was acquainted in the Muski had the aspect of a mendicant; and whilst Mohammed's neighbors sold phials of essence and tiny boxes of pastilles to the patrons of Messrs. Cook, were not the silent caravans following the ancient desert routes laden with great crates of sweet merchandise from the manufactory at Shubra? To the city of Mecca alone Mohammed sent annually perfumes to the value of two thousand pounds sterling; he manufactured three kinds of incense exclusively for the royal house of Persia; and his wares were known from Alexandria to Kashmir, and prized alike in Stambûl and Tartary. Well might he watch with tolerant smile the more showy activities of his less fortunate competitors.

The shop of Mohammed er-Rahmân was at the end of the street remote from the Hamzâwi (Cloth Bazaar), and as I stood up to resume my labors my mood of gloomy abstraction was changed as much by a certain atmosphere of expectancy—I cannot otherwise describe it—as by the familiar smells of the place. I had taken no more than three paces onward into the Sûk ere it seemed to me that all business had suddenly become suspended; only the Western element of the throng remained outside whatever influence had claimed the Orientals. Then presently the visitors, also becoming aware of this expectant hush as I had become aware of it, turned almost with one accord, and following the direction of the merchants' glances, gazed up the narrow street towards the Mosque of el-Ashraf.

And here I must chronicle a curious circumstance. Of the Imám Abû Tabâh I had seen nothing for several weeks, but at this moment I suddenly found myself thinking of that remarkable man. Whilst any mention of his name, or nickname—for I could not believe "Tabâh" to be patronymic—amongst the natives led only to pious ejaculations indicative of respectful fear, by the official world he was tacitly disowned. Yet I had indisputable evidence to show that few doors in Cairo, or indeed in all Egypt, were closed to him; he came and went like a phantom. I should never have been surprised, on entering my private apartments at Shepheard's, to have found him seated therein, nor did I question the veracity of a native acquaintance who assured me that he had met the mysterious *imám* in Aleppo on the same morning that a letter from his partner in Cairo had arrived mentioning a visit by Abû Tabâh to el-Azhar. But throughout the native city he was known as the Magician and was very generally regarded as a master of the *ginn.* Once more depositing my burden upon the ground, then, I gazed with the rest in the direction of the mosque.

It was curious, that moment of perfumed silence, and my imagination, doubtless inspired by the memory of Abû Tabâh, was carried back to the days of the great *khalîfs,* which never seem far removed from one in those mediæval streets. I was transported to the Cairo of Harûn al Raschîd, and I thought that the Grand Wazîr on some mission from Baghdad was visiting the Sûk el-Attârin.

Then, stately through the silent group, came a black-robed, white-turbaned figure outwardly similar to many others in the bazaar, but followed by two tall muffled negroes. So still was the place that I could hear the tap of his ebony stick as he strode along the centre of the street.

At the shop of Mohammed er-Rahmân he paused, exchanging a few words with the merchant, then resumed his way, coming down the Sûk towards me. His glance met mine, as I stood there beside the box; and, to my amazement, he saluted me with smiling dignity and passed on. Had he, too, mistaken me for Saïd—or had his all-seeing gaze detected beneath my disguise the features of Neville Kernaby?

As he turned out of the narrow street into the Hamzâwi, the commercial uproar was resumed instantly, so that save for this horrible doubt which had set my heart beating with uncomfortable rapidity, by all the evidences now about me his coming might have been a dream.

III

Filled with misgivings, I carried the box along to the shop; but Mohammed er-Rahmân's greeting held no hint of suspicion.

"By fleetness of foot thou shalt never win Paradise," he said.

"Nor by unseemly haste shall I thrust others from the path," I retorted.

"It is idle to bandy words with any acquaintance of Abdul the Porter's," sighed Mohammed; "well do I know it. Take up the box and follow me."

With a key which he carried attached to a chain about his waist, he unlocked the ancient door which alone divided his shop from the outjutting wall marking a bend in the street. A native shop is usually nothing more than a double cell; but descending three stone steps, I found myself in one of those cellar-like apartments which are not uncommon in this part of Cairo. Windows there were none, if I except a small square opening, high up in one of the walls, which evidently communicated with the narrow courtyard separating Mohammed's establishment from that of his neighbor, but which admitted scanty light and less ventilation. Through this opening I could see what looked like the uplifted shafts of a cart. From one of the rough beams of the rather lofty ceiling a brass lamp hung by chains, and a quantity of primitive chemical paraphernalia littered the place; old-fashioned alembics, mysterious looking jars, and a sort of portable furnace, together with several tripods and a number of large, flat brass pans gave the place the appearance of some old alchemist's den. A rather handsome ebony table, intricately carved and inlaid with mother-of-pearl and ivory, stood before a cushioned *dîwan* which occupied that side of the room in which was the square window.

"Set the box upon the floor," directed Mohammed, "but not with such undue dispatch as to cause thyself to sustain an injury."

That he had been eagerly awaiting the arrival of the box and was now burningly anxious to witness my departure, grew more and more apparent with every word. Therefore—

"There are asses who are fleet of foot," I said, leisurely depositing my load at his feet; "but the wise man regulateth his pace in accordance with three things: the heat of the sun; the welfare of others; and the nature of his burden."

"That thou hast frequently paused on the way from Shubra to reflect upon these three things," replied Mohammed, "I cannot doubt; depart, therefore, and ponder them at leisure, for I perceive that thou art a great philosopher."

"Philosophy," I continued, seating myself upon the box, "sustaineth the mind, but the activity of the mind being dependent upon the welfare of the stomach, even the philosopher cannot afford to labor without hire."

At that, Mohammed er-Rahmân unloosed upon me a long pent-up torrent of invective—and furnished me with the information which I was seeking.

"O son of a wall-eyed mule!" he cried, shaking his fists over me, "no longer will I suffer thy idiotic chatter! Return to Abdul the Porter, who employed thee, for not one *faddah* will I give thee, calamitous mongrel that thou art I Depart! for I was but this moment informed that a lady of high station is about to visit me. Depart! lest she mistake my shop for a pigsty."

But even as he spoke the words, I became aware of a vague disturbance in the street, and—

"Ah!" cried Mohammed, running to the foot of the steps and gazing upwards, "now am I utterly undone! Shame of thy parents that thou art, it is now unavoidable that the Lady Zuleyka shall find thee in my shop. Listen, offensive insect—thou art Saïd, my assistant. Utter not one word; or with this"—to my great alarm he produced a dangerous-looking pistol from beneath his robe—"will I blow a hole through thy vacuous skull!"

Hastily concealing the pistol, he went hurrying up the steps, in time to perform a low salutation before a veiled woman who was accompanied by a Sûdanese servant-girl and a negro. Exchanging some words with her which I was unable to detect, Mohammed er-Rahmân led the way down into the apartment, wherein I stood, followed by the lady, who in turn was followed by her servant. The negro remained above. Perceiving me as she entered, the lady, who was attired with extraordinary elegance, paused, glancing at Mohammed.

"My lady," he began immediately, bowing before her, "it is Saïd my assistant, the slothfulness of whose habits is only exceeded by the impudence of his conversation."

She hesitated, bestowing upon me a glance of her beautiful eyes. Despite the gloom of the place and the *yashmak* which she wore, it was manifest that she was good to look upon. A faint but exquisite perfume stole to my nostrils, whereby I knew that Mohammed's charming visitor was none other than the Lady Zuleyka.

"Yet," she said softly, "he hath the look of an active young man."

"His activity," replied the scent merchant, "resideth entirely in his tongue."

The Lady Zuleyka seated herself upon the *dîwan,* looking all about the apartment.

"Everything is in readiness, Mohammed?" she asked.

"Everything, my lady."

Again the beautiful eyes were turned in my direction, and, as their inscrutable gaze rested upon me, a scheme—which, since it was never carried out, need not be described—presented itself to my mind. Following a brief but eloquent silence—for my answering glances were laden with significance:—

"O Mohammed," said the Lady Zuleyka indolently, "in what manner doth a merchant, such as thyself, chastise his servants when their conduct displeaseth him?"

Mohammed er-Rahmân seemed somewhat at a loss for a reply, and stood there staring foolishly.

"I have whips for mine," murmured the soft voice. "It is an old custom of my family."

Slowly she cast her eyes in my direction once more.

"It seemed to me, O Saïd," she continued, gracefully resting one jeweled hand upon the ebony table, "that thou hadst presumed to cast love-glances upon me. There is one waiting above whose duty it is to protect me from such insults. Miska!"—to the servant girl—"summon El-Kimri (The Dove)."

Whilst I stood there dumbfounded and abashed the girl called up the steps:

"El-Kimri! Come hither!"

Instantly there burst into the room the form of that hideous negro whom I had glimpsed above; and—

"O Kimri," directed the Lady Zuleyka, and languidly extended her hand in my direction, "throw this presumptuous clown into the street!"

My discomfiture had proceeded far enough, and I recognized that, at whatever risk of discovery, I must act instantly. Therefore, at the moment that El-Kimri reached the foot of the steps, I dashed my left fist into his grinning face, putting all my weight behind the blow, which I followed up with a short right, utterly outraging the pugilistic proprieties, since it was well below the belt. El-Kimri bit the dust to the accompaniment of a human discord composed of three notes—and I leaped up the steps, turned to the left, and ran off around the Mosque of el-Ashraf, where I speedily lost myself in the crowded Ghuriya.

Beneath their factitious duskiness my cheeks were burning hotly: I was ashamed of my execrable artistry. For a druggist's assistant does not lightly make love to a duchess!

IV

I spent the remainder of the forenoon at my house in the Darb el-Ahmar heaping curses upon my own fatuity and upon the venerable head of Abdul the Know-all. At one moment it seemed to me that I had wantonly destroyed a golden opportunity, at the next that the seeming opportunity had been a mere mirage. With the passing of noon and the approach of evening I sought desperately for a plan, knowing that if I failed to conceive one by midnight, another chance of seeing the famous prescription would probably not present itself for twelve months.

At about four o'clock in the afternoon came the dawn of a hazy idea, and since it necessitated a visit to my rooms at Shepheard's, I washed the paint off my face and hands, changed, hurried to the hotel, ate a hasty meal, and returned to the Darb el-Ahmar, where I resumed my disguise.

There are some who have criticized me harshly in regard to my commercial activities at this time, and none of my affairs has provoked greater acerbitude than that of the perfume called "Breath of Allah." Yet I am at a loss to perceive wherein my perfidy lay; for my outlook is sufficiently socialistic to cause me to regard with displeasure the conserving by an individual of something which, without loss to himself, might reasonably be shared by the community. For this reason I have always resented the way in which the Moslem veils the faces of the pearls of his *harêm*. And whilst the success of my present enterprise would not render the Lady Zuleyka the poorer, it would enrich and beautify the world by delighting the senses of men with a perfume more exquisite than any hitherto known.

Such were my reflections as I made my way through the dark and deserted bazaar quarter, following the Shâria el-Akkadi to the Mosque of el-Ashraf. There I turned to the left in the direction of the Hamzâwi, until, coming to the narrow alley opening from it into the Sûk el-Attârin, I plunged into its darkness, which was like that of a tunnel, although the upper parts of the houses above were silvered by the moon.

I was making for that cramped little courtyard adjoining the shop of Mohammed er-Rahmân in which I had observed the presence of one of those narrow high-wheeled carts peculiar to the district, and as the entrance thereto from the Sûk was closed by a rough wooden fence I anticipated little difficulty in gaining access. Yet there was one difficulty which I had not foreseen, and which I had not met with had I arrived, as I might easily have arranged to do, a little earlier. Coming to the corner of the Street of the Perfumers, I cautiously protruded my head in order to survey the prospect.

Abû Tabâh was standing immediately outside the shop of Mohammed er-Rahmân!

My heart gave a great leap as I drew back into the shadow, for I counted his presence of evil omen to the success of my enterprise. Then, a swift revelation, the truth burst in upon my mind. He was there in the capacity of *imám* and attendant magician at the mystical "Blessing of the fumes"! With cautious tread I retraced my steps, circled round the Mosque and made for the narrow street which runs parallel with that of the Perfumers and into which I knew the courtyard beside Moham- med's shop must open. What I did not know was how I was going to enter it from that end.

I experienced unexpected difficulty in locating the place, for the height of the buildings about me rendered it impossible to pick up any familiar landmark. Finally, having twice retraced my steps, I determined that a door of old but strong workmanship set in a high, thick wall must communicate with the courtyard; for I could see no other opening to the right or left through which it would have been possible for a vehicle to pass.

Mechanically I tried the door, but, as I had anticipated, found it to be securely locked. A profound silence reigned all about me and there was no window in sight from which my operations could be observed. There- fore, having planned out my route, I determined to scale the wall. My first foothold was offered by the heavy wooden lock which projected fully six inches from the door. Above it was a crossbeam, and then a gap of sever- al inches between the top of the gate and the arch into which it was built. Above the arch projected an iron rod from which depended a hook; and if I could reach the bar it would be possible to get astride the wall.

I reached the bar successfully, and although it proved to be none too firmly fastened, I took the chance and without making very much noise found myself perched aloft and looking down into the little court. A sigh of relief escaped me; for the narrow cart with its disproportionate wheels stood there as I had seen it in the morning, its shafts pointing gauntly upward to where the moon of the Prophet's nativity swam in a cloudless sky. A dim light shone out from the square window of Mo- hammed er-Rahmân's cellar.

Having studied the situation very carefully, I presently perceived to my great satisfaction that whilst the tail of the cart was wedged under a crossbar, which retained it in its position, one of the shafts was in reach of my hand. Thereupon I entrusted my weight to the shaft, swinging out over the well of the courtyard. So successful was I that only faint creak- ing sound resulted; and I descended into the vehicle almost silently.

Having assured myself that my presence was undiscovered by Abû Tabâh, I stood up cautiously, my hands resting upon the wall, and peered through the little window into the room. Its appearance had changed somewhat. The lamp was lighted and shed a weird and subdued illumination upon a rough table placed almost beneath it. Upon this table were scales, measures, curiously shaped flasks, and odd-looking chemical apparatus which might have been made in the days of Avicenna himself. At one end of the table stood an alembic over a little pan in which burnt a spirituous flame. Mohammed er-Ramân was placing cushions upon the *dîwan* immediately beneath me, but there was no one else in the room. Glancing upward, I noted that the height of the neighboring building prevented the moonlight from penetrating into the courtyard, so that my presence could not be detected by means of any light from without; and, since the whole of the upper part of the room was shadowed, I saw little cause for apprehension within.

At this moment came the sound of a car approaching along the Shâria esh-Sharawâni. I heard it stop, near the Mosque of el-Ashraf, and in the almost perfect stillness of those tortuous streets from which by day arises a very babel of tongues I heard approaching footsteps. I crouched down in the cart, as the footsteps came nearer, passed the end of the courtyard abutting on the Street of the Perfumers, and paused before the shop of Mohammed er-Rahmân. The musical voice of Abû Tabâh spoke and that of the Lady Zuleyka answered. Came a loud rapping, and the creak of an opening door: then—

"Descend the steps, place the coffer on the table, and then remain immediately outside the door," continued the imperious voice of the lady. "Make sure that there are no eavesdroppers."

Faintly through the little window there reached my ears a sound as of some heavy object being placed upon a wooden surface, then a muffled disturbance as of several persons entering the room; finally, the muffled bang of a door closed and barred . . . and soft footsteps in the adjoining street!

Crouching down in the cart and almost holding my breath, I watched through a hole in the side of the ramshackle vehicle that fence to which I have already referred as closing the end of the courtyard which adjoined the Sûk el-Attârin. A spear of moonlight, penetrating through some gap in the surrounding buildings, silvered its extreme edge. To an accompaniment of much kicking and heavy breathing, into this natural limelight arose the black countenance of "The Dove." To my unbounded joy I perceived that his nose was lavishly decorated with sticking-plaster and that his right eye was temporarily off duty. Eight fat fingers clutching at the top of the woodwork, the bloated negro regarded the apparently empty yard for a space of some three seconds, ere lowering his ungainly bulk to the level of the street again. Followed a faint "pop" and a gurgling quite unmistakable. I heard him walking back to the door, as I cautiously stood up and again surveyed the interior of the room.

V

Egypt, as the earliest historical records show, has always been a land of magic, and according to native belief it is to-day the theater of many super-natural dramas. For my own part, prior to the episode which I am about to relate, my personal experiences of the kind had been limited and unconvincing. That Abû Tabâh possessed a sort of uncanny power akin to second sight I knew, but I regarded it merely a a form of telepathy. His presence at the preparation of the secret perfume did not surprise me, for a belief in the efficacy of magical operations prevailed, as I was aware, even among the more cultured Moslems. My scepticism, however, was about to be rudely shaken.

As I raised my head above the ledge of the window and looked into the room, I perceived the La Zuleyka seated on the cushioned *dîwan,* her hands resting upon an open roll of parchment which lay upon the table beside a massive brass chest of antique native workmanship. The lid of the chest was raised, and the interior seemed to be empty, but near it upon the table I observed a number of gold-stoppered vessels of Venetian glass and each of which was of a different color.

Beside a brazier wherein glowed a charcoal fire, Abû Tabâh stood; and into the fire he cast alternately strips of paper bearing writing of some sort and little dark brown pastilles which he took from a sandal-wood box set upon a sort of tripod beside him. They were composed of some kind of aromatic gum in which benzoin seemed to predominate, and the fumes from the brazier filled the room with a blue mist.

The *imám,* in his soft, musical voice, was reciting that chapter of the Korân called "The Angel." The weird ceremony had begun. In order to achieve my purpose I perceived that I should have to draw myself right up to the narrow embrasure and rest my weight entirely upon the ledge of the window. There was little danger in the maneuver, provided I made no noise; for the hanging lamp, by reason of its form, cast no light into the upper part of the room. As I achieved the desired position I became painfully aware of the pungency of the perfume with which the apartment was filled.

Lying there upon the ledge in a most painful attitude, I wriggled forward inch by inch further into the room, until I was in a position to use my right arm more or less freely. The preliminary prayer concluded, the measuring of the perfumes had now actually commenced, and I readily perceived that without recourse to the parchment, from which the Lady Zuleyka never once removed her hands, it would indeed be impossible to discover the secret. For, consulting the ancient prescription, she would select one of the gold-stoppered bottles, unscrew it, direct that so many grains should be taken from it, and never removing her gaze from Mohammed er-Rahmân whilst he measured out the correct quantity, would restopper the vessel and so proceed. As each was placed in a wide-mouthed glass jar by the perfumer, Abû Tabâh, extending his hands over the jar, pronounced the names:

"Gabraîl Mikaîl, Israfîl, Israîl."

Cautiously I raised to my eyes the small but powerful opera-glasses to procure which I had gone to my rooms at Shepheard's. Focussing them upon the ancient scroll lying on the table beneath me, I discovered, to my joy, that I could read the letters quite well. Whilst Abû Tabâh began to recite some kind of incantation in the course of which the names of the Companions of the Prophet frequently occurred, I commenced to read the writing of Avicenna.

"In the name of God, the Compassionate, the Merciful, the High, the Great. . ."

So far had I proceeded and no further when I became aware of a curious change in the form of the Arabic letters. They seemed to be moving, to be cunningly changing places one with another as if to trick me out of grasping their meaning!

The illusion persisting, I determined that it was due to the unnatural strain imposed upon my vision, and although I recognized that time was precious I found myself compelled temporarily to desist, since nothing was to be gained by watching these letters which danced from side to side of the parchment, sometimes in groups and sometimes singly, so that I found myself pursuing one slim Arab A (*'Alif*) entirely up the page from the bottom to the top where it finally disappeared under the thumb of the Lady Zuleyka!

Lowering the glasses I stared down in stupefaction at Abû Tabâh. He had just cast fresh incense upon the flames, and it came home to me, with a childish and unreasoning sense of terror, that the Egyptians who called this man the Magician were wiser than I. For whilst I could no longer hear his voice, I now could *see* the words issuing from his mouth! They formed slowly and gracefully in the blue clouds of vapour some four feet above his head, revealed their meaning to me in letters of gold, and then faded away towards the ceiling!

Old-established beliefs began to totter about me as I became aware of a number of small murmuring voices within the room. They were the voices of the perfumes burning in the brazier. Said one, in a guttural tone:

"I am Myrrh. My voice is the voice of the Tomb."

And another softly: "I am Ambergris. I lure the hearts of men."

And a third huskily: "I am Patchouli. My promises are lies."

My sense of smell seemed to have deserted me and to have been replaced by a sense of hearing. And now this room of magic began to expand before my eyes. The walls receded and receded, until the apartment grew larger than the interior of the Citadel Mosque; the roof shot up so high that I knew there was no cathedral in the world half as lofty. Abû Tabâh, his hands extended above the brazier, shrank to minute dimensions, and the Lady Zuleyka, seated beneath me, became almost invisible.

The project which had led me to thrust myself into the midst of this feast of sorcery vanished from my mind. I desired but one thing: to depart, ere reason utterly deserted me. But, to my horror, I discovered that my muscles were become rigid bands of iron! The figure of Abû Tabâh was drawing nearer; his slowly moving arms had grown serpentine and his eyes had changed to pools of flame which seemed to summon me. At the time when this new phenomenon added itself to the other horrors, I seemed to be impelled by an irresistible force to jerk my head downwards: I heard my neck muscles snap metallically: I *saw* a scream of agony spurt forth from my lips . . . and I saw upon a little ledge immediately below the square window a little *mibkharah,* or incense burner, which hitherto I had not observed. A thick, oily brown stream of vapor was issuing from its perforated lid and bathing my face clammily. Sense of smell I had none; but a chuckling, demoniacal voice spoke from the *mibkharah,* saying—

"I am *Hashish!* I drive men mad! Whilst thou hast lain up there like a very fool, I have sent my vapors to thy brain and stolen thy senses from thee. It was for this purpose that I was set here beneath the window where thou couldst not fail to enjoy the full benefit of my poisonous perfume. . . ."

Slipping off the ledge, I fell . . . and darkness closed about me.

VI

My awakening constitutes one of the most painful recollections of a not uneventful career; for, with aching head and tortured limbs, I sat upright upon the floor of a tiny, stuffy, and uncleanly cell! The only light was that which entered by way of a little grating in the door. I was a prisoner; and, in the same instant that I realized the fact of my incarceration, I realized also that I had been duped. The weird happenings in the apartment of Mohammed er-Rahmân had been hallucinations due to my having inhaled the fumes of some preparation of *hashish,* or Indian hemp. The characteristic sickly odor of the drug had been concealed by the pungency of the other and more odoriferous perfumes; and because of the position of the censer containing the burning *hashish,* no one else in the room had been affected by its vapor. Could it have been that Abû Tabâh had known of my presence from the first?

I rose, unsteadily, and looked out through the grating into a narrow passage. A native constable stood at one end of it, and beyond him I obtained a glimpse of the entrance hall. Instantly I recognized that I was under arrest at the Bâb el-Khalk police station!

A great rage consumed me. Raising my fists I banged furiously upon the door, and the Egyptian policeman came running along the passage.

"What does this mean, *shawêsh?*" I demanded. "Why am I detained here? I am an Englishman. Send the superintendent to me instantly."

The policeman's face expressed alternately anger, surprise, and stupefaction.

"You were brought here last night, most disgustingly and speechlessly drunk, in a cart!" he replied.

"I demand to see the superintendent."

"Certainly, certainly, *effendim!*" cried the man, now thoroughly alarmed. "In an instant, *effendim!*"

Such is the magical power of the word "Inglîsi" (Englishman).

A painfully perturbed and apologetic native official appeared almost immediately, to whom I explained that I had been to a fancy dress ball at the Gezira Palace Hotel, and, injudiciously walking homeward at a late hour, had been attacked and struck senseless. He was anxiously courteous, sending a man to Shepheard's with my written instructions to bring back a change of apparel and offering me every facility for removing my disguise and making myself presentable. The fact that he palpably disbelieved my story did not render his concern one whit the less.

I discovered the hour to be close upon noon, and, once more my outward self, I was about to depart from the Place Bâb el-Khalk, when, into the superintendent's room came Abû Tabâh! His handsome ascetic face exhibited grave concern as he saluted me.

"How can I express my sorrow, Kernaby Pasha," he said in his soft faultless English, "that so unfortunate and unseemly an accident should have befallen you? I learned of your presence here but a few moments ago, and I hastened to convey to you an assurance of my deepest regret and sympathy."

"More than good of you," I replied. "I am much indebted."

"It grieves me," he continued suavely, "to learn that there are footpads infesting the Cairo streets, and that an English gentleman may not walk home from a ball safely. I trust that you will provide the police with a detailed account of any valuables which you may have lost. I have here"—thrusting his hand into his robe—"the only item of your property thus far recovered. No doubt you are somewhat short-sighted, Kernaby Pasha, as I am, and experience a certain difficulty in discerning the names of your partners upon your dance programme."

And with one of those sweet smiles which could so transfigure his face, Abû Tabâh handed me my opera-glasses!

The Whispering Mummy

Felix Bréton and I were the only occupants of the raised platform at the end of the hall; and the inartistic performance of the bulky dancer who occupied the stage promised to be interminable. From motives of sheer boredom I studied the details of her dress—a white dress, fitting like a vest from shoulder to hip, and having short, full sleeves under which was a sort of blue gauze. Her hair, wrists, and ankles glittered with barbaric jewelry and strings of little coins.

A deafening orchestra consisting of tambourines, shrieking Arab viols, and the inevitable *daràbukeh,* surrounded the performer in a half-circle; and three other large-sized *ghawâzi* mingled their shrill voices with the barbaric discords of the musicians. I yawned.

"As a quest of local color, Bréton," I said, "this evening's expedition can only be voted a dismal failure."

Felix Bréton turned to me, with a smile, resting his elbows upon the dirty little marble-topped table. He looked sufficiently like an artist to have been merely a painter; yet his gruesome picture "Le Roi S'Amuse" had proved the salvation of the previous Salon.

"Have patience," he said; "it is Shejeret ed-Durr (Tree of Pearls) that we have come to see, and she has not yet appeared."

"Unless she appears shortly," I replied, stifling another yawn, "I shall disappear."

But even as I spoke, there arose a hum of excitement throughout the crowded room; the fat dancer, breathless from her unpleasing exertions, resumed her seat; and all the performers turned their heads towards a door at the side of the stage. A veiled figure entered, with slow, lithe step; and her appearance was acclaimed excitedly. Coming to the centre of the stage, she threw off her veil with a swift movement, and

confronted the audience, a slim, barbaric figure. I glanced at Felix Bréton. His eyes were glittering with excitement. Here at last was the
ghazîyeh of romance, the *ghazîyeh* of the Egyptian monuments; a true
daughter of that mysterious tribe who, in the remote past of tile Nile-
land, wove spells of subtle moon-magic before the golden Pharaoh.

A monstrous crash from the musicians opened the music of the
dance—the famous Gazelle dance—which commenced to a measure of
long, monotonous cadences. Shejeret ed-Durr began slowly to move her
arms and body in that indescribable manner which, like the stirring of
palm fronds, speaks the veritable language of the voluptuous Orient.
The attendant dancers clashing their miniature cymbals, the measure
quickened, and swift passion informed the languorous body, which magically became transformed into that of a leaping nymph, a bacchante, a
living illustration of Keats' wonder-words:

> "Like to a moving vintage, down they came,
>   Crown'd with green leaves, and faces all aflame;
>   All madly dancing through the pleasant valley,
>   To scare thee, Melancholy!"

At the conclusion of her dance, Shejeret ed-Durr, resuming her veil,
descended to the floor of the hall and passed from table to table, exchanging light badinage with those patrons known to her.

"Do you think you could induce her to come up here, Kernaby?"
said Bréton excitedly; "she is simply the ideal model for my 'Danse Funébre.'"

"Any inducement other than our presence in this select part of the
establishment," I replied, offering him a cigarette, "is unnecessary. She
will present herself with all reasonable despatch."

Indeed, I had seen the dark eyes glance many times towards us, as
we sat there in distinguished isolation; and, even as I spoke, the girl was
ascending the steps, from whence she approached our table, smiling in
friendly fashion. Bréton's surprise was rather amusing when she confi-
dently seated herself, giving an order to the cross-eyed waiter in close
attendance. It would be our privilege, of course, to pay the bill. Of its
being a privilege, no one could doubt who had observed the envious
glances cast in our direction by less favored patrons.

As Bréton spoke no Arabic, the task of interpreter devolved upon me; and I was carrying on quite mechanically when my attention was drawn to a peculiarly sinister-looking person seated alone at a table close beside the corner of the stage. I remembered having observed him address some remark to Shejeret ed-Durr, and having noted that she seemed to avoid him. Now, he was directing upon us a glare so electrically baleful that when I first detected it I was conscious of a sort of shock. The man was rather oddly dressed, wearing a black turban and a sort of loose robe not unlike the *burnûs* of the desert Arabs. I concluded that he belonged to some religious order, and that his bosom was inflamed with a hatred of a most murderous character towards myself, Felix Bréton, and the dancer.

I endeavored, without attracting the girl's notice, to indicate to Bréton the presence of the Man of the Glare; but the artist was so engrossed in contemplation of Shejeret ed-Durr and kept me so busy interpreting, that I abandoned the attempt in despair. Having made his wishes evident to her, the girl readily consented to pose for him; and when next I glanced at the table near the stage, the Man of the Glare had disappeared.

What induced me to look towards the rear of the platform upon which we were seated I know not, unless I did so in obedience to a species of hypnotic suggestion; but something prompted me to glance over my shoulder. And, for the second time that night, I encountered the gaze of mysterious eyes. From a little square window these compelling eyes regarded me fixedly, and presently I distinguished the outline of a head surmounted by a white turban.

The second watcher was Abû Tabâh!

What business could have brought the mysterious *imám* to such a place was a problem beyond my powers of conjecture, but that he was silently directing me to depart with all speed I presently made out. Having signified, by a gesture, that I had grasped the purport of his message, I turned again to Bréton, who was struggling to carry on a conversation with Shejeret ed-Durr in his native French.

I experienced some difficulty in inducing him to leave, but my arguments finally prevailed, and we passed out into the dimly lighted street. About us in the darkness pipes wailed, and there was the dim throbbing of the eternal *darábukeh*. We were in that part of El-Wasr adjoining the notorious Square of the Fountain. Discordant woman voices filled the night, and strange figures flitted from the shadows into the light streaming from the open doorways. It was the centre of secret Cairo, the midnight city; and three paces from the door of the dance hall, a slim, black-robed figure suddenly appeared at my elbow, and the musical voice of Abû Tabâh spoke close to my ear:

"Be on the terrace of Shepheard's in half an hour."

The mysterious figure melted again into the shadows about us.

II

On the deserted hotel balcony, Abû Tabâh awaited me.

"It was indeed fortunate, Kernaby Pasha," he said, "that I observed you this evening."

"I am greatly obliged to you," I replied, "for watching over me with such paternal solicitude. May I inquire what danger I have incurred?"

I was angrily conscious of feeling like a schoolboy suffering reproof.

"A very great danger," Abû Tabâh assured me, his gentle, musical voice expressing real concern. "Ahmad es-Kebîr is the lover of the dancer called Shejeret ed-Durr, although she who is of the *ghawâzi*, of Keneh does not return his affections."

"Ahmad es-Kebîr?—do you refer to a malignant, looking person in a black turban?" I inquired.

Abû Tabâh gravely inclined his head.

"He is one of the *Rifa'îyeh*, the Black *Darwîshes*. They practise strange rites and are by some are credited with supernatural powers. For you the danger is not so great as for your friend, who seemed to be speaking words of love to the *ghazîyeh*."

I laughed shortly.

"You are mistaken, Abû Tabâh," I replied; "his interest was not of the character which you suppose. He is an artist and merely desired the girl to pose for him."

Abû Tabâh shrugged his shoulders.

"She is an unveiled woman," he said contemptuously, "but love in the heart of such a one as Ahmad is a terrible passion, consuming the vitals and rendering whom it afflicts either a partaker of Paradise or as one of the evil *ginn*."

"In the particular case under consideration," I said, "it would seem distinctly to have produced the latter and less agreeable symptoms."

"Let your friend step warily," advised Abû Tabâh; "for some who have aroused the enmity of the Black *Darwîshes* have met with strange ends, nor has it been possible to fix responsibility upon any member of the order."

"You think my poor friend, Felix Bréton, may be discovered some morning in an unpleasantly messy condition?"

"The Black *Darwîshes* do not employ the knife," answered Abû Tabâh; "they employ strange and more subtle weapons."

I stared hard at him in the darkness. I thought I knew my Cairo, but this sounded unpleasantly mysterious. However—

"I am indebted to you, Abû Tabâh," I said, "for your timely warning. As you know, I always personally avoid any possibility of misunderstanding in regard to my relations with Egyptian womenfolk."

"With some rare exceptions," agreed Abû Tabâh, "particulars of which escape my memory at the moment, you have always been a model of discretion, Kernaby Pasha."

"I will warn my friend," I said hastily, "of the view of his conduct mistakenly taken by the gentleman in the black turban."

"It is well," replied Abû Tabâb; "we shall meet again ere long."

With that and the customary dignified salutations he departed, leaving me wondering what hidden significance lay in his words, "we shall meet again ere long."

Experience had taught me that Abû Tabâh's warnings were not to be lightly dismissed, and I knew enough of the fanaticism of those strange Eastern sects whereof the *Rifa'îyeh,* or Black *Darwîshes,* was one, to realize that it would prove an unhealthy amusement to interfere with their domestic affairs. Felix Bréton, who possessed the rare gift of capturing and transferring to canvas the atmosphere of the East with the opulent colorings and vivid contrasts which constitute its charm, had nevertheless but little practical experience of the manners and customs of the golden Orient. He had leased a large studio situated on the roof of a fine old Cairene palace hidden away behind the Street of the

Booksellers and almost in the shadow of the Mosque of el-Azhar. His romantic spirit had prompted him after a time to give up his rooms at the Continental and to take up his abode in the apartment adjoining the studio; that is to say, completely to cut himself off from European life and to become an inhabitant of the Oriental city. With his imperfect knowledge of the practical side of native life in the East, I did not envy him; but I was fully alive to his danger, isolated as he was from the European community, indeed from modernity; for out of the boulevards of modern Cairo into the streets of the *Arabian Nights* is but a step, yet a step that bridges the gulf of centuries.

As I entered his studio on the following morning, I discovered him at work upon the extraordinary picture "Danse Funébre." Shejeret ed-Durr was posing in the dress of an ancient priestess of Isis. Bréton briefly greeted me, waving his hand towards a cushioned diwan before which stood a little coffee-table bearing decanters, siphons, cigarettes, and other companionable paraphernalia. Making myself comfortable, I studied the picture and the model.

"Danse Funébre" was an extraordinary conception, representing an elaborately furnished modern room, apparently that of an antiquary or Egyptologist; for a multitude of queer relics decorated the walls, cabinets, and the large table at which a man was seated. Boldly represented immediately to the left of his chair stood a mummy in an ornate sarcophagus, and forth from the swathed figure into the light cast downwards from an antique lamp, floated a beautiful spirit shape—that of an Egyptian priestess. Upon her face was an expression of intense anger, as, her fingers crooked in sinister fashion, she bent over the man at the table.

The mummy and sarcophagus depicted on the canvas stood before me against the wall of the studio, the lid resting beside the case. It, was moulded, as is sometimes seen, to represent the face and figure of the occupant and was as fine an example of the kind as I had met with. The mummy was that of a priestess and dancer of the Great Temple at Philæ, and it had been lent by the museum authorities for the purpose of Bréton's picture.

His enthusiasm at first seeing Shejeret ed-Durr was explainable by the really uncanny resemblance which the girl bore to the modeled figure. Studying her, from my seat on the *dîwan,* as she posed in that gauzy raiment depicted upon the lid of the sarcophagus, it seemed indeed that the ancient priestess was reborn in the form of Shejeret ed-Durr the *ghazîyeh.* Bréton had evidently tabooed make-up, with the exception of the characteristic black bordering to the eyes (which appeared in the presentment of the servant of Isis); and seen now in its natural coloring the face of the dancing-girl had undoubted beauty.

Presently, whilst the model rested, I informed Bréton of my conversation with Abû Tabâh; but, as I had anticipated, he was sceptical to the point of derision.

"My dear Kernaby," he said, "is it likely that I am going to interrupt my work now that I have found such an inspiring model, because some ridiculous *darwîsh* disapproves?"

"It is highly unlikely," I admitted; "but do not make the mistake of treating the matter lightly. You are right off the map here, and Cairo is not Paris."

"It is a great deal safer!" he cried in his boisterous fashion, "and infinitely more interesting."

But my mind was far from easy; for in the dark eyes of the model, when their glance rested upon Felix Bréton, there was that to have aroused poisonous sentiments in the bosom of the Man of the Glare.

III

During the course of the following month I saw Felix Bréton two or three times, and he was enthusiastic about the progress of his picture and the beauty of his model. The first hint that I received of the strange idea which was to lead to stranger happenings came one afternoon when he had called upon me at Shepheard's.

"Do you believe in reincarnation, Kernaby?" he asked suddenly.

I stared at him in surprise.

"Regardless of my personal views on the matter," I replied, "in what way does the subject interest you?"

Momentarily he hesitated; then—

"The resemblance between Yâsmîna" (this was the real name of Shejeret ed-Durr) "and the priestess of Isis," he said, "appears to me too marked to be explainable by mere coincidence. If the mummy were my personal, property I should unwrap it—"

"Do you seriously desire me to believe that you regard Yâsmîna as a reincarnation of the elder lady?"

"That or a lineal descendant," he answered. "The tribe of the *Ghawâzi* is of unknown antiquity and may very well be descended from those temple dancers of the days of the Pharaohs. If you have studied the ancient wall paintings, you cannot have failed to observe that the dancing girls represented have entirely different forms from those of any other women depicted and from those of the ordinary Egyptian women of to-day."

His enthusiasm was tremendous; he was one of those uncomfortable fanatics who will ride a theory to the death.

"I cannot say that I have noticed it," I replied. "Your knowledge of the female form divine is doubtless more extensive than mine."

"My dear Kernaby," he cried excitedly, "to the trained eye the difference is extraordinary. Until I saw Yâsmîna I had believed the peculiar form to which I refer to be extinct like the blue enamel and the sacred lotus. If it is not reincarnation it is heredity."

I could not help thinking that it more closely resembled insanity than either; but since Bréton had made no reference to the wearer of the black turban, I experienced less anxiety respecting his physical than his mental welfare.

Three days later there was a dramatic development. Drifting idly into Bréton's studio one morning I found him pacing the place in despair and glaring at his unfinished canvas like a man distraught.

"Where is Shejeret ed-Durr?" I inquired.

"Gone!" he replied. "She disappeared yesterday and I can find no trace of her."

"Surely the excellent Suleyman, proprietor of the dancing establishment, can assist you?"

"I tell you," cried Bréton savagely, "that she has disappeared. No one knows what has become of her."

I looked at him in dismay. He presented a mournful spectacle. He was unshaven and his dark hair was wildly disordered. His despair was more acute than I should have supposed possible in the circumstances; and I concluded that his interest in Yâsmîna was deeper than I had assumed or that I was incapable of comprehending the artistic temperament. I suppose the Gallic blood in him had something to do with it, but I was unspeakably distressed to observe that the man was on the verge of tears.

Consolation was impossible, and I left him pacing his empty studio distractedly. That night at an unearthly hour, long after I had retired to my own apartments, he came to Shepheard's. Being shown into my room, and the servant having departed—

"Yâsmîna is dead!" he burst out, standing there, a disheveled figure, just within the doorway.

"What!" I exclaimed, standing up from the table at which I had been writing and confronting him. "Dead? Do you mean—"

"He has murdered her!" said Bréton, in a dull monotonous voice— "that fiend of whom you warned me."

I was appalled; for I had been utterly unprepared for such a tragedy. "Who discovered her?"

"No one discovered her; she will never be discovered! He has buried her body in some secret spot in the desert."

My amazement grew with every word that he uttered, and presently—

"Then how in Heaven's name did you learn of her murder?" I asked.

Felix Bréton, who had begun to pace up and down the room, a truly pitiable figure, paused and looked at me wildly.

"You will think that I am mad, Kernaby," he said; "but I must tell you—I must tell someone. I could see that you were incredulous when I spoke to you of reincarnation, but I was right, Kernaby, I was right! Either that or my reason is deserting me."

My opinion inclined distinctly in the direction of the latter theory, but I remained silent, watching Bréton's haggard face.

"To-night," he continued, "as I sat looking at my unfinished picture and trying to imagine what could have become of Yâsmîna, the mummy—the mummy of the priestess—*spoke to me!*"

I slowly sank back into my chair. I was now assured that Felix Bréton had formed a sudden and intense infatuation for Yâsmîna and that her mysterious disappearance had deranged his sensitive mind. Words failed me; I could think of nothing to say; and bending towards me his haggard face—

"It whispered to me," he said, "in her voice—in my own language, French, as I have taught it to her; just a few imperfect words, but sufficient to convey to me the story of the tragedy. Kernaby, what does it mean? Is it possible that her spirit, released from the body of Yâsmîna, has returned to that which I firmly believe it formerly inhabited? . . ."

I had had the misfortune to be a party to some distressing scenes, but few had affected me so unpleasantly as this. That poor Felix Bréton was raving I could not doubt, but having persuaded him to spend the night at Shepheard's and having seen him safely to bed, I returned to my own room to endeavor to work out the problem of what steps I should take regarding him on the morrow.

In the morning, however, he seemed more composed, having shaved and generally rendered himself more presentable; but the wild look still lingered in his eyes and I could see that the strange obsession had secured a firm hold upon him. He discussed the matter quite calmly during breakfast, and invited met to visit the scene of this supernatural happening. I assented, and hailing *arabîyeh* we drove together to the studio.

There was nothing abnormal in the appearance of the place, but I examined the mummy and the mummy case with a new curiosity; for if Felix Bréton was not mad (and this was a point upon which I recognized my incompetence to decide) the phantom voice was clearly the product of some trick. However, I was unable to discover anything to account for it. The sarcophagus stood against the outer wall of the studio and near to a large lattice window before which was draped a heavy tapestry curtain for the purpose of excluding undesirable light upon that side of the model's throne. There was no balcony outside the window, which was fully thirty feet from the street below; therefore unless someone had been hiding in the window recess beside the sarcophagus, trickery appeared to be out of the question. Turning to Bréton, who was watching me haggardly—

"You searched the recess last night?" I said.

"I did—immediately. There was no one there. There was no one anywhere in the studio; and when I looked out of the open window, the street below was deserted from end to end."

Naturally, I took it for granted that he would avoid the place, at any rate by night; and I said as much, as we passed along the Mûski together. I can never forget the wildness in his eyes as he turned to me.

"I must go back, Kernaby," he said. "It seems like desertion, base and cowardly."

IV

Bréton did not join me at dinner that evening as we had arranged that he should do, and towards the hour of ten o'clock, growing more and more uneasy on his behalf, I set out for the studio, half hoping that I should meet him. I saw nothing of him, however, as I crossed the Ezbekîyeh Gardens and the Atabet el-Khadrá into the Mûski. From thence onward to the Rondpoint the dark and narrow streets were almost deserted, and from the corner of the Shâria el-Khordâgîya to the Street of the Bookbinders I met with no living thing save a lean and furtive cat.

My footsteps echoed hollowly from wall to wall of the overhanging buildings, as I approached the door giving access to the courtyard from which a stair communicated with the studio above. The moonlight, slanting down into the ancient place, left more than half of it in densest shadow, but just touched the railing of the balcony and the lower part of the *mushrabîyeh* screen masking what once had been the *harêm* apartments from the view of one entering the courtyard. Far above me, through an open lattice, a dim light shone out, though vaguely. This part of the house was bathed in the radiance of the moon, which dimmed that of the studio lamp; for the open window was the window of Bréton's studio.

The door at the foot of the stairs was partly open, and I ascended slowly, since the place was quite dark and I was forced to feel my way around the eccentric turnings introduced by an Arab architect to whom simplicity had evidently been an abomination.

A modern door had been fitted to the studio; and although this door was also unfastened, I rapped loudly, but, receiving no answer, entered the studio. It was empty. The lamp was lighted, as I had observed from below, and a faint aroma of Turkish tobacco smoke hung in the air. Clearly, Bréton had left but a few moments earlier; and I judged it probable that he would be returning very shortly, for had he set out for Shepheard's he would not have left his door unlocked, and in any event

I should have met him on the way. Therefore, having glanced into the inner room, which, latterly, Bréton had been using as a bedroom, I sat down on the *dîwan* and prepared to await his return.

The lamp whose light I had seen shining through the window was that which hung before the model's throne, and the curtain which usually draped the window recess had been partially pulled aside, so that from where I sat I could see part of the centre lattice, which was open. My mind at this time was entirely occupied with uneasy speculations regarding Bréton, and although I had glanced more than once at the large unfinished picture on the easel, from which the face of Shejeret ed-Durr peered out across the shoulder of the seated man, and several times had looked at the mummy set upright in its painted sarcophagus, no sense of the uncanny had touched me or in any way prepared me for the amazing manifestation which I was about to witness.

How long I had sat there I cannot say exactly; possibly for ten minutes or a quarter of an hour: when, suddenly, an eerie whisper crept through the stillness of the big room!

Since I had more than once been temporarily tricked into belief in the supernatural, by means of certain ingenious devices, I did not readily fall a victim to the mysterious nature of the present occurrence. Yet I must confess that my heart gave a great leap and I was forced to exert all my will to control my nerves. I sat quite still, listening intently for a repetition of that evil whisper. Then, in the stillness, it came again.

"Felix," it breathed, "because of you I lie dead in a grave in the desert. . . . I died for you, Felix, and now I am so lonely. . . ."

The whispering voice offered no clue to the age or the sex of the speaker; for a true whisper is toneless. But the words, as Bréton had declared, were uttered in broken French and spoken with a curious accent.

It ceased, that ghostly whispering; and I realized that my nerves could stand no more of it; for that it came or seemed to come from the mummy of the priestess was a fact as undeniable as it was horrible.

Resorting to action, I sprang up and leaped across the room, grasping first at the curtain draped in the window on the right of the sarcophagus. I jerked it fully aside. The recess was empty. All three lattices were open, on the right, left, and in the centre of the window; but, craning out from the latter, I saw the street below to be vacant from end to end.

Stepping back into the room, and metaphorically clutching my courage with both hands, I approached the sarcophagus, peered behind it, all around it, and, finally, into the swathed face of the mummy itself. Nothing rewarded my search. But the studio of Felix Bréton seemed to have become icily cold; at any rate I found myself to be shivering; and walking deliberately, although it cost me a monstrous effort to do so, I descended the dark winding stairway into the courtyard, and, on regaining the street, discovered to my intense annoyance that my brow was wet with cold perspiration.

I had taken no more than ten paces in the direction of the Sûk es-Sûdan when I heard the sound of approaching footsteps, and for some reason (I can only suppose as a result of my highly strung condition) I stepped into the shelter of a narrow gateway, where I could see without being seen, and there awaited the appearance of the one who approached.

It was Felix Bréton, his face showing ghastly in the moonlight as he turned the corner. I could not be certain if a mere echo had deceived me, but I thought I could detect faintly the softer footfalls of someone who was following him. From my cover I had an uninterrupted view of the entrance to the house which I had just left; and without showing myself I watched Bréton approach the door. At its threshold he seemed to hesitate; and in that brief hesitancy were illustrated the conflicting emotions driving the man. I recalled the words he had spoken to me that morning. "I must go back, Kernaby; it seems like desertion, base and cowardly." He opened the door and disappeared.

As he did so, a second figure crossed from the shadows on the opposite side of the street—that is, the side upon which I was concealed; and in turn advanced towards the door. As he passed my hiding-place I acted. Without an instant's hesitation I hurled myself upon him.

How he avoided that furious attack—if he did avoid it—or whether in the darkness I miscalculated my spring, I do not know to this day: I only know that I missed my objective, stumbled, recovered myself . . . and turned with clenched fists to find *Abû Tabâh* confronting me!

"Kernaby Pasha!" he cried.

"Abû Tabâh!" said I dazedly.

"I perceive that I am not alone in my anxiety for the welfare of M. Felix Bréton."

"But why were you following him? I narrowly missed assaulting you."

"Very narrowly," he agreed in his gentle manner; "but you ask me why I was following M. Bréton. I was following him because I have seen so many of those who have crossed the path of the Black *Darwîshes* meet with violent and inexplicable deaths."

"Murder?" I whispered.

"Not murder—suicide. Therefore, observing, as I had anticipated, a strangeness in your friend's behavior, I have watched him."

"The strangeness of his behavior is easily accounted for," I said. And excitedly, for the horror of the episode in the studio was still strongly upon me, I told him of the whispering mummy.

"These are very dreadful things of which you speak, Kernaby Pasha," he admitted, "but I warned you that it was ill to incur the enmity of the Black *Darwîshes.* That there is a scheme afoot to compass the self-destruction or insanity of your friend is now evident to me; and he has brought this calamity upon himself; for the words which he believed to be spoken by the spirit of the girl Yâsmîna would not have affected him so unpleasantly if his attitude towards her had been marked by proper restraint and the affair confined within suitable limitations."

"Quite so. But although the Black *Darwîshes* may be both malignant and clever, that uncanny whispering is beyond the control of natural forces."

"Such is not my opinion," replied Abû Tabâh. "A spirit does not mistake one person for another; and the whispering voice addressed itself to Felix, when Felix was not present. I believe, Kernaby Pasha, that you are the possessor of a pair of excellent opera-glasses? May I suggest that you return to Shepheard's and procure them."

V

The platform of the minaret seemed very cold to the touch of my stockinged feet; for I had left my shoes at the entrance to the mosque below in accordance with custom; and now, from the wooden balcony, I overlooked the neighboring roof's of Cairo, and Abû Tabâh, beside me, pointed to where a vague patch of light broke the darkness beneath us to the left.

"The window of M. Felix Bréton's studio," he said.

Raising the glasses to his eyes, he gazed in that direction, whilst I also peered thither and succeeded in making out the well of the courtyard and the roofs of the buildings to right and left of it. It was not evident to me for what Abû Tabâh was looking, and when presently he lowered the glasses and turned to me I expressed my doubts in words.

"It is surely evident," I said, speaking, as I now almost invariably did to the *imám,* in English, of which he had a perfect mastery, "that we have little chance of discovering anything from here, since nothing was visible from the studio window. Furthermore, who save Yâsmîna could have spoken in the manner which I have related and in broken French?"

"An eavesdropper," he replied, "might have profited by the lessons which Yâsmîna received from M. Bréton; and all vocal characteristics are lost in a whisper. In the second place, Yâsmîna is not dead."

"What!" I cried.

Although, when Bréton had informed me of her death, I myself had doubted him, for some reason the ghostly whisper had convinced me as it had convinced him.

"She has been kept a prisoner during the past week in a house belonging to one of the Black *Darwîshes,*" continued Abû Tabâh; "but my agents succeeded in tracing her this morning. By my orders, however, she has not been allowed to return to her home."

"And what was the object of those orders?"

"That I might learn for what purpose she had been made to disappear," replied Abû Tabâh; "and I have learned it to-night."

"Then you think that the whispering mummy—"

He suddenly clutched my arm.

"Quick! raise your glasses!" he said softly. "On the roof of the house to the left of the light. There is the whispering mummy!"

Strung up to a high pitch of excitement, I gazed through the glasses in the direction indicated by my companion. Without difficulty I discerned him—a man wearing a black turban—who crept like some ungainly cat along the flat roof, carrying in his hand what looked like one of those sugar canes which pass for a delicacy among the natives, but which to European eyes appear more suitable for curtain-poles than sweetmeats. Springing perilously across a yawning gulf, the wearer of the black turban gained the roof of the studio, crept along for some little distance further, and then, lying prone, began slowly to lower the bamboo rod in the direction of the lighted window.

I found that unconsciously I had suspended my respiration, and now, breathlessly, as the truth came home to me—

"It is a speaking-tube!" I cried. "I cannot see the end of it, but no doubt it is curved so as to protrude through the side of the lattice window. Do you look, Abû Tabâh: I propose to act."

Thrusting the glasses into the _imám's_ hand, I took my Colt repeater from my pocket, and, having peered for some seconds steadily in the direction of the dimly visible _Darwîsh,_ I opened fire! I had fired five shots in the heat of my anger at that sinister crouching figure, ere Abû Tabâh seized my wrist.

"Stop!" he cried; "do you forget where you stand?"

Truly I had forgotten in my indignation, or I should not have outraged his feelings by firing from the minaret of a mosque. But sufficient of my wrath remained to occasion me a thrill of satisfaction, when, peering through the dusk, I saw the _Darwîsh_ throw up his arms and disappear from view.

"There is blood in the courtyard," said Abû Tabâh; "but Ahmad es-Kebîr has fled. Therefore he still lives, and his anger will be not the less but the greater. Depart from Cairo, M. Bréton: it is my counsel to you."

"But," cried Felix Bréton, glaring wildly at the big canvas on the easel, "I must finish my picture. As Yâsmîna is alive, she must return, and I must finish my picture!"

"Yâsmîna cannot return," replied Abû Tabâh, fixing his weird eyes upon the speaker. "I have caused her to be banished from Cairo." He raised his hand, checking Bréton's hot words ere they were uttered. "Recriminations are unavailing. Her presence disturbs the peace of the city, and the peace of the city it is my duty to maintain."

Lord of the Jackals

In those days, of course (said the French agent, looking out across the sea of Yûssuf Effendis which billowed up against the balcony to where, in the moonlight, the minarets of Cairo pointed the way to God), I did not occupy the position which I occupy to-day. No, I was younger, and more ambitious; I thought to carve in the annals of Egypt a name for myself such as that of De Lesseps.

I had a scheme—and there were those who believed in it—for extending the borders of Egypt. Ah! my friends, Egypt after all is but a double belt of mud following the Nile, and terminated east and west by the desert. The desert! It was the dream of my life to exterminate that desert, that hungry gray desert; it was my plan—a foolish plan as I know now—to link the fertile Fáyûm to the Oases! How was this to be done? Ah!

Why should I dig up those buried skeletons? It was not done; it never could be done; therefore, let me not bore you with how I had proposed to do it. Suffice it that my ambitions took me far off the beaten tracks, far, even, from the caravan roads—far into the gray heart of the desert.

But I was ambitious, and only nineteen—or scarcely twenty. At nineteen, a man who comes from St. Rémy fears no obstacle which Fate can place in his way, and looks upon the world as a grape-fruit to be sweetened with endeavor and sucked empty.

It was in those days, then, that I learned as your Rudyard Kipling has also learned that "East is East"; it was in those days that I came face to face with that "mystery of Egypt" about which so much is written, has always been written, and always will be written, but concerning which so few people, so very few people, know anything whatever.

Yes, I, René de Flassans, saw with my own eyes a thing that I knew to be magic, a thing whereat my reason rebelled—a thing which my poor European intelligence could not grapple, could not begin to explain.

69

It was this which you asked me to tell you, was it not? I will do so with pleasure, because I know that I speak to men of honor, and because it is good for me, now that I cannot count the gray hairs in my beard, to confess how poor a thing I was when I could count every hair upon my chin—and how grand a thing I thought myself.

One evening, at the end of a dreadful day in the saddle—beneath a sky which seemed to reflect all the fires of hell, a day passed upon sands simply smoking in that merciless sun—I and my native companions came to an encampment of Arabs.

They were Bedouins[1]—the tribe does not matter at the moment—and, as you may know, the Bedouin is the most hospitable creature whom God has yet created. The tent of the Sheikh is open to any traveller who cares to rest his weary limbs therein. Freely he may partake of all that the tribe has to offer, food and drink and entertainment; and to seek to press payment upon the host would be to insult a gentleman.

That is desert hospitality. A spear that stands thrust upright in the sand before the tent door signifies that whosoever would raise his hand against the guest has first to reckon with the Sheikh. Equally it would be an insult to erect one's own tent in the neighborhood of a Bedouin encampment.

Well, my friends, I knew this well, for I was no stranger to the nomadic life, and accordingly, without fear of the fierce-eyed throng who came forth to meet us, I made my respects to the Sheikh Saïd Mohammed, and was reckoned by him as a friend and a brother. His tent was placed at my disposal and provisions were made for the suitable entertainment of those who were with me.

You know how dusk falls in Egypt? At one moment the sky is a brilliant canvas, glorious with every color known to art, at the next the curtain—the wonderful veil of deepest violet—has fallen; the stars break through it like diamonds through the finest gauze; it is night, velvet, violet night. You see it here in this noisy modern Cairo. In the lonely desert it is ten thousand times grander, ten thousand times more impressive; it speaks to the soul with the voice of the silence. Ah, those desert nights!

---

1. This incorrect but familiar spelling is retained throughout.

So was the night of which I speak and having partaken of the fare which the Sheikh caused to be set before me—and Bedouin fare is not for the squeamish stomach—I sipped that delicious coffee which, though an acquired taste, is the true nectar, and looked out beyond the four or five palm trees of this little oasis to where the gray carpet of the desert grew black as ebony and met the violet sweep of the sky.

Perhaps I was the first to see him; I cannot say; but certainly he was not perceived by the Bedouins, although one stood on guard at the entrance to the camp.

How can I describe him? At the time, as he approached in the moonlight with a shambling, stooping gait, I felt that I had never seen his like before. Now I know the reason of my wonder, and the reason of my doubt. I know what it was about him which inspired a kind of horror and a revulsion—a dread.

Elfin locks he had, gray and matted, falling about his angular face, shading his strange, yellow eyes. His was dressed in rags, in tatters; he was furtive, and he staggered as one who is very weak, slowly approaching out of the vastness.

Then it appeared as though every dog in the camp knew of his coming. Out from the shadows of the tents they poured, those yapping mongrels. Never have I seen such a thing. In the midst of the yellowish, snarling things, at the very entrance to the camp, the wretched old man fell, uttering a low cry.

But now, snatching up a heavy club which lay close to my hand, I rushed out of the tent. Others were thronging out too, but, first of them all, I burst in among the dogs, striking, kicking, and shouting. I stooped and raised the head of the stranger.

Mutely he thanked me, with half-closed eyes. A choking sound issued from his throat, and he clutched with his hands and pointed to his mouth.

An earthenware jar, containing cool water, stood beside a tent but a few yards away. Hurling my club at the most furious of the dogs, which, with bared fangs, still threatened to attack the recumbent man, I ran and seized the *dorak,* regained his side, and poured water between his parched lips.

The throng about me was strangely silent, until, as the poor old man staggered again to his feet, supported by my arm, a chorus arose about me—one long, vowelled word, wholly unfamiliar, although my Arabic was good. But I noted that all kept a respectful distance from myself and the man whom I had succored.

Then, pressing his way through the throng came the Sheikh Saïd Mohammed. Saluting the ragged stranger with a sort of grim respect, he asked him if he desired entertainment for the night.

The other shook his head, mumbling, pointed to the water jar, and by dint of gnashing his yellow and pointed teeth, intimated that he required food.

Food was brought to him hurriedly. He tied it up in a dirty cloth, grasped the water jar, and, with never a glance at the Arabs, turned to me. With his hand he touched his brow, his lips, and his breast in salute; then, although tottering with weakness, he made off again with that queer, loping gait.

The camp dogs began to howl, and a strange silence fell upon the Arabs about me. All stood watching the departing figure until it was lost in a dip of the desert, when the watchers began to return again to their tents.

Saïd Mohammed took my hand, and in a few direct and impressive words thanked me for having spared him and his tribe from a grave dishonor. Need I say that I was flattered? Had you met him, my friends, that fine Bedouin gentleman, polished as any noble of old France, fearless as a lion, yet gentle as a woman, you would know that I rejoiced in being able to serve him even so slightly.

Two of the dogs, unperceived by us, had followed the weird old man from the camp; for suddenly in the distance I heard their savage growls. Then, these growls were drowned in such a chorus of howling—the howling of jackals—as I had never before heard in all my desert wanderings. The howling suddenly subsided . . . but the dogs did not return.

I glanced around, meaning to address the Sheikh, but the Sheikh was gone.

Filled with wonder, then, respecting this singular incident, I entered the tent—it was at the farther end of the camp—which had been placed at my disposal, and lay down, rather to reflect than to sleep. With my mind confused in thoughts of yellow-eyed wanderers, of dogs, and of jackals, sleep came.

How long I slept I cannot say; but I was awakened as the cool fingers of dawn were touching the crests of the sand billows. A gray and dismal light filled the tent, and something was scratching at the flap.

I sat up immediately, quite wide awake, and taking my revolver, ran to the entrance and looked out.

A slinking shape melted into the shadows of the tent adjoining mine, and I concluded that a camp dog had aroused me. Then, in the early morning silence, I heard a faint call, and peering through the gloom to the east saw, in black silhouette, a solitary figure standing near the extremity of the camp.

In those days, my friends, I was a brave fellow—we are all brave at nineteen—and throwing a cloak over my shoulders I strode intrepidly towards this figure. I was within ten paces when a hand was raised to beckon me.

It was the mysterious stranger! Again he beckoned to me, and I approached yet nearer, asking him if it was he who had aroused me.

He nodded, and by means of a grotesque kind of pantomime ultimately made me understand that he had caused me to be aroused in order to communicate something to me. He turned, and indicated that we were to walk away from the camp. I accompanied him without hesitation.

Although the camp was never left unguarded, no one had challenged us; and, a hundred yards beyond the outermost tent, this strange old man stopped and turned to me.

First, he pointed back to the camp, then to myself, then out along the caravan road towards the Nile.

"Do you mean," I asked him—for I perceived that he was dumb or vowed to silence—"that I am to leave the camp?"

He nodded rapidly, his strange yellow eyes gleaming.

"Immediately?" I demanded.

Again he nodded.

"Why?"

Pantomimically he made me understand that death threatened me if I remained—that I must leave the Bedouins before sunrise.

I cannot convey to you any idea of the mad earnestness of the man. But, alas! youth regards the counsels of age with nothing but contempt; moreover, I thought this man mad, and I was unable to choke down a sort of loathing which he inspired in me.

I shook my head then, but not unkindly; and, waving my hand, prepared to leave him. At that, with a sorrow in his strange eyes which did not fail to impress me, he saluted me with gravity, turned, and passed out of sight.

Although I did not know it at the time, I had chosen of two paths the one that led through fire.

I slept little after this interview—if it was a real interview and not a dream—and feeling tired and unrefreshed, I saw the sun rise purple and angry over the distant hills.

You know what *khamsin* is like, my friends? But you cannot know what *simoom* is like—*simoom* in the heart of the desert! It came that morning—a wall of sand so high as to shut out the sunlight, so dense as to turn the day into night, so suffocating that I thought I should never live through it!

It was apparent to me that the Bedouins were prepared for the storm. The horses, the camels and the asses were tethered in an enclosure specially strengthened to exclude the choking dust, and with their cloaks about their heads the men prepared for the oncoming of this terror of the desert.

My God! it was a demon which sought to blind me, to suffocate me, and which clutched at my throat with strangling fingers of sand! This, I told myself, was the danger which I might have avoided by quitting the camp before sunrise.

Indeed, it was apparent to me that if I had taken the advice so strangely offered, I might now have been safe in the village of the Great Oasis for which I was bound. But I have since seen that the *simoom* was a minor danger, and not the real one to which this weird being had referred.

The storm passed, and every man in the encampment praised the merciful God who had spared us all. It was in the disturbance attendant upon putting the camp in order once more that I saw her.

She came out from the tent of Saïd Mohammed, to shake the sand from a carpet; the newly come sunlight twinkled upon the bracelets which clasped her smooth brown arms as she shook the gaily colored mat at the tent door. The sunlight shone upon her braided hair, upon her slight robe, upon her silver anklets, and upon her tiny feet. Transfixed I stood watching—indeed, my friends, almost holding my breath. Then the sunlight shone upon her eyes, two pools of mysterious darkness into which I found myself suddenly looking.

The face of this lovely Arab maiden flushed, and drawing the corner of her robe across those bewitching eyes, she turned and ran back into the tent.

One glance—just one glance, my friends! But never had Ulysses' bow propelled an arrow more sure, more deadly. I was nineteen, remember, and of Provence. What do you foresee! You who have been through the world, you who once were nineteen.

I feigned a sickness, a sickness brought about by the sandstorm, and taking base advantage of that desert hospitality which is unbounded, which knows no suspicion, and takes no count of cost, I remained in the tent which had been vacated for me.

In this voluntary confinement I learned little of the doings of the camp. All day I lay dreaming of two dark eyes, and at night when the jackals howled I thought of the wanderer who had counseled me to leave. One day, I lay so; a second; a third again; and the women of Saïd Mohammed's household tended me, closely veiled of course. But in vain I waited for that attendant whose absence was rendering my feigned fever a real one—whose eyes burned like torches in my dreams and for the coming of whose little bare feet across the sand to my tent door I listened hour by hour, day by day, in vain—always in vain.

But at nineteen there is no such thing as despair, and hope has strength to defy death itself. It was in the violet dusk of the fourth day, as I lay there with a sort of shame of my deception struggling for birth in my heart, that she came.

She came through the tent door bearing a bowl of soup, and the rays of the setting sun outlined her fairy shape through the gossamer robe as she entered.

At that my poor weak little conscience troubled me no more. How my heart leaped, leaped so that it threatened to choke me, who had come safe through a great sandstorm.

There is fire in the Southern blood at nineteen, my friends, which leaps into flame beneath the glances of bright eyes.

With her face modestly veiled, the Bedouin maid knelt beside me, placing the wooden bowl upon the ground. My eager gaze pierced the *yashmak,* but her black lashes were laid upon her cheek, her glorious eyes averted. My heart—or was it my vanity?—told me that she regarded me at least with interest, that she was not at ease in my company; and as, having spoken no word, having ventured no glance, she rose again to depart, I was emboldened to touch her hand.

Like a startled gazelle she gave me one rapid glance, and was gone!

She was gone—and my very soul gone with her! For hours I lay, not so much as thinking of the food beside me—dreaming of her eyes. What were my plans? Faith! Does one have plans at nineteen where two bright eyes are concerned?

Alas, my friends, I dare not tell you of my hopes, yet upon those hopes I lived. Oh, it is glorious to be nineteen and of Provence; it is glorious when all the world is young, when the fruit is ripe upon the trees and the plucking seems no sin. Yet, as we look back, we perceive that at nineteen we were scoundrels.

The Bedouin girl is a woman when a European woman is but a child, and Sakina, whose eyes could search a man's soul, was but twelve years of age—twelve! Can you picture that child of twelve squeezing a lover's heart between her tiny hands, entwining his imagination in the coils of her hair?

You, my friend, may perhaps be able to conceive this thing, for you know the East, and the women of the East. At ten or eleven years of age many of them are adorable; at twenty-one most of them are *passé;* at twenty-six all of them—with rare exceptions—are shrieking hags.

But to you, my other friends, who are strangers to our Oriental ways, who know not that the peach only attains to perfect ripeness for one short hour, it may be strange, it may be horrifying, that I loved, with all the ardor which was mine, this little Arab maiden, who, had she been born in France, would not yet have escaped from the nursery. But I digress.

The Arabs were encamped, of course, in the neighborhood of a spring. It lay in a slight depression amid the tiny palm-grove. Here, at sunset, came the women with their pitchers on their heads, graceful of carriage, veiled, mysterious.

Many peaches have ripened and have rotted since those days of which I speak, but now—even now—I am still enslaved by the mystery of Egypt's veiled women. Untidy, bedraggled, dirty, she may be, but the real Egyptian woman when she bears her pitcher upon her head and glides, stately, sinuously, through the dusk to the well, is a figure to en-chain the imagination.

Very soon, then, the barrier of reserve which, like the screen of the *harêm,* stands between Eastern women and love, was broken. My trivial scruples I had cast to the winds, and feigning weakness, I would sally forth to take the air in the cool of the evening; this two days later.

My steps, be assured, led me to the spring; and you who are men of the world will know that Sakina, braving the reproaches of the Sheikh's household, neglectful of her duties, was last of all the women who came to the well for water.

I taught her to say my name—René! How sweet it sounded from her lips, as she strove in vain to roll the 'ʀ' in our Provençal fashion. Some *ginnee* most certainly presided over this enchanted fountain, for despite the nearness of the camp our rendezvous was never discovered, our meetings were never detected.

With her pitcher upon the ground beside her, she would sit with those wistful, wonderful eyes upraised to mine, and sway before the ar-dor of my impassioned words as a young and tender reed sways in the Nile breeze. Her budding soul was a love lute upon which I played in ecstasy; and when she raised her red lips to mine . . . Ah! those nights in the boundless desert! God is good to youth, and harsh to old age!

Next to Saïd Mohammed, her father, Sakina's brother was the finest horseman of the tribe, and his white mare their fleetest steed. I had cast covetous eyes upon this glorious creature, my friends, and secretly had made such overtures as were calculated to win her confidence.

Within two weeks, then, my plans were complete—up to a point. Since they were doomed to failure, like my great scheme, I shall not trouble you with their details, but an hour before dawn on a certain night I cut the camel-hair tethering of the white mare, and, undetected, led the beautiful creature over the silent sands to a cup-like depression, a thousand yards distant from the camp.

The Bedouin who was upon guard that night had with him a gourd of *'erksoos.* This was customary, and I had chosen an occasion when the duty of filling the sentinel's gourd had fallen upon Sakina; to his *'erksoos* I had added four drops of dark brown fluid from my medicine chest.

It was an hour before dawn, then, when I stood beside the white mare, watching and listening; it was an hour before dawn when she for whom my great scheme was forgotten, for whom I was about to risk the anger, the just anger, of men amongst the most fierce in the known world, came running fleetly over the hillocks down into the little valley, and threw herself into my arms. . . .

When dawn burst in gloomy splendor over the desert, we were still five hours' ride from the spot where I had proposed temporarily to conceal myself, with perhaps an hour's start of the Arabs. I knew the desert ways well enough, but the ghostly and desolate place in which I now found myself nevertheless filled me with foreboding.

A seam of black volcanic rock split the sands for a great distance, forming a kind of natural wall of forbidding aspect. In places this wall was pierced by tunnel-like openings; I think they may have been prehistoric tombs. There was no scrap of verdure visible, north, south, east or west; only desolation, sand, grayness, and this place, ghostly and wan with that ancient sorrow, that odor of remote mortality which is called "the dust of Egypt."

Seated before me in the saddle, Sakina looked up into my face with a never-changing confidence, having her little brown fingers interlocked about my neck. But her strength was failing. A short rest was imperative.

Thus far I had detected no evidence of pursuit and, descending from the saddle, I placed my weary companion upon a rock over which I had laid a rug, and poured out for her a draught of cool water.

Bread and dates were our breakfast fare; but bread and dates and water are nectar and ambrosia when they are sweetened with kisses. Oh! the glorious madness of youth! Sometimes, my friends, I am almost tempted to believe that the man who has never been wicked has never been happy!

Picture us then, if you can, set amid that desolation, which for us was a rose-garden, eating of that unpalatable food—which for us was the food of the gods!

So we remained awhile, deliriously happy, though death might terminate our joys ere we again saw the sun, when something . . . *something* spoke me . . .

Understand me, I did not say that *someone* spoke, I did not say that anything *audible* spoke. But I know that, unlocking those velvet arms which clung to me, I stood up slowly—and, still slowly, turned and looked back at the frowning black rocks.

Merciful God! My heart beats wildly now when I recall that moment.

Motionless as a statue, but in a crouching attitude, as if about to leap down, he who had warned me so truly stood upon the highest point of the rocks watching us!

How long did I remain thus?

I cannot pretend to say; but when I turned to Sakina—she lay trembling on the ground, with her face hidden in her hands.

Then down over the piled-up rocks, this mysterious and ominous being came leaping. Old man though he was, he descended with the agility of a mountain goat—and sometimes, in the difficult places, *he went on all fours.*

Crossing the intervening strip of sand, he stood before me. You have seen the reproach in the eyes of a faithful dog whose master has struck him unjustly? Such a reproach shone out from the yellow eyes of this desert wanderer. I cannot account for it; I can say no more. . . .

It was impossible for me to speak; I trembled violently; such a fear and such a madness of sorrow possessed me that I would have welcomed any death—to have freed me from that intolerable reproach.

He suddenly pointed towards the horizon where against the curtain of the dawn black figures appeared.

I fell upon my knees beside Sakina. I was a poor, pitiable thing; the madness of my passion had left me, and already I was within the great

Shadow; I could not even weep; I knew that I had brought Sakina out into that desolate place—to die.

And now the man whose ways were unlike human ways began to babble insanely, gesticulating and plucking at me. I cannot hope to make you feel one little part of the emotion with which those instants were laden. Sakina clung to me trembling in a way I can never forget— never, never forget. And the look in her eyes! even now I cannot bear to think of it, I cannot bear—

Those almost colorless lizards which dart about in the desert places with incredible swiftness were now coming forth from their nests; and all the while the black figures, unheard as yet, were approaching along the path of the sun.

My mad folly grew more apparent to me every moment. I realized that this which so rapidly was overtaking me had been inevitable from the first. The strange wild man stood watching me with that intolerable glare, so that my trembling companion shrank from him in horror.

But evidently he was seeking to convey some idea to me. He gesticulated constantly, pointing to the approaching Arabs and then over his shoulder to, the frowning rock behind. Since it was too late for flight— for I knew that the white mare with a double burden could never outpace our pursuers—it occurred to me at the moment when the muffled beat of hoofs first became audible, that this hermit of the rocks was endeavoring to induce me to seek some hiding-place with which no doubt he was acquainted.

How I cursed the delay which had enabled the Arabs to come up with us! I know, now, of course, that even had I not delayed, our ultimate capture was certain. But at the moment, in my despair, I thought otherwise.

And now I cursed the stupidity which had prevented me from following this weird guide; I even thought wrathfully of the poor frightened child, whose weakness had necessitated the delay and whose fears had contributed considerably to this later misunderstanding.

The pursuing party, numbering four, and led by Saïd Mohammed, was no more than five hundred yards away when I came to my senses. The hermit now was tugging at my arm with frightful insistence; his eyes were glaring insanely, and he chattered in an almost pitiable manner.

"Quick!" I cried, throwing my arm about Sakina, "up to the rocks. This man can hide us!"

"No, no!" she whispered, "I dare not—"

But I lifted her, and signing to the singular being to lead the way, staggered forward despairingly.

The distance was greater than it appeared, the climb incredibly difficult. My guide held out his hand to me to assist me to mount the slippery rocks; but I had much ado to proceed and also to support Sakina.

Her terror of the man and of the place to which he was leading us momentarily increased. Indeed, it seemed that she was becoming mad with fear. When the man paused before an opening in the rocks not more than fifteen or sixteen inches in height, and wildly waving his arms in the air, his elfin locks flying about his shoulder, his eyes glassy, intimated that we were to crawl in—Sakina writhed free of my grasp and bounded back some three or four paces down the slope.

"Not in there!" she cried, holding out her little hands to me pitifully, "I dare not! He would devour us!"

At the foot of the slope, Saïd Mohammed, who had dismounted from his horse, and who, far ahead of the others, was advancing towards us, at that moment raised his gun and fired. . . .

Can I go on?

It is more years ago than I care to count, but it is fresher in my mind than the things of yesterday. A lonely old age is before me, my friends—for I have been a solitary man since that shot was fired. For me it changed the face of the world, for me it ended youth, revealing me to myself for what I was.

Something more nearly resembling human speech than any sound he had yet uttered burst from the lips of the wild man as the report of Saïd Mohammed's shot whispered in echoes through the mysterious labyrinths beneath us.

Fate had stood at the Sheikh's elbow as he pulled the trigger.

With a little soft cry—I hear it now, gentle, but having in it a world of agony—Sakina sank at my feet . . . and her blood began to trickle over the black rocks on which she lay.

The man who professes to describe to you his emotions at such a frightful moment is an impostor. The world grew black before my eyes;

every emotion of which my being was capable became paralysed.

I heard nothing, I saw nothing but the little huddled figure, that red stream upon the black rock, and the agonized love in the blazing eyes of Sakina. Groaning, I threw myself down beside her, and as she sighed out her life upon my breast, I knew—God help me—that what had been but a youthful amour, was now a life's tragedy; that for me the light of the world had gone out, that I should never again know the warmth of the sun and the gladness of the morning. . . .

The cave man, with a dog-like fidelity, sought now to drag me from my dead love, to drag me into that gloomy lair which she had shrunk from entering. His incoherent mutterings broke in upon my semi-coma; but I shook him off, I shrieked curses at him. . . .

Now the Bedouins were mounting the slope, not less than a hundred yards below me. In the growing light I could see the face of Saïd Mohammed. . . .

The man beside me exerted all his strength to drag me back into the gallery or cave—I know not what it was; but with my arms locked about Sakina I lay watching the pursuers coming closer and closer.

Then, those persistent efforts suddenly ceased, and dully I told myself that this weird being, having done his best to save me, had fled in order to save himself.

I was wrong.

You have asked me for a story of the magic of Egypt, and although, as you see, it has cost me tears—oh! I am not ashamed of those tears, my friends!—I have recounted this story to you. You say, where is the magic? and I might reply: the magic was in the changing of my false love to a true. But there was another magic as well, and it grew up around me now at this moment when I lay inert. waiting for death.

From behind me, from above me, arose a cry—a cry. You may have heard of the Bedouin song, the 'Mizmûnne':

> "Ya men melek ana dêri waat sa jebb,
> Id el' ish hoos' a beb hatsa azât ta lebb."

You may have heard how when it is sung in a certain fashion, flowers drop from their stalks! Also, you may have doubted this, never having heard a magical cry.

I do not doubt it, my friends! For I have heard a magical cry—this cry which arose from behind me! It started some chord in my dulled consciousness which had never spoken before. I turned my head—and there upon the highest point of the rocks stood the cave man. He suddenly stretched forth his hands.

Again he uttered that uncanny, that indescribable cry. It was not human. It was not animal. Yet it was nearer to the cry of an animal than to any sound made by the human species. His eyes gleamed with an awful light, his spare body had assumed a strange significance; he was transfigured.

A third time he uttered the cry, and out from one of those openings in the rock which I have mentioned, crept a jackal. You know how a jackal avoids the day, how furtive, how nocturnal a creature it is? but there in the golden glory which proclaimed the coming of the sun, black silhouettes moved.

A great wonder possessed me, as the first jackal was followed by a second, by a third, by a fourth, by a fifth. Did I say a fifth? . . . By five hundred—by five thousand!

From every visible hole in the rocks, jackals poured forth in packs. Wonder left me, fear left me; I forgot my sorrow, I became a numbed intelligence amid a desert of jackals. Over a sea of moving furry backs, I saw that upstanding crag and the weird crouching figure upon it. Right and left, above and below, jackals moved . . . and all turned their heads towards the approaching Bedouins!

Again—again I heard that dreadful cry. The jackals, in a pack, thousands strong, began to advance upon the Bedouins! . . .

Not east or west, north or south, could you hope to find a braver man than was the Sheikh Saïd Mohammed; but—he fled!

I saw the four horsemen riding like furies into the morning sun. The white mare, riderless, galloped with them—and the desert behind was yellow with jackals! For the last time I heard the cry.

The jackals began to return!

Forgive me, dear friends, if I seem an emotional fool. But when I recovered from the swoon which blotted out that unnatural spectacle, the wizard—for now I knew him for nothing less—had dug a deep trench—and had left me, alone.

Not a jackal was in sight; the sun blazed cruelly upon the desert. With my own hands I laid my love to rest in the sands. No cross, no crescent marks her resting-place; but I left my youth upon her grave, as a last offering.

You may say that, since I had sinned so grievously, since I had betrayed the noble confidence of Saïd Mohammed, my host, I escaped lightly.

Ah! you do not know!

And what of the strange being whose gratitude I had done so little to merit but yet which knew no bounds? It is of him that I will tell you.

Years later—how many it does not matter, but I was a man with no illusions—my restless wanderings (I being still a desert bird-of-passage) brought me one night to a certain well but rarely visited. It lay in a depression, like another well that I am fated often to see in my dreams, and, as one approached, the crowns of the palm trees which grew there appeared above the mounds of sand.

I was alone and tired out; the next possible camping-place—for I had no water—was many miles away. Yet it was written that I should press on to that other distant well, weary though I was.

First, then, as I came up, I perceived numbers of vultures in the air; and I began to fear that someone near to his end lay at the well. But when, from the top of a mound, I obtained a closer view, I saw a sight that, after one quick glance, caused me to spur up my tired horse and to fly—fly, with panic in my, heart.

The brilliant moon bathed the hollow in light and cast dense shadows of the palm stems upon the slope beyond. By the spring, his fallen face ghastly in the moonlight, in a clear space twenty feet across, lay a dead man.

Even from where I sat I knew him; but, had I doubted, other evidence was there of his identity. As I mounted the slope, thousands of fiery eyes were turned upon me.

God! that arena all about was alive with jackals—jackals, my friends, eaters of carrion—which, silent, watchful, guarded the wizard dead, who, living, had been their lord!

Harûn Pasha

I

I will tell you this story (said Ferrier of the Egyptian Civil) with one reservation; comments are to be reserved for some future time. I can only tell you what I saw with my own eyes and heard with my own ears; I offer no explanation; I pass on the story; you can take it or leave it.

Some of you will remember Dunlap—I don't mean Robert Dunlap, who is chief officer of the Pekin, but Jack Dunlap his cousin, the irrigation man who used to be stationed at Assuan.

You remember the build of the beggar?—the impression of scaffolding his figure conveyed? I always used to think of him as an iron framework, and he had the most hard-bitten head-piece I have ever struck; steel blue eyes and a mouth that was born shut. The dash of ginger in his hair, complexion, and constitution made up a Scotch brew that was very strongly flavored.

He came down to Cairo one spring, and a lot of us got together in the club—on a Sunday night, I remember, it was. The conversation got along that silly line; what we were all doing, and why we were doing it, what we had really intended to do, and how Fate had butted in and made sailors of those that had meant to be parsons, engineers of the poets, and tramps of the chaps who had proposed to become financiers.

Well, we had traveled up and down this blind alley for hours, I should think, when Dunlap mounted on his hind legs and took the rug with the proposition that nothing—nothing—was impossible of achievement to the man of single purpose. Someone put up an extreme case; asking Dunlap how he should handle the business of the son of a respectable greengrocer who, with singleness of purpose, proposed to become king of England.

85

He said it was not a fair case, but he accepted the challenge; and the way this junior greengrocer, under Dunlap's guidance, plunged into politics, got elected M.P., wormed himself into the confidence of the entire Empire by a series of brilliant campaigns conducted from John o' Groats to Van Diemen's Land; induced the reigning monarch, publicly, to advocate his own abdication; established a sort of commonwealth with his ex-Majesty on the board and Dunlap occupying a post between that of a protoctol and a Roman Cæsar—well, it was wonderful.

Of course, you can judge of the lateness of the hour from the fact that a group of moderately intelligent men tolerated, and contributed to, a chat of this nature. But what brings me down to the story is the few words which I exchanged with Dunlap at the break-up of the party, when he was leaving.

His cousin Robert, as you know, is well on the rippity side; but Jack, with all his fine capacity for heather-dew, had always struck me as something of a psalmster. I've heard that Bacchus holds the keys of truth, and it may be right; for out on the steps of the club, I said to Jack Dunlap:

"It seems you don't practise what you preach?"

"Don't I?" he snapped hardly. "What do you suppose I am doing here?"

"Engineering, I take it. Do you aspire to a pedestal beside De Lesseps?"

"De Lesseps be damned!" he retorted sourly. "Look at these."

He held out his hands, hardened with manual toil—the hands of a grinder.

"Clearly you are a glutton for work," I said.

"I am aiming at never doing another hand's stroke in my life," he replied, with an odd glint in his blue eyes. "My idea of life—*life,* mind you, not mere existence—is to be a pasha—one of the old school, with gate porters, orange trees, fountains, slaves, mosaic pavements, a marble bath."

He mixed his ambitions oddly.

"Someone to do all the shifting for me, and even the thinking; to hold a book in front of me if I wanted to read, to poke my pipe in my mouth, and to take it out when I wanted to blow smoke rings—and to *know* when I wanted it taken out without being told."

"On your showing, you are traveling by the wrong road."

"Am I?" he snapped viciously. "Just wait awhile."

That was all the indication I had of Dunlap's ideas, and remembering the time of night and other circumstances, I did not count upon it worth a brass farthing; putting it down to the heather-dew rather than to any innate viciousness of the man. But listen to the sequel, which shifts us up just about twelve months, to the spring of the following year, in fact.

II

I had seen no more of Dunlap, and concluded that he was back in Assuan, or somewhere on the river, foozling with his irrigation again. I never had the clearest conception of the work of his department, by the way. An irrigation man once started to explain to me about his section, mixing up surveying paraphernalia in his talk, telling me something about an allowance of half an inch variation in half a mile of bank, or chat to that effect; but I couldn't quite make it out. My impression of Dunlap at business was very hazy; I pictured him measuring the bank of the Nile with a six-foot rule, and periodically kneeling down in the smelly mud to footle with a spirit-level. But he was a Senior Wrangler, as you remember, and a man, too, of more substantial accomplishments, and he drew five hundred a year from the Egyptian Government; so that probably I underestimated his usefulness.

At any rate, I had forgotten his iron framework and mahogany countenance, together with his response (under the afflatus of heather-dew) at the time of which I am now speaking.

A little matter had cropped up which touched me on a weak spot; and with a mob of jabbering Egyptians and one very placid Bedouin flooding my room, I found myself thinking again of Dunlap and envying him his intimate acquaintance with Arabic.

Although I had been in the country quite twice as long as Dunlap, my Arabic was far from perfect, for I have always been a rotten linguist. Dunlap, as I now remembered, might have passed for a native (excepting his Scottish headpiece), and I ascribed his proficiency to an inherent trick of mimicry. There was something of the big ape about him; and after one function at which we both were present, I remember how he convulsed the entire club with an imitation of a certain highly placed

Egyptian dignitary, voice and gesture being equal in comic effect to Cyril Maude at his best. In fact, if you notice, you will find that the best linguists, as a rule, have a marked apish streak in their composition.

Well, here was I at my wits' ends to grasp twenty points of view at one and the same time; no two expressed in quite the same dialect, and each orator more excited than another. You know the brutes?

That got me thinking of Dunlap, and even after the incident was closed, I found myself thinking of him. Some friends from home were staying at Shepheard's, and of course they had claimed me as dragoman; not that I objected in the least, for one of the party—when it was possible to dodge her mother—was, well, a very agreeable companion, you understand.

On this particular morning we were doing the bazaars. I have found by comparison that the average tourist knows far more of the Mûski than the average resident; in the same way, I suppose that for information regarding the Tower of London or the British Museum, one must go, not to a Cockney, but to an American visitor. At any rate, my party told me more than I could tell them, and my job degenerated into that of a mere interpreter. In the matter of purchases, I possibly saved them money, but their knowledge of the wares was miles ahead of my own. These up-to-date guide books must be very useful reading, I think.

Although I had tried hard to rush them past that dangerous quarter, the *Gôhargîya,* the ladies of the party had discovered a shop where little trays of loose gems, turquoises, rubies, bits of lapis-lazuli, and so forth, were displayed snarefully.

After that I knew where I could find them up to any time before lunch; I knew they were safe enough for the rest of the morning; and accepting my defeat at the hands of the jewel merchant who turned his slow eyes upon me and shrugged apologetically, I drifted off, after a decent interval (leaving young Forrest, who, mysteriously, had turned up, to do the cavalierly), intending to visit my acquaintance, Hassan, in the *Sûk el-Attârin* (Street of the Perfumers), not twenty yards away.

You know Hassan? A large, mysterious figure in the shadows of his little shop, smoking amber-scented cigarettes as though he liked them, and turning his sleepy eyes slowly upon each passer-by. Well, I drifted around in his direction.

Right at the corner of the street, a big limousine was standing; an up-to-date car, fawn cushions, silver-plated fittings, and simply stuffed with fresh-cut flowers. A useful-looking Nubian was chauffeur, and on the step squatted a fat and resplendent being in all the glory of much gold braid.

These *harêm* guards are rarely seen in Cairo nowadays—they belong to the other picturesque Oriental institutions which have begun to fade with the cresent of Islâm. There was something startlingly incongruous about this full-grown specimen, that bloated representative of Eastern despotism squatting on the step of an up-to-date French car.

It was a kind of all-round shock; I cannot describe how it struck me. It was something like running into Martin Luther at the Grand National or Nero, say, at an aviation meeting.

This was a frightfully hot morning, and the adipose object on the car step was slumbering blissfully. A moment later I spotted the charge which he was guarding with such sedulous care. She was seated in Hassan's shop—well back in the shadows—a gauzy white vision, all eyes and *yashmak.* A confidential female servant accompanied her. They made a pleasing picture enough, and a more suitable setting could not well be found. It was an illustrated page of the *Arabian Nights,* and it appealed strongly even to my jaded perceptions.

Of course, I was not going to interrupt the *tête-à-tête;* but from where I stood I could observe the group very well whilst remaining myself unobserved. It presently became evident that the lady of the *yashmak,* under the pretence of purchasing perfumes, was merely killing time, and my interest increased as the hour of noon grew near and the artistic group remained unbroken. You know the Mosque of El-Ashraf by Hassan's shop? Its minaret almost overhung the place. Well, in due course, out popped the *mueddin.*

"*La il aha illa Allah. . . .*"

There he was a very sweet-voiced singer, as I noted at the time, telling them there was no God but God, and all the rest of it; and presently he worked round to the side of the gallery overlooking Hassan's shop.

Then I could see which way the wind blew. He seemed to be deliberately singing at the picturesque trio—and the dark eyes of the lady of the *yashmak* were lifted upward—in reverence, perhaps; but I hardly thought so.

There was no doubt about the *mueddin's* final glance, as he turned and retired from the gallery. I remained where I was until the *yashmak* left the shop; and as she had to pass quite close to me in order to rejoin the waiting car, I had a good look at her.

It was just an impression, of course, an impression of red lips under the white gauze, an oval Oriental outline, with very fine eyes—notably fine, where fine eyes are common—and a little exquisitely chiseled nose; a bewitching face. Just that one glimpse I had and a vague impression of rustling silk with the tap of high heels. A faint breath of musk still proclaimed itself above the less pleasing odors of the street; then, the female attendant having cuffed the slumbering Silenus into wakefulness, the car moved off and this *harêm* lily vanished from the bazaar.

I knew that my party was safe for another half an hour, at any rate, so I nipped along to Hassan's shop. Of course, he began brazenly by declaring that no ladies had been there that morning. I had expected it, and the attitude confirmed my suspicions.

Presently, when his boy had made fresh coffee, and Hassan, from the black cabinet, had produced some real cigarettes, we got more intimate. There was a scarcity of European visitors that morning; and excepting one interruption by a party of four American ladies, I had Hassan to myself for half an hour.

He raised his fat finger to his lips when I pressed my question, and rolled his eyes fearfully.

"She is from the palace of Harûn Pasha," he whispered with more sidelong glances. "Ah! *effendim,* I fear. . . ."

We smoked awhile; then—

"The Pasha's wife?" I inquired.

"It is the Lady Zohara," he said.

This did not add greatly to my information; but I continued: "And the *mueddin?*"

"Ah!—do not whisper it. . . . That is my brother, Saïd!"

"He raises his eyes very high?"

"Not so, *effendim;* it is she who raises her eyes. I fear—I fear for Saïd. The Pasha . . . you have heard of him?"

"I may have heard his name," I replied; "but I am quite unfamiliar with his reputation."

Hassan shook his head gloomily.

"He is the last of his race," he explained; "the race of the Khalifs. He inhabits the ancient palace—but much has been rebuilt, and much added—in Old Cairo, close behind the Coptic Church. . . ."

"I did not know that such a palace even existed."

Again Hassan raised his finger to his lips.

"He is not like the other pashas," he said; "in the house of Harûn Pasha are observed to-day all the old customs as in the day of his great ancestor Harûn al-Raschid."

"But a motor-car!"

"Ah, *effendim,* he does not scorn to employ modern comforts, nor do I mean that he is a strict Moslem. But you saw the one who sat upon the step? The *harêm* of the Pasha is well guarded; not only by such as he, but by the Nubians and by the other mutes."

"Mutes!"

"He has many slaves. His agent in Mecca procures for him the pick of the market."

"But there is no such thing as slavery in Egypt!"

"Do the slaves know that, *effendim?*" he asked simply. "Those who have tongues are never seen outside the walls—unless they are guarded by those who have no tongue!"

It was a curious sidelight upon a more curious possibility and I was much impressed.

"Your brother—"

"Alas! I have warned him! I fear, most sincerely I fear, that one dark night the same will befall him that befell the son of my cousin, Ali."

"And what was that?"

"He climbed the wall of the Pasha's garden. There is a fig tree growing close beside it at one place. Someone assisted him to descend on the other. But he had been betrayed; the Nubian mutes took him—and they—"

He bent and whispered in my ear.

"Impossible!" I cried—"impossible! *báss! báss!*"

"Not so, *effendim*—nor was that all. After that they—"

"Enough, Hassan, enough!" I cried. *"Usbûr!"*

Hassan sighed, raising fearful eyes to the minaret.

III

There has been nothing you are likely to disbelieve so far; but now—well, I specified at the beginning—no comments. Let me tell the story in my own way, and you have permission to think what you please.

There was a dance at Shepheard's that night, and young Forrest rather interfered with my plans again as to one of the members of the English party; I think I have referred to her before? That sent me home in a bad humor—at least not home; for as I was standing over by the Ezbekîyeh Gardens, wondering whether to go along to "Jimmy's" or not, I formed a sudden determination to go and have a look at the abode of Harûn Pasha instead!

Mind you, I was not surprised to have lived in Cairo all these years without having heard of the place; I had learned things about the Mûski in the morning, from my tourist friends, which had revealed to me something of my pitiable ignorance. But I was determined to mend my ways, so to speak, and I thought I would turn my restless mood to good purpose, by improving my knowledge of my neighbors.

I induced the torpid driver of an _arabîyeh_ to drive me out to Old Cairo. He obviously considered me to be even more demented than the rest of my countrymen, but since the fare would be a substantial one, he tackled the job. Mad expedition? Quite so; but you appreciate the mood?

After we had passed a certain quarter—a quarter which never sleeps—there was nothing livelier than decayed tombs _en route._ In the chill of the evening I began to weigh up my own foolishness appreciatively, but having got so far as the Coptic Church—you know the church I mean?—I was not going back unsatisfied; so I told my man to wait, and started off to look for the famous palace.

I must say the scene was impressive; a sky full of diamonds and a moon just bursting with light. The liquid night-sounds of the Nile alone disturbed the silence, and the buildings might have been made of mother-o'-pearl, so flawless and pure did they seem, gleaming there under the moon.

Well, I wandered up some narrow streets—past ruins of former important houses, and all that—until I found myself in the shadow of a high wall which obviously was kept in good repair. I followed this for some distance, and I could see trees on the other side; at one place a perfect mat of those purple flowers hung over the top; gorgeous things; the name begins with a B, but I can never remember it. This seemed promising, and as there was not a soul in sight, nor, on the visible evidences, a habitable building near me, I began to fossick for a likely place to climb up.

Presently I found the spot, and at the same time confirmation of my belief that these were the precincts of the Pasha. A fig tree grew beside the wall, affording an admirable means of reaching the top—a natural ladder. In a jiffy I was up . . . and overlooking one of the most glorious gardens I had ever seen or dreamt of!

It must have been planned by an artist simply soaked in the lore of the Orient. It set me thinking of Edmond Dulac's illustrations to the *Arabian Nights.* Apart from those pages, you never saw anything like it, I swear. The position of each tree was a study; the arrangement of the flowerbeds was poetic—that is the only word for it; there was a pond with marble seats around and a flight of steps with big copper urns filled with growing flowers, mosaic paths, and lesser pools with fountains playing. I peered down into the water, and the moon rays glittered magically upon the scales of the golden carp which darted there. And all this fairy prospect was no more than an introduction, as it were, a sort of lead-up, to the Aladdin's Palace beyond.

I saw now that what with palms and the natural rise of the land back from the Nile, the wonderful palace, with its terraces and gleaming domes, must actually be invisible from all points; a more secret locality one could not well imagine.

As to this magician's abode, which lay before me, I shall not attempt to describe it. But turn to the illustrations which I have mentioned, or to those of Burton's big edition; I will leave it to the artist's and your imagination to fill up the canvas.

Lights shone out from a hundred windows. Out of the ghostly, tomb-like silence of Old Cairo, I had clambered into a sort of fairyland; I stood there with the spray from a fountain wetting me, and rubbed my eyes. Honestly, I should not have been surprised to find myself dreaming. Well, you may be sure I was not going back yet; there was not a living soul to be seen in the gardens, and I meant to have a peep into the palace, whatever the chances.

The likeliest point, as I soon determined, was to the west—where a long, low wing of the building extended, and was lost, if I may use the term, in a great bank of verdure and purple blooms. I took full advantage of the ample shadow cast by the trees, and came right up under the white wall without mishap.

To my right, the wall was obviously modern, but to my left, although in the distance and under the moon it had seemed uniform, it was built of sandstone blocks and was evidently of great age. The palace proper, you understand, was fully forty yards east; the place before me was a sort of low extension and evidently had no real connection with the residential part.

Just above my head was a square window, iron-barred, but this did not look promising, and cautiously, for I was hampered by the creepers which grew under the wall, I felt my way further west. Presently I encountered a pointed door of black, time-seared wood, and heavily iron-studded. Then, with alarming suddenness, the quietude of my adventure was broken; things began to move with breathless rapidity.

A most dreadful screaming and howling split the stillness and made me jump like a startled frog!

The sound of a lash on bare flesh reached me from some place behind the pointed door. Screams for mercy in thick, guttural Arabic, mingled and punctuated with horrifying shrieks of pain, informed my ignorance unmistakably that mediæval methods yet ruled in the civilized Near East.

Screams and supplications merged into a dull moaning; but the whistle of the lash continued uninterruptedly. Then that too ceased, and dimly came the sounds of a muffled colloquy; a sort of gurgling talk that got me wondering.

I had just time to creep away and conceal myself behind a thick clump of bushes, when the door was thrown open, and the most gigantic negro I have ever set eyes upon appeared in the opening, outlined against the smoky glare from within. He had one gleaming bare arm about the neck of an insensible man, and he dragged him out into the garden as one might drag a heavy sack; dropping him all in a quivering heap upon the very spot which I had just vacated!

The negro, who was stripped to the waist and whose glistening body reminded me of a bronze statue of Hercules, stood looking down at the insensible victim, with a hideous leer. I ventured to raise myself ever so slightly; and in the ghastly, sweat-bedaubed face of the tortured man—whose bare shoulders were bloody from the lash—I recognized the Silenus of the limousine!

In response to a guttural inarticulate muttering by the black giant, a second Nubian, of scarcely lesser dimensions, emerged from the dungeon with a jar of water. He drenched the swooning man, evidently in order to revive him; and, when the wretched being ultimately fought his way back to agonized consciousness—to my horror he was seized, dragged in through the doorway again, and once more I heard the whistle of the lash being applied to his lacerated back, the skin of which was already in ribbons.

I suppose there are times when the most discreet man is snatched outside himself by circumstances? The door of this beastly torture-room had not been reclosed, and before I could realize what I was about, I found myself inside!

The wretched victim had been hauled up to a beam by his bound wrists, and the huge Nubian was putting all his strength into the wielding of the cat-o'-nine-tails, drawing blood with every stroke; whilst his assistant hung on to the rope running through a pulley-block in the low ceiling.

All in a sort of whirl (I was raving mad with indignation) I got amongst the trio, and landed a clip on the jaw of the son of Erebus which made his teeth rattle like castanets.

Down came the fat sufferer all in a heap in his own blood. Down went my man, and began to cough out broken molars. Then it was my turn; and down I went with the second mute on top of me, and the pair of us were playing hell all about the blood-spattered floor—up, down, under, over—straining, punching, kicking . . . then my antagonist introduced gouging, and I had to beat the mat.

It had been a stiff bout, and the stinking shambles were whirling about me like a bloody maelstrom. When things settled down a bit, I found myself lying in a small cell skewered up like a pullet, and with a prospect of iron grating and stone-flagged passage before me. I was more than a trifle damaged, and my head was singing like a kettle. If I had thought that I dreamed before, it was a struggle now to convince myself that this was not a nightmare.

Amid the rattling of chains and dropping of bars, a fantastic procession was filing down the passage. First came a hideous, crook-backed apparition, hook-nosed, and bearing a lantern. Behind him appeared two guards with glittering scimitars. Behind the guards walked a fourth personage, black-robed and white-turbaned—a sort of dignified dragoman, carrying an enormous bunch of keys.

The iron grating of my dungeon was unlocked and raised, and I was requested, in Arabic, to rise and follow. Realizing that this was no time for funny business, I staggered to my feet, and between the two Scimitars marched unsteadily through a maze of passages with doors unlocked and locked behind us, stairs ascended and stairs descended.

From empty passages, our journey led us to passages richly carpeted and softly lighted. By a heavy door opening on to the first of the latter, we left the squinting man; and, with the two Scimitars and Black Robe, I found myself crossing a lofty pavilion.

The floor was of rich mosaic, and priceless carpets were spread about in artistic confusion. Above my head loomed a great dome, lighted by stained glass windows in which the blue of lapis-lazuli predominated. By golden chains from above swung golden lamps burning perfumed oil and flooding the pavilion with a mellow blue light. There were inlaid tables and cabinets; great blue vases of exquisite Chinese porcelain stood in niches of the wall. The walls were of that faintly amber-tinted alabaster which is quarried in the Mokattam Hills; and there were fragile columns of some delicately azure-veined marble, rising, graceful and slender, ethereal as pencils of smoke, to a balcony high above my head; then, from this, a second series of fairy columns crept in blue streaks up into the luminous shadows of the dome.

We crossed this place, my heel taps echoing hollowly and before a curtained door took pause. An impressive interval of perfumed silence; then in response to the muffled clapping of hands, the curtain was raised and I was thrust into a smaller apartment beyond.

I found myself standing before a long *dîwan,* amid an opulence of Oriental appointment which surpassed anything which I could have imagined. The atmosphere was heavy with the odor of burning perfumes, and, whereas the lofty pavilion afforded a delicate study in blue, this chamber was voluptuously amber—amber-shaded lamps, amber cushions, amber carpets; everywhere the glitter of amber and gold.

Amid the amber sea, half immersed in the golden silks of the daïs, reclined a large and portly Sheikh; full and patriarchal his beard, wherein played amber tints, lofty and serene his brow, sweeping up to the snowy turban. From a mouthpiece of amber and gold he inhaled the scented smoke of a *narghli*. Behind him, upon a cushioned stool, knelt a female whose beauty of face and form was unmistakable, since it was undisguised by the filmy artistry of her attire. With a gigantic fan of peacock's feathers, she cooled the Sheikh, and dispersed the flies which threatened to disturb his serenity. A second houri received in her hands the amber mouthpiece as it fell from her lord's lips; a third, who evidently had been playing upon a lute, rose and glided from the apartment like an opium vision, as I entered between the guardian Scimitars.

I found myself thinking of Saint Saen's music to *Samson and Delilah;* the barbaric strains of the exquisite bacchanale were beating on my brain.

Black Robe advanced and knelt upon the floor of the *dïwan.*

"We have brought the wretched malefactor into your glorious presence," he said.

The Pasha (for I knew, beyond doubt, that I stood before Harûn Pasha) raised his eyes and fixed a stern gaze upon me. He gazed long and fixedly, and an odd change took place in his expression. He seemed about to address me, then, apparently changing his mind, he addressed the recumbent figure at his feet.

"Have the slaves returned with the female miscreant and her partner in Satan?" he demanded sternly.

"Lord of the age," replied the other, rising upon his knees, "they are expected."

"Let them be brought before me," directed the Pasha, "upon the instant of their arrival. Has Misrûn confessed his complicity?"

"He fainted beneath the lash, excellency, but confessed that he slept—that pig who prayed without washing and whose birth was a calamity—on several occasions when accompanying the lady Zohara."

"Leave us!" cried the Pasha. "But, first, unbind the prisoner."

He swept his arm around comprehensively, and everyone withdrew from the apartment, including the Scimitars (one of whom cut my lashings) and the lady of the fan. I found myself alone with Harûn Pasha.

IV

"Sit here beside me!" directed the Pasha.

Being yet too dazed for wonder or protest, I obeyed mechanically. My exact situation was not clear to me at the moment and I was a long way off knowing how to act.

"I am much disturbed in mind, and my bosom is contracted," continued the Pasha, with a certain benignity, "by reason of a conspiracy in my _harêm,_ which came to a head this night, and which led to the loss of the pearl of my household, a damsel who cost me her weight in gold, who entangled me in the snare of her love and pierced me with anguish. Know, O young Inglîsi, that love is difficult. Alas! she who had captivated my reason by her loveliness fled with a shame of the Moslems who defamed the sacred office of _mueddin!_ In truth he is naught but the son of a disease and a consort of camels. My soul cries out to Allah and my mind is a nest of wasps. Relate to me your case, that it may turn me from the contemplation of my sorrows. At another time, it had gone hard with you, and penalties of a most unfortunate description had been visited upon your head, O disturber of my peace; but since this child of filth and progeny of mules has shattered it forever, your lesser crime comes but as a diversion. Relate to me the matters which have brought you to this miserable pass."

There was some still little voice in my mind which was trying to speak to me, if you understand what I mean. But what with the suffocating perfume of ambergris (or it may have been frankincense), my incredible surroundings, and the buzzing of my maltreated skull, I simply could not think connectedly.

A memory was struggling for identification in my addled brain; but whether it was due to something I had seen, heard, or smelled, I could not for the life of me make out. I heard myself spinning my own improbable yarn as one listens to a dreary. and boresome recitation; I didn't seem to be the raconteur; my mind was busy about that amber room furiously chasing that hare-like memory, which leaped and doubled, dived under the silken cushions popped up behind the Pasha, and flicked its ears at me from amid the feathers of the peacock fan.

I driveled right on to the end of my story, mechanically, without having got my mind in proper working order; and when the Pasha spoke again—there was that wretched memory still dodging me, sometimes almost within my grasp, but always just eluding it.

"Your amusing narrative has diverted me," said the Pasha; and he clapped his hands three times.

It never occurred to me, you will note, to assert myself in any way; I accepted the lordly condescensions of this singular personage without protest. You will be wondering why I didn't kick up a devil of a hullabaloo—declare that I had come in response to screams for assistance—wave the dreaded name of the British Agent under the Pasha's nose, and all that. I can only say that I didn't; I was subdued; in fact I was down, utterly down and out.

Black Robe entered with eyes averted.

"Well, wretched vermin!" roared the Pasha in sudden wrath; "do you tell me they are not here?"

The man, with his head bumping on the carpet, visibly trembled.

"Most noble," he replied hoarsely, "your lowly slave has exerted himself to the utmost—"

"Out! son of a calamity!" shouted the Pasha—and before my astonished eyes he raised the heavy *narghli* and hurled it at the bowed head of the man before him.

It struck the white turban with a resounding crack, and then was shattered to bits upon the floor. It was a blow to have staggered a mule. But Black Robe, without apparent loss of dignity, rose and departed, bowing.

The Pasha sat rocking about, and plucking madly at his beard.

"O Allah!" he cried, "how I suffer." He turned to me, "Never since the day that another of your race (but, this one, a true son of Satan) came to my palace, have I tasted so much suffering. You shall judge of my clemency, O imprudent stranger, and pacify your heart with the spectacle of another's punishment."

He clapped his hands twice. This time there was a short delay, which the Pasha suffered impatiently; then there entered the squint-eyed man, together with the two Scimitars.

"I would visit the dungeon of the false Pasha," said my singular host; and, rising to his feet, he placed his hand upon my shoulder and indicated that we were to proceed from the apartment.

Led by Crook Back, in whose hand the gigantic bunch of keys rattled unmelodiously, and followed by the Scimitars, we proceeded upon our way; and it was beyond the powers of my disordered brain to dismiss the idea that I was taking part in a Christmas pantomime. Many steps were descended; many heavy doors unbolted and unbarred, bolted and barred behind us; many stone-paved passages, reminding me of operatic scenery, were traversed ere we came to one tunnel more gloomy than the rest.

Upon the right was a blank stone wall, upon the left, a series of doors, black with age and heavily iron-studded. The only illumination was that furnished by the lantern which Crook Back carried.

Before one of the doors the Pasha paused.

"In which is Misrûn?" he demanded.

"In the next, excellency," replied the jailer—for such I took to be the office of the hunchback.

As he spoke, he held the lantern to the grating.

I found myself peering into a filthy dungeon, the reek of which made me ill; and there, upon the stone floor, lay poor Silenus! He raised his eyes to the light.

"Lord of the age," he moaned, lifting his manacled wrists, "glory of the universe, sun of suns! I have confessed my frightful sin, and most dire misfortunes. Of your sublime mercy, take pity upon the meanest thing that creeps upon the earth—"

"Proceed!" said the Pasha.

And with the moaning cries of Misrûn growing fainter behind us, we moved along the passage. Before a second door, we halted again, and the jailer raised the lantern.

"Look upon this!" cried the Pasha to me—"I look well, and look long!"

Shudderingly I peered in between the bars. It had come home to me how I was utterly at the mercy of this man's moods. If he had chosen to have me hurled into one of his dungeons, what prospect of release would have been mine? Who would ever know of my plight? No one! And beyond doubt I was in the realm of an absolute monarch. I silently thanked my lucky stars that my lot was not the lot of him who occupied this second dungeon.

As the dim light, casting shadow bars across the filthy floor, picked out the features of the prisoner, I gave a great start. Save that the beard was more gray, longer, filthy and unkempt, and that, in place of the nearly shaven skull, this unhappy being displayed dishevelled locks, the captive might easily have passed for the Pasha.

I met the eye of this terrible despot.

"Look upon the false Pasha," he said; "look upon the one who thought to dispossess me! For years, by his own miserable confession, he studied me in secret. When I journeyed to my estates in Assuan" (I started again) "he was watching—watching—always watching. His scheme, which was whispered into his ear by the Evil One, was no plant of sudden growth, but a tree, that, from a seed of Satan planted in fertile soil, had flourished exceedingly, tended by the hand of villainous ambition."

I clutched at the bars for support. The stench of the place was simply indescribable; but it was neither the stench nor the bizarre incidents of the night which accounted for my dizziness: it was the sudden tangibility of that hitherto elusive memory.

In build, in complexion, in certain mannerisms underlying the dignified assumption, Harûn Pasha might well have been the twin brother of Jack Dunlap!

A frightful possibility burst upon me like a bomb; clutching the bars with quivering hands, I stared and stared at the wretched impostor in the cell. *Could* it be? Had he been mad enough to make some attempt upon the Pasha? And was this his end?

I looked around again. I searched the bearded features of the Pasha with eager gaze. Good God! either I was going mad, or incredible things had been done, were being done, in Cairo.

I had not seen Dunlap for a year, remember, and in the ordinary way I did not see him more than half a dozen times in twelve months, so that, all things considered, it was not so remarkable that I had overlooked the resemblance. A full beard and mustache, artificially darkened eyelashes, a shaven head and a white turban, are effectual disguises; but if you can imagine Dunlap—the Dunlap you remember—so arrayed, then you have Harûn Pasha. Imagine Harûn Pasha, dirty, bedraggled, a hopeless captive . . . and you have the prisoner who crouched upon the straw in that noisome dungeon!

For the second time that night I was lifted out of myself. I turned on the man beside me in a blazing fury.

"You villain!" I shouted at him, and clenched my fists—"do you *dare* to confine a Britisher in your stinking cellars. By God! sir . . ."

Harûn Pasha clapped his hand over my mouth; the two guards had me by the arms from behind. But my cries had aroused the man in the dungeon, and, as I was dragged down the passage, these moaning words reached me, spoken in Arabic:

"Help! help! Englishman! A crime has been committed! I appeal to Lord—"

A door was slammed fast with a resounding bang, and the rest of the captive's appeal was lost to me. One of my guards had substituted his hand for that of the Pasha, but now it was removed; and; speechless with rage, I found myself being thrust up stone stairs—and I realized that by a moment's indiscretion, I had ruined everything.

Back in the amber apartment once more, with the two Scimitars at the door and Harûn Pasha reclining upon the cushions, I found speech.

"What are you going to do with me?" I demanded.

"My son," replied the Pasha with benignity, "I pardon all! Your great courage and address, together with the modesty of your deportment, and the spirit of adventure which has brought you to your present unfortunate case, plead for you in a manner which my clemency cannot resist. It is my unhappy lot often to be called upon to punish. Tonight, those gloomy dungeons which you have seen will echo, alas, with the howls of miserable wretches who are responsible for the loss of the pearl of my soul; for I am persuaded that she has fled with the son of offal who profaned the words of Allah from the minaret. This being so, I would temper my proper severity with a merciful deed. You shall never speak of what you have seen within these walls, save in terms suitably disguised. You shall never seek to return, nor, by speech with any man, to confirm whatsoever you may suspect. Upon this warranty, you shall depart in peace."

He clapped his hands twice, and a houri of most bewitching aspect glided into the *dîwan.*

"Bring sherbet!" ordered the Pasha.

The maiden departed; and whilst I was yet trying to come to a decision (the Pasha had mentioned no alternative, but my imagination was equal to the task of supplying one!) she returned with a tray upon which were porcelain cups and two vessels of beautifully chased gold.

Harûn Pasha decocted a sparkling beverage, and, with his own hands, passed the brimming cup to me.

I knew you would not believe it; but I warned you, and I made a stipulation. Your idea is that I must be a poor sort of animal to accept so dishonorable a compromise? I agree. But the situation was even more peculiarly difficult than is apparent to you at the moment. Without seeking the information, I learned from Hassan of the Scent Bazaar that his brother had indeed fled with the beauteous Lady Zohara, no one knew whither; and this confirmation of the Pasha's sorrows touched a very tender spot in my heart!

Then there is another little point.

When the Pasha removed the elaborate stopper from the first of the golden vessels to which I have just referred, my eye alone perceived that a bottle, bearing a familiar black and white label, was contained in this golden casing. The flavor of the decoction with which we sealed our infamous bargain clinched the matter.

I was absolutely thrust out of the presence chamber before I had time for another word; but, looking back from the door and meeting the eye of the Pasha, I encountered a most portentous wink. Therefore I have stuck to my bargain.

Oh! I have not given much away. The Pasha is not called Harûn, and the palace is nowhere near the Coptic Church in Old Cairo. Because, you see, I only knew one man who winked in quite that elaborate fashion—and his name was Jack Dunlap!

In the Valley of the Sorceress

I

ondor wrote to me three times before the end (said Neville, Assistant-Inspector of Antiquities, staring vaguely from his open window at a squad drilling before the Kasr-en-Nîl Barracks). He dated his letters from the camp at Deir-el-Bahari. Judging from these, success appeared to be almost within his grasp. He shared my theories, of course, respecting Queen Hatasu, and was devoting the whole of his energies to the task of clearing up the great mystery of Ancient Egypt which centres around that queen.

For him, as for me, there was a strange fascination about those defaced walls and roughly obliterated inscriptions. That the queen under whom Egyptian art came to the apogee of perfection should thus have been treated by her successors; that no perfect figure of the wise, famous, and beautiful Hatasu should have been spared to posterity; that her very cartouche should have been ruthlessly removed from every inscription upon which it appeared, presented to Condor's mind a problem only second in interest to the immortal riddle of Gizeh.

You know my own views upon the matter? My monograph, "Hatasu, the Sorceress," embodies my opinion. In short, upon certain evidences, some adduced by Theodore Davis, some by poor Condor, and some resulting from my own inquiries, I have come to the conclusion that the source—real or imaginary—of this queen's power was an intimate acquaintance with what nowadays we term, vaguely, magic. Pursuing her studies beyond the limit which is lawful, she met with a certain end, not uncommon, if the old writings are to be believed, in the case of those who penetrate too far into the realms of the Borderland.

For this reason—the practice of black magic—her statues were dishonored, and her name erased from the monuments. Now, I do not

105

propose to enter into any discussion respecting the reality of such practices; in my monograph I have merely endeavored to show that, according to contemporary belief, the queen was a sorceress. Condor was seeking to prove the same thing; and when I took up the inquiry, it was in the hope of completing his interrupted work.

He wrote to me early in the winter of 1908, from his camp by the Rock Temple. Davis's tomb, at Bibân el-Mulûk, with its long, narrow passage, apparently had little interest for him; he was at work on the high ground behind the temple, at a point one hundred yards or so due west of the upper platform. He had an idea that he should find there the mummies of Hatasu—and another; the latter, a certain Sen-Mût, who appears in the inscriptions of the reign as an architect high in the queen's favor. The archæological points of the letter do not concern us in the least, but there was one odd little paragraph which I had cause to remember afterwards.

"A girl belonging to some Arab tribe," wrote Condor, "came racing to the camp two nights ago to claim my protection. What crime she had committed, and what punishment she feared, were far from clear; but she clung to me, trembling like a leaf, and positively refused to depart. It was a difficult situation, for a camp of fifty native excavators, and one highly respectable European enthusiast, affords no suitable quarters for an Arab girl—and a very personable Arab girl. At any rate, she is still here; I have had a sort of lean-to rigged up in a little valley east of my own tent, but it is very embarrassing."

Nearly a month passed before I heard from Condor again; then came a second letter, with the news that on the eve of a great discovery— as he believed—his entire native staff—the whole fifty—had deserted one night in a body! "Two days' work," he wrote, "would have seen the tomb opened—for I am more than ever certain that my plans are accurate. Then I woke up one morning to find every man Jack of my fellows missing! I went down into the village where a lot of them live, in a towering rage, but not one of the brutes was to be found, and their relations professed entire ignorance respecting their whereabouts. What caused me almost as much anxiety as the check in my work was the fact that Mahâra—the Arab girl—had vanished also. I am wondering if the thing has any sinister significance."

Condor finished with the statement that he was making tremendous efforts to secure a new gang. "But," said he, "I shall finish the excavation) if I have to do it with my own hands."

His third and last letter contained even stranger matters than the two preceding it. He had succeeded in borrowing a few men from the British Archæological camp in the Fáyûm. Then, just as the work was re-starting, the Arab girl, Mahâra, turned up again, and entreated him to bring her down the Nile, "at least as far as Dendera. For the vengeance of her tribesmen," stated Condor, "otherwise would result not only in her own death, but in mine! At the moment of writing I am in two winds what to do. If Mahâra is to go upon this journey, I do not feel justified in sending her alone, and there is no one here who could perform the duty," etc.

I began to wonder, of course; and I had it in mind to take the train to Luxor merely in order to see this Arab maiden, who seemed to occupy so prominent a place in Condor's mind. However, Fate would have it otherwise; and the next thing I heard was that Condor had been brought into Cairo, and was at the English hospital.

He had been bitten by a cat—presumably from the neighboring village; and although the doctor at Luxor dealt with the bite at once, traveled down with him, and placed him in the hand of the Pasteur man at the hospital, he died, as you remember, in the night of his arrival, raving mad; the Pasteur treatment failed entirely.

I never saw him before the end, but they told me that his howls were horribly like those of a cat. His eyes changed in some way, too, I understand; and, with his fingers all contracted, he tried to scratch everyone and everything within reach.

They had to strap the poor beggar down, and even then he tore the sheets into ribbons.

Well, as soon as possible, I made the necessary arrangements to finish Condor's inquiry. I had access to his papers, plans, etc., and in the spring of the same year I took up my quarters near Deir-el-Bahari, roped off the approaches to the camp, stuck up the usual notices, and prepared to finish the excavation, which, I gathered, was in a fairly advanced state.

My first surprise came very soon after my arrival, for when, with the plan before me, I started out to find the shaft, I found it, certainly, but only with great difficulty.

It had been filled in again with sand and loose rock right to the very top!

II

All my inquiries availed me nothing. With what object the excavation had been thus closed I was unable to conjecture. That Condor had not reclosed it I was quite certain, for at the time of his mishap he had actually been at work at the bottom of the shaft, as inquiries from a native of Suefee, in the Fáyûm, who was his only companion at the time, had revealed.

In his eagerness to complete the inquiry, Condor, by lantern light, had been engaged upon a solitary night-shift below, and the rabid cat had apparently fallen into the pit; probably in a frenzy of fear, it had attacked Condor, after which it had escaped.

Only this one man was with him, and he, for some reason that I could not make out, had apparently been sleeping in the temple—quite a considerable distance from Condor's camp. The poor fellow's cries had aroused him, and he had met Condor running down the path and away from the shaft.

This, however, was good evidence of the existence of the shaft at the time, and as I stood contemplating the tightly packed rubble which alone marked its site, I grew more and more mystified, for this task of reclosing the cutting represented much hard labor.

Beyond perfecting my plans in one or two particulars, I did little on the day of my arrival. I had only a handful of men with me, all of whom I knew, having worked with them before, and beyond clearing Condor's shaft I did not intend to excavate further.

Hatasu's Temple presents a lively enough scene in the daytime during the winter and early spring months, with the streams of tourists constantly passing from the white causeway to Cook's Rest House on the edge of the desert. There had been a goodly number of visitors that day to the temple below, and one or two of the more curious and venturesome had scrambled up the steep path to the little plateau which was the scene of my operations. None had penetrated beyond the notice boards, however, and now, with the evening sky passing through those innumerable shades which defy palette and brush, which can only be distinguished by the trained eye, but which, from palest blue melt into exquisite pink, and by some magical combination form that deep violet which does not exist to perfection elsewhere than in the skies of Egypt, I found myself in the silence and the solitude of "the Holy Valley."

I stood at the edge of the plateau, looking out at the rosy belt which marked the course of the distant Nile, with the Arabian hills vaguely sketched beyond. The rocks stood up against that prospect as great black smudges, and what I could see of the causeway looked like a gray smear upon a drab canvas. Beneath me were the chambers of the Rock Temple, with those wall paintings depicting events in the reign of Hatasu which rank among the wonders of Egypt.

Not a sound disturbed my reverie, save a faint clatter of cooking utensils from the camp behind me—a desecration of that sacred solitude. Then a dog began to howl in the neighboring village. The dog ceased, and faintly to my ears came the note of a reed pipe. The breeze died away, and with it the piping.

I turned back to the camp, and, having partaken of a frugal supper, turned in upon my campaigner's bed, thoroughly enjoying my freedom from the routine of official life in Cairo, and looking forward to the morrow's work pleasurably.

Under such circumstances a man sleeps well; and when, in an uncanny gray half-light, which probably heralded the dawn, I awoke with a start, I knew that something of an unusual nature alone could have disturbed my slumbers.

Firstly, then, I identified this with a concerted howling of the village dogs. They seemed to have conspired to make night hideous; I have never heard such an eerie din in my life. Then it gradually began to die away, and I realized, secondly, that the howling of the dogs and my own awakening might be due to some common cause. This idea grew upon me, and as the howling subsided, a sort of disquiet possessed me, and, despite my efforts to shake it off, grew more urgent with the passing of every moment.

In short, I fancied that the thing which had alarmed or enraged the dogs was passing from the village through the Holy Valley, upward to the Temple, upward to the plateau, and was approaching me.

I have never experienced an identical sensation since, but I seemed to be audient of a sort of psychic patrol, which, from a remote *pianissimo,* swelled *fortissimo,* to an intimate but silent clamor, which beat in some way upon my brain, but not through the faculty of hearing, for now the night was deathly still.

Yet I was persuaded of some *approach*—of the coming of something sinister, and the suspense of waiting had become almost insupportable, so that I began to accuse my Spartan supper of having given me nightmare, when the tent-flap was suddenly raised, and, outlined against the paling blue of the sky, with a sort of reflected elfin light playing upon her face, I saw an Arab girl looking in at me!

By dint of exerting all my self-control I managed to restrain the cry and upward start which this apparition prompted. Quite still, with my fists tightly clenched, I lay and looked into the eyes which were looking into mine.

The style of literary work which it has been my lot to cultivate fails me in describing that beautiful and evil face. The features were severely classical and small, something of the Bisharîn type, with a cruel little mouth and a rounded chin, firm to hardness. In the eyes alone lay the languor of the Orient; they were exceedingly—indeed, excessively—long and narrow. The ordinary ragged, picturesque finery of a desert girl bedecked this midnight visitant, who, motionless, stood there watching me.

I once read a work by Pierre de l'Ancre, dealing with the Black Sabbaths of the Middle Ages, and now the evil beauty of this Arab face threw my memory back to those singular pages, for, perhaps owing to the reflected light which I have mentioned, although the explanation scarcely seemed adequate, those long, narrow eyes shone catlike in the gloom.

Suddenly I made up my mind. Throwing the blanket from me, I leapt to the ground, and in a flash had gripped the girl by the wrists. Confuting some lingering doubts, she proved to be substantial enough. My electric torch lay upon a box at the foot of the bed, and, stooping, I caught it up and turned its searching rays upon the face of my captive.

She fell back from me, panting like a wild creature trapped, then dropped upon her knees and began to plead—began to plead in a voice and with a manner which touched some chord of consciousness that I could swear had never spoken before, and has never spoken since.

She spoke in Arabic, of course, but the words fell from her lips as liquid music in which lay all the beauty and all the deviltry of the "Siren's Song." Fully opening her astonishing eyes, she looked up at me, and, with her free hand pressed to her bosom, told me how she had fled from an unwelcome marriage; how, an outcast and a pariah, she had hidden in the desert places for three days and three nights, sustaining life only by means of a few dates which she had brought with her, and quenching her thirst with stolen water-melons.

"I can bear it no longer, *effendim.* Another night out in the desert, with the cruel moon beating, beating, beating upon my brain, with creeping things coming out from the rocks, wriggling, wriggling, their many feet making whisperings in the sand—ah, it will kill me! And I am for ever outcast from my tribe, from my people. No tent of all the Arabs, though I fly to the gates of Damascus, is open to me, save I enter in shame, as a slave, as a plaything, as a toy. My heart"—furiously she beat upon her breast—"is empty and desolate, *effendim.* I am meaner than the lowliest thing that creeps upon the sand; yet the God that made that creeping thing made me also—and you, you, who are merciful and strong, would not crush any creature because it was weak and helpless."

I had released her wrist now, and was looking down at her in a sort of stupor. The evil which at first I had seemed to perceive in her was effaced, wiped out as an artist wipes out an error in his drawing. Her dark beauty was speaking to me in a language of its own; a strange language, yet one so intelligible that I struggled in vain to disregard it. And her voice, her gestures, and the witch-fire of her eyes were whipping up my blood to a fever heat of passionate sorrow—of despair. Yes, incredible as it sounds, despair!

In short, as I see it now, this siren of the wilderness was playing upon me as an accomplished musician might play upon a harp, striking this string and that at will, and sounding each with such full notes as they had rarely, if ever, emitted before.

Most damnable anomaly of all, I—Edward Neville, archæologist, most prosy and matter-of-fact man in Cairo, perhaps—*knew* that this nomad who had burst into my tent, upon whom I had set eyes for the first time scarce three minutes before, held me enthralled; and yet, with her wondrous eyes upon me, I could summon up no resentment, and could offer but poor resistance.

"In the Little Oasis, *effendim,* I have a sister who will admit me into her household, if only as a servant. There I can be safe, there I can rest. O *Inglîsi,* at home in England you have a sister of your own! Would you see her pursued, a hunted thing from rock to rock, crouching for shelter in the lair of some jackal, stealing that she might live—and flying always, never resting, her heart leaping for fear, flying, flying, with nothing but dishonor before her?"

She shuddered and clasped my left hand in both her own convulsively, pulling it down to her bosom.

"There can be only one thing, *effendim,*" she whispered. "Do you not see the white bones bleaching in the sun?"

Throwing all my resolution into the act, I released my hand from her clasp, and, turning aside, sat down upon the box which served me as chair and table, too.

A thought had come to my assistance, had strengthened me in the moment of my greatest weakness; it was the thought of that Arab girl mentioned in Condor's letters. And a scheme of things, an incredible scheme, that embraced and explained some, if not all, of the horrible circumstances attendant upon his death, began to form in my brain.

Bizarre it was, stretching out beyond the realm of things natural and proper, yet I clung to it, for there, in the solitude, with this wildly beautiful creature kneeling at my feet, and with her uncanny powers of fascination yet enveloping me like a cloak, I found it not so improbable as inevitably it must have seemed at another time.

I turned my head, and through the gloom sought to look into the long eyes. As I did so they closed and appeared as two darkly luminous slits in the perfect oval of the face.

"You are an impostor!" I said in Arabic, speaking firmly and deliberately. "To Mr. Condor"—I could have sworn that she started slightly at sound of the name—"you called yourself Mahâra. I know you, and I will have nothing to do with you."

But in saying it I had to turn my head aside, for the strangest, maddest impulses were babbling up in my brain in response to the glances of those half-shut eyes.

I reached for my coat, which lay upon the foot of the bed, and, taking out some loose money, I placed fifty piastres in the nerveless brown hand.

"That will enable you to reach the Little Oasis, if such is your desire," I said. "It is all I can do for you, and now—you must go."

The light of the dawn was growing stronger momentarily, so that I could see my visitor quite clearly. She rose to her feet, and stood before me, a straight, slim figure, sweeping me from head to foot with such a glance of passionate contempt as I had never known or suffered.

She threw back her head magnificently, dashed the money on the ground at my feet, and, turning, leaped out of the tent.

For a moment I hesitated, doubting, questioning my humanity, testing my fears; then I took a step forward, and peered out across the plateau. Not a soul was in sight. The rocks stood up gray and eerie, and beneath lay the carpet of the desert stretching unbroken to the shadows of the Nile Valley.

III

We commenced the work of clearing the shaft at an early hour that morning. The strangest ideas were now playing in my mind, and in some way I felt myself to be in opposition to definite enmity. My excavators labored with a will, and, once we had penetrated below the first three feet or so of tightly packed stone, it became a mere matter of shoveling, for apparently the lower part of the shaft had been filled up principally with sand.

I calculated that four days' work at the outside would see the shaft clear to the base of Condor's excavation. There remained, according to his own notes, only another six feet or so; but it was solid limestone—the roof of the passage, if his plans were correct, communicating with the tomb of Hatasu.

With the approach of night, tired as I was, I felt little inclination for sleep. I lay down on my bed with a small Browning pistol under the pillow, but after an hour or so of nervous listening drifted off into slumber. As on the night before, I awoke shortly before the coming of dawn.

Again the village dogs were raising a hideous outcry, and again I was keenly conscious of some ever-nearing menace. This consciousness grew stronger as the howling of the dogs grew fainter, and the sense of *approach* assailed me as on the previous occasion.

I sat up immediately with the pistol in my hand, and, gently raising the tent flap, looked out over the darksome plateau. For a long time I could perceive nothing; then, vaguely outlined against the sky, I detected something that moved above the rocky edge.

It was so indefinite in form that for a time I was unable to identify it, but as it slowly rose higher and higher, two luminous eyes—obviously feline eyes, since they glittered greenly in the darkness—came into view. In character and in shape they were the eyes of a cat, but in point of size they were larger than the eyes of any cat I had ever seen. Nor were they jackal eyes. It occurred to me that some predatory beast from the Sûdan might conceivably have strayed thus far north.

The presence of such a creature would account for the nightly disturbance amongst the village dogs; and, dismissing the superstitious notions which had led me to associate the mysterious Arab girl with the phenomenon of the howling dogs, I seized upon this new idea with a sort of gladness.

Stepping boldly out of the tent, I strode in the direction of the gleaming eyes. Although my only weapon was the Browning pistol, it was a weapon of considerable power, and, moreover, I counted upon the well-known cowardice of nocturnal animals. I was not disappointed in the result.

The eyes dropped out of sight, and as I leaped to the edge of rock overhanging the temple a lithe shape went streaking off in the greyness beneath me. Its coloring appeared to be black, but this appearance may have been due to the bad light. Certainly it was no cat, was no jackal; and once, twice, thrice my Browning spat into the darkness.

Apparently I had not scored a hit, but the loud reports of the weapon aroused the men sleeping in the camp, and soon I was surrounded by a ring of inquiring faces.

But there I stood on the rock-edge, looking out across the desert in silence. Something in the long, luminous eyes, something in the sinuous, flying shape had spoken to me intimately, horribly.

Hassan es-Sugra, the headman, touched my arm, and I knew that I must offer some explanation.

"Jackals," I said shortly. And with no other word I walked back to my tent.

The night passed without further event, and in the morning we addressed ourselves to the work with such a will that I saw, to my satisfaction, that by noon of the following day the labor of clearing the loose sand would be completed.

During the preparation of the evening meal I became aware of a certain disquiet in the camp, and I noted a disinclination on the part of the native laborers to stray far from the tents. They hung together in a group, and whilst individually they seemed to avoid meeting my eye, collectively they watched me in a furtive fashion.

A gang of Moslem workmen calls for delicate handling, and I wondered if, inadvertently, I had transgressed in some way their iron-bound code of conduct. I called Hassan es-Sugra aside.

"What ails the men?" I asked him. "Have they some grievance?"

Hassan spread his palms eloquently.

"If they have," he replied, "they are secret about it, and I am not in their confidence. Shall I thrash three or four of them in order to learn the nature of this grievance?"

"No thanks all the same," I said, laughing at this characteristic proposal. "If they refuse to work to-morrow, there will be time enough for you to adopt those measures."

On this, the third night of my sojourn in the Holy Valley by the Temple of Hatasu, I slept soundly and uninterruptedly. I had been looking forward with the keenest zest to the morrow's work, which promised to bring me within sight of my goal, and when Hassan came to awaken me, I leaped out of bed immediately.

Hassan es-Sugra, having performed his duty, did not, as was his custom, retire; he stood there, a tall, angular figure, looking at me strangely.

"Well?" I said.

"There is trouble," was his simple reply. "Follow me, Neville Effendi."

Wondering greatly, I followed him across the plateau and down the slope to the excavation. There I pulled up short with a cry of amazement.

Condor's shaft was filled in to the very top, and presented, to my astonished gaze, much the same aspect that had greeted me upon my first arrival!

"The men—" I began.

Hassan es-Sugra spread wide his palms.

"Gone!" he replied. "Those Coptic dogs, those eaters of carrion, have fled in the night."

"And this"—I pointed to the little mound of broken granite and sand—"is their work?"

"So it would seem," was the reply; and Hassan sniffed his sublime contempt.

I stood looking bitterly at this destruction of my toils. The strangeness of the thing at the moment did not strike me, in my anger; I was only concerned with the outrageous impudence of the missing workmen, and if I could have laid hands upon one of them it had surely gone hard with him.

As for Hassan es-Sugra, I believe he would cheerfully have broken the necks of the entire gang. But he was a man of resource.

"It is so newly filled in," he said, "that you and I, in three days, or in four, can restore it to the state it had reached when those nameless dogs, who regularly prayed with their shoes on, those devourers of pork, began their dirty work."

His example was stimulating. *I* was not going to be beaten, either.

After a hasty breakfast, the pair of us set to work with pick and shovel and basket. We worked as those slaves must have worked whose toil was directed by the lash of the Pharaoh's overseer. My back acquired an almost permanent crook, and every muscle in my body seemed to be on fire. Not even in the midday heat did we slacken or stay our toils; and when dusk fell that night a great mound had arisen beside Condor's shaft, and we had excavated to a depth it had taken our gang double the time to reach.

When at last we threw down our tools in utter exhaustion, I held out my hand to Hassan, and wrung his brown fist enthusiastically. His eyes sparkled as he met my glance.

"Neville Effendi," he said, "you are a true Moslem!"

And only the initiated can know how high was the compliment conveyed.

That night I slept the sleep of utter weariness yet it was not a dreamless sleep, or perhaps it was not so deep as I supposed, for blazing cat-eyes encircled me in my dreams, and a constant feline howling seemed to fill the night.

When I awoke the sun was blazing down upon the rock outside my tent, and, springing out of bed, I perceived, with amazement, that the morning was far advanced. Indeed, I could hear the distant voices of the donkey-boys and other harbingers of the coming tourists.

Why had Hassan es-Sugra not awakened me?

I stepped out of the tent and called him in a loud voice. There was no reply. I ran across the plateau to the edge of the hollow.

Condor's shaft had been reclosed to the top!

Language fails me to convey the wave of anger, amazement, incredulity, which swept over me. I looked across to the deserted camp and back to my own tent; I looked down at the mound, where but a few hours before had been a pit, and seriously I began to question whether I was mad or whether madness had seized upon all who had been with me. Then, pegged down upon the heap of broken stones, I perceived, fluttering, a small piece of paper.

Dully I walked across and picked it up. Hassan, a man of some education, clearly was the writer. It was a pencil scrawl in doubtful Arabic, and, not without difficulty, I deciphered it as follows:

"Fly, Neville Effendi! This is a haunted place!"

Standing there by the mound, I tore the scrap of paper into minute fragments, bitterly casting them from me upon the ground. It was incredible; it was insane.

The man who had written that absurd message, the man who had undone his own work, had the reputation of being fearless and honorable. He had been with me before a score of times, and had quelled petty mutinies in the camp in a manner which marked him a born overseer. I could not understand; I could scarcely believe the evidence of my own senses.

What did I do?

I suppose there are some who would have abandoned the thing at once and for always, but I take it that the national traits are strong within me. I went over to the camp and prepared my own breakfast; then, shouldering pick and shovel, I went down into the valley and set to work. What ten men could not do, what two men had failed to do, one man was determined to do.

It was about half an hour after commencing my toils, and when, I suppose, the surprise and rage occasioned by the discovery had begun to wear off, that I found myself making comparisons between my own case and that of Condor. It became more and more evident to me that events—mysterious events—were repeating themselves.

The frightful happenings attendant upon Condor's death were marshaling in my mind. The sun was blazing down upon me, and distant voices could be heard in the desert stillness. I knew that the plain below was dotted with pleasure-seeking tourists, yet nervous tremors shook me. Frankly, I dreaded the coming of the night.

Well, tenacity or pugnacity conquered, and I worked on until dusk. My supper despatched, I sat down on my bed and toyed with the Browning.

I realized already that sleep, under existing conditions, was impossible. I perceived that on the morrow I must abandon my one-man enterprise, pocket my pride, in a sense, and seek new assistants, new companions.

The fact was coming home to me conclusively that a menace, real and not mythical, hung over that valley. Although, in the morning sunlight and filled with indignation, I had thought contemptuously of Hassan es-Sugra, now, in the mysterious violet dusk so conducive to calm consideration, I was forced to admit that he was at least as brave a man as I. And he had fled! What did that night hold in keeping for me?

I will tell you what occurred, and it is the only explanation I have to give of why Condor's shaft, said to communicate with the real tomb of Hatasu, to this day remains unopened.

There, on the edge of my bed, I sat far into the night, not daring to close my eyes. But physical weariness conquered in the end, and, although I have no recollection of its coming, I must have succumbed to sleep, since I remember—can never forget—a repetition of the dream, or what I had assumed to be a dream, of the night before.

A ring of blazing green eyes surrounded me. At one point this ring was broken, and in a kind of nightmare panic I leaped at that promise of safety, and found myself outside the tent.

Lithe, slinking shapes hemmed me in—cat shapes, ghoul shapes, veritable figures of the pit. And the eyes, the shapes, although they were the eyes and shapes of cats, sometimes changed elusively, and became the wicked eyes and the sinuous, writhing shapes of women. Always the ring was incomplete, and always I retreated in the only direction by which retreat was possible. I retreated from those cat-things.

In this fashion I came at last to the shaft, and there I saw the tools which I had left at the end of my day's toil.

Looking around me, I saw also, with such a pang of horror as I cannot hope to convey to you, that the ring of green eyes was now unbroken about me.

And it was closing in.

Nameless feline creatures were crowding silently to the edge of the pit, some preparing to spring down upon me where I stood. A voice seemed to speak in my brain; it spoke of capitulation, telling me to accept defeat, lest, resisting, my fate be the fate of Condor.

Peals of shrill laughter rose upon the silence. The laughter was mine.

Filling the night with this hideous, hysterical merriment, I was working feverishly with pick and with shovel filling in the shaft.

The end? The end is that I awoke, in the morning, lying, not on my bed, but outside on the plateau, my hands torn and bleeding and every muscle in my body throbbing agonisingly. Remembering my dream—for even in that moment of awakening I thought I had dreamed—I staggered across to the valley of the excavation.

Condor's shaft was reclosed to the top.

The Haunting of Low Fennel

T here's Low Fennel," said Major Dale.

We pulled up short on the brow of the hill. Before me lay a little valley carpeted with heather, purple slopes hemming it in A group of four tall firs guarded the house, which was couched in the hollow of the dip —a low, rambling building, in parts showing evidence of great age and in other parts of the modern improver.

"That's the new wing," the Major continued, raising his stick; "projecting out this way. It's the only addition I've made to the house, which, as it stood, had insufficient accommodation for the servants."

"It is a quaint old place."

"It is, and I'm loath to part with it, especially as it means a big loss."

"Have you formed any theories since wiring me?"

"None whatever. I've always been a skeptic, Addison, but if Low Fennel is not haunted, I'm a Dutchman, by the Lord Harry!"

I laughed reassuringly, and the two of us descended the slope to the white gate giving access to a trim gravel path flanked by standard roses. Mrs. Dale greeted us at the door. She was, as I had heard, much younger than the Major, and a distinctly pretty woman. In so far Dame Rumour was confirmed; other things I had heard of her, but I was not yet in a position to pass judgment.

She greeted me cordially enough, although women are usually natural actresses. I thought that she did not suspect the real object of my visit. Tea was served in a delightful little drawing room which bore evidence of having but recently left the hands of London decorators, but when presently I found myself alone with my host in the Major's peculiar sanctum, the real business afoot monopolized our conversation.

The room which Major Dale had appropriated as a study was on the ground floor of the new wing—the wing which he himself had had built onto Low Fennel. In regard to its outlook it was a charming apartment enough, with roses growing right up to the open window, so that their perfume filled the place, and beyond, a prospect of golden gorse slopes and fir-clad hills.

Sporting prints decorated the walls, and the library was entirely, or almost entirely, made up of works on riding, hunting, shooting, racing, and golf, with a sprinkling of Whyte-Melville and Nat Gould novels and a Murray handbook or two. It was a most cosy room, probably because it was so untidy, or, as Mrs. Dale phrased it, "so manny."

On a side table was ranked enough liquid refreshment to have inebriated a regiment, and, in one corner, cigar boxes and tobacco tins were stacked from the floor some two feet up against the wall. We were soon comfortably ensconced, then, the Major on a hard leather couch, and I in a deep saddlebag chair.

"It's an awkward sort of thing to explain," began Dale, puffing away at a cigar and staring through the open window; "because, if you're to do anything, you will want full particulars."

I nodded.

"Well," he continued, "you've heard how that blackguard Ellis let me down over those shares? The result?—I had to sell the Hall—Fennel Hall, where a Dale has been since the time of Elizabeth! But still, never mind! that's not the story. This place, Low Fennel, is really part of the estate, and I have leased it from Meyers, who has bought the Hall. It was formerly the home farm, but since my father's time it has not been used for that purpose. The New Farm is over the brow of the hill there, on the other side of the high road; my father built it."

"Why?"

"Well—" Dale shifted uneasily, and a look of perplexity crossed his jolly red face—"there were stories—uncomfortable stories. To cut a long story short, Seager—a man named Seager, who occupied it at the time I was at Sandhurst—was found dead here, or something; I never was clear as to the particulars, but there was an inquiry and a lot of fuss, and, in short, no one would occupy the property. Therefore the governor built the New Farm."

"Low Fennel has been empty for many years then?"

"No, sir; only for one. Ord, the head gardener at the Hall, lived here up till last July. The old story about Seager was dying out, you see;

but Ord must have got to hear about it—or I've always supposed so. At any rate, in July—a dam' hot July, too, almost if not quite as hot as now—Ord declined to live here any longer."

"On what grounds?"

"He told me a cock-and-bull story about his wife having seen a horrible-looking man with a contorted face peering in at her bedroom window! I questioned the woman, of course, and she swore to it."

He mopped his heated brow excitedly and burnt several matches before he succeeded in relighting his cigar.

"She tried to make me believe that she woke up and saw this apparition, but I bullied the truth out of her, and, as I expected, the man Ord had come home the worse for drink. I made up my mind that the contorted face was the face of her drunken husband—whom she had declined to admit, and who therefore had climbed the ivy to get in at the open window."

"She denied this?"

"Of course she denied it; they both did; but, from evidence obtained at the Three Keys in the village, I proved that Ord had returned home drunk that night. Still—" he shrugged his shoulders ponderously—"the people declined to remain in the place, so what could I do? Ord was a good gardener, and his drunken habits in no way interfered with his efficiency. He gained nothing out of the matter except that, instead of keeping Low Fennel, a fine house, I sent him to live in one of the Valley Cottages. He lives there now, for he's still head gardener at the Hall."

I made an entry in my notebook.

"I must see Ord," I said.

"I should," agreed the Major in his loud voice; "you'll get nothing out of him. He's the most pig-headed liar in the county! But to continue. The place proved unlettable. All the old stories were revived, and I'm told that people cheerfully went two miles out of their way in order to avoid passing Low Fennel at night! When I sold the Hall and decided to lease the place from the new proprietor, believe me it was almost hidden in a wilderness of weeds and bushes which had grown up around it. By the Lord Harry, I don't think a living soul had approached within a hundred yards of the house since the day that the Ords quitted it! But it suited my purpose, being inexpensive to keep up;

and by adding this new wing I was enabled to accommodate such servants as we required. The horses and the car had to go, of course, and with them a lot of my old people, but we brought the housekeeper and three servants, and when a London firm had rebuilt, renovated, decorated, and so forth, it began to look habitable."

"It's a charming place," I said with sincerity.

"Is it!" snapped the Major, tossing his half-smoked cigar on to a side table and selecting a fresh one from a large box at his elbow. "Help yourself, the bottle's near you. Is it! . . . Hullo! what have we here?"

He broke off, cigar in hand, as the sound of footsteps upon the gravel path immediately outside the window became audible. Through the cluster of roses peered a handsome face, that of a dark man whose soft grey hat and loose tie lent him a sort of artistic appearance.

"Oh, it's you, Wales!" cried the Major, but without cordiality. "See you in half an hour or so; little bit of business in hand at the moment. Marjorie's somewhere about."

"All right!" called the new arrival, and, waving his hand, passed on.

"It's young Aubrey Wales," explained Dale, almost savagely biting the end from his cigar, "son of Sir Frederick Wales, and one of my neighbours. He often drops in."

Mentally considering the Major's attitude, certain rumours which had reached me, and the youth and beauty of Mrs. Dale, I concluded that the visits of Aubrey Wales were not too welcome to my old friend. But he resumed in a louder voice than ever:

"It was last night that the fun began. I can make neither head nor tail of it. If the blessed place is haunted, why have we seen nothing of the ghost during the two months or so we have lived at Low Fennel? The fact remains that nothing unusual happened until last night. It came about owing to the infernal heat.

"Mrs. Alson, the housekeeper, came down about two o'clock, intending, so I understand, to get a glass of cider from the barrel in the cellar. She could not sleep owing to the heat, and felt extremely thirsty. There's a queer sort of bend in the stair—I'll show you in a minute; and as she came down and reached this bend she met a man, or a thing, who was going up! The moonlight was streaming in through the window right upon that corner of the stair, and the apparition stood fully revealed.

"I gather that it was that of an almost naked man. Mrs. Alson naturally is rather reticent on the point, but I gather that the apparition was inadequately clothed. Regarding the face of the thing she supplies more details. Addison—" the Major leant forward across the table—"it was the face of a demon, a contorted devilish face, the eyes crossed, and glaring like the eyes of a mad dog!

"Of course the poor woman fainted dead away on the spot. She might have died there if it hadn't been for the amazing heat of the night. This certainly was the cause of her trouble, but it also saved her. About three o'clock I woke up in a perfect bath of perspiration. I never remember such a night, not even in India, and, as Mrs. Alson had done an hour earlier, I also started to find a drink. Addison! I nearly fell over her as she lay swooning on the stair!"

He helped himself to a liberal tot of whisky, then squirted soda into the glass.

"For once in a way I did the right thing, Addison. Not wishing to alarm Marjorie, I knocked up one of the maids, and when Mrs. Alson had somewhat, recovered, gave her into the girl's charge. I sat downstairs here in this room until she could see me, and then got the particulars which I've given you. I wired you as soon as the office was open; for I said to myself, 'Dale, the devilry has begun again. If Marjorie gets to hear of it there'll be hell to pay. She won't live in the place.'"

He stood up abruptly, as a ripple of laughter reached us from the garden.

"Suppose we explore the scene of the trouble?" he suggested, moving toward the door.

I thought in the circumstance our inspection might be a hurried one therefore:

"Should you mind very much if I sought it out for myself?" I said. "It is my custom in cases of the kind to be alone if possible."

"My dear fellow, certainly!"

"My ramble concluded, I will rejoin Mrs. Dale and yourself—say on the lawn?"

"Good, good!" cried the Major, throwing open the door. "An opening has been made on the floor above corresponding with this, and communicating with the old stair. Go where you like; find out what you can; but remember—not a word to Marjorie."

2

Filled with the liveliest curiosity, I set out to explore Low Fennel. First I directed my attention to the exterior, commencing my investigations from the front. That part of the building on either side of the door was evidently of Tudor date, with a Jacobean wing to the west containing apartments overlooking the lawn—the latter a Georgian addition; while the new east wing, built by Major Dale, carried the building out almost level with the clump of fir trees and into the very heart of the ferns and bushes which here grew densely.

There was no way around on this side, and not desiring to cross the lawn at present, I passed in through the house to the garden at the back. This led me through the northern part of the building and the servants' quarters, which appeared to be of even greater age than the front of the house. The fine old kitchen in particular was suggestive of the days when roasting was done upon a grand scale.

Beyond the flower garden lay the kitchen garden, and beyond that the orchard. The latter showed evidences of neglect, bearing out the Major's story that the place had been unoccupied for twelve months; but it was evident, nevertheless, that the soil had been cultivated for many generations. Thus far I had discovered nothing calculated to assist me in my peculiar investigation, and entering the house I began a room-to-room quest, which, beyond confirming most of my earlier impressions, afforded little data.

The tortuous stairway, which had been the scene of the event described by my host, occupied me for some time, and I carefully examined the time-blackened panels, and tested each separate stair, for in houses like Low Fennel secret passages and "priest-holes" were to be looked for. However, I found nothing, but descending again to the hall I made a small discovery.

There were rooms in Low Fennel which one entered by descending or ascending two or three steps, but this was entirely characteristic of the architectural methods of the period represented. I was surprised, however, to find that one mounted three steps in order to obtain access to the passage leading to the new wing. I had overlooked this peculiarity hitherto, but now it struck me as worthy of attention. Why should a modern architect introduce such a device? It could only mean that the ground was higher on the east side of the building, and that, for some reason, it had proved more convenient to adopt the existing foundations than to level the site.

I returned to the hallway and stood there deep in thought, when the contact of a rough tongue with my hand drew my attention to a young Airedale terrier who was anxious to make my acquaintance. I patted his head encouragingly, and, having reviewed the notes made during my tour of inspection, determined to repeat the tour in order to check them.

The Airedale accompanied me, behaving himself with admirable propriety as we passed around the house and then out through the kitchens into the garden. It was not until my journey led me back to the three steps communicating with the new wing that my companion seemed disposed to desert me.

At first I put down his attitude to mere canine caprice. But when he persistently refused to be encouraged, I began to ascribe it to something else.

Suddenly grasping him by the collar, I dragged him up the steps, along the corridor, and into the Major's study. The result was extraordinary. I think I have never seen a dog in quite the same condition; he whimpered and whined most piteously. At the door he struggled furiously, and even tried to snap at my hand. Then, as I still kept a firm grip upon him, he set out upon a series of howls which must have been audible for miles around. Finally I released him, having first closed the study door and lowered the window. What followed was really amazing.

The Airedale hurled himself upon the closed door, scratching at it furiously, with intermittent howling; then, crouching down, he turned his eyes upon me with a look in them, not savage, but truly piteous. Seeing that I did not move, the dog began to whimper again; when, suddenly making up his mind, as it seemed, he bounded across the room and went crashing through the glass of the closed window into the rose bushes, leaving me standing looking after him in blank wonderment.

3

Aubrey Wales stayed to dinner, and since he had no opportunity of dressing, his presence afforded a welcome excuse for the other members of the party. The night was appallingly hot; the temperature being such as to preclude the slightest exertion. The Major was an excellent host, but I could see that the presence of the younger man irritated him, and at times the conversation grew strained; there was an uncomfortable tension. So that altogether I was not sorry when Mrs. Dale left the table and the quartet was broken up. On closer acquaintance I perceived that Wales was even younger than I had supposed, and therefore I was the more inclined to condone his infatuation for the society of Mrs. Dale, although I felt less sympathetically disposed toward her for offering him the encouragement which rather openly she did.

Ere long, Wales left Major Dale and myself for the more congenial society of the hostess; so that shortly afterwards, when the Major, who took at least as much wine as was good for him, began to doze in his chair, I found myself left to my own devices. I quitted the room quietly, without disturbing my host, and strolled around onto the lawn, smoking a cigarette, and turning over in my mind the matters responsible for my presence at Low Fennel.

With no definite object in view, I had wandered towards the orchard, when I became aware of a whispered conversation taking place somewhere near me, punctuated with little peals of laughter. I detected the words "Aubrey" and "Marjorie" (Mrs. Dale's name), and, impatiently tossing my cigarette away, I returned to the house, intent upon arousing the Major and terminating this tête-à-tête. That it was more, on Mrs. Dale's part, than a harmless flirtation, I did not believe; but young Wales was not a safe type of man for that sort of amusement.

The Major, sunk deep in his favourite chair in the study, was snoring loudly, and as I stood contemplating him in the dusk I changed my mind and, retracing my steps, joined the two in the orchard, proclaiming my arrival by humming a popular melody.

"Has he fallen asleep?" asked Mrs. Dale, turning laughing eyes upon me.

I studied the piquant face ere replying. Her tone and her expression had reassured me, if further assurance were necessary, that my old friend's heart was in safe keeping; but she was young and gay; it was a case for diplomatic handling.

"India leaves its mark on all men," I replied lightly; "but I have no doubt that the Major is wide-awake enough now."

My words were an invitation; to which, I was glad to note, she responded readily enough.

"Let's come and dig him out of that cavern of his!" she said, and linking her right arm in that of Wales, and her left with mine, she turned us about toward the house.

Dusk was now fallen, and lights shone out from several windows of Low Fennel. Suddenly, an upper window became illuminated, and Mrs. Dale pointed to this.

"That is my room," she said to me; "isn't it delightfully situated? The view from the window is glorious."

"I consider Low Fennel charming in every way," I replied.

Clearly she knew nothing of the place's sinister reputation, which seemed to indicate that she employed herself little with the domestic side of the household; otherwise she must undoubtedly have learnt of the episode of the man with the contorted face, if not from the housekeeper, from the maid. It was a tribute to the reticence of the servants that the story had spread no further; but the broken study window and the sadly damaged Airedale already afforded matter for whispered debate among them, as I had noted with displeasure.

The "digging out" of the Major did not prove to be an entire success. He was in one of his peculiar moods, which I knew of old, and rather surly, being pointedly rude on more than one occasion to Wales. He had some accounts to look into, or professed to have, and the three of us presently left him alone. It was now about ten o'clock, and Aubrey Wales made his departure, shaking me warmly by the hand and expressing the hope that we should see more of one another. He could not foresee that the wish was to be realized in a curious fashion.

Mrs. Dale informed me that the Major in all probability would remain immured in his study until a late hour, which I took to be an intimation that she wished to retire. I therefore pleaded weariness as a result of my journey, and went up to my room, although I had no intention of turning in. I opened the two windows widely, and the heavy perfume of some kind of tobacco plant growing in the beds below grew almost oppressive. The heat of the night was truly phenomenal; I might have been, not in an English home county, but in the Soudan. An absolute stillness reigned throughout Low Fennel, and, my hearing being peculiarly acute, I could detect the chirping of the bats which flitted restlessly past my windows.

It was difficult to decide how to act. My experience of so-called supernatural appearances had strengthened my faith in the theory set forth in the paper "Chemistry of Psychic Phenomena"—which had attracted unexpected attention a year before. Therein I classified hauntings under several heads, basing my conclusions upon the fact that such apparitions are invariably localized; often being confined, not merely to a particular room, for instance, but to a certain wall, door, or window. I had been privileged to visit most of the famous haunted homes of Great Britain, and this paper was the result; but in the case of Low Fennel I found myself nonplussed, largely owing to lack of data. I hoped on the morrow to make certain inquiries along lines suggested by oddities in the structure of the house itself and by the nature of the little valley in which it stood.

When meditating, I never sit still, and while marshalling my ideas I paced the room from end to end, smoking the whole time. Both windows, and also the door, were widely opened. The amazing heat wave which we were then experiencing promised to afford me a valuable clue, for I had proved to my own satisfaction that the apparitions variously known as "controls" and "elementals" not infrequently coincided with abrupt climatic changes, thunder-storms, or heat waves, or with natural phenomena, such as landslides, and the like.

This pacing led me from end to end of the room, between the open door and the large, dressing table facing it. It was as I returned from the door towards the dressing table that I became aware of the presence of the *contorted face.*

My peculiar studies had brought me into contact with many horrible apparitions, and if familiarity had failed to breed contempt, at least it had served to train my nerves for the reception of such sudden and ghastly appearances. I should be avoiding the truth, however, if I claimed to have been unmoved by the vision which now met me in the mirror. I drew up short, with one sibilant breath, and then stood transfixed.

Before me was a reflection of the open door, and of part of the landing and stairs beyond it. The landing lights were extinguished, and therefore the place beyond the door lay in comparative darkness. But, crawling in, serpent fashion, inch by inch, silently, intently, so that the head, throat, and hands were actually across the threshold, came a creature which seemed to be entirely naked! It had the form of a man, but the face, the dreadful face which was being pushed forward slowly across the carpet with head held sideways so that one ear all but touched the floor, was the face, not of a man, but of a ghoul!

I clenched my teeth hard, staring into the mirror and trying to force myself to turn and confront, not the reflection, but the reality. Yet for many seconds I was unable to accomplish this. The baleful, protruding eyes glared straight into mine from the glass. The chin and lower lip of this awful face seemed to be drawn up so as almost to meet the nose, entirely covering the upper lip, and the nostrils were distended to an incredible degree, whilst the skin had a sort of purple tinge unlike anything I had seen before. The effect was grotesque in the true sense of the word; for the thing was clearly grimacing at me, yet God knows there was nothing humorous in that grimace!

Nearer it came and nearer. I could hear the heavy body being drawn across the floor; I could hear the beating of my own heart . . . and I could hear a whispered conversation which seemed to be taking place somewhere immediately outside my room.

At the moment that I detected the latter sound, it seemed that the apparition detected it also. The protruding eyes twisted in the head, rolling around ridiculously but horribly. Despite the dread which held me, I identified the whisperers and located their situation. Mrs. Dale was at her open window, and Aubrey Wales was in the garden below.

The thought crossed my mind and was gone—but gone no quicker than the contorted face. By a sort of backward, serpentine movement, the thing which had been crawling into my room suddenly retired and was swallowed up in the shadows of the landing.

I turned and sprang toward the open door, the fever of research hot upon me, and my nerves in hand again. At the door. I paused and listened intently. No sound came to guide me from the darkened stair, and when, stepping quietly forward and leaning over the rail, I peered down into the hall below, nothing stirred, no shadow of the many there moved to tell of the passage of any living thing. I paused irresolute, unable to doubt that I was in the presence of an authentic apparition. But how to classify it?

Slowly I returned to my room, and stood there, thinking hard, and all the while listening for the slightest sound from within or without the house.

The whispered conversation continued, and I stole quietly to one of the windows and leant out, looking to the left, in the direction of the new wing. A light burnt in the Major's study, whereby I concluded that he was still engaged with his accounts, if he had not fallen asleep. Between my window and the new wing, and on a level with my eyes, was the window of Mrs. Dale's room; and in the bright moonlight I could see her leaning out, her elbows on the ledge. Her bare arms gleamed like marble in the cold light, and she looked statuesquely beautiful. Wales I could not see, for a thick, square-clipped hedge obstructed my view . . . but I saw something else.

Lizard fashion, a hideous unclad shape crawled past beneath me among the tangle of ivy and low plants about the foot of the fir trees. The moonlight touched it for a moment, and then it was gone into denser shadows. . . .

A consciousness of impending disaster came to me, but, because of its very vagueness, found me unprepared. Then suddenly I saw young Wales. He sprang into view above the hedge, against which, I presume, he had been crouching; he leapt high in the air as though from some menace on the ground beneath him. I have never heard a more horrifying scream than that which he uttered.

"My God!" he cried, "Marjorie! Marjorie!" and yet again: "Marjorie! *save me!*"

Then he was down, still screaming horribly, and calling on the woman for aid—as though she could have aided him. The crawling thing made no sound, but the dreadful screams of Wales sank slowly into a sort of sobbing, and then into a significant panting which told of his dire extremity.

I raced out of the room and down the dark stair into the hall. Everywhere I was met by locked doors which baffled me. I had hoped to reach the garden by way of the kitchens, but now I changed my plan and turned my attention to the front door. It was bolted, but I drew the bolts one after the other, and got the door open.

Outside, the landscape was bathed in glorious moonlight, and a sort of grey mist hovered over the valley like smoke. I ran around the angle of the house onto the lawn, and went plunging through flower beds heedlessly to the scene of the incredible conflict.

I almost fell over Wales as he lay inert upon the gravel path. The shadows veiled him so that I could not see his face; but when, groping with my bands, I sought to learn if his heart still pulsed, I failed to discover any evidence that it did. With my hand thrust against his breast and my ear lowered anxiously, I listened, but he gave no sign of life, lying as still as all else around me.

Now this stillness was broken. Excited voices became audible, and doors were being unlocked here and there. First of all the household, Mrs. Dale appeared, enveloped in a lace dressing gown.

"Aubrey!" she cried tremulously, "what is it? Where are you?"

"He is here, Mrs. Dale," I answered, standing up, "and in a bad way, I fear."

"For Heaven's sake, what has happened to him? Did you hear his awful cries?"

"I did," I said shortly.

Standing with the moonlight full upon her, Mrs. Dale sought him in the shadows of the hedge—and I knew that by the manner of his frightened outcry the man lying unconscious at my feet had forfeited whatever of her regard he had enjoyed. She was dreadfully alarmed, not so much on his behalf, as by the mystery of the attack upon him. But now she composed herself, though not without visible effort.

"Where is he, Mr. Addison?" she said firmly, "and what has happened to him?"

A man, who proved to be a gardener, now appeared upon the scene.

"Help me to carry him in," I said to this new arrival; "perhaps he has only fainted."

We gathered up the recumbent body and carried it through the kitchens into the breakfast room, where there was a deep couch. All the servants were gathered at the foot of the stairs, frightened and useless, but the outcry did not seem to have aroused Major Dale.

Mrs. Dale and I bent over Wales. His face was frightfully congested, whilst his tongue protruded hideously; and it was evident, from the great discoloured weals which now were coming up upon his throat, that he had been strangled, or nearly so. I glanced at the white face of my hostess and then bent over the victim, examining him more carefully. I stood upright again.

"Do you know first aid, Mrs. Dale?" I asked abruptly.

She nodded, her eyes fixed intently upon me.

"Then help to employ artificial respiration," I said, "and let one of the girls get ammonia, if you have any, and a bowl of hot water. We can patch him up, I think, without medical aid—which might be undesirable."

Mrs. Dale seemed fully to appreciate the point, and in business-like fashion set to work to assist me. Wales had just opened his eyes and begun to clutch at his agonized throat, when I heard a heavy step descending from the new wing—and Major Dale, in his dressing gown, joined us. His red face was more red than usual, and his eyes were round with wonder.

"What the devil's the matter?" he cried; "what's everybody up for?"

"There has been an accident, Major," I said, glancing around at the servants, who stood in a group by the door of the breakfast room; "I can explain more fully later."

Major Dale stepped forward and looked down at Wales.

"Good God!" he said hoarsely, "it's young Wales, by the Lord Harry!—what's he doing here?"

Mrs. Dale, standing just behind me, laid her hand upon my arm; and, unseen by the Major, I turned and pressed it reassuringly.

4

The following day I lunched alone with the Major, Mrs. Dale being absent on a visit. It had been impossible to keep the truth from her (or what we knew of it) and at present I could not quite foresee the issue of last night's affair. Young Wales, who had been driven home in a car sent from his place at a late hour, had not since put in an appearance; and it was sufficiently evident that Mrs. Dale would not welcome him should he do so, the hysterical panic which he had exhibited on the previous night having disgusted her. She had not said so in as many words, but I did not doubt it.

"Well, Addison," said the Major as I entered, "have you got the facts you were looking for?"

"Some of them," I replied, and opening my notebook I turned to the pages containing notes made that morning.

The Major watched me with intense curiosity, and almost impatiently awaited my next words. The servant having left the room:

"In the first place," I began, glancing at the notes, "I have been consulting certain local records in the town, and I find that in the year 1646 a certain Dame Pryce occupied a cabin which, according to one record, 'stood close beside unto ye Lowe Fennel.'"

"That is, close beside this house?" interjected the Major excitedly.

"Exactly," I said. "She attracted the attention of one of the many infamous wretches who disfigure the history of that period: Matthew Hopkins, the self-styled Witch-Finder General. This was a witch-ridden age, and the man Hopkins was one of those who fattened on the credulity of his fellows, receiving a fee of twenty shillings for every unhappy woman discovered and convicted of witchcraft. Poor Pryce was 'swum' in a local pond (a test whereby the villain Hopkins professed to discover if the woman were one of Satan's band, or otherwise) and burnt alive in Reigate market-place on June 23, 1646."

"By God!" said the Major, who had not attempted to commence his lunch, "that's a horrible story!"

"It is one of the many to the credit of Matthew Hopkins," I replied; "but, without boring you with the details of this woman's examination and so forth, I may say that what interests me most in the case is the date—June 23."

"Why? I don't follow you."

"Well," I said, "there's a hiatus in the history of the place after that, except that even in those early days it evidently suffered from the reputation of being haunted; but without troubling about the interval, consider the case of Seager, which you yourself related to me. Was it not in the month of June that he was done to death here?"

"By Gad!" cried the Major, his face growing redder than ever, "you're right!—and hang it all, Addison! it was in July—last July—that the Ords cleared out!"

"I remember your mentioning," I continued, smiling at his excitement, "that it was a very hot month."

"It was."

"From a mere word dropped by one of the witnesses at the trial of poor Pryce I have gathered that the month in which she was convicted of practising witchcraft in her cabin adjoining Low Fennel (as it stood in those days) was a tropically hot month also."

Major Dale stared at me uncomprehendingly.

"I'm out of my depth, Addison—wading hopelessly. What the devil has the heat to do with the haunting?"

"To my mind everything. I may be wrong, but I think that, if the glass were to fall to-night, there would be no repetition of the trouble."

"You mean that it's only in very hot weather—" ⸻

"In phenomenally hot weather, Major—the sort that we only get in England perhaps once in every ten years. For the glass to reach the altitude at which it stands at present, in two successive summers, is quite phenomenal, as you know."

"It's phenomenal for it to reach that point at all," said the Major, mopping his perspiring forehead; "it's simply Indian, simply Indian, sir, by the Lord Harry!"

"Another inquiry," I continued, turning over a leaf of my book, "I have been unable to complete, since, in order to interview the people who built your new wing, I should have to run up to London."

"What the blazes have they to do with it?"

"Nothing at all, but I should have liked to learn their reasons for raising the wing three feet above the level of the hallway."

Between the heat and his growing excitement, Major Dale found himself at a temporary loss for words. Then:

"They told me," he shouted at the top of his voice, "they told me at the time that it was something about —that it was due to the plan—that it was—"

"I can imagine that they had some ready explanation," I said, "but it may not have been the true one."

"Then what the—what the—is the true one?"

"The true one is that the new wing covers a former mound."

"Quite right; it does."

"If my theory is correct, it was upon this mound that the cabin of Dame Pryce formerly stood."

"It's quite possible; they used to allow dirty hovels to be erected alongside one's very walls in those days—quite possible."

"Moreover, from what I've learnt from Ord—whom I interviewed at the Hall—and from such accounts as are obtainable of the death of Seager, this mound, and not the interior of Low Fennel as it then stood, was the scene of the apparitions."

"You've got me out of my depth again, Addison. What d'you mean?"

"Seager was strangled outside the house, not inside."

"I believe that's true," agreed the Major, still shouting at the top of his voice, but gradually growing hoarser; "I remember they found him lying on the step, or something."

"Then again, the apparition with the contorted face which peered in at Mrs. Ord—"

"Lies, all lies!"

"I don't agree with you, Major. She was trying to shield her husband, but I think she saw the contorted face right enough. At any rate, it's interesting to note that the visitant came from outside the house again."

"But," cried the Major, banging his fist upon the table, "it wanders about inside the house, and—and—damn it all!—it goes outside as well!"

"Where it goes," I interrupted quietly, "is not the point. The point is, where it comes from."

"Then where do you believe it comes from?"

"I believe the trouble arises, in the strictest sense of the word, from the same spot whence it arose in the days of Matthew Hopkins, and from which it had probably arisen ages before Low Fennel was built."

"What the—"

"I believe it to arise from the ancient barrow, or tumulus, above which you have had your new wing erected."

Major Dale fell back in his chair, temporarily speechless, but breathing noisily; then:

"Tumulus!" he said hoarsely; "d'you mean to tell me the house is built on a dam' burial ground?"

"Not the whole house," I corrected him; "only the new wing."

"Then is the place haunted by the spirit of some uneasy Ancient Briton or something of that sort, Addison? Hang it all! you can't tell me a fairy tale like that! A ghost going back to pre-Roman days is a bit too ancient for me, my boy—too hoary, by the Lord Harry!"

"I have said nothing about an Ancient British ghost—you're flying off at a tangent!"

"Hang it all, Addison! I don't know what you're talking about at all, but nevertheless your hints are sufficiently unpleasant. A tumulus! No man likes to know he's sleeping in a graveyard, not even if it is two or three thousand years old. D'you think the chap who surveyed the ground for me knew of it?"

"By the fact that he planned the new wing so as to avoid excavation, I think probably he did. He was wise enough to surmise that the order might be cancelled altogether and the job lost if you learnt the history of the mound adjoining your walls."

"A barrow under the study floor!" groaned the Major—"damn it all! I'll have the place pulled down—I won't live in it. Gad! if Marjorie knew, she would never close her eyes under the roof of Low Fennel again—I'm sure she wouldn't, I know she wouldn't. But what's more, Addison, the thing, whatever it is, is dangerous—infernally dangerous. It nearly killed young Wales!" he added, with a complacency which was significant.

"It was the fright that nearly killed him," I said shortly.

Major Dale stared across the table at me.

"For God's sake, Addison," he said, "what does it mean? What unholy thing haunts Low Fennel? You've studied these beastly subjects, and I rely upon you to make the place clean and good to live in again."

"Major," I replied, "I doubt if Low Fennel will ever be fit to live in. At any time an abnormal rise of temperature might produce the most dreadful results."

"You don't mean to tell me—"

"If you care to have the new wing pulled down and the wall bricked up again, if you care to keep all your doors and windows fastened securely whenever the thermometer begins to exhibit signs of rising, if you avoid going out on hot nights after dusk, as you would avoid the plague—yes, it may be possible to live in Low Fennel."

Again the Major became speechless, but finally:

"What d'you mean, Addison?" he whispered; "for God's sake, tell me. What is it?—what is it?"

"It is what some students have labelled an 'elemental' and some a 'control,'" I replied; "it is something older than the house, older, perhaps, than the very hills, something which may never be classified, something as old as the root of all evil, and it dwells in the Ancient British tumulus."

5

As I had hoped, for my plans were dependent upon it, the mercury towered steadily throughout that day, and showed no signs of falling at night; the phenomenal heat wave continued uninterruptedly. The household was late retiring, for the grey lord Fear had imposed his will upon all within it. Every shadow in the rambling old building became a cavern of horrors, every sound that disturbed the ancient timbers a portent and a warning.

That the servants proposed to leave *en masse* at the earliest possible moment was perfectly evident to me; in a word, all the dark old stories which had grown up around Low Fennel were revived and garnished, and new ones added to them. The horror of the night before had left its mark upon everyone, and the coming of dusk brought with it such a dread as could almost be felt in the very atmosphere of the place. Ghostly figures seemed to stir the hangings, ghostly sighs to sound from every nook of the old hall and stairway; baleful eyes looked in at the open windows, and the shrubberies were peopled with hosts of nameless things whispering together in evil counsel.

Mrs. Dale was as loath to retire as were the servants, more especially since the Major and I were unable to disguise from her our intention of watching for the strange visitant that night. But finally we prevailed upon her to depart, and she ran upstairs as though the legions of the lost pursued her, slamming and locking her door so that the sound echoed all over the house.

We had told her nothing, of course, of my discoveries and theories, but nevertheless the cat was out of the bag; the affair of the night before had spoilt our scheme of secrecy.

In the Major's study we made our preparations. The windows were widely opened, and the door was ajar. Not a breath of wind disturbed the stillness of the night, and although Major Dale had agreed to act exactly as I might direct, he stared in almost comic surprise when he learnt the nature of these directions.

Placing two large silk handkerchiefs upon the table, I saturated them with the contents of a bottle which I had brought in my pocket and handed one of the handkerchiefs to him.

"Tie that over your mouth and nostrils," I said, "and whatever happens don't remove it unless I tell you."

"But, Addison—"

"You know the compact, Major? If you aren't prepared to assist I must ask you to retire. To-night might be the last chance, perhaps, for years."

Growling beneath his breath, Major Dale obeyed, and, a humorous figure enough, stretched himself upon the couch, staring at me round-eyed. I also fastened a handkerchief about my head.

"It would perhaps be better," I said, my voice dimmed by the wet silk, "if we avoided conversation as much as possible."

Standing up, I rolled back a corner of the carpet, exposing the floor planks, and with a brace-and-bit, which I had in my pocket, I bored a round hole in one of these. Into it I screwed a tube, attached to a little watch-like contrivance, twisting the face of the dial so that I could study it from where I proposed to sit. Then I took up my post, smothering a laugh as I noted the expression upon that part of the Major's red face which was visible to me.

Thus began the business of that strange night. Half an hour passed in almost complete silence, save for Dale's audible breathing—he being by no means an ideal companion for such an investigation. But, having agreed to assist me, in justice to my old friend I must say that he did his best to stick to the bargain, and to play his part in what obviously he regarded as an insane comedy.

At about the expiration of this thirty minutes, I thought I heard a door open somewhere in the house. Listening intently, and glancing at my companion, I received no confirmation of the idea. Evidently the Major had heard nothing. Again I thought I heard a sound—as of the rustling of silk upon the stair, or in an upper corridor; finally I was almost certain that the floor of the room above (viz., the Major's bedroom) creaked very slightly.

At that I saw my companion glance upward, then across at me, with a question in his eyes. But not desiring to disturb the silence I merely shook my head.

An hour passed. There had been no repetition of the slight sounds to which I have referred, and the stillness of Low Fennel was really extraordinary. A thermometer, which I had placed upon, the table near to my elbow, recorded the fact that the temperature of the room had not abated a fraction of a point since sunset, and, sitting still though I was, I found myself bathed in perspiration. Despite the open door and windows, not a breath of air stirred in the place, but the room was laden with the oppressive perfume of those night-scented flowers which I have mentioned elsewhere, for it was faintly perceptible to me, despite the wet silk.

Once, a bat flew half in at one of the windows, striking its wings upon the glass, but almost immediately it flew out again. A big moth fluttered around the room, persistently banging its wings against the lamp shade. But nothing else within or without the house stirred, if I except the occasional restless movements of the Major.

Then all at once—and not gradually, as I had anticipated—the meter at my feet began to register. Instantly, I looked to the thermometer. It had begun to fall.

I glanced across at Major Dale. He was staring at something which seemed to have attracted his attention in a distant corner of the room.

Glancing away from the meter, the indicator of which was still moving upward, I looked in the same direction. There was much shadow there, but nevertheless I could not doubt that a very faint vapour was forming in that corner . . . rising—rising—rising—slowly higher and higher.

It proceeded from some part of the floor concealed by the big saddlebag chair—the Major's favourite dozing place (probably from a faulty floor board), and it was rising visibly, inch upon inch, as I watched, until it touched the ceiling above. Then, like a column of smoke, it spread out, mushroom fashion; it crept in ghostly coils along the cornices, spreading, a dim grey haze, until it obscured a great part of the ceiling.

Again I looked across at the Major. He was staring at the phenomenon with eyes which were glassy with amazement. I could see that momentarily he expected the vapour to take shape, to form into some ghoulish thing with a contorted face and clutching, outstretched fingers.

But this did not happen. The vapour, which was growing more fine and imperceptible, began to disperse. I glanced from corner to corner of the room, then down to the meter on the floor. The indicator was falling again.

Still I made no move, although I could hear Major Dale fidgeting nervously, but I looked across at him . . . and a dreadful change had come over his face. He was sitting upright upon the couch, the edge of which he clutched with one hand, while with the other he combed the air in a gesture evidently meant to attract my attention. He was trying to speak, but only a guttural sound issued from his throat. His staring eyes were set in a glare of stark horror upon the door of the study.

Swiftly I turned—to see the door slowly opening; to see, low down upon the bare floor—for I had removed the carpet from that corner of the room—a ghastly, contorted face, held sideways with one ear almost touching the ground, and with the lower lip and the chin drawn up as though they were of rubber, almost to the tip of the nose!

The eyes glared up balefully into mine, the hair hung a dishevelled mass about the face, and I had a glimpse of one bare shoulder pressed upon the floor.

Wider and wider opened the door; and further into the room crept the horrible apparition. . . .

The light gleamed equally upon the hideous, contorted face and upon the rounded shoulders and slim white arms. . . .

It was a woman!

In a flash of inspiration my doubts were resolved; *I understood.* Leaning across the table, I extinguished the lamp . . . in the same instant that Major Dale, uttering an inarticulate, choking cry, sprang to his feet and toppled forward, senseless, upon the floor!

The study became plunged in darkness, but into the long corridor, beyond the open door, poured the cold illumination of the moon. Framed in the portal uprose a slim figure, seeming like a black silhouette upon a silvern background, or a wondrous statue in ebony. Elfin, dishevelled locks crowned the head; the pose of the form was as that of a startled dryad or a young Bacchante; poised for a joyous leap. . . .

Thus, for an instant, like some exquisite dream of Phidias visualized, the figure stood . . . then had fled away down the corridor and was gone!

6

Close upon a month had elapsed. Major Dale and I sat in my study in London.

"Young Aubrey Wales has gone abroad," I said. "He's ashamed to show up again, I suppose."

"H'm!" growled the Major—"I've got nothing to crow about, myself, by the Lord Harry! There's courage and courage, sir! I've been 'over the top' a time or two, but I'd never qualify for the D.S.O. as a ghost hunter!—never, by Gad!—never!"

He reached out for the decanter; then withdrew his hand. "Doctor's orders," he muttered. "Discipline must be maintained!"

"It was the sudden excitement which precipitated the seizure," I said, glancing at the altered face of my old friend. "I was wrong to expose you to it; but of course I did not know that the doctor had warned you."

"And now," said the Major, sighing loudly as he filled his tumbler with plain soda water—"what have you to tell me?"

"In the first place—have you definitely decided to leave Low Fennel for good?"

"Certainly—not a doubt on the point! We're leasing a flat in town here while we look around."

"Good! Because I very much doubt if the place could ever be rendered tenable. . . ."

"Then it's really haunted?"

"Undoubtedly."

"By what, Addison? Tell me that!—by what?"

"By a grey vapour."

Major Dale's eyes began to protrude, and:

"Addison," he said hoarsely—"don't joke about it!—don't joke. It was not a grey vapour that strangled Seager. . . ."

"Certainly it was not. Seager was strangled by some wholly inoffensive person—we shall probably never know his identity—who had fallen asleep among the bushes on the mound, close beside the house. . . ."

"But, man alive! I've *seen* the beastly thing, with my own eyes! You've seen it! Wales saw it! Mrs. Ord saw it! . . ."

"Mrs. Ord saw her husband."

"Ah! you're coming round to my belief about the Ords!"

"Decidedly I am."

"But what did Wales see—eh? And what did *I* see?"

"You saw the vapour in operation."

The Major fell back in his chair with an expression upon his face which I cannot hope to describe. Words failed him altogether.

"I had come prepared for something of the sort," I continued rapidly; "for I have investigated several cases of haunting—notably in the Peak district—which have proved to be due to an emanation from the soil—a vapour. But the effect of such vapour, in the other cases, was to induce delusions of sight in nearly every instance (although, in two, the delusions were of hearing).

"In other words, the person affected by this vapour was drugged, and, during the drugged state, perceived certain visions. I made the mistake, at first, of supposing that Low Fennel came within the same category. The classical analogy, of course, is that of the Sibyls, who delivered the oracular responses from the tripod, under the afflatus of a vapour said to arise from the sacred subterranean stream called Kassotis. The theory is, therefore, by no means a new one!"

Major Dale stared dully, but made no attempt to interrupt me.

"There are probably many spots, in England alone," I continued, "thus affected; but, fortunately, few of them have been chosen as building sites. Barrows and tumuli of the Stone and Bronze ages, and also Roman shrines, seem frequently to be productive of such emanations. The barrow beside Low Fennel (and now under the new wing) is a case in point.

"Sudden atmospheric changes seem to be favourable to the formation of the vapour. The barrow in Peel Castle, Isle of Man, is peculiarly susceptible to thunder-storms, for instance, while that at Low Fennel emits a vapour only after a spell of intense heat, and at the exact moment when the temperature begins to fall again. In the case of a sustained heat wave this would take place at some time during each night.

"And now for the particular in which the vapour at Low Fennel differs from other, similar emanations. It is not productive of delusions of sight; it induces a definite and unvarying form of transient insanity!"

Major Dale moved slightly, but still did not speak.

"Dame Pryce was the first recorded victim of the vapour. She was accused of witchcraft by a neighbour who testified to having seen her transform herself into a hideous and unrecognizable hag—whereas, in her proper person, she seems to have been a comely old lady. Lack of evidence compels us to dismiss the case of Seager, but consider that of the Ords. The man Ord, on his own confession, had fallen asleep outside the house. He became a victim of the vapour—and his own wife failed to recognize him.

"To what extent the mania so produced is homicidal remains to be proved; the gas is rare and difficult to procure, so that hitherto analysis has not been attempted. My own theory is that the subject remains harmless provided that, while under the mysterious influence, he does not encounter any person distasteful to him. Thus, Seager may have met his death at the hands of some tramp who had been turned away from the house.

"As to the symptoms: they seem to be quite unvarying. The subject strips, contorts his face out of all semblance to humanity (and always in a particular fashion) and crawls, lizard-like, upon the ground, with the head held low, in an attitude of listening. That it is possible so to contort the face as to render it unrecognizable is seen in some cases of angina pectoris, of course.

"The subject apparently returns to the spot from whence he started and sinks into profound sleep, as is seen in some cases of somnambulism; and—like the somnambulist, again—he acquires incredible agility. How you yourself came, twice, under the influence of the vapour, is easily explained. The first time—when the housekeeper saw you—you had actually been in bed; and the second time, as you have told me, you had gone upstairs, undressed, and then slipped on your dressing gown in order to complete some work in the study. Instead of completing the work, you dozed in your chair—and we know what followed! In the case of—Mrs. Dale . . ."

"God! Addison," said the Major huskily, and stood up, clutching the chair arms— "Addison! You are trying to tell me that—what I saw was . . . *Marjorie!* . . ."

I nodded gravely.

"Without letting her suspect my reason for making the inquiries, I learnt that on that last night at Low Fennel, feeling dreadfully lonely and frightened, she determined to run along to the new wing—which seemed a safer place—and to wait in your room until you came up. She fell asleep, and . . ."

"Addison . . . can a mere 'vapour' produce such . . ."

"You mean, is the vapour directed or animated by some discarnate, evil intelligence? My dear Dale, you are taking us back to the theory of elemental spirits, and I blankly refuse to follow you!"

The Valley of the Just

A Story of the Shan Hills

Merciless sun beat down upon the little caravan, winding its way upward and ever upward to the hill land. Beneath stretched a panorama limned in feverish greens and unhealthy yellows; scarlike rocks striated the jungle clothing the foothills, and through the dancing air, viewed from the arid heights, they had the appearance of running water. Swamps to the southeast showed like unhealing wounds upon the face of the landscape; beyond them spread the muddy river waters, the bank of the stream proper being discernible only by reason of a greater greenness in the palm-tops: venomous green slopes beyond them again, a fringe of dwarfed forest, and the brazen skyline.

Right of the path rose volcanic rock, gnarled, twisted and contorted as with the agonies of some mighty plague, which in a forgotten past had seized upon the very bowels of the world, and had contorted whole mountains, and laid waste vast forests and endless plains. Above, the cruel sun; ahead, more plague-twisted rocks, with sandy scars dancing like running water; and, all around, the breathless stillness, the swooning stillness of tropical midday. North, south, east, and west, that haze of heat, that silence unbroken, lay like an accursed mantle upon Burma.

Moreen Fayne could scarcely support herself upright in the saddle; her head throbbed incessantly, and the veil which she wore could not protect her eyes from the maddening glare of the sun. But although at any moment during the past hour she could have slipped insensible from her saddle, she sat stiffly upright, her dauntless eyes looking straight ahead, her small mouth set with masculine sternness, and her hands clenched—the physical reflection of a mental effort whereby, alone, she was enabled to pursue the journey.

Just in front of her paced Ramsa Lal. His stride had not varied from the lowlands, through the foothills, nor on the rocky mountain paths. He had looked neither right nor left, but had walked, walked, walked. At times Moreen had been hard put to it to choke down the hysterical screams which had risen in her throat; madness had threatened her, as she watched, in dumb misery, that silent striding man. Yet she knew that it was only the presence of this tireless, immobile guide which had enabled her to go on; although he never directed one glance towards her, she knew that his steady march was meant for encouragement.

Behind, like the tail of a scorpion, trailed the native retinue, and on the end of the tail, where the sting would be, her husband rode. This simile had occurred to her at once, and she allowed her mind to dwell upon the idea as an invalid will consider imaginary designs upon the wall paper of the sick-room.

Sometimes there was a sliding of hoofs and a sound of stumbling; sometimes her own pony lost his footing. On such occasion, there would be mechanical cries of encouragement from the natives, and perhaps a growling curse from the man who brought up the rear of the little company. The road wound through a frowning chasm, where lizards and other creeping things darted into holes to right and left of their progress. Grateful shadow ruled a while, and a stifled sigh escaped from Moreen's lips. Ramsa Lal paced straightly onward, the others came stumbling behind; fifty yards ahead the ravine opened out, and once more deathly heat poured unchecked upon their heads.

Again Moreen all but lost control of herself; her fortitude threatened to slip from her; so that she bit her lips until pain filled her eyes with burning tears. The, effort to control herself proved successful, but left her white and quivering. She felt impelled to speak to Ramsa Lal, and constrained herself only with a second effort of which her will was barely capable. Then she saw that speech, which would be dangerous, was unnecessary; the man's wonderful intuition had enabled him to hear that crying of the soul, and he was answering her.

His brown fingers were clutching and unclutching convulsively, and as he swung his arm, he would clench his right fist and beat the air. For a moment he acted thus, and then, as if he knew that she had seen, and understood, his fingers hung limply again, and his arm swung loosely as before.

A sort of plateau was reached, and in a natural clearing, where giant bamboos ranged back to the tangled, creeper-laden boughs of the forest trees, the voice of Fayne cried a halt. Ramsa Lal was beside Moreen's pony in a trice, and he so screened her exhausted descent from the saddle, setting her down upon an hospitable bank hard by, that she was enabled to maintain her inflexible attitude, when presently her husband came striding along to stand looking down on her, where she sat. His blackly pencilled brows were drawn together, and the pale blue eyes shone out, saturnine, from cavernous sockets. His handsome face was heavily lined, and in the appearance, in the whole attitude of the man, was something aggressive, a violence markedly repellent. Moreen locked her hands behind her, the fingers twining and intertwining, but she raised a pale face to his, from which by a last supreme effort of will she had driven all traces of emotion.

So they remained for a moment, while the servants busied themselves with the baggage; he, with feet wide apart, staring down at her, and slashing at the air with a fly whisk, and she meeting his gaze with a stony calm pitiful to behold, had there been any soul capable of pity to see her. Ramsa Lal was directing operations.

"Here," said Fayne, "we camp."

His voice would have told a skilled observer that which the facial lines and a certain odd puffiness of skin more than suggested, that Roger Fayne was not a temperate man.

Moreen made no sign, but simply sat watching the speaker.

"It's a delightful situation," he continued, "and your ambition, frequently expressed in Mandalay, to see something of Burma other than bridge parties and polo matches, at last is realized."

He spoke with a seeming sincerity that had carried conviction to any save the most skeptical. But Moreen made no sign.

"Here," continued, he, "you may feast your eyes upon the glories of a Burma forest. Those flowering creepers, festooned from bough to bough, are peculiar to this district, and if you care to explore further, you will be rewarded by the discovery of some fine orchids. Note, also, the perfume of the flowers."

He turned away to supervise the work of camping.

Ramsa Lal already had one of the tents nearly erected, and Moreen watched his deft fingers at work with an anxiety none the less because it was masked. She knew that collapse was imminent. That cruel march under a pitiless sun had had due effect, but it had not broken her spirit. She knew that she had reached the end of her strength, but she showed no sign of weakness before her husband.

It was done at last, and Ramsa Lal held the tent cloth aside and bowed.

Moreen stood up, clenched her teeth together grimly, and staggered forward. As the tent flap was dropped she sank down beside the camp bedstead, and her head fell upon the covering.

2

Dusk fell, a quick curtain, and the lamps of night shone out with glorious brilliancy, illuminating the little plateau. The tents gleamed whitely in that cold radiance; there was a dancing redness to show where the fire had been built, with figures grouped dimly around it. On a jagged rock, which started up from the very heart of a thicket, black against the newly risen moon, was silhouetted the figure of Roger Fayne. Night things swept the air about him and rustled in the canebrake below him; the fire crackled in the neighbouring camp; sometimes a murmur came from the group of natives.

But, heedless of these matters, Moreen's husband stood on the rocky eminence looking back upon the way they had come, looking down to the distant river valley.

For many minutes he remained so, but presently, clambering down, heavily forced his way through undergrowth to the little camp. Passing the tents, he walked back to the dip of the pathway, and paused again, watching and listening; then turned and strode to the fire, grasped Ramsa Lal by the shoulder, and drew him away from the others.

"Come here!" he directed tersely.

At the head of the pathway he bade him halt.

"Listen!" he directed.

Ramsa Lal stood in an attitude of keen attention, and Fayne watched him with feverish anxiety, which he was wholly unable to conceal.

"Do you hear it?" he demanded—"hoofs on the path!"

Ramsa Lal shook his head.

"I hear nothing, sahib."

"Put your ear to the ground, and listen. I tell you I saw figures moving away below there, and I heard—hoofs, stumbling hoofs."

The man knelt down upon the ground, and, bending forward, lowered his head. Fayne watched him, and with growing anxiety, so that, what with this and the pallid moonlight, his face appeared ghastly.

But again Ramsa Lal stood up, shaking his head.

"Nothing, sahib," he repeated.

Roger Fayne suddenly grasped him by the shoulders, spinning him about, and dragging him forward, so that the dusky face was but inches removed from hiss own. He glared into the man's eyes.

"Are you lying to me?" he demanded, "are you lying?"

"I swear it is the truth: why should I lie to you, sahib?"

"You want them—"

Fayne broke off abruptly and thrust the man away from him. A different expression had crept into his face, an expression in which there was something furtive. He spun around upon his heel and stepped to the tent where Moreen was. Raising the flap slightly:

"Good-night," he called, and turned away.

Ramsa Lal had gone back to the fireside; and Fayne, following a moment of hesitancy, strode with his regular, military gait to a tent erected in the furthermost corner of the clearing. He had stooped to enter, when he hesitated, remaining there bent forward—and listening.

From the opposite side of the distant fire Ramsa Lal, though few would have suspected the fact, was watching. Evidently enough, the leader of the little company was obsessed with his delusion that someone or something clambered up the steep path beneath. Suddenly shrugging his shoulders, Fayne stooped yet lower and dived into the tent.

One of the natives threw fresh fuel upon the fire, and a stream of sparks sped up through the clear air in a widening trail ever growing fainter.

There was a crackling, a murmur of voices, and then a new silence. This in turn was broken by the distant howling of dogs, and in the near stillness one might have heard faint shrieking of bats, who now were embarked upon their nocturnal voyagings.

A shrill, wild scream burst suddenly from the heart of the trees in the east, rose eerily upon the night, and died away. But the group about the fire moved not at all, for this dreadful screaming but marked an animal tragedy of the Burma forests. So furred things howled and screamed and moaned in the woodlands, feathered things piped and hooted around and above, and the bats, uncanny creatures of the darkness who seem to have kinship neither with fur nor feather, chirped faintly overhead.

Once there was a distant, hollow booming like the sound of artillery, which echoed down the mountain gorges, and seemed to roll away over lowland swamps, to die, inaudible, by the remote river bank.

Yet no one stirred; for this mysterious gunnery is a phenomenon met with in that district, inexplicable, weird, but no novelty to one who has camped in the Shan Hills.

A second time later in the night phantom guns boomed; and again their booming died away in the far valleys. The fire was getting low, now.

3

Moreen lay, sleepless, wide-eyed, staring up at the roof of the tent. She had eaten, could eat, nothing, but she was consumed by a parching thirst. The sounds of the night had no terrors for her; indeed, she scarcely noticed them, for she had other and more dreadful things to think of.

Ramsa Lal had been her father's servant: him she could trust. But the others—the others were Roger Fayne's. They were no more than spies upon her; guards.

What did it mean, this sudden dash from the bungalow into the hills? It amused her husband to pretend that it was a pleasure trip, but the equipment was not of the sort one takes upon such occasions, and one is not usually dragged from bed at midnight to embark upon such a journey. It was additionally improbable in view of the fact that up to the moment of departure Roger had not spoken to her, except in public, for six months. The dreadful, forced marches were breaking her down, and she knew that he was drinking heavily. What, in God's name, would be the end of it?

Weakly, she raised herself into a sitting position, groping for and lighting a candle. From her handbag she took out a letter, the last she had received from home before this mad flight. There was something in it which had frightened her at the time, but which, viewed in the light of recent events, was unspeakably horrifying.

During the long estrangement between Roger and herself she had learnt, and had paid for her knowledge with bitter tears, that there was a side to his character which he had carefully concealed from her before marriage; the dark, saturnine facet of her husband's nature had dawned upon her suddenly. That had been the beginning of her disillusionment; a disillusionment which has come to more than one English girl during the first twelve months of married life in an Indian bungalow.

Then, of course, the gap had widened, and six months later had become a chasm quite impassable except in the interests of social propriety. Anglo-Indian society is notable for divorces, and poor Moreen very early in her married life fully understood the reason.

She held the letter to the dim light and read it again attentively. Allowing a certain discount for her mother's changeless animosity towards Roger Fayne, it yet remained a startling letter. Much of it consisted in feckless condolences, characteristic but foolish; the passage, however, which she read and reread by the dim, flickering light was as follows:

"Mr. Harringay in his last letter begged of me to come out by the next boat to Rangoon," her mother wrote. *"He has quite opened my eyes to the truth, Moreen, not in, such a way as to shock me all at once, but gradually. I always distrusted Roger Fayne and never disguised the fact from you. I knew that his previous life had been far from irreproachable, but his treatment of you surpasses even my expectations. I know all, my poor darling! and I know something which you do not know. His father did not die in Colombo at all he died in a madhouse! and there are two other known dipsomaniacs in Roger Faytte's family—"*

A hand reached over Moreen's shoulder and tore the letter from her.

She turned with a cry—and looked up into her husband's quivering face! For a moment he stood over her, his left fist clenching and unclenching, and his pale blue eyes glassy with anger. Then chokingly he spoke:

"So you carry one of his letters about with you?"

The veins were throbbing visibly upon his temples. Moreen clutched at the blanket but did not speak, dared not move, for if ever she had looked into the face of a madman it was at this moment when she looked into the face of Roger Fayne.

He suddenly grabbed the candle and, holding it close to the letter, began to read. His hands were perfectly steady, showing the tremendous nerve tension under which he laboured. Then his expression changed, but nothing of the maniac glare left his eyes.

"From your mother," he said hoarsely, "and full of two things—your wrongs, *your* wrongs! and Jack Harringay—Jack Harringay—always Jack Harringay . . . Damn Jack Harringay!"

He put down the candle and began to tear the letter into tiny fragments, pouring forth the while a disconnected murmur of blasphemous language. Moreen, who felt that consciousness was slipping from her, crouched there with a face deathly pale.

Fayno began to laugh softly as he threw the torn-up letter from him piece by piece.

"Damn Jack Harringay!" he said again. He turned blazing eyes towards his wife. "You lying, baby-faced hypocrite! Why don't you admit that he is—"

He stopped; words died upon his lips, and he stood there shaking all over and with a sort of stark horror in his eyes dreadful to see.

"Why don't you?" he muttered—and looked at her almost pathetically—"why of course you can't—no one can—"

He reeled and clutched at the tent flap, then stumblingly made his way out.

"No one can," came back in a shaky whisper—"no one can—"

Moreen heard him staggering away, until the sound of his uncertain footsteps grew inaudible. A distant howling rose upon the night, and, nearer to the clearing, sounded a sort of tapping, not unlike that of a woodpecker. Some winged creature was fluttering over the tent.

4

Dawn saw that dreadful march resumed. Fayne now exhibited unmistakable traces of his course of heavy drinking. He brought up the rear as hitherto, and often tarried far behind where some peculiar formation of the path enabled him to study country already traversed. He had altered the route of the march, and now they were leaving the Shan Hills upon the northeast and dipping down to a chasm-like valley through which ran a tributary of the Selween River. Since the dry season was commenced the entire country beneath them showed through a haze of heat and dust.

They had made a crude and hasty breakfast as strangers having nothing in common who by chance share a table. Moreen no longer doubted that her husband was mad, for he muttered to himself and was ever glancing over his shoulder. This and his constant watching of the path behind spoke of some secret terror from which he fled.

Towards noon, they skirted a village whose inhabitants poured forth *en bloc* to watch the passing of this unfamiliar company. A faint hope that some European might be there died in Moreen's breast. Her position was a dreadful one. Led by a madman—of this she was persuaded—and surrounded by natives who, if not actively hostile, were certainly unfriendly, with but one man to whom she could look for the slightest aid, she was proceeding further and further from civilization into unknown wildernesses.

What her husband's purpose might be she could not conceive. She was unable to think calmly, unable to formulate any plan. In the dull misery of a sick dream she rode forward speculating upon the awakening.

Midday heat in the valley was so great that a halt became imperative. They camped at the edge of a dense jungle where banks of rotten vegetation, sun-dried upon the top, lay heaped about the bamboo stems. None but a madman would have chosen to tarry in such a spot; and Fayne's servants went about their work with many a furtive glance at their master. Ramsa Lal's velvety eyes showed a great compassion, but Moreen offered no protest. She was in an unreal frame of mind and her will was merely capable of a mute indifference: any attempt to assert herself must have meant a sudden breakdown. Something in her brain was strained to utmost tension; any further effort had snapped it.

In the hour of the greatest heat Roger Fayne went out alone, offering no explanation of his intentions and leaving no word as to the time of his return. Moreen only learnt of his departure from Ramsa Lal. She received the news with indifference and asked no questions. Inert she lay in the little tent looking out at the wall of jungle where it uprose but twenty yards away. So the day wore on. Mechanically she trifled with food when Ramsa Lal placed it before her, but, although the man's attitude palpably was one of uneasiness, she did not question him, and he departed in silence. It was an incredible situation.

Throughout the afternoon nothing occurred to break this dread monotony save that once there arose a buzz of conversation, and she became dimly aware that someone from the native village which they had passed in the morning had come into the camp. After a time the sounds had died away again, and Ramsa Lal had stepped into view, looking towards her interrogatively; but although she recognized his wish to speak to her, the inertia which now claimed mind and body prevailed, and she offered him no encouragement to intrude upon her misery.

Thus the weary hours passed, until even to the dulled perceptions of Moreen sounds of unrest and uneasiness pervading the camp began to penetrate. Yet Roger did not return. The insect and reptile life of a Burmese jungle moved around her, but she was curiously indifferent to everything. Without alarm she brushed a venomous spider, fully one inch in girth, from the camp bedstead, and dully watched it darting away into jungle undergrowth.

Darkness swept down, and tropical night things raised their mingled voices; then came Ramsa Lal.

"Forgive me, mem-sahib," he said, "but I must speak to you."

She half-reclined, looking at him as he stood, a dimly seen figure, before her.

"The men from the village," he continued, "come to say that we may not camp. It is holy ground from this place away"—he waved his arm vaguely—"to the end of the jungle where the river is."

"I can do nothing, Ramsa Lal."

"I fear—for him."

"Fayne Sahib?"

"He goes into the jungle to look for something. What does he go to look for? Why does he not return?"

Moreen made no reply.

"All of them there"—he indicated the direction of the native servants—"know this place. They are already afraid, and, with those from the village coming to warn us, they get more afraid still. This is a haunted place, mem-sahib."

Moreen sat up, shaking off something of the lassitude which possessed her

"What do you mean?"

"In that jungle," Ramsa Lal replied, "there is buried a temple, a very old temple, and in the temple there is buried one who was a holy man. His spirit watches over this place, and none may rest here because of him—"

"But the men of the village came here," said Moreen.

"Before sunset, mem-sahib. No man would come here after dark. Look! you will see—they are frightened."

Languidly, but with some awakening to the demands of the situation, Moreen stepped out of the tent and looked across to where, about a great fire, the retinue huddled in a circle. Ramsa Lal stood beside her with something contemptuous in the bearing of his tall figure.

"A spell lies upon all this valley, mem-sahib," he said. "Therefore it is called the Valley of the Just."

"Why?"

"Because only the just may stay within its bounds through the night."

Moreen stared affrightedly.

"Do you mean that they die in the night, Ramsa Lal?"

"In the night, mem-sahib, before the dawn."

"By what means?"

Ramsa Lal spread his palms eloquently.

"Who knows?" he replied. "It is a haunted place."

"And are you afraid?"

"I am not afraid, for I have passed a night in the Valley of the Just many years ago, and I live."

"You were alone?"

"With two others, mem-sahib."

"And the others?"

"One was bitten by a snake an hour before dawn, and the other, who was an upright man, lives today."

Moreen shuddered.

"Do you know—" she still hesitated to broach this subject with the man—"do you know where—Fayne Sahib has gone?"

"It is said, mem-sahib, that a stream runs through the jungle close beside the old temple, a stream which bubbles up from a cavern and which is supposed to come underground from the Ruby Mine plateau. He goes early in the morning to look for rubies—so I think."

Moreen tapped the ground with her foot.

"Do you think—" again she hesitated—"that he is afraid of something? Of something—where we have come from?"

Ramsa Lal bowed low.

"I cannot tell," he replied, "but we shall know before sunrise."

For a moment Moreen scarcely grasped the significance of his words; then their inner meaning became apparent to her.

"Make me some coffee, Ramsa. Lal," she said; am cold—very cold."

She reentered the tent, lighting the lamp.

The Valley of the Just! What irony, that her husband should have selected this spot to camp in! She sat deep in thought, when presently Ramsa Lal entered with coffee. He had just set down the tray when the sound of a distant cry brought him rigidly upright. He stood listening intently. The sound was repeated—nearer it seemed—a sort of hoarse scream, terrible to hear—impossible to describe.

Moreen rose to her feet and followed the man out of the tent. Someone—someone who kept crying out—was plunging heavily through the jungle towards the camp.

The men about the fire were on their feet now. Obviously they would have fled, but the prospect of flight into haunted darkness was one more terrible than that of remaining where they were.

It ceased, that strange cry; but whoever was approaching could be heard alternately groaning and laughing madly.

Then out from the thicket on the west into the red light of the fire burst a fearful figure. It was that of Roger Fayne, wild eyed, and with face which seemed to be of a dull grey. He staggered and almost fell, but kept on for a few more paces and then collapsed in a heap almost at Moreen's feet, amid the clatter of the strange loot wherewith he was laden.

This consisted of a number of golden vessels heavily encrusted with gems, a huge golden salver, and a dozen or more ropes of gigantic rubies!

Amid these treasures, the ransom of a sultan, the price of a throne, he lay writhing convulsively.

Ramsa Lal was first to recover himself. He leapt forward, seized the prostrate man by the shoulders and dragged him into the tent, past Moreen. Having effected this he raised his eyes in a mute question. She nodded, and while Ramsa Lal seized Fayne's shoulders, Moreen grasped his ankles, and together they lifted him up onto the bed.

He lay there, rolling from side to side. His eyes were wide open, glassy and unseeing; a slight froth was upon his lips, his fists rose and fell in regular, mechanical beats, corresponding with the convulsive movements of his knees.

Moreen dropped down beside him.

"Ramsa Lal! Ramsa Lal! What shall I do? What has happened to him?"

Ramsa Lal ripped the collar from Fayne's neck in order to aid his respiration. Then, quietly signing to Moreen to hold the lamp, he began to search the exposed surface of skin. Evidently he failed to find that for which he was looking. He glanced down at the ankles, but Fayne wore thick putties, and Ramsa Lal shook his head in a puzzled way.

"It is like the bite of a hamadryad," he said softly, "but there is no mark."

"What shall I do?" moaned Moreen—"what shall I do?"

There was a frightened murmur from the entrance, where the native servants stood in a group, peering in. Moreen stood up.

"Hot water, Ramsa Lal!" she said. "We must give him brandy."

"But it is useless, mem-sahib; he has not been bitten—there is no mark; it may be a fever from the jungle."

Moreen beat her hands together helplessly.

"We must do *something!*" she said; "we must do *something.*"

A sudden change took place in Roger Fayne. Convulsive movements ceased, and he lay quiet, and breathing quite regularly. The glassy look began to fade from his eyes, and with every appearance of being in full possession of his senses, he stared at Moreen and spoke:

"You shall repent of your words, Harringay," he said in a quiet voice. "You have deliberately accused me of faking the cards. I don't give a damn for any of you. Why should I attempt such a thing? I could buy and sell you all! . . ."

Moreen dropped slowly back upon her knees again, white to the lips, watching her husband. With the same appearance of perfect sanity, but now addressing empty air, he continued:

"In my tent—my wife will tell you it is true—my wife, Harringay, do you hear?—I have jewelled cups and strings of rubies, enough to buy up Mandalay! I blundered onto them in that old ruined temple, back in the jungle, not five hundred yards from your bungalow. Harringay—think of it—a treasure room like that, within sight of your veranda! There are snakes there, snakes, you understand, in hundreds; but it is worth risking for a big fortune like mine."

"He mixes time and place," murmured Ramsa Lal. "He talks to the commissioner sahib in Mandalay of what is here in the Valley of the Just."

Moreen nodded, catching her breath hysterically.

"You see," continued the delirious man. "I am as rich as Midas. Why should I want to cheat you? Don't talk to me of what you would do for my wife's sake! Keep your favours, thank you!"

With a contemptuous smile, Fayne threw his head back upon the pallet. Then came another change; the look of stark horror which Moreen had seen once before crept into the grey face; and her husband raised himself in bed, glaring wildly into shadows beyond the lamp.

"You are a spirit!" The words came in a thrilling, eerie whisper. "Oh, God! I understand. Yes! I came away from Harringay's bungalow. My wife was asleep, and I sat drinking until I had emptied the whisky decanter."

He bent forward as if listening.

"Yes, I went back. I went back to reason with him. No! as God is my witness I did not plan it! I went back to reason with him."

Again the uncanny attitude was resumed; then:

"I stepped in through the veranda, and there he sat with Moreen's photograph in his hand. Listen to me—*listen!*" There was an agony of entreaty in his voice; it rose to a thin scream—"My wife's photograph! Do you hear me? Do you understand? *Moreen's* photograph!—and as I stood behind him, he raised it to his lips—he—"

Fayne stopped abruptly, as if checked by a spoken word; and with wildly beating heart Moreen found herself listening for the phantom voice. She could hear the breathing of the natives clustered behind her; but no other sound save a distant howling in the jungle was audible, until her husband began again:

"I struck him down—from behind, yes, from behind. His blood poured over the picture. You understand I was mad. If you are just—and is not this called the Valley of the Just?—you cannot condemn me. Why did I run away? I was not in my right mind; I had—been drinking, as I told you; I was mad. If I was not mad I should never have bolted, never have drawn suspicion—on myself."

He fell back as if exhausted, then once more struggled upright and began to peer about him. When he spoke again, his voice, though weak, was more like his own.

"Moreen!" he said—"where the devil are you? Why can't you give me a drink?"

Suddenly, he seemed to see her, and he drew his brows together in the old, ugly frown.

"Damn you!" he said. "I have found you out! I am a rich man now, and when I have gone to England, see what Jack Harringay will do for you. I will paint London red! I have looted the old temple, and they are after me, they "

The words merged into a frightful scream. Fayne threw up his hands and fell back insensible upon the bed.

"Mem-sahib! Mem-sahib, you must be brave!" It was Ramsa Lal who spoke; he supported Moreen with his arm. "There is a spell upon this place. No medicine, nothing, can save him. There is only one thing—"

Moreen controlled herself by one of those giant efforts of which she was capable.

"Tell me," she whispered—"what must we do?"

Ramsa Lal removed his arm, saw that she could stand unsupported, and bent forward over the unconscious man. Following a rapid examination, he signed to her to leave the tent. They came out into a white blaze of moonlight—and there at their feet lay the glittering loot of the haunted temple, a dazzlement of rainbow sparks.

"Only for such a thing as this," said Ramsa Lal, "dare I go, but not one of us will see another dawn if we do not go." He pointed to the heap of treasure. "Mein-sahib must come also."

"But—my husband—"

"He must remain," he said. "It is of his own choosing."

5

The temple stood in a kind of clearing. Grotesquely horrible figures guarded its time-worn entrance. Moreen drew a deep breath of relief on emerging from the jungle path by which, amid the rustle of retreating snakes, they had come, but shrank back affrighted from the blackness of the ruined doorway. Ramsa Lal placed the lantern upon the stump of a broken pillar, where its faint yellow light was paled by moon rays.

"It is *you* who must restore," he said.

One by one he handed her the jewel-encrusted vessels and hung the ropes of rubies upon her arm.

She nodded, and as Ramsa Lal took up the lantern and began to descend the steps within, followed him.

"No foot save his," came back to her, "has trod these sacred steps for ages. The secret of the jungle path is known only to a few. . . ."

"How do you—know the way?"

Ramsa Lal did not reply.

They traversed a short tunnel; a heavy door was thrust open; and Moreen found herself standing in a small pillared hall. Through a window high in one wall, overgrown with tangled vegetation, crept a broken moonbeam. Directly before her was the carven figure of a grotesque deity. A long, heavily clamped chest stood before it like an altar step.

She staggered forward, deposited her priceless burden upon the floor, and mechanically began to raise the lid of the chest.

"Not that one, mem-sahib!" The voice of Ramsa Lal rose shrilly— "not that one! . . ."

But he spoke too late. Moreen realized that there were three divisions in the chest, each having a separate lid. As she raised the one in the centre, a breath of fetid air greeted her nostrils, and she had a vague impression that this was no chest but the entrance to a deep pit. Then all these thoughts were swept away by the crowning horror which appeared out of the subterranean darkness.

A great winged creature, clammily white, rose towards her, passed beneath her upraised hands and sailed into the darkness on the right. She heard it flapping its great bat wings against the wall—heard them beating upon a pillar—then saw it coming back towards her into the moonlight—and knew no more.

6

"Mem-sahib!"

Moreen opened her eyes. She lay, propped against a saddle, in the camp beyond the jungle. She shuddered icily.

"Ramsa Lal—how—"

"I carried the mem-sahib! The treasures of the temple I restored to their resting place—"

"And the—the other—"

"The door that the mem-sahib opened she opened by the decree of Fate. It was not for Ramsa Lal to close it. That is a passage—"

"Yes?"

"—to the tomb of the great one who is buried in the temple!"

"Oh! heavens! that white thing " She raised her hands to her face. "But—the camp—"

"The camp is deserted! They all fled from—"

Moreen sat up.

"From what?"

From one who came for something we forgot!"

"Roger!—"

"There was a ring upon Fayne Sahib's finger. I saw it, and knew where it came from, but forgot to remove it."

Moreen stood up and turned towards the nearer tent. Ramsa Lal gently detained her.

"Not that way, mem-sahib."

"But I must see him! I must, I *must* tell him that he wrongs me, cruelly, wickedly! You heard his words——Oh, God! can he have——"

"It would be useless to tell him, mem-sahib—he could not hear you! But that what you would tell him is true I know well; for see—it is the dawn!"

"Ramsa Lal! . . ."

"The unjust cannot stay in this valley through a night and live to see the dawn, mem-sahib!"

7

At about that same hour, Deputy Commissioner Jack Harringay opened his eyes and looked wonderingly at a grey-haired, white-aproned nurse who sat watching him.

"Don't speak, Mr. Harringay," she said soothingly. "You have been very ill, but you are on the high road to recovery now."

"Nurse! . . ."

"Please don't speak; I know what you would ask. There has been no scandal. The attack upon you was put down to robbers. You have been delirious, Mr. Harringay, and have told me—many things. I am old enough, or nearly old enough, to be your mother, so you will not mind my telling you that a love like yours deserves reward. God has spared your life: be sure it was with a purpose—"

The Master of Hollow Grange

Jack Dillon came to Hollow Grange on a thunderous black evening when an ebony cloud crested the hill-top above, and, catching the upflung rays of sunset, glowed redly like the pall of Avalon in the torchlight. Through the dense ranks of firs cloaking the slopes a breeze, presaging the coming storm, whispered evilly, and here in the hollow the birds were still.

The man who had driven him from the station glanced at him with a curiosity thinly veiled.

"What about your things, sir?" he inquired.

Dillon stared rather blankly at the ivy-covered lodge, which, if appearances were to be trusted, was unoccupied.

"Wait a moment; I will ring," he said curtly; for this curiosity, so ill concealed, had manifested itself in the manner of the taxi driver from the moment that Dillon had directed him to drive to Hollow Grange.

He pushed open the gate and tugged at the iron ring which was suspended from the wall of the lodge. A discordant clangour rewarded his efforts, the cracked note of a bell that spoke from somewhere high up in the building, that seemed to be buffeted to and fro from fir to fir, until it died away, mournfully, in some place of shadows far up the slope. In the voice of the bell there was something furtive, something akin to the half-veiled curiosity in the eyes of the man who stood watching him; something fearful, too, in both, as though man and bell would whisper: "Return! Beware of disturbing the dwellers in this place."

But Dillon angrily recalled himself to the realities. He felt that these ghostly imaginings were born of the Boche-maltreated flesh, were products of lowered tone; that he would have perceived no query in the glance of the taxi driver and heard no monkish whisper in the clang of the bell had he been fit, had he been fully recovered from the effects of his wound. Monkish whisper? Yes, that was it—his mind had supplied, automatically, an aptly descriptive term: the cracked bell spoke with the voice of ancient monasteries, had in it the hush of cloisters and the sigh of renunciation.

"Hang it all!" muttered Dillon. "This won't do."

A second time he awoke the ghostly bell-voice, but nothing responded to its call; man, bird, and beast had seemingly deserted Hollow Grange. He was conscious of a sudden nervous irritation as he turned brusquely and met the inquiring glance of the taxi man.

"I have arrived before I was expected," he said. "If you will put my things in the porch here I will go up to the house and get a servant to fetch them. They will be safe enough in the meantime."

His own words increased his irritability; for were they not in the nature of an apology on behalf of his silent and unseen host? Were they not a concession to that nameless query in the man's stare? Moreover, deep within his own consciousness, some vague thing was stirring; so that, the man dismissed and promptly departing, Dillon stood glancing from the little stack of baggage in the lodge porch up the gloomy, narrow, and over-arched drive indignantly aware that he also carried a question in his eyes.

The throb of the motor mounting the steep, winding lane grew dim and more dim until it was borne away entirely upon a fitful breeze. Faintly he detected the lowing of cattle in some distant pasture; the ranks of firs whispered secretly, one to another, and the pall above the hills grew blacker and began to extend over the valley.

Amid that ominous stillness of nature he began to ascend the cone-strewn path. Evidently enough, the extensive grounds had been neglected for years; and that few pedestrians, and fewer vehicles, ever sought Hollow Grange was demonstrated by the presence of luxuriant weeds in the carriageway. Having proceeded for some distance, until the sheer hillside seemed to loom over him like the wall of a tower, Dillon paused, peering about in the ever growing darkness. He was aware of a physical chill; certainly no ray of sunlight ever penetrated to this tunnel through the firs. Could he have mistaken the path and be proceeding, not toward the house, but away from it and into the midnight of the woods mantling the hills?

There was something uncomfortable in that reflection; momentarily

he knew a childish fear of the darkening woods and walked forward rapidly, self-assertively. Ten paces brought him to one of the many bends
in the winding road—and there, far ahead, as though out of some cavern
in the very hillside, a yellow light shone.

He pressed on with greater assurance until the house became visible. Now he perceived that he had indeed strayed from the carriage-
sweep in some way, for the path that he was following terminated at the
foot of a short flight of moss-covered brick steps. He mounted the steps
and found himself at the bottom of a terrace. The main entrance was far
to his left and separated from the terrace by a neglected lawn. That por-
tion of the place was Hanoverian and ugly, while the wing nearest to
him was Tudor and picturesque. Excepting the yellow light shining out
from a sunken window almost at his feet, no illuminations were visible
about the house, although the brewing storm had already plunged the
hollow into premature night.

Indeed, there was no sign of occupancy about the strange-looking
mansion, which might have hidden forgotten for centuries in the horse-
shoe of the hills. He had sought for rest and quiet; here he should find
them. The stillness of the place was of that sort which almost seems to
be palpable; that can be seen and felt. A humid chill arose apparently
from the terrace, with its stone pavings outlined in moss, crept up from
the wilderness below and down from the fir woods above.

A thought struggled to assume form in his mind. There was something reminiscent about this house of the woods, this silent house which
struck no chord of human companionship, in which was no warmth of
life or love. Suddenly the thought leapt into complete being.

This was the palace of the sleeping beauty to which he had penetrated.
It was the fairy tale dear to childhood which had been struggling for expression in his mind ever since he had emerged from the trees onto the
desolate terrace. With the departure of the station cab had gone the last
link with to-day, and now he was translated to the goblin realm of fable.

He had crossed the terrace and the lawn and, stood looking through
an open French window into a room that evidently adjoined the hall. A
great still darkness had come, and on a little table in the room a reading
lamp was burning. It had a quaint mosaic shade which shut in much of the
light but threw a luminous patch directly on a heap of cushions strewn

upon the floor. Face downward in this silken nest, her chin resting upon her hands and her elfin curly brown hair tousled bewitchingly, lay a girl so audaciously pretty that Dillon hesitated to accept the evidence of his eyes.

The crunching of a piece of gravel beneath his foot led to the awakening of the sleeping beauty. She raised her head quickly and then started upright, a lithe, divinely petite figure in a green velvet dress, having short fur-trimmed sleeves that displayed her pretty arms. For an instant it was a startled nymph that confronted him; then a distracting dimple appeared in one fair cheek, and:

"Oh! how you frightened me!" said the girl, speaking with a slight French accent which the visitor found wholly entrancing. "You must be Jack Dillon? I am Phryné."

Dillon bowed.

"How I envy Hyperides!" he said.

A blush quickly stained the lovely face of Phryné, and the roguish eyes were lowered, whereby the penitent Dillon, who had jested in the not uncommon belief that a pretty girl is necessarily brainless, knew that the story of the wonder-woman of Thespiæ was familiar to her modern namesake.

"I am afraid," declared Phryné, with a return of her mischievous composure, "that you are very wicked."

Dillon, who counted himself a man of the world, was temporarily at a loss for a suitable rejoinder. The cause of his hesitancy was twofold. In the first place he had reached the age of disillusionment, whereat a man ceases to believe that a perfectly lovely woman exists in the flesh, and in the second place he had found such a fabulous being in a house of gloom and silence to which, a few moments ago, he had deeply regretted having come.

His father, who had accepted the invitation from an old college friend on his son's behalf, had made no mention of a Phryné, whereas Phryné clearly took herself for granted and evidently knew all about Jack Dillon. The latter experienced a volcanic change of sentiment; Hollow Grange was metamorphosed, and assumed magically the guise of a Golden House, an Emperor's pleasure palace, a fair, old-world casket holding this lovely jewel. But who was she?—and in what spirit should he receive her bewildering coquetries?

"I trust," he said, looking into the laughing eyes, "that you will learn to know me better."

Phryné curtsied mockingly.

"You have either too much confidence in your own character or not enough in my wisdom," she said

Dillon stepped into the room, and, stooping, took up a book which lay open upon the floor. It was a French edition of *The Golden Ass* of Apuleius.

The hollow was illuminated by a blinding flash of lightning, and Phryné's musical laughter was drowned in the thunder that boomed and crashed in deepening peals over the hills. In a sudden tropical torrent the rain descended, as Dr. Kassimere entered the room.

2

Jack Dillon leant from his open window and looked out over the valley to where a dull red glow crowned the hill-top. There was a fire somewhere in the neighbourhood of the distant town; probably a building had been struck by lightning. The storm had passed, although thunder was still audible dimly, like the roll of muffled drums or a remote bombardment. Stillness had reclaimed Hollow Grange.

He was restless, uneasy; he sought to collate his impressions of the place and its master. Twelve years had elapsed since his one previous meeting with Dr. Kassimere, and little or no memory of the man had remained. So much had intervened; the war—and Phryné. Now that he was alone and could collect his ideas he knew of what Dr. Kassimere's gaunt, wide-eyed face had reminded him: it was of Thoth, the ibis-headed god whose figure he had seen on the walls of the temples during his service in Egypt.

"Kassimere was always a queer fish, Jack," his father had said; "but most of his eccentricities were due to his passion for study. The Grange is the very place Sir Francis" (the specialist) "would have chosen for your convalescence, and you'll find nothing dangerously exciting in Kassimere's atmosphere!"

Yet there was that about Dr. Kassimere which he did not and could not like; his quietly cordial welcome, his courteous regret that his guest's arrival by an earlier train (a circumstance due to reduced service) had led to his not being met at the station; the charming simplicity with which he confessed to the smallness of his household, and to the pleasure which it afforded him to have the son of an old comrade beneath his roof—all these kindly overtures had left the bird-like eyes cold, hard, watchful, calculating. The voice was the voice of a friend and a gentleman, but the face was the face of Thoth.

The mystery of Phryné was solved in a measure. She was Dr. Kassimere's adopted daughter and the orphaned child of Louis Devant, the famous Paris cartoonist, who had died penniless at the height of his success. In his selection of a name for her, the brilliant and dissolute artist had exhibited a breadth of mind which Phryné inherited in an almost embarrassing degree.

Her mental equipment was bewildering: the erudition of an Oxford don spiced with more than a dash of Boul' Mich', which made for complexity. Her curious learning was doubtless due to the setting of a receptive mind amid such environment, but how she had retained her piquant vivacity in Hollow Grange was less comprehensible. The servants formed a small and saturnine company; only two—the housekeeper, Mrs. Harman, a black and forbidding figure, and Madame Charny, French companion—sleeping in the house. Gawly, a surly creature who neglected the gardens and muttered savagely over other duties, together with his wife, who cooked, resided at the lodge. There were two maids, who lived in the village. . . .

The glow from the distant fire seemed to be reflected upon the firs bordering the terrace below; then Dillon, watching the dull red light, remembered that Dr. Kassimere's laboratory adjoined the tiny chapel, and that, though midnight drew near, the doctor was still at work there.

Owls and other night birds hooted and shrieked among the trees, and many bats were in flight. He found himself thinking of the pyramid bats of Egypt, and of the ibis-headed Thoth who was the scribe of the underworld.

Dr. Kassimere had made himself medically responsible for his case and had read attentively the letters which Dillon had brought from his own physician. He was to prescribe on the following day, and to-night the visitor found Morpheus a treacherous god. Furtive activities disturbed the house, or so it seemed to the sleepless man tossing on his bed; alert intelligences within Hollow Grange responded to the night life of the owls without, and he seemed to lie in the shadow of a watchfulness that never slumbered.

3

"There's many a fine walk hereabouts," said the old man seated in the armchair in the corner of the Threshers' Inn bar parlour.

Dillon nodded encouragingly.

"There's Ganton-on-the-Hill," continued the ancient. "You can see the sea from there in clear weather; and many's the time I've heard the guns in France from Upper Crobury of a still night. Then, four mile away, there's the haunted Grange, though nobody's allowed past the gate. Not as nobody wants to be," he added reflectively.

"The haunted Grange?" questioned Dillon. "Where is that?"

"Hollow Grange?" said the old man. "Why, it lies—"

"Oh, Hollow Grange—yes! I know where Hollow Grange is, but I was unaware that it was reputed to be haunted."

"Ah," replied the other pityingly, "you're new to these parts; I see that the minute I set eyes on you. Maybe you was wounded in France, and you're down here to get well, like?"

"Quite so. Your deductive reasoning is admirable."

"Ah," said the sage, chuckling with self-appreciation, "I ain't lived in these here parts for nigh on seventy-five years without learning to use my eyes, I ain't. For seventy-four years and seven months," he added proudly, "I ain't been outside this here county where I was born, and I can use my eyes, I can; I know a thing, I do, when I see it. Maybe it was providence, as you might say, what brought you to the Threshers' to-day."

"Quite possibly," Dillon admitted.

"He was just such another as you," continued the old man with apparent irrelevance. "You don't happen to be stopping at Hainingham Vicarage?"

"No," replied Dillon.

"Ah! he was stopping at Hainingham Vicarage, and he'd been wounded in France. How he got to know Dr. Kassimere I can't tell you; not at parson's, anyway. Parson won't never speak to him. Only last Sunday week he preached agin him; not in so many words, but I could see his drift. He spoke about them heathen women livin' on an island—sort of female Robinson Crusoes, I make 'em out, I do—as saves poor shipwrecked sailors from the sea and strangles of 'em ashore."

Dillon glanced hard at the voluble old man.

"The sirens?" he suggested, conscious of a sudden hot surging about his heart.

"Ah, that's the women I mean."

"But where is the connection?"

"Ah, you're new to these parts, you are. That Dr. Kassimere he keeps a siren down in Hollow Grange. They see her—these here strangers (same as the shipwrecked sailors parson told about)—and it's all up with 'em."

Dillon stifled a laugh in which anger would have mingled with contempt. To think that in the twentieth century a man of science was like, to meet with the fate of Dr. Dee in the days of Elizabeth! Truly there were dark spots in England. But could' he credit the statement of this benighted elder that a modern clergyman had actually drawn an analogy between Phryné Devant and the sirens? It was unbelievable.

"What was the unhappy fate," he asked, masking his intolerance, "of the young man staying at the Vicarage?"

"The same as them afore him," came the startling reply; "for he warn't the first, and maybe"—with a shrewd glance of the rheumy old eyes—"he won't be the last. Them sirens has the powers of darkness. I know, 'cause I've seen one—her at the Grange; and though I'm an old man, nigh on seventy-five, I'll never forget her face, I won't, and the way she smiled at me!"

"But," persisted Dillon patiently, "what became of this particular young man, the one who was staying at the Vicarage?"

The ancient sage leant forward in his chair and tapped the speaker upon the knee with the stem of his clay pipe.

"Ask them as knows," he said, with impressive solemnity. "Nobody else can tell you!"

And, having permitted an indiscreet laugh to escape him, not another word on the subject could Dillon induce the old man to utter, he strictly confining himself, in his ruffled dignity, to the climatic conditions and the crops.

When Dillon, finally, set out upon the four-mile walk back to the Grange, he realized, with annoyance, that the senile imaginings of his bar-parlour acquaintance lingered in his mind. That Dr. Kassimere dwelt outside the social life of the county he had speedily learnt; but for this he had been prepared. That he might possibly be, not a recluse, but a pariah, was a new point of view. Trivial things, to which hitherto he had paid scant attention, began to marshal themselves as evidence. The two village "helpers," he knew, received extravagant wages, because, as Phryné had confessed, they had "found it almost impossible to get girls to stay." Why?

Of the earlier guest, or guests, who had succumbed to the siren lure of Phryné, he had heard no mention. Why? Save at meal times he rarely saw his host, who frankly left him to the society of Phryné. Again—why? Dr. Kassimere, in his jealously locked laboratory, was at work day and night upon his experiments. What were these experiments? What was the nature of the doctor's studies?

He had now been for nearly three weeks at Hollow Grange, and never had Dr. Kassimere spoken of his work. And Phryné? The sudden new thought of Phryné was so strange, so wonderful and overwhelming, that it reacted physically; and he pulled up short in the middle of a field path, as though some palpable obstacle blocked the way.

Why had he set out alone that day, when all other days had been spent in the girl's company? He had deliberately sought solitude—because of Phryné; because he wanted to think calmly, judicially, to arraign himself before his own judgment, remote from the witchery of her presence. He had tried to render his mind a void, wherein should linger not one fragrant memory of her delicate beauty and charm, so that he might return unbiased to his judgment. He had returned; he was judged.

He loved Phryné madly, insanely. His future, his life, lay in the hollow of her hands.

4

"Yes," admitted Phryné, "it is true. There were two of them."

"And"—Dillon hesitated—"were they in love with you?"

"Of course," said Phryné naïvely.

"But you—"

Phryné shook her curly head.

"I rather liked the French boy, but I do not believe anything that a Frenchman says to a girl; and Harry, the other, was handsome, but so silly. . . ."

"So you did not love either of them?"

"Of course not."

"But," said Dillon, and impulsively he swept her into his arms, "you are going to love me."

One quick upward glance she gave, but instantly lowered her eyes and withheld her bewitching face from him.

"Am I?" she whispered. "You are so conceited."

But as she spoke the words he kissed her, and she surrendered sweetly, nestling her head against his shoulder for a moment. Then, leaping back, bright-eyed and blushing, she turned and ran like a startled fawn across the terrace and into the house.

He saw no more of her until dinner time, and spent the interval in a kind of suspended consciousness that was new and perturbing. Within him life pulsed at delirious speed, but the universe seemed to have slowed upon its course so that each hour became as two. Throughout dinner, Phryné was deliciously shy to the point of embarrassment; and Dillon, who several times surprised the bird-eyes of Dr. Kassimere studying the girl's face, detained his host, and being a young man of orderly mind, formally asked his consent to an engagement.

The doctor's joy was seemingly so unfeigned that Dillon almost liked him for a moment. He placed no obstacle in the path of the suitor for his adopted daughter's hand, graciously expressing every confidence in the future. His joy was genuine enough, Dillon determined; but from what source did it actually spring? The Thoth-like eyes were exultant, and all the old mistrust poured back in a wave upon the younger man. Was this distrust becoming an obsession? Why should he eternally be seeking an ulterior motive for every act in this man's life?

He went to look for Phryné, and found her in the spot where he had first seen her, prone in a nest of cushions. She sprang up as he entered the room, and glanced at him in that new way which set his heart leaping. . . .

And because of the magic of her presence, it was not until later, when he stood alone in his own room, that he could order the facts gleaned from her.

There was some grain of truth in the story of the ancient gossip at the Threshers', after all. A young French lieutenant of artillery had received an invitation to spend a leave at Hollow Grange. His Gallic soul had been fired by Phryné's beauty, and although his advances had been met with rebuff, he had asked Dr. Kassimere's permission to pay his court to the girl. On the same evening he had departed hurriedly, and Phryné had supposed, since the doctor never referred to him again, that he had been sent about his business. Then came a strange letter which Phryné had shown to Dillon. Its tone throughout was of passionate anger, and one passage recurred again and again to Dillon's mind. "I would give my life for you gladly," it read, "but my soul belongs to God. . . ."

Phryné had counted him demented, and Dr. Kassimere had agreed with her. But there was Harry Waynwright, nephew of the vicar of St. Peter's at Hainingham. An accidental meeting with Phryné had led to a courtesy call—and the inevitable. It had all the seeming of a case of love-sickness, and the unhappy youth grew seriously ill. From pestering her daily he changed his tactics to studiously avoiding her, until, meeting her in the village one morning, he greeted her with, "I can't do it, Phryné! Tell him I can't do it. He can rely upon my word; but I'm going away to try to forget!"

Dr. Kassimere had professed entire ignorance of the meaning of the words. A faint shadow had crossed Phryné's face as she spoke of these matters, but, as a result of her extraordinary beauty, she was somewhat callous where languishing admirers were concerned, and she had dismissed the gloomy twain with a shrug of her charming shoulders.

"Mad!" she had said. "It seems my fate always to meet madmen!"

The night silence had descended again upon Hollow Grange, disturbed only by the mournful cry of the owl and the almost imperceptible note of the bat. But to the nervous alertness of Dillon, a deep unrest seemed to stir within the house; yet—an unrest not physical but spiritual; it was as the shadow of a sleepless watcher—a shadow creeping over his soul.

What was the explanation lying at the back of it all? Vainly he sought for a theory, however wild, however improbable, that should embrace all the facts known to him and serve either to banish his black doubts or to focus them. Upon one thing he had determined: There was something or someone in Hollow Grange that he *feared,* some centre from whence fear radiated.

Phryné, for one fleeting moment, had revealed to him that she, too, had known this formless dread, but only latterly; probably from lack of a more definite date, she had spoken of this fear as first visiting her at about the time of the Frenchman's advent.

"Slowly, he has changed towards me," she had whispered, referring to Dr. Kassimere. "He watches me, sometimes, in a strange way. Oh, he has been so good, so very kind and good, but—I shall be glad when—"

Could some part of the mystery be explained away by the doctor's increasing absorption in his studies, which led him to regard the charge of a ward, and a wayward one at that, as unduly onerous and disturbing? Might it not fairly be supposed that ignorant superstition and the ravings of unrequited passion accounted for the rest?

At the nature of Dr. Kassimere's studies he could not even guess. The greater number of the works in the library related to mysticism in one form or another, although there was a sprinkling of exact science to leaven the whole.

"He can rely upon my word," Waynwright had said. Regarding what, or regarding whom, had he given his word?

The cry of a night hawk came, as if in answer; the hoot of an owl, as if in mockery. Out beyond the terrace a dull red light showed from Dr. Kassimere's laboratory.

5

Enlightenment came about in this fashion: Seeking to quench a feverish thirst, Dillon discovered that no glass had been left in his room. He determined to fetch one from the buffet cupboard downstairs. Softly, in slippered feet, he descended the stairs and was crossing the hallway when he kicked something—a small book, he thought—that lay there upon the floor. Groping, he found it, slipped it into the pocket of his dressing gown, and entered the dining room. He found a tumbler without difficulty, in the dark, noted the presence of a heavy, oppressive odour, and returned upstairs. Now he made another discovery. He had forgotten the nightly draught of medicine prescribed by Dr. Kassimere; a new unopened phial stood upon the dressing table.

He mixed himself a mild whisky and soda from the decanter and siphon which his host's hospitality caused nightly to be placed in his room, and then, seized by a sudden thought, took out the little book which he had found in the hall.

It was a faded manuscript, in monkish Latin; a copy of an unpublished work of Paracelsus. Many passages had been rendered into English, and the translations, in Dr. Kassimere's minute, cramped writing, were interposed between the bound pages. In these again were interpolated marginal notes, some in the shape of unintelligible symbols, others in that of chemical formulae. Several passages were marked in red ink. And, having perused the first of these which he chanced upon, a clammy moisture broke out upon his skin, accompanied by so marked a nervous trembling that he was forced to seat himself upon the bed.

The secret of this man's ghastly life work was in his hands; he knew, now, what bargain Dr. Kassimere had proposed to the Frenchman and to the other; he knew why he had adopted the lovely daughter of Louis Devant—and he knew why he, Jack Dillon, had been invited to Hollow Grange. That such a ghoul in human shape could live and have his being amid ordinary mankind was a stupendous improbability which, ten minutes earlier, he would have laughed to scorn.

"My God!" he whispered. "My God!"

His glance fell upon the unopened phial on his dressing table, and from his soul a silent thanksgiving rose to heaven that he had left it untasted. He realized that his own case differed from those of his predecessors in two particulars: He was actually in residence under Dr. Kassimere's roof and receiving treatment from the man's hands. No option was to be offered to *him;* the great experiment, the *Magnum Opus,* was to be performed without his consent!

And Phryné!—Phryné, the other innocent victim of this fiend's lust for knowledge! The thought restored his courage. More than life itself depended upon his coolness and address; he must act, at once. The monstrous possibility hinted at by Von Hohenheim in his earliest published work, *Practica D. Theophrasti Paracelsi,* printed at Augsburg in 1529, was, in this hideous pamphlet, elaborated and brought within the bounds of practical experiment.

He crept to the door, opened it, and stood listening intently. That silence which seemed like a palpable cloud—a cloud masking the presence of one who watched—lay over the house. Slowly he descended to the hall and dropped the horror which the evil genius of Von Hohenheim had conceived, upon the spot where it had lain when his foot had discovered it.

A creaking sound warned him of someone's approach, and he had barely time to slip behind some draperies ere a cowled figure bearing a lantern came out into the hall. It was Dr. Kassimere, wearing a loose gown having a monkish hood—and he was searching for something.

Nothing in his experience—not the blood lust seen in the eyes of men in battle—had prepared him for that which transfigured the face of Dr. Kassimere. The strange semblance, of Thoth was there no more; it had given place to another, more active malevolence, to a sort of Satanic *eagerness* indescribably terrifying; it was the face of one possessed.

Like some bird of grey he pounced upon the book, thrust it into the pocket of his gown, and began furtively to retrace his steps. As he entered the big dining room, Dillon was close upon his heels.

Dr. Kassimere passed into the small room beyond and turned from thence into the library. Dillon, observing every precaution, followed. From the library the doctor entered the short, narrow passage leading to that quaint relic of bygone days and ways—the tiny chapel. At the entrance Dillon paused, watchful. Once, the man in the monkish robe turned, on the time-worn step of the altar, and looked back over his shoulder, revealing a face that might well have been that of Asmodeus himself.

On the left of the altar was the cupboard wherein, no doubt, in past ages, the priest had kept his vestments. The oppressive odour which Dillon had first observed in the dining room was very perceptible in the chapel; and as Dr. Kassimere opened the door of the cupboard and stepped within, an explanation of the presence of this deathly smell in the house occurred to Dillon's mind. The laboratory adjoined the Grange on this side; here was a private entrance known to, and used by, Dr. Kassimere alone.

His surmise proved to be correct. Occasioning scarcely a sound, the secret door opened, and a fiery glow leapt out across the altar steps, accompanied by a wave of heated air laden with the nauseous, unnamable smell. Within the redly lighted doorway, Dr. Kassimere paused and glanced at a watch which he wore upon his wrist. Then for a moment he disappeared, to reappear carrying a small squat bottle and a contrivance of wire and gauze the sight of which created in Dillon a sense of physical nausea. It was a chloroform mask! Both he placed upon a vaguely seen table and again approached the door.

Weakly, Dillon fell back, pressing himself closely against the chapel wall, as the doctor, this time leaving the secret entrance open—with a purpose in view which the watcher shudderingly recognized—recrossed the chapel and went off, softly treading, in the direction of the library.

All his courage, moral and physical, was called upon now, and knowing, by some intuition of love, what and whom he should find there, he stepped unsteadily into Dr. Kassimere's laboratory. . . .

That there were horrors—monstrosities that may not be described, whose names may not be written—in the place, he realized, in some subconscious fashion; but—prone upon a low metal couch of most curious workmanship lay Phryné, still—white; perfect in her pale beauty as her namesake who posed for Praxiteles.

Dillon reeled, steadied himself, and sank upon his knees by the couch.

"Phryné!" he whispered, locking his arms about her—"my Phryné! . . ."

Then he remembered the gauze mask and even detected the sickly, sweet smell of the anaesthetic. Anger gave him new strength; he raised the girl in his arms and turned towards the door communicating with the chapel.

Framed in the opening was the hooded figure of Dr. Kassimere, confronting him. His face was immobile again, with the immobility of ibis-headed Thoth; his eyes were hard, his voice was cold.

"What is the meaning of this outrage?" he demanded sternly. "Phryné has been taken suddenly ill; an immediate operation may be necessary—"

"Out of my way!" said Dillon, advancing past a huge glass jar filled with reddish liquid that stood upon a pedestal between the couch and the door.

"Be careful, you fool!" shrieked Dr. Kassimere, frenziedly, his calm dropping from him like a cloak and a new and dreadful light coming into the staring eyes.

But he was too late. Dillon's foot had caught the pedestal. With a resounding crash the thing overturned; as Dr. Kassimere sprang forward, he slipped in the slimy stream that was pouring over the laboratory floor—and fell. . . .

Laying Phryné upon the altar, her head resting against the age-worn communion rails, Dillon turned and closed the secret door dividing the house of God from the house of Satan. One glimpse, in the red furnace glow, he had of Dr. Kassimere, writhing upon the slimy floor, shrieking, blaspheming—and fighting, fighting madly, as a man fights for life and more than life. . . .

He had not yet carried the unconscious girl beyond the dining room, when, above that other smell, he detected the odour of burning wood. A fire had broken out in the laboratory.

*   *   *

Mrs. Jack Dillon mourns her guardian (no trace of whom was ever found in the charred remains of Hollow Grange) to this day; for she retains no memory of the night of the great fire, but believes that, overcome by the fumes, she was rescued and carried insensible from the house, by her lover. In the latter's bosom the grim secret is locked, with the memory of a demoniac figure, fighting, fighting. . . .

The Curse of a Thousand Kisses

Introductory

Saville Grainger will long be remembered by the public as a brilliant journalist and by his friends as a confirmed misogynist. His distaste for the society of women amounted to a mania, and to Grainger a pretty face was like a red rag to a bull. This was all the more extraordinary and, for Grainger, more painful, because he was one of the most handsome men I ever knew—very dark, with wonderful flashing eyes and the features of an early Roman—or, as I have since thought, of an aristocratic Oriental; aquiline, clean-cut, and swarthy. At any mixed gathering at which he appeared, women gravitated in his direction as though he possessed some magnetic attraction for the sex; and Grainger invariably bolted.

His extraordinary end—never explained to this day—will be remembered by some of those who read of it; but so much that affected whole continents has occurred in the interval that to the majority of the public the circumstances will no longer be familiar. It created a considerable stir in Cairo at the time, as was only natural, but when the missing man failed to return, the nine days' wonder of his disappearance was forgotten in the excitement of some new story or another.

Briefly, Grainger, who was recuperating at Mena House after a rather severe illness in London, went out one evening for a stroll, wearing a light dust-coat over his evening clothes and smoking a cigarette. He turned in the direction of the Great Pyramid—and never came back. That is the story in its bald entirety. No one has ever seen him since—or ever reported having seen him.

If the following story is an elaborate hoax—perpetrated by Grainger himself, for some obscure reason remaining in hiding, or by another well acquainted with his handwriting—I do not profess to say. As to how

181

it came into my possession, that may be told very briefly. Two years after Grainger's disappearance I was in Cairo, and although I was not staying at Mena House I sometimes visited friends there. One night as I came out of the hotel to enter the car which was to drive me back to the Continental, a tall native, dressed in white and so muffled up that little more of his face than two gleaming eyes was visible, handed me a packet—a roll of paper, apparently—saluted me with extraordinary formality, and departed.

No one else seemed to have noticed the man, although the chauffeur, of course, was nearly as close to him as I was, and a servant from the hotel had followed me out and down the steps. I stood there in the dusk, staring at the packet in my hand and then after the tall figure—already swallowed up in the shadow of the road. Naturally I assumed that the man had made some mistake, and holding the package near the lamp of the car I examined it closely.

It was a roll of some kind of parchment, tied with a fragment of thin string, and upon the otherwise blank outside page my name was written very distinctly!

I entered the car, rather dazed by the occurrence, which presented several extraordinary features, and, unfastening the string, began to read. Then, in real earnest, I thought I must be dreaming. Since I append the whole of the manuscript I will make no further reference to the contents here, but will content myself with mentioning that it was written—with dark-brown ink—in Saville Grainger's unmistakable hand upon some kind of parchment or papyrus which has defied three different experts to whom I have shown it, but which, in short, is of unknown manufacture. The twine with which it was tied proved to be of finely plaited reed.

That part of Grainger's narrative, if the following amazing statement is really the work of Grainger, which deals with events up to the time that he left Mena House—and the world—I have been able to check. The dragoman, Hassan Abd-el-Kebîr, was still practising his profession at Mena House at the time of my visit, and he confirmed the truth of Grainger's story in regard to the heart of lapis-lazuli, which he had seen, and the meeting with the old woman in the Milski—of which Grainger had spoken to him.

For the rest, the manuscript shall tell Grainger's story.

The Manuscript

Two years have elapsed since I quitted the world, and the presence in Egypt of a one-time colleague, of which I have been advised, prompts me to put on record these particulars of the strangest, most wonderful, and most beautiful experience which has ever befallen any man. I do not expect my story to be believed. The skepticism of the material world of Fleet Street will consume my statement with its devouring fires. But I do not care. The old itching to make a "story" is upon me. As a "story" let this paper be regarded.

Where the experience actually began I must leave to each reader to judge for himself. I, personally, do not profess to know, even now. But the curtain first arose upon that part of the story which it is my present purpose to chronicle one afternoon near the corner of the Street of the Silversmiths in Cairo. I was wandering in those wonderful narrow, winding lanes, unaccompanied, for I am by habit a solitary being; and despite my ignorance of the language and customs of the natives I awakened to the fact that a link of sympathy—of silent understanding—seemed to bind me to these busy brown men.

I had for many years cherished a secret ambition to pay a protracted visit to Egypt, but the ties of an arduous, profession hitherto had rendered its realization impossible. Now, a stranger in a strange, land, I found myself *at home.* I cannot hope to make evident to my readers the completeness of this recognition. From Shepheard's, with its throngs of cosmopolitan travellers and its hosts of pretty women, I had early fled in dismay to the comparative quiet of Mena House. But the only real happiness I ever knew—indeed, as I soon began to realize, had ever known—I found among the discordant cries and mingled smells of perfume and decay in the native city. The desert called to me sweetly, but it was the people, the shops, the shuttered houses, the noise and the smells of the Eastern streets which gripped my heart.

Delightedly I watched the passage of those commercial vehicles, narrow and set high upon monstrous wheels, which convey loads of indescribable variety along streets no wider than the "hall" of a small suburban residence. The Parsees in the Khân Khalil with their carpets and shining silkware, the Arab dealers, fierce swarthy tradesmen from the desert, and the smoothtongued Cairenes upholding embroidered cloths and gauzy *yashmaks* to allure the eye—all these I watched with a kind of gladness that was almost tender, that was unlike any sentiment I had ever experienced toward my fellow creatures before.

Mendicants crying the eternal *"Bakshîsh!" Sakhas* with their skins of Nile water, and the other hundred and one familiar figures of the quarter filled me with a great and glad contentment.

I purposely haunted the Mûski during the heat of the day because at that hour it was comparatively free from the presence of Europeans and Americans. Thus, on the occasion of which I write, coming to the end of the street in which the shops of the principal silversmiths are situated, I found myself to be the only white man (if I except the Greeks) in the immediate neighbourhood.

A group of men hurrying out of the street as I approached it first attracted my attention. They were glancing behind them apprehensively as though at a rabid dog. Then came a white-bearded man riding a tiny donkey and also glancing back apprehensively over his shoulder. He all but collided with me in his blind haste; and, stepping quickly aside to avoid him, I knocked down an old woman who was coming out of the street.

The man who had been the real cause of the accident rode off at headlong speed, and I found myself left with the poor victim of my clumsiness in a spot which seemed miraculously to have become deserted. If the shopkeepers remained in their shops, they were invisible, and must have retreated into the darkest corners of the caves in the wall which constitute native emporiums. Pedestrians there were none.

I stooped to the old woman, who lay moaning at my feet . . . and as I did so, I shrank. How can I describe the loathing, the repulsion which I experienced? Never in the whole of my career had I seen such a hideous face. A ragged black veil which she wore had been torn from its brass fastenings as she fell, and her countenance was revealed in all its appalling ugliness. Yellow, shrivelled, toothless, it was scarcely human; but, above all, it repelled because of its aspect of *extreme age.* I do not mean that it was like the face of a woman of eighty; it was like that of a woman who had miraculously survived decease for several centuries! It was a witch face, a deathly face.

And as I shrank, she opened her eyes, moaning feebly, and groping with claw-like hands as if darkness surrounded her Furthermore I saw a new pain, and a keener pain, light up those aged eyes. She had detected my involuntary movement of loathing.

Those who knew me will bear testimony to the fact that I was not an emotional man or one readily impressed by any kind of human appeal. Therefore they will wonder the more to learn that this pathetic light in the old woman's eyes changed my revulsion to a poignant sorrow. I had roughly knocked her from her feet and now hesitated to assist her to rise again! Truly, she was scorned and rejected by all. A wave of tenderness that cannot be described, that could not be resisted, swept over me. My eyes grew misty, and a great remorse claimed me.

"Poor old soul!" I whispered.

Stooping, I gently raised the shrivelled, ape-like head, resting it against my knee; and, bending down, I kissed the old woman on the brow!

I record the fact, but even now, looking back upon its happening, and seeking to recapture the cold, solitary Saville Grainger who has left the world, I realize the wonder of it. That *I* should have given rein to such an impulse! That such an impulse should have stirred me! Which phenomenon was the more remarkable?

The result of my act—regretted as soon as performed—was singular. The aged, hideous creature sighed in a manner I can never forget, and an expression that almost lent comeliness to her features momentarily crept over her face. Then she rose to her feet with difficulty, raised her hands as if blessing me, and muttering something in Arabic went shuffling along the deserted street, stooping as she walked.

Apparently the episode had passed unnoticed. Certainly if anyone witnessed it he was well concealed. But, conscious of a strange embarrassment, with which were mingled other tumultuous emotions, I turned out of the Street of the Silversmiths and found myself amid the normal activities of the quarter again. The memory of the Kiss was repugnant, I wanted to wipe my lips—but something seemed to forbid the act; a lingering compassion that was almost a yearning.

For once in my life I desired to find myself among normal, healthy, moderately brainless Europeans. I longed for the smell of cigar smoke, for the rattle of the cocktail shaker and the sight of a pretty face. I hurried to Shepheard's.

2

The same night, after dinner, I walked out of Mena House to look for Hassan Abd-el-Kebîr, the dragoman with whom I had contracted for a journey, by camel, to Sakhara on the following day. He had promised to attend at half-past eight in order to arrange the time of starting in the morning, together with some other details.

I failed to find him, however, among the dragomans and other natives seated outside the hotel, and to kill time I strolled leisurely down the road toward the electric-tram terminus. I had taken no more than ten paces, I suppose, when a tall native, muffled to the tip of his nose in white and wearing a white turban, appeared out of the darkness beside me, thrust a small package into my hand, and, touching his brow, his lips and his breast with both hands, bowed and departed. I saw him no more.

Standing there in the road, I stared at the little package stupidly. It consisted of a piece of fine white silk fastened about some small, hard object. Evidently, I thought, there had been a mistake. The package could not have been intended for me.

Returning to the hotel, I stood near a lamp and unfastened the silk, which was delicately perfumed. It contained a piece of lapis-lazuli carved in the form of a heart, beautifully mounted in gold and bearing three Arabic letters, inlaid in some way, also in gold!

At this singular ornament I stared harder than ever. Certainly the muffled native had made a strange mistake. This was a love token—and emphatically not for *me!*

I was standing there lost in wonderment, the heart of lapis-lazuli in my palm, when the voice of Hassan disturbed my stupor.

"Ah, my gentleman, I am sorry to be late, but—"

The voice ceased. I looked up.

"Well?" I said.

Then I, too, said no more. Hassan Abd-el-Kebîr was glaring at the ornament in my hand as though I had held, not a very choice example of native jewelry, but an adder or a scorpion!

"What's the matter?" I asked, recovering from my surprise. "Do you know to whom this amulet belongs?"

He muttered something in guttural Arabic ere replying to my question. Then:

"It is the heart of lapis," he said, in a strange voice. "It is the heart of lapis!"

"So much is evident," I cried, laughing. "But does it alarm you?"

"Please," he said softly, and held out a brown hand—"I will see."

I placed the thing in his open palm, and he gazed at it as one might imagine an orchid hunter would gaze at a new species of Odontoglossum.

"What do the figures mean?" I asked.

"They form the word *alf,*" he replied.

"*Alf?* Somebody's name!" I said, still laughing.

"In Arab it means ten hundred," he whispered.

"A thousand?"

"Yes—one thousand."

"Well?"

Hassan returned the ornament to me, and his expression was so strange that I began to grow really annoyed. He was looking at me with a mingling of envy and compassion which I found to be quite insufferable.

"Hassan," I said sternly, "you will tell me all you know about this matter. One would imagine that you suspected me of stealing the thing!"

"Ah, no, my gentleman!" he protested earnestly. "But I will tell you, yes, only you will not believe me."

"Never mind. Tell me."

Thereupon Hassan Abd-el-Kebîr told me the most improbable story to which I had ever listened. Since to reproduce it in his imperfect English, with my own frequent interjections, would be tedious, I will give it in brief. Some of the historical details, imperfectly re-fated by Hassan as I learned later, I have corrected.

In the reign of the Khalif El-Mamûm—a son of Hárûn er-Rashid and brother of the prototype of Beckford's *Vathek*—one Shawar was Governor of Egypt, and the daughter of the Governor, Scheherazade, was famed throughout the domains of the Khalif as the most beautiful maiden in the land. Wazirs and princes sought her hand in vain. Her heart was given to a handsome young merchant of Cairo, Ahmad er-Madâ, who was also the wealthiest man in the city. Shâwar, although an indulgent father, would not hear of such a union, however, but he hesitated to destroy his daughter's happiness by forcing her into an unwelcome marriage. Finally, passion conquered reason in the breasts of the lovers, and they fled, Scheherazade escaping from the palace of her father by means of a rope ladder smuggled into the *harêm* apartments by a slave whom Ahmad's gold had tempted, and meeting Ahmad outside the gardens where he waited with a fleet horse.

Even the guard at the city gate had been bought by the wealthy merchant, and the pair succeeded in escaping from Cairo.

The extensive possessions of Ahmad were confiscated by the enraged father, and a sentence of death was passed upon the absent man—to be instantly put into execution in the event of his arrest anywhere within the domain of the Khalif.

Exiled in a distant oasis, the sheikh of which was bound to Ahmad by ties of ancient friendship, the prospect which had seemed so alluring to Scheherazade became clouded. Recognizing this change in her attitude, Ahmad er-Mâdi racked his brains for some scheme whereby he might recover his lost wealth and surround his beautiful wife with the luxury to which she had been accustomed. In this extremity he had recourse to a certain recluse who resided in a solitary spot in the desert far from the haunts of men and who was widely credited with magical powers.

It was a whole week's journey to the abode of the wizard, and, unknown to Ahmad, during his absence a son of the Khalif, visiting Egypt, chanced to lose his way on a hunting expedition and came upon the secret oasis in which Scheherazade was hiding. This prince had been one of her most persistent suitors.

The ancient magician consented to receive Ahmad, and the first boon which the enamoured young man craved of him was that he might grant him a sight of Scheherazade. The student of dark arts consented. Bidding Ahmad to look into a mirror, he burned the secret perfumes and uttered the prescribed incantation. At first mistily, and then quite clearly, Ahmad saw Scheherazade, standing in the moonlight beneath a tall palm tree—her lips raised to those of her former suitor!

At that the world grew black before the eyes of Ahmad. And he, who had come a long and arduous journey at the behest of love, now experienced an equally passionate hatred. Acquainting the magician with what he had seen, he demanded that he should exercise his art in visiting upon the false Scheherazade the most terrible curse that it lay within his power to invoke!

The learned man refused; whereupon Ahmad, insane with sorrow and anger, drew his sword and gave the magician choice of compliance or instant death. The threat sufficed. The wizard performed a ghastly conjuration, calling down upon Scheherazade the curse of an ugliness beyond that of humanity, and which should remain with her not for the ordinary span of a lifetime but for incalculable years, during which she should continue to live in the flesh, loathed, despised, and shunned of all!

"Until one thousand compassionate men, unasked and of their own free will, shall each have bestowed a kiss upon thee," was the exact text of the curse. "Then thou shalt regain thy beauty, thy love—and death."

Ahmad er-Mâdi staggered out from the cavern, blinded by a hundred emotions—already sick with remorse; and one night's stage on his return journey dropped dead from his saddle . . . stricken by the malignant will of the awful being whose power he had invoked! I will conclude this wild romance in the words of Hassan, the dragoman, as nearly as I can recall them.

"And so," he said, his voice lowered in awe, "Scheherazade, who was stricken with age and ugliness in the very hour that the curse was spoken went out into the world, my gentleman. She begged her way from place to place, and as the years passed by accumulated much wealth in that manner. Finally, it is said, she returned to Cairo, her native city, and there remained. To each man who bestowed a kiss upon her—and such men were rare—she caused a heart of lapis to be sent, and upon, the heart was engraved in gold the number of the kiss! It is said that these gifts ensured to those upon whom they were bestowed the certain possession of their beloved! Once before, when I was a small child, I saw such an amulet, and the number upon it was nine hundred and ninety-nine."

The thing was utterly incredible, of course; merely a picturesque example of Eastern imagination; but just to see what effect it would have upon him, I told Hassan about the old woman in the Mûski. I had to do so. Frankly, the coincidence was so extraordinary that it worried me. When I had finished:

"It was she Scheherazade," he said fearfully. "And it was the *last* kiss!"

"What then?" I asked.

"Nothing, my gentleman. I do not know!"

3

Throughout the expedition to Sakhâra on the following day I could not fail to note that Hassan was covertly watching me—and his expression annoyed me intensely. It was that compound of compassion and resignation which one might bestow upon a condemned man.

I charged him with it, but of course he denied any such sentiment. Nevertheless, I knew that he entertained it, and, what was worse, I began, in an uncomfortable degree, to share it with him! I cannot make myself clearer. But I simply felt the normal world to be slipping from under my feet, and, no longer experiencing a desire to clutch at modernity as I had done after my meeting with the old woman, I found myself to be reconciled to my fate!

To my fate? . . . to what fate? I did not know; but I realized, beyond any shade of doubt, that something tremendous, inevitable, and ultimate was about to happen to me. I caught myself unconsciously raising the heart of lapis-lazuli to my lips! Why I did so I had no idea; I seemed to have lost identity. I no longer knew myself.

When Hassan parted from me at Mena House that evening he could not disguise the fact that he regarded the parting as final; yet my plans were made for several weeks ahead. Nor did I quarrel with the man's curious attitude. I regarded the parting as final, also!

In a word, I was becoming reconciled—to something. It is difficult, all but impossible, to render such a frame of mind comprehensible, and I shall not even attempt the task, but leave the events of the night to speak for themselves.

After dinner I lighted a cigarette, and avoiding a particularly persistent and very pretty widow who was waiting to waylay me in the lounge, I came out of the hotel and strolled along in the direction of the Pyramid.

Once I looked back—bidding, a silent farewell to Mena House! Then I took out the heart of lapis-lazuli from my pocket and kissed it rapturously—kissed it as I had never kissed any object or any person in the whole course of my life!

And why I did so I had no idea.

All who read my story will be prepared to learn that in this placid and apparently feeble frame of mind I slipped from life, from the world. It was not so. The modern man, the Saville Grainger once known in Fleet Street, came to life again for one terrible, strenuous moment . . . and then passed out of life for ever.

Just before I reached the Pyramid, and at a lonely spot in the path—for this was not a "Sphinx and Pyramid night"—that is to say, the moon was not at the full—a tall, muffled native appeared at my elbow. He was the same man who had brought me the heart of lapis-lazuli, or his double. I started.

He touched me lightly on the arm.

"Follow," he said—and pointed ahead into the darkness below the plateau.

I moved off obediently. Then—suddenly, swiftly, came revolt. The modern man within me flared into angry life. I stopped dead, and:

"Who are you? Where are you leading me?" I cried.

I received no reply.

A silk scarf was slipped over my head by someone who, silently, must have been following me, and drawn tight enough to prevent any loud outcry but not so as to endanger my breathing. I fought like a madman. I knew, and the knowledge appalled me, that I was fighting for life. Arms like bands of steel grasped me; I was lifted, bound and carried—I knew not where. . . .

Placed in some kind of softly padded saddle, or, as I have since learned, into a *shibrîyeh* or covered litter on a camel's back, I felt the animal rise to its ungainly height and move off swiftly. As suddenly as revolt had flamed up, resignation returned. I was contented. My bonds were unnecessary; my rebellion was ended. I yearned, wildly, for the end of the desert journey! Someone was calling me and all my soul replied.

For hours, as it seemed, the camel raced ceaselessly on. Absolute silence reigned about me. Then, in the distance I heard voices, and the gait of the camel changed. Finally the animal stood still. Came a word of guttural command, and the camel dropped to its knees. Pillowed among a pile of scented cushions, I experienced no discomfort from this usually painful operation.

I was lifted out of my perfumed couch and set upon my feet. Having been allowed to stand for a while until the effects of remaining so long in a constrained position had worn off, I was led forward into some extensive building. Marble pavements were beneath my feet, fountains played, and the air was heavy with burning ambergris.

I was placed with my back to a pillar and bound there, but not harshly. The bandage about my head was removed. I stared around me.

A magnificent Eastern apartment met my gaze—a great hall open on one side to the desert. Out upon the sands I could see a group of men who had evidently been my captors and my guards. The one who had unfastened the silk scarf I could not see, but I heard him moving away behind the pillar to which I was bound.

Stretched upon a luxurious couch before me was a woman.

If I were to seek to describe her I should inevitably fail, for her loveliness surpassed everything which I had ever beheld—of which I had ever dreamed. I found myself looking into her eyes, and in their depths I found all that I had missed in life, and lost all that I had found.

She smiled, rose, and taking a jewelled dagger from a little table beside her, approached me. My heart beat until I felt almost suffocated as she came near. And when she bent and cut the silken lashing which bound me, I knew such rapture as I had hitherto counted an invention of Arabian poets. I was raised above the joys of common humanity and tasted the joy of the gods. She placed the dagger in my hand.

"My life is thine," she said "Take it."

And clutching at the silken raiment draping her beautiful bosom, she invited me to plunge the blade into her heart!

The knife dropped, clattering upon the marble pavement. For one instant I hesitated, watching her, devouring her with my eyes; then I swept her to me and pressed upon her sweet lips the thousand and first kiss. . . .

(NOTE.—The manuscript of Saville Grainger finishes here.)

The Man with the Shaven Skull

A STRANGE DISAPPEARANCE

Pull that light lower," ordered Inspector Wessex. "There you are, Mr. Harley; what do you make of it?"

Paul Harley and I bent gingerly over the ghastly exhibit to which the C.I.D. official had drawn our attention, and to view which we had journeyed from Chancery Lane to Wapping.

This was the body of a man dressed solely in ragged shirt and trousers. But the remarkable feature of his appearance lay in the fact that every scrap of hair from chin, lip, eyebrows and skull had been shaved off!

There was another facial disfigurement, peculiarly and horribly Eastern, which my pen may not describe.

"Impossible to identify!" murmured Harley. "Yes, you were right, Inspector; this is a victim of Oriental deviltry. Look here, too!"

He indicated three small wounds, one situated on the left shoulder and the others on the forearm of the man.

"The divisional surgeon cannot account for them," replied Wessex. "They are quite superficial, and he thinks they may be due to the fact that the body got entangled with something in the river."

"They are due to the fact that the man had a birthmark on his shoulder and something—probably a name or some device—tattooed on his arm," said Harley quietly. "Some few years ago, I met with a similar case in the neighbourhood of Stambûl. A woman," he added, significantly.

Detective-Inspector Wessex listened to my companion with respect, for apart from his established reputation as a private inquiry-agent which had made his name familiar in nearly every capital of the civilized world, Paul Harley's work in Constantinople during the six months preceding war with Turkey had merited higher reward than it had ever received.

Had his recommendations been adopted the course of history must have been materially changed.

"You think it's a Chinatown case, then, Mr. Harley?"

"Possibly," was the guarded answer.

Paul Harley nodded to the constable in charge, and the ghastly figure was promptly covered up again. My friend stood staring vacantly at Wessex, and presently:

"The chief actor, I think, will prove to be not Chinese," he said, turned, and walked out.

"If there's any development," remarked Wessex as the three of us entered Harley's car, which stood at the door, "I will, of course, report to you, Mr. Harley. But in the absence of any clue or mark of identification, I fear the verdict will be, 'Body of a man unknown,' etc., which has marked the finish of a good many in this cheerful quarter of London."

"Quite so," said Harley, absently. "It presents extraordinary features, though, and may not end as you suppose. However—where do you want me to drop you, Wessex; at the Yard?"

"Oh no," answered Wessex. "I made a special visit to Wapping just to get your opinion on the shaven man. I'm really going down to Deepbrow to took into that new disappearance case; the daughter of the gamekeeper. You'll have read of it?"

"I have," said Harley shortly.

Indeed, readers of the daily press were growing tired of seeing on the contents bills: "Another girl missing." The circumstance (which might have been no more than coincidence) that three girls had disappeared within the last eight weeks leaving no trace behind, had stimulated the professional scribes to link the cases, although no visible link had been found, and to enliven a somewhat dull journalistic season with theories about "a new Mormon menace."

The vanishing of this fourth girl had inspired them to some startling headlines, and the case had interested me personally for the reason that I was acquainted with Sir Howard Hepwell, one of whose gamekeepers was the stepfather of the missing Molly Clayton. Moreover, it was hinted that she had gone away in the company of Captain Ronald Vane, at that time a guest of Sir Howard's at the Manor.

In fact, Sir Howard had 'phoned to ask me if I could induce Harley to run down, but my friend had expressed himself as disinterested in a common case of elopement. Now, as Wessex spoke, I glanced aside at Harley, wondering if the fact that so celebrated a member of the C.I.D. as Detective-Inspector Wessex had been put in charge would induce him to change his mind.

We were traversing a particularly noisy and unsavoury section of the Commercial Road, and although I could see that Wessex was anxious to impart particulars of the case to Harley, so loud was the din that I recognized the impossibility of conversing, and therefore:

"Have you time to call at my rooms, Wessex?" I asked.

"Well," he replied, "I have three-quarters of an hour."

"You can do it in the car," said Harley suddenly. "I have been asked to look into this case myself, and before I definitely decline I should like to hear your version of the matter."

Accordingly, we three presently gathered in my chambers, and Wessex, with one eye on the clock, outlined the few facts at that time in his possession respecting the missing girl.

Two days before the news of the disappearance had been published broadcast under such headings as I have already indicated, a significant scene had been enacted in the gamekeeper's cottage.

Molly Clayton, a girl whose remarkable beauty had made her a central figure in numerous scandalous stories, for such is the charity of rural neighbours, was detected by her stepfather, about eight in the evening, slipping out of the cottage.

"Where be ye goin', hussy?" he demanded, grasping her promptly by the arm.

"For a walk!" she replied defiantly.

"A walk wi' that fine soger from t' Manor!" roared Bramber furiously. "You'll be sorry yet, you barefaced gadabout! Must I tell you again that t' man's a villain?"

The girl wrenched her arm from Bramber's grasp, and blazed defiance from her beautiful eyes.

"He knows how to respect a woman—what you don't!" she retorted hotly.

"So I don't respect you, my angel?" shouted her stepfather. "Then you know what you can do! The door's open and there's few'll miss you!"

Snatching her hat, the girl, very white, made to go out. Whereat the gamekeeper, a brutal man with small love for Molly, and maddened by her taking him at his word, seized her suddenly by her abundant fair hair and hauled her back into the room.

A violent scene followed, at the end of which Molly fainted and Bramber came out and locked the door.

When he came back about half-past nine the girl was missing, She did not reappear that night, and the police were advised in the morning. Their most significant discovery was this:

Captain Ronald Vane, on the night of Molly's disappearance, had left the Manor House, after dining alone with his host, Sir Howard Hepwell, saying that he proposed to take a stroll as far as the Deep Wood.

He never returned!

From the moment that Gamekeeper Bramber left his cottage and the moment when Sir Howard Hepwell parted from his guest after dinner, the world to which these two people, Molly Clayton and Captain Vane, were known, knew them no more!

I was about to say that they were never seen again. But to me has fallen the task of relating how and where Paul Harley and I met with Captain Vane and Molly Clayton.

At the end of the Inspector's account:

"H'm," said Harley, glancing under his thick brows in my direction, "could you spare the time, Knox?"

"To go to Deepbrow?" I asked with interest.

"Yes; we have ten minutes to catch the train."

"I'll come," said I. "Sir Howard will be delighted to see you, Harley."

II

THE CLUE OF THE PHOTOGRAPHS

"What do you make of it, Inspector?" asked my friend.

Detective-Inspector Wessex smiled, and scratched his chin.

"There was no need for me to come down!" he replied. "And certainly no need for you, Mr. Harley!"

Harley bowed, smiling, at the implied compliment.

"It's a common or garden elopement!" continued the detective. "Vane's reputation is absolutely rotten, and the girl was clearly infatuated.

He must have cared a good bit, too. He'll be cashiered, as sure as a gun!"

Leaving Sir Howard at the Manor, we had joined Inspector Wessex at a spot where the baronet's preserves bordered a narrow lane. Here the ground was soft, and the detective drew Harley's attention to a number of footprints by a stile.

"I've got evidence that he was seen here with the girl on other occasions. Now, Mr. Harley, I'll ask you to look over these footprints."

Harley dropped to his knees and made a brief but close examination of the ground round about. One particularly clear imprint of a pointed toe he noticed especially; and Wessex, diving into the pocket of his light overcoat, produced a patent-leather shoe, such as is used for evening wear.

"He had a spare pair in his bag," he explained nonchalantly, "and his man did not prove incorruptible!"

Harley took the shoe and placed it in the impression. It fitted perfectly!

"This is Molly Clayton, I take it?" he said, indicating the prints of a woman's foot.

"Yes," assented Wessex. "You'll notice that they stood for some little time and then walked off, very close together."

Harley nodded absently.

"We lose them along here," continued Wessex, leading up the lane; "but at the corner by the big haystack they join up with the tracks of a motor-car! I ask for nothing clearer! There was rain that afternoon, but there's been none since."

"What does the Captain's man think?"

"The same as I do! He's not surprised at any madness on Vane's part, with a pretty woman in the case!"

"The girl left nothing behind—no note?"

"Nothing."

"Traced the car?"

"No. It must have been hired or borrowed from a long distance."

Where the tracks of the tires were visible we stopped, and Harley made a careful examination of the marks.

"Seems to have had a struggle with her," he said, dryly.

"Very likely!" agreed Wessex, without interest.

Harley crawled about on the ground for some time, to the great detriment of his Harris tweeds, but finally arose, a curious expression on his face—which, however, the detective evidently failed to observe.

We returned to the Manor House where Sir Howard was awaiting us, his good-humoured red face more red than usual; and in the library, with its sporting prints and its works for the most part dealing with riding, hunting, racing, and golf (except for a sprinkling of Nat Gould's novels and some examples of the older workmanship of Whyte-Melville), we were presently comfortably ensconced. On a side table were placed a generous supply of liquid refreshments, cigars and cigarettes; so that we made ourselves quite comfortable, and Sir Howard restrained his indignation, until each had a glass before him and all were smoking.

"Now," he began, "what have you got to report, gentlemen? You, Inspector," he pointed with his cigar toward Wessex, "have seen Vane's man and all of you have been down to look at these damned tracks. I only want to hear one thing; that you expect to trace the disgraceful couple. I'll see to it"—his voice rose almost to a shout—"that Vane is kicked out of the service, and as to that shameless brat of Bramber's, I wish her no worse than the blackguard's company!"

"One moment, Sir Howard, one moment," said Harley quietly; "there are always two sides to a case."

"What do you mean, Mr. Harley? There's only one side that interests me—the outrage inflicted upon my hospitality by this dirty guest of mine. For the girl I don't give twopence; she was bound to come to a bad end."

"Well," said Harley, "before we pronounce the final verdict upon either of them I should like to interview Bramber. Perhaps," he added, turning to Wessex, "it would be as well if Mr. Knox and I went alone. The presence of an official detective sometimes awes this class of witness."

"Quite right, quite right!" agreed Sir Howard, waving his cigar vigorously. "Go and see Bramber, Mr. Harley; tell him that no blame attaches to himself whatever; also, tell him with my compliments that his stepdaughter is—"

"Quite so, quite so," interrupted Harley, endeavouring to hide a smile. "I understand your feelings, Sir Howard, but again I ask you to reserve your verdict until all the facts are before us."

As a result, Harley and I presently set out for the gamekeeper's cottage, and as the man had been warned that we should visit him, he was on the porch smoking his pipe. A big, dark, ugly fellow he proved to be, of a very forbidding cast of countenance. Having introduced ourselves:

"I always knowed she'd come to a bad end!" declared Gamekeeper Bramber, almost echoing Sir Howard's words. "One o' these gentlemen o' hers was sure to be the finish of her!"

"She had other admirers—before Captain Vane?"

"Aye! the hussy! There was a black-faced villain not six months since! He got t' vain cat to go to London an' have her photograph done in a dress any decent woman would 'a' blushed to look at! Like one o' these Venuses up at t' Manor! Good riddance! She took after her mother!"

The violent old ruffian was awkward to examine, but Harley persevered.

"This previous admirer caused her to be photographed in that way, did he? Have you a copy?"

"No!" blazed Bramber. "What I found I burnt! He ran off, like I told her he would—an' her cry'n' her eyes out! But the pretty soger dried her tears quick enough!"

"Do you know this man's name?"

"No. A foreigner, he was."

"Where were the photographs done—in London, you say?"

"Aye."

"Do you know by what photographer?"

"I don't! An' I don't care! Piccadilly they had on 'em, which was good enough for me."

"Have you her picture?"

"No!"

"Did she receive a letter on the day of her disappearance?"

"Maybe."

"Good day!" said Harley. "And let me add that the atmosphere of her home was hardly conducive to ideal conduct!"

Leaving Bramber to digest this rebuke, we came out of the cottage. Dusk was falling now, and by the time that we regained the Manor the place was lighted up. Inspector Wessex was waiting for us in the library, and:

"Well?" he said, smiling slightly as we entered.

"Nothing much," replied Harley dryly, "except that I don't wonder at the girl's leaving such a home."

"What's that! What!" roared a big voice, and Sir Howard came into the room. "I tell you, Bramber only had one fault as a stepfather; he wasn't heavy-handed enough. A bad lot, sir, a bad lot!"

"Well, sir," said Inspector Wessex, looking from one to another, "personally, beyond the usual inquiries at railway stations, etc., I cannot see that we can do much here. Don't you agree with me, Mr. Harley?"

Harley nodded.

"Quite," he replied.

"There is a late train to town which I think we could catch if we started at once."

"Eh?" roared Sir Howard; "you're not going back to-night? Your rooms are ready for you, damn it!"

"I quite appreciate the kindness, Sir Howard," replied Harley; "but I have urgent business to attend to in London. Believe me, my departure is unavoidable."

The blue eyes of the baronet gleamed with the simple cunning of his kind.

"You've got something up your sleeve," he roared. "I know you have, I know you have!"

Inspector Wessex looked at me significantly, but I could only shrug my shoulders in reply; for in these moods Harley was as inscrutable as the Sphinx.

However, he had his way, and Sir Howard hurriedly putting a car in commission, we raced for the local station and just succeeded in picking up the express at Claybury.

Wessex was rather silent throughout the journey, often glancing in my friend's direction, but Harley made no further reference to the case beyond outlining the interview with Bramber, until, as we were parting at the London terminus, Wessex to report to Scotland Yard and I to go to Harley's rooms:

"How long do you think it will take you to find that photographer,

Wessex?" he asked. "Piccadilly is a sufficient clue."

"Well," replied the Inspector, "nothing can be done to-night, of course, but I should think by mid-day tomorrow the matter should be settled."

"Right," said Harley shortly. "May I ask you to report the result to me, Wessex?"

"I will report without fail."

III
ALI OF CAIRO

It was not until the evening of the following day that Harley rang me up, and:

"I want you to come round at once," he said urgently. "The Deep-brow case is developing along lines which I confess I had anticipated, but which are dramatic nevertheless."

Knowing that Harley did not lightly make such an assertion, I put aside the work upon which I was engaged and hurried around to Chancery Lane. I found my friend, pipe in mouth, walking up and down his smoke-laden study in a state which I knew to betoken suppressed excitement, and:

"Did Wessex find your photographer?" I asked on entering.

"Yes," he replied. "A first-class man, as I had anticipated. As I had further anticipated he did a number of copies of the picture for the foreign gentleman—about fifty, in fact!"

"Fifty!"

"Yes! Does the significance of that fact strike you?" asked Harley, a queer smile stealing across his tanned, clean-shaven face.

"It is an extraordinary thing for even an ardent admirer to have so many reproductions done of the same picture!"

"It is! I will show you now what I found trodden into one of the footprints where the struggle took place beside the car."

Harley produced a piece of thick silk twine.

"What is it?"

"It is a link, Knox—a link to seek which I really went down to Deep-brow." He stared at me quizzically, but my answering look must have been a blank one. "It is part of the tassel of one of those red cloth caps commonly called in England, a fez!"

He continued to stare at me and I to stare at the piece of silk; then:

"What is the next move?" I demanded. "Your new clue rather bewilders me."

"The next move," he said, "is to retire to the adjoining room and make ourselves look as much like a couple of Oriental commercial travellers as our correctly British appearance will allow!"

"What!" I cried.

"That's it!" laughed Harley. "I have a perpetual tan, and I think I can give you a temporary one which I keep in a bottle for the purpose."

Twenty minutes later, then, having quitted Harley's chambers by a back way opening into one of those old-world courts which abound in this part of the metropolis, two quietly attired Eastern gentlemen got into a cab at the corner of Chancery Lane and proceeded in the direction of Limehouse.

There are haunts in many parts of London whose very existence is unsuspected by all but the few; haunts unvisited by the tourist and even unknown to the copy-hunting pressman. Into a quiet thoroughfare not three minutes' walk from the busy life of West India Dock Road, Harley led the way. Before a door sandwiched in between the entrance to a Greek tobacconist's establishment and a boarded shop-front, he paused and turned to me.

"Whatever you see or hear," he cautioned, "express no surprise. Above all, show no curiosity."

He rang the bell beside the door, and almost immediately it was opened by a Negress, grossly and repellently ugly.

Harley pattered something in what sounded like Arabic, whereat the Negress displayed the utmost servility, ushering us into an ill-lighted passage with every evidence of respect. Following this passage to its termination, an inner door was opened, and a burst of discordant music greeted us, together with a wave of tobacco smoke. We entered.

Despite my friend's particular injunctions to the contrary I gave a start of amazement.

We stood in the doorway of a fairly large apartment having a divan round three of its sides. This divan was occupied by ten or a dozen men of mixed nationalities—Arabs, Greeks, lascars, and others. They smoked cigarettes for the most part and sipped *Mokha* from little cups. A girl was performing a wriggling dance upon the square carpet occupying the centre of the floor, accompanied by a Nubian boy who twanged upon a guitar, and by most of the assembled company, who clapped their hands to the music or droned a low, tuneless dirge.

Shortly after our entrance the performance terminated, and the girl retired through a curtained doorway at the farther end of the room. Our presence being now observed, suspicious glances were cast in our direction, and a very aged man, who sat smoking a *narghli* near the door by which the girl had made her exit, gravely waved towards us the amber mouthpiece which he held in his hand.

Harley walked straight across to him, I close at his heels. The light of a lamp which hung close by fell fully upon my friend's face; and, rising from his seat, the old man greeted him with the dignified and graceful salutation of the East. At his request we seated ourselves beside him, and, while we all three smoked excellent Turkish cigarettes, Harley and he conversed in a low tone. Suddenly, at some remark of my friend's, our strange host rose to his feet, an angry frown contracting his heavy eyebrows.

Silence fell upon the company.

In a loud and peremptory voice he called out something in Arabic.

Instantly I detected a fellow near the entrance door, and whom I had not hitherto observed, slipping furtively into the shadow, with a view, as I thought, to secret departure. He seemed to be deformed in some way and had the most evil, pock-marked face I had ever beheld in my life. Angrily, the majestic old man recalled him. Whereupon, with a sort of animal snarl quite indescribable, the fellow plucked out a knife! Two men who had been on the point of seizing him fell back, and:

"Hold him!" shouted Harley, springing forward—"hold him! It's Ali of Cairo!"

But Harley was too late. Turning, the strange and formidable-looking Oriental ran like the wind! Ere hand could be raised to stay him he was through the doorway!

"That settles it," said Harley grimly, as once more I found myself in a cab beside him. "I was right; but he'll forestall us!"

"*Who* will forestall us?" I asked in bewilderment.

"The biggest villain in Europe, Asia, or Africa!" cried my companion. "I have wasted precious time to-day. I might have known." He drummed irritably upon his knees. "The place we have just left is a sort of club, you understand, Knox, and Hákim is the proprietor or host as well as being an old gentleman of importance and authority in the Moslem world. I told him of my suspicions—which step I should have taken earlier—and they were instantly confirmed. My man was there—recognized me—and bolted! He'll forestall us."

"But my dear fellow," I said patiently—"who is this man, and what has he to do with the Deepbrow case?"

"He is the blackest, scoundrel breathing!" answered Harley bitterly. "As to what he has to do with the case—why did he bolt? At any rate, I know where to find him now—and we *may* not be too late after all."

"But who and what is this man?"

"He is Ali of Cairo! As to *what* he is—you will soon learn."

IV

THE HOUSE BY THE RIVER

On quitting the singular Oriental club, Harley had first raced off to a public telephone, where he had spoken for some time—as I now divined—to Scotland Yard. For when we presently arrived at the headquarters of the Metropolitan Police, I was surprised to find Inspector Wessex awaiting us. Leaning out of the cab window:

"Yes?" called Harley excitedly. "Was I right?"

"You were, Mr. Harley," answered Wessex, who seemed to be no less excited than my companion. "I got the man's reply an hour ago."

"I knew it!" said Harley shortly. "Get in, Wessex; we haven't a minute to waste."

The Inspector joined us in the cab, having first given instructions to the chauffeur. As we set out once more:

"You have had very little time to make the necessary arrangements," continued my friend.

"Time enough," replied Wessex. "They will not be expecting us."

"I'm not so sure of it. One of the biggest villains in the civilized world recognized me three minutes before I called you up and then made good his escape. However, there is at least a fighting chance."

Little more was said from that moment until the end of the drive, both my companions seeming to be consumed by an intense eagerness to reach our destination. At last the cab drew up in a deserted street. I had rather lost my bearings; but I knew that we were once more somewhere in the Chinatown area, and:

"Follow us until we get into the house," Harley said to Inspector Wessex, "and wait out of sight. If you hear me blow this whistle, bring up the men you have posted—as quick as you like! But make it your particular business to see that *no one gets out!*"

Into a pitch-dark yard we turned, and I felt a shudder of apprehension upon observing that it was the entrance to a wharf. Dully gleaming in the moonlight, the Thames, that grave of many a ghastly secret, flowed beneath us. Emerging from the shadow of the archway, we paused before a door in the wall on our left.

At that moment something gleamed through the air, whizzed past my ear, and fell with a metallic jingle on the stones!

Instinctively we both looked up.

At an unlighted window on the first floor I caught a fleeting glimpse of a dark face.

"You were right!" I said. "Ali of Cairo has forestalled us!"

Harley stooped and picked up a knife with a broad and very curious blade. He slipped it into his pocket, nonchalantly.

"All evidence!" he said. "Keep in the shadow and bend down. I am going to stand on your shoulders and get into that window!"

Wondering at his daring, I nevertheless obeyed; and Harley succeeded, although not without difficulty, in achieving his purpose. A moment after he had disappeared in the blackness of the room above.

"Stand clear, Knox!" I heard.

Two of the cushion seats sometimes called "poof-ottomans" were thrown down, and:

"Up you come!" called Harley. "I'll grasp your hands if you can reach."

It proved no easy task, but I finally managed to scramble up beside my friend—to find myself in a dark and stuffy little room.

"This way!" said Harley rapidly—"upstairs."

He led the way without more ado, but it was with serious misgivings that I stumbled up a darkened stair in the rear of my greatly daring friend.

A pistol cracked in the darkness—and my fez was no longer on my head!

Harley's repeater answered, and we stumbled through a heavily curtained door into a heated room, the air of which was laden with some Eastern perfume. In the dim light from a silken-shaded lantern a figure showed, momentarily, darting across the place before us.

Again Harley's pistol spoke, but, as it seemed, ineffectively.

I had little enough opportunity to survey my surroundings; yet even in those brief, breathless moments I saw enough of the place wherein we stood to make me doubt the evidence of my senses! Outside, I knew, lay a dingy wharf, amid a maze of mean streets; here was an opulently furnished apartment with a strong Oriental note in the decorations!

Snatching an electric torch from his pocket, Harley leaped through a doorway draped with rich Persian tapestry, and I came close on his heels. Outside was darkness. A strong draught met us; and, passing along a carpeted corridor, we never halted until we came to a room filled with the weirdest odds and ends, apparently collected from every quarter of the globe.

Crack!

A bullet flattened itself on the wall behind us!

"Good job he can't shoot straight!" rapped Harley.

The ray of the torch suddenly picked out the head and shoulders of a man who was descending through a trap in the floor! Ere we had time to shoot he was gone! I saw his brown fingers relax their hold—and a bundle which he had evidently hoped to take with him was left lying upon the floor.

Together we ran to the trap and looked down.

Slowly moving tidal water flowed darkly beneath us! For twenty breathless seconds we watched—but nothing showed upon the surface.

"I hope his swimming is no better than his shooting," I said.

"It can avail him little," replied Harley grimly; "a river-police boat is waiting for anyone who tries to escape from that side of the house. We are by no means alone in this affair, Knox. But, firstly, what have we here!" He took up the bundle which the fugitive had deserted. "Something incriminating when Ali of Cairo dared not stay to face it out! He would never have deserted this place in the ordinary way. That fellow who was such a bad shot was left behind, when the news of our approach reached here, to make a desperate attempt to remove some piece of evidence! I'll swear to it. But we were too soon for him!"

All the time he was busily removing the pieces of sacking and scraps of Oriental stuff with which the bundle was fastened; and finally he drew out a dress-suit, together with the linen, collar, shoes, and underwear—a complete outfit, in fact—and on top of the whole was a soft gray felt hat!

Eagerly Harley searched the garments for some name of a maker by which their owner might be identified. Presently, inside the lining of the breast pocket, where such a mark is usually found, he discovered the label of a well-known West End firm.

"The police can confirm it, Knox!" he said, looking up, his face slightly flushed with triumph; "but I, personally, have no doubt!"

"You may have no doubt, Harley," I retorted, "but I am full of doubt! What is the significance of this discovery to which you seem to attach so much importance?"

"At the moment," replied my friend, "never mind; I still have hopes—although they have grown somewhat slender—of making a much more important discovery."

"Why not permit the police to aid in the search?"

"The police are more useful in their present occupation," he replied. "We are dealing with the most cunning knave produced by East or West, and I don't mean to let him slip through my fingers if he is in this house! Nevertheless, Knox, I am submitting you to rather an appalling risk, I know; for our man is desperate, and if he is still in the place will prove as dangerous as a cornered rat."

"But the man who dropped through the trap?"

"The man who dropped through the trap," said Harley, "was not Ali of Cairo—and it is Ali of Cairo for whom I am looking!"

"The hunchback we saw to-night?"

Harley nodded, and having listened intently for a few moments, proceeded again to search the singular apartments of the abode. In each was evidence of Oriental occupancy; indeed, some of the rooms possessed a sort of *Arabian Nights* atmosphere. But no living creature was to be seen or heard anywhere: It was while the two of us, having examined every inch of wall, I should think, in the building, were standing staring rather blankly at each other in the room with the lighted lantern, that I saw Harley's expression change.

"Why," he muttered, "is this one room illuminated—and all the others in darkness?"

Even then the significance of this circumstance was not apparent to me. But Harley stared critically at an electric switch which was placed on the immediate right of the door and then up at the silk-shaded lantern which lighted the room. Crossing, he raised and lowered the switch rapidly, but the lamp continued to burn uninterruptedly!

"Ah!" he said—"a good trick!"

Grasping the wooden block to which the switch was attached, he turned it bodily—and I saw that it was a masked knob; for in the next moment he had pulled open the narrow section of wall—which proved to be nothing less than a cunningly fitted door!

A small, dimly lighted apartment was revealed, the Oriental note still predominant in its appointments, which, however, were few, and which I scarcely paused to note. For lying upon a mattress in this place was a pretty, fair-haired girl!

She lay on her side, having one white arm thrown out and resting limply on the floor, and she seemed to be in a semi-conscious condition, for although her fine eyes were widely opened, they had a glassy, witless look, and she was evidently unaware of our presence.

"Look at her pupils," rapped Harley. "They have drugged her with *bhang!* Poor, pretty fool!"

"Good God!" I cried. "Who is this, Harley?"

"Molly Clayton!" he answered. "Thank heaven we have saved *one* victim from Ali of Cairo."

V

THE HAREN AGENCY

Owing to the instrumentality of Paul Harley, the public never learned that the awful riverside murder called by the Press in reference to the victim's shaven skull "the barber atrocity" had any relation to the Deepbrow case. It was physically impossible to identify the victim, and Harley had his own reasons for concealing the truth. The house on the wharf with its choice Oriental furniture was seized by the police; but, strange to relate, no arrest was made in connection with this most gruesome outrage. The man who dropped through the trap had been wounded by one of Harley's shots, and he sank for the last time under the very eyes of the crew of the police cutter.

It was at a late hour on the night of this concluding tragedy that I learned the amazing truth underlying the case. Wessex was still at work in the East End upon the hundred and one formalities which attached to his office, and Harley and I sat in the study of my friend's chambers in Chancery Lane.

"You see," Harley was explaining. "I got my first clue down at Deepbrow. The tracks leading to the motor-car. They showed—to anyone not hampered by a preconceived opinion—that the girl and Vane had not gone on together (since the man's footprints proved him to have been *running*), but that *she* had gone first and that *he* had run after her! Arguments: (*a*) He heard the approach of the car; or (*b*) he heard her call for help. In fact, it almost immediately became evident to me that someone else had met her at the end of the lane; probably someone who expected her, and whom she was going to meet when she, accidentally, encountered Vane! The captain was not attired for an elopement, and, more significant still, he said he should stroll to the Deep Wood, and that was where he did stroll to; for it borders the road at this point!

"I had privately ascertained, from the postman, that Molly Clayton actually received a letter on that morning! This resolved my last doubt. She was not going to meet Vane on the night of her disappearance."

"Then whom?"

"The old love! He who some months earlier had had over fifty seductive pictures of this undoubtedly pretty girl prepared for a purpose of his own!"

"Vane interfered?"

"When the girl saw that they meant to take her away, she no doubt made a fuss! He ran to the rescue! They had not reckoned on his being there, but these are clever villains, who leave no clues—except for one who has met them on their own ground!"

"On their own ground! What do you mean, Harley? Who are these people?"

"Well—where do you suppose those fifty photographs went?"

"I cannot I conjecture!"

"Then I will tell you. The turmoil in the East has put wealth and power into unscrupulous hands. But even before the war there were marts, Knox—open marts—at which a negro girl might be purchased for some £30, and a Circassian for anything from £250 to £500! Ah! You stare! But I assure you it was so. Here is the point, though: there were, and still are, private dealers! Those photographs were circulated among the *nouveaux riches* of the East! They were employed in the same way that any other merchant employs a catalogue. They reached the hands of many an opulent and abandoned 'profiteer' of Damascus, Stambûl—where you will. Molly's picture would be one of many. Remember that hundreds of pretty girls disappear from their homes—taking the whole of the world—every year. Clearly, English beauty is popular at the moment! And," he added bitterly, "the arch-villain has escaped!"

"Ali of Cairo!" I cried. "Then Ali of Cairo—"

"Is the biggest *slave-dealer* in the East!"

"Good God! Harley—at last I understand!"

"I was slow enough to understand it myself, Knox. But once the theory presented itself I asked Wessex to get into immediate touch with the valet he had already interviewed at Deepbrow. It was the result of his inquiry to which he referred when we met him at Scotland Yard to-night. Captain Vane had a large mole *on his shoulder* and a girl's name, together with a small device, tattooed *on his forearm*—a freak of his Sandhurst days—"

"Then 'the man with the shaven skull'—"

"Is Captain Ronald Vane! May he rest in peace. But I never shall until the crook-back dealer in humanity has met his just deserts."

The White Hat

I

MAJOR JACK RAGSTAFF

Hallo! Innes," said Paul Harley as his secretary entered. "Someone is making a devil of a row outside."

"This is the offender, Mr. Harley," said Innes, and handed my friend a visiting card.

Glancing at the card, Harley read aloud:

"Major J. E. P. Ragstaff, Cavalry Club."

Meanwhile a loud harsh voice, which would have been audible in a full gale, was roaring in the lobby.

"Nonsense!" I could hear the Major shouting. "Balderdash! There's more fuss than if I had asked for an interview with the Prime Minister. Piffle! Balderdash!"

Innes's smile developed into a laugh, in which Harley joined, then:

"Admit the Major," he said.

Into the study where Harley and I had been seated quietly smoking, there presently strode a very choleric Anglo-Indian. He wore a horsy check suit and white spats, and his tie closely resembled a stock. In his hand he carried a heavy malacca cane, gloves, and one of those tall, light-gray hats commonly termed white. He was below medium height, slim and wiry; his gait and the shape of his legs, his build, all proclaimed the dragoon. His complexion was purple, and the large white teeth visible beneath a bristling gray moustache added to the natural ferocity of his appearance. Standing just within the doorway:

"Mr. Paul Harley?" he shouted.

It was apparently an inquiry, but it sounded like a reprimand.

My friend, standing before the fireplace, his hands in his pockets and his pipe in his mouth, nodded brusquely.

"I am Paul Harley," he said. "Won't you sit down?"

Major Ragstaff, glancing angrily at Innes as the latter left the study, tossed his stick and gloves on to a settee, and drawing up a chair seated himself stiffly upon it as though he were in a saddle. He stared straight at Harley, and:

"You are not the sort of person I expected, sir," he declared. "May I ask if it is your custom to keep clients dancin' on the mat and all that— on the blasted mat, sir?"

Harley suppressed a smile, and I hastily reached for my cigarette-case which I had placed upon the mantelshelf.

"I am always naturally pleased to see clients, Major Ragstaff," said Harley, "but a certain amount of routine is necessary even in civilian life. You had not advised me of your visit, and it is contrary to my custom to discuss business after five o'clock."

As Harley spoke the Major glared at him continuously, and then:

"I've seen you in India!" he roared; "damme! I've seen you in India!—and, yes! in Turkey! Ha! I've got you now sir!" He sprang to his feet. "You're the Harley who was in Constantinople in 1912."

"Quite true."

"Then I've come to the wrong shop."

"That remains to be seen, Major."

"But I was told you were a private detective, and all that."

"So I am," said Harley quietly. "In 1912 the Foreign Office was my client. I am now at the service of anyone who cares to employ me."

"Hell!" said the Major.

He seemed to be temporarily stricken speechless by the discovery that a man who had acted for the British Government should be capable of stooping to the work of a private inquiry agent. Staring all about the room with a sort of naïve wonderment, he drew out a big silk handkerchief and loudly blew his nose, all the time eyeing Harley questioningly. Replacing his handkerchief he directed his regard upon me, and:

"This is my friend, Mr. Knox," said Harley; "you may state your case before him without hesitation, unless—"

I rose to depart, but:

"Sit down, Mr. Knox! Sit down, sir!" shouted the Major. "I have no dirty linen to wash, no skeletons in the cupboard or piffle of that kind. I simply want something explained which I am too thick-headed—too damned thick-headed, sir—to explain myself."

He resumed his seat, and taking out his wallet extracted from it a small newspaper cutting which he offered to Harley.

"Read that, Mr. Harley," he directed. "Read it aloud."

Harley read as follows:

> "Before Mr. Smith, at Marlborough Street Police Court, John Edward Bampton was charged with assaulting a well-known clubman in Bond Street on Wednesday evening. It was proved by the constable who made the arrest that robbery had not been the motive of the assault, and Bampton confessed that he bore no grudge against the assailed man, indeed, that he had never seen him before. He pleaded intoxication, and the police surgeon testified that although not actually intoxicated, his breath had smelled strongly of liquor at the time of his arrest. Bampton's employers testified to a hitherto blameless character, and as the charge was not pressed the man was dismissed with a caution."

Having read the paragraph, Harley glanced at the Major with a puzzled expression.

"The point of this quite escapes me," he confessed.

"Is that so?" said Major Ragstaff. "Is that so, sir? Perhaps you will be good enough to read *this.*"

From his wallet he took a second newspaper cutting, smaller than the first, and gummed to a sheet of club notepaper. Harley took it and read as follows:

> "Mr. De Lana, a well-known member of the Stock Exchange, who met with a serious accident recently, is still in a precarious condition."

The puzzled look on Harley's face grew more acute, and the Major watched him with an expression which I can only describe as one of fierce enjoyment.

"You're thinkin' I'm a damned old fool, ain't you?" he shouted suddenly.

"Scarcely that," said Harley, smiling slightly, "but the significance of these paragraphs is not apparent, I must confess. The man Bampton would not appear to be an interesting character, and since no great damage has been done, his drunken frolic hardly comes within my sphere. Of Mr. De Lana, of the Stock Exchange, I never heard, unless he happens to be a member of the firm of De Lana and Day?"

"He's not a member of that firm, sir," shouted the Major. "He *was,* up to six o'clock this evenin'."

"What do you mean exactly?" inquired Harley, and the tone of his voice suggested that he was beginning to entertain doubts of the Major's sanity or sobriety; then:

"He's dead!" declared the latter. "Dead as the Begum of Bangalore! He died at six o'clock. I've just spoken to his widow on the telephone."

I suppose I must have been staring very hard at the speaker, and certainly Harley was doing so, for suddenly directing his fierce gaze toward me:

"You're completely treed, sir, and so's your friend!" shouted Major Ragstaff.

"I confess it," replied Harley quietly; "and since my time is of some little value I would suggest, without disrespect, that you explain the connection, if any, between yourself, the drunken Bampton, and Mr. De Lana, of the Stock Exchange, who died, you inform us, at six o'clock this evening as the result, presumably, of injuries received in an accident."

"That's what I'm here for!" cried Major Ragstaff. "In the first place, then, I am the party, although I saw to it that my name was kept out of print, whom the drunken lunatic assaulted."

Harley, pipe in hand, stared at the speaker perplexedly.

"Understand me," continued the Major, "I am the person—I, Jack Ragstaff—he assaulted. I was walkin' down from my quarters in Maddox Street on my way to dine at the club, same as I do every night o' my life, when this flamin' idiot sprang upon me, grabbed my hat"—he took up his white hat to illustrate what had occurred—"not this one, but one like it—pitched it on the ground and jumped on it!"

Harley was quite unable to conceal his smiles as the excited old soldier dropped his conspicuous head-gear on the floor and indulged in a vigorous pantomime designed to illustrate his statement.

"Most extraordinary," said Harley. "What did you do?"

"What did I do?" roared the Major. "I gave him a crack on the head with my cane, and I said things to him which couldn't be repeated in court. I punched him, and likewise hoofed him, but the hat was completely done in. Damn crowd collected, hearin' me swearin' and bellowin'. Police and all that; names an' addresses and all that balderdash. Man lugged away to guard-room and me turnin' up at the club with no hat. Damn ridiculous spectacle at my time of life."

"Quite so," said Harley soothingly; "I appreciate your annoyance, but I am utterly at a loss to understand why you have come here, and what all this has to do with Mr. De Lana, of the Stock Exchange."

"He fell out of the window!" shouted the Major.

"Fell out of a window?"

"Out of a window, sir, a second floor window ten yards up a side street! Pitched on his skull—marvel he wasn't killed outright!"

A faint expression of interest began to creep into Harley's glance, and:

"I understand you to mean, Major Ragstaff," he said deliberately, "that while your struggle with the drunken man was in progress Mr. De Lana fell out of a neighbouring window into the street?"

"Right!" shouted the Major. "Right, sir!"

"Do you know this Mr. De Lana?"

"Never heard of him in my life until the accident occurred. Seems to me the poor devil leaned out to see the fun and overbalanced. Felt responsible, only natural, and made inquiries. He died at six o'clock this evenin', sir."

"H'm," said Harley reflectively. "I still fail to see where I come in. From what window did he fall?"

"Window above a sort of teashop, called Café Dame—damn silly name. Place on a corner. Don't know name of side street."

"H'm. You don't think he was pushed out, for instance?"

"Certainly not!" shouted the Major; "he just fell out, but the point is, he's dead!"

"My dear sir," said Harley patiently, "I won't dispute that point; but what on earth do you want of me?"

"I don't know what I want!" roared the Major, beginning to walk up and down the room, "but I know I ain't satisfied, not easy in my mind, sir. I wake up of a night hearin' the poor devil's yell as he crashed on the pavement. That's all wrong. I've heard hundreds of death-yells, but"—he took up his malacca cane and beat it loudly on the table—"I haven't woke up of a night dreamin' I heard 'em again."

"In a word, you suspect foul play?"

"I don't suspect anything!" cried the other excitedly, "but someone mentioned your name to me at the club—said you could see through concrete, and all that—and here I am. There's something wrong, radically wrong. Find out what it is and send the bill to me. Then perhaps I'll be able to sleep in peace."

He paused, and again taking out the large silk handkerchief blew his nose loudly. Harley glanced at me in rather an odd way, and then:

"There will be no bill, Major Ragstaff," he said; "but if I can see any possible line of inquiry I will pursue it and report the result to you."

II

A CURIOUS OUTRAGE

"What do you make of it, Harley?" I asked. Paul Harley returned a work of reference to its shelf and stood staring absently across the study.

"Our late visitor's history does not help us much," he replied. "A somewhat distinguished army career, and so forth, and his only daughter, Sybil Margaret, married the fifth Marquis of Ireton. She is, therefore, the noted society beauty, the Marchioness of Ireton. Does this suggest anything to your mind?"

"Nothing whatever," I said blankly.

"Nor to mine," murmured Harley.

The telephone bell rang.

"Hallo!" called Harley. "Yes. That you, Wessex? Have you got the address? Good. No, I shall remember it. Many thanks. Good-bye."

He turned to me.

"I suggest, Knox," he said, "that we make our call and then proceed to dinner as arranged."

Since I was always glad of an opportunity of studying my friend's methods I immediately agreed, and ere long, leaving the lights of the two big hotels behind, our cab was gliding down the long slope which leads to Waterloo Station. Thence through crowded, slummish high-roads we made our way via Lambeth to that dismal thoroughfare,

Westminster Bridge Road, with its forbidding, often windowless, houses, and its peculiar air of desolation.

The house for which we were bound was situated at no great distance from Kensington Park, and telling the cabman to wait, Harley and
I walked up a narrow, paved path, mounted a flight of steps, and rang
the bell beside a somewhat time-worn door, above which was an old-
fashioned fanlight dimly illuminated from within.

A considerable interval elapsed before the door was opened by a
marvellously untidy servant girl who had apparently been interrupted in
the act of blackleading her face. Partly opening the door, she stared at
us agape, pushing back wisps of hair from her eyes and with every
movement daubing more of some mysterious black substance upon her
countenance.

"Is Mr. Bampton in?" asked Harley.

"Yus, just come in. I'm cookin' his supper."

"Tell him that two friends of his have called on rather important
business."

"All right," said the black-faced one. "What name is it?"

"No name. just say two friends of his."

Treating us to a long, vacant stare and leaving us standing on the
step, the maid (in whose hand I perceived a greasy fork) shuffled along
the passage and began to mount the stairs. An unmistakable odour of
frying sausages now reached my nostrils. Harley glanced at me quizzically, but said nothing until the Cinderella came stumbling downstairs
again. Without returning to where we stood:

"Go up," she directed. "Second floor, front. Shut the door, one of
yer."

She disappeared into gloomy depths below as Harley and I, closing
the door behind us, proceeded to avail ourselves of the invitation.
There was very little light on the staircase, but we managed to find our
way to a poorly furnished bed-sitting-room where a small table was
spread for a meal. Beside the table, in a chintz-covered arm-chair, a
thick-set young man was seated smoking a cigarette and having a copy of
the *Daily Telegraph* upon his knees.

He was a very typical lower middle-class, nothing-in-particular young
man, but there was a certain truculence indicated by his square jaw, and

that sort of self-possession which sometimes accompanies physical strength was evidenced in his manner as, tossing the paper aside, he stood up.

"Good evening, Mr. Bampton," said Harley genially. "I take it"—pointing to the newspaper—"that you are looking for a new job?"

Bampton stared, a suspicion of anger in his eyes, then, meeting the amused glance of my friend, he broke into a smile very pleasing and humorous. He was a fresh-coloured young fellow with hair inclined to redness, and smiling he looked very boyish indeed.

"I have no idea who you are," he said, speaking with a faint north-country accent, "but you evidently know who I am and what has happened to me."

"Got the boot?" asked Harley confidentially.

Bampton, tossing the end of his cigarette into the grate, nodded grimly.

"You haven't told me your name," he said, "but I think I can tell you your business." He ceased smiling. "Now look here, I don't want any more publicity. If you think you are going to make a funny newspaper story out of me change your mind as quick as you like. I'll never get another job in London as it is. If you drag me any further into the limelight I'll never get another job in England."

"My dear fellow," replied Harley soothingly, at the same time extending his cigarette-case, "you misapprehend the object of my call. I am not a reporter."

"What!" said Bampton, pausing in the act of taking a cigarette, "then what the devil are you?"

"My name is Paul Harley, and I am a criminal investigator."

He spoke the words deliberately, having his eyes fixed upon the other's face; but although Bampton was palpably startled there was no trace of fear in his straightforward glance. He took a cigarette from the case, and:

"Thanks, Mr. Harley," he said. "I cannot imagine what business has brought you here."

"I have come to ask you two questions," was the reply. "Number one: Who paid you to smash Major Ragstaff's white hat? Number two: How much did he pay you?"

To these questions I listened in amazement, and my amazement was evidently shared by Bampton. He had been in the act of lighting his cigarette, but he allowed the match to burn down nearly to his fingers and then dropped it with a muttered exclamation in the fire. Finally:

"I don't know how you found out," he said, "but you evidently know the truth. Provided you assure me that you are not out to make a silly-season newspaper story, I'll tell you all I know."

Harley laid his card on the table, and:

"Unless the ends of justice demand it," he said, "I give you my word that anything you care to say will go no further. You may speak freely before my friend, Mr. Knox. Simply tell me in as few words as possible what led you to court arrest in that manner."

"Right," replied Bampton, "I will." He half closed his eyes, reflectively. "I was having tea in the Lyons' café, to which I always go, last Monday afternoon about four o'clock, when a man sat down facing me and got into conversation."

"Describe him!"

"He was a man rather above medium height. I should say about my own build; dark, going gray. He had a neat moustache and a short beard, and the look of a man who had travelled a lot. His skin was very tanned, almost as deeply as yours, Mr. Harley. Not at all the sort of chap that goes in there as a rule. After a while he made an extraordinary proposal. At first I thought he was joking, then when I grasped the idea that he was serious I concluded he was mad. He asked me how much a year I earned, and I told him Peters and Peters paid me £150. He said: 'I'll give you a year's salary to knock a man's hat off!'"

As Bampton spoke the words he glanced at us with twinkling eyes, but although for my own part I was merely amused, Harley's expression had grown very stern.

"Of course, I laughed," continued Bampton, "but when the man drew out a fat wallet and counted ten five-pound notes on the table I began to think seriously about his proposal. Even supposing he was cracked, it was absolutely money for nothing.

"'Of course,' he said, 'you'll lose your job and you may be arrested, but you'll say that you had been out with a few friends and were a little excited, also that you never could stand white hats. Stick to that story and the balance of a hundred pounds will reach you on the following morning.'

"I asked him for further particulars, and I asked him why he had picked me for the job. He replied that he had been looking for some time for the right man; a man who was strong enough physically to accomplish the thing, and someone"—Bampton's eyes twinkled again—"with a dash of the devil in him, but at the same time a man who could be relied upon to stick to his guns and not to give the game away.

"You asked me to be brief, and I'll try to be. The man in the white hat was described to me, and the exact time and place of the meeting. I just had to grab his white hat, smash it, and face the music. I agreed. I don't deny that I had a couple of stiff drinks before I set out, but the memory of that fifty pounds locked up here in my room and the further hundred promised, bucked me up wonderfully. It was impossible to mistake my man; I could see him coming toward me as I waited just outside a sort of little restaurant called the Café Dame. As arranged, I bumped into him, grabbed his hat and jumped on it."

He paused, raising his hand to his head reminiscently.

"My man was a bit of a scrapper," he continued, "and he played hell. I've never heard such language in my life, and the way he laid about me with his cane is something I am not likely to forget in a hurry. A crowd gathered, naturally, and (also naturally) I was 'pinched.' That didn't matter much. I got off lightly; and although I've been dismissed by Peters and Peters, twenty crisp fivers are locked in my trunk there, with the ten which I received in the City."

Harley checked him, and:

"May I see the envelope in which they arrived?" he asked.

"Sorry," replied Bampton, "but I burned it. I thought it was playing the game to do so. It wouldn't have helped you much, though," he added; "it was an ordinary common envelope, posted in the City, address typewritten, and not a line enclosed."

"Registered?"

"No."

Bampton stood looking at us with a curious expression on his face, and suddenly:

"There's one point," he said, "on which my conscience isn't easy. You know about that poor devil who fell out of a window? Well, it would never have happened if I hadn't kicked up a row in the street. There's no doubt he was leaning out to see what the disturbance was about when the accident occurred."

"Did you actually see him fall?" asked Harley.

"No. He fell from a window several yards behind me in the side street, but I heard him cry out, and as I was lugged off by the police I heard the bell of the ambulance which came to fetch him."

He paused again and stood rubbing his head ruefully.

"H'm," said Harley; "was there anything particularly remarkable about this man in the Lyons' café?"

Bampton reflected silently for some moments, and then:

"Nothing much," he confessed. "He was evidently a gentleman, wore a blue top-coat, a dark tweed suit, and what looked like a regimental tie, but I didn't see much of the colours. He was very tanned, as I have said, even to the backs of his hands—and oh, yes! there was one point: He had a gold-covered tooth."

"Which tooth?"

"I can't remember, except that it was on the left side, and I always noticed it when he smiled."

"Did he wear any ring or pin which you would recognize?"

"No."

"Had he any oddity of speech or voice?"

"No. Just a heavy, drawling manner. He spoke like thousands of other cultured Englishmen. But wait a minute—yes! There was one other point. Now I come to think of it, his eyes very slightly slanted upward."

Harley stared.

"Like a Chinaman's?"

"Oh, nothing so marked as that. But the same sort of formation."

Harley nodded briskly and buttoned up his overcoat.

"Thanks, Mr. Bampton," he said; "we will detain you no longer!"

As we descended the stairs, where the smell of frying sausages had given place to that of something burning—probably the sausages:

"I was half inclined to think that Major Ragstaff's ideas were traceable to a former touch of the sun," said Harley. "I begin to believe that he has put us on the track of a highly unusual crime. I am sorry to delay dinner, Knox, but I propose to call at the Café Dame."

III

A CRIMINAL GENIUS

On entering the doorway of the Café Dame we found ourselves in a narrow passage. In front of us was a carpeted stair, and to the right a glass-panelled door, communicating with a discreetly lighted little dining room which seemed to be well patronized. Opening the door Harley beckoned to a waiter, and:

"I wish to see the proprietor," he said.

"Mr. Meyer is engaged at the moment, sir," was the reply.

"Where is he?"

"In his office upstairs, sir. He will be down in a moment."

The waiter hurried away, and Harley stood glancing up the stairs as if in doubt what to do.

"I cannot imagine how such a place can pay," he muttered. "The rent must be enormous in this district."

But even before he ceased speaking I became aware of an excited conversation which was taking place in some apartment above.

"It's scandalous!" I heard, in a woman's shrill voice. "You have no right to keep it! It's not your property, and I'm here to demand that you give it up." A man's voice replied in voluble broken English, but I could only distinguish a word here and there. I saw that Harley was interested, for catching my questioning glance, he raised his finger to his lips enjoining me to be silent.

"Oh, that's the game, is it?" continued the female voice. "Of course you know it's blackmail?"

A flow of unintelligible words answered this speech, then:

"I shall come back with someone," cried the invisible woman, "who will *make* you give it up!"

"Knox," whispered Harley in my ear, "when that woman comes down, follow her! I'm afraid you will bungle the business, and I would not ask you to attempt it if big things were not at stake. Return here; I shall wait."

As a matter of fact, his sudden request had positively astounded me, but ere I had time for any reply a door suddenly banged open above and a respectable-looking woman, who might have been some kind of upper servant, came quickly down the stairs. An expression of intense indignation rested upon her face, and without seeming to notice our presence she brushed past us and went out into the street.

"Off you go, Knox!" said Harley.

Seeing myself committed to an unpleasant business, I slipped out of the doorway and detected the woman five or six yards away hurrying in the direction of Piccadilly. I had no difficulty in following her, for she was evidently unsuspicious of my presence, and when presently she mounted a westward-bound 'bus I did likewise, but while she got inside I went on top, and occupied a seat on the near side whence I could observe anyone leaving the vehicle.

If I had not known Paul Harley so well I should have counted the whole business a ridiculous farce, but recognizing that something underlay these seemingly trivial and disconnected episodes, I lighted a cigarette and resigned myself to circumstance.

At Hyde Park Corner I saw the woman descending, and when presently she walked up Hamilton Place I was not far behind her. At the door of an imposing mansion she stopped, and in response to a ring of the bell the door was opened by a footman, and the woman hurried in. Evidently she was an inmate of the establishment; and conceiving that my duty was done when I had noted the number of the house, I retraced my steps to the corner; and, hailing a taxicab, returned to the Café Dame.

On inquiring of the same waiter whom Harley had accosted whether my friend was there:

"I think a gentleman is upstairs with Mr. Meyer," said the man.

"In his office?"

"Yes, sir."

Thereupon I mounted the stairs and before a half-open door paused. Harley's voice was audible within, and therefore I knocked and entered.

I discovered Harley standing by an American desk. Beside him in a revolving chair which, with the desk, constituted the principal furniture of a tiny office, sat a man in a dress-suit which had palpably not been made for him. He had a sullen and suspiciously Teutonic cast of countenance, and he was engaged in a voluble but hardly intelligible speech as I entered.

"Ha, Knox!" said Harley, glancing over his shoulder, "did you manage?"

"Yes," I replied.

Harley nodded shortly and turned again to the man in the chair.

"I am sorry to give you so much trouble, Mr. Meyer," he said, "but I should like my friend here to see the room above."

At this moment my attention was attracted by a singular object which lay upon the desk amongst a litter of bills and accounts. This was a piece of rusty iron bar somewhat less than three feet in length, and which once had been painted green.

"You are looking at this tragic fragment, Knox," said Harley, taking up the bar. "Of course"—he shrugged his shoulders—"it explains the whole unfortunate occurrence. You see there was a flaw in the metal at this end, here"—he indicated the spot—"and the other end had evidently worn loose in its socket."

"But I don't understand."

"It will all be made clear at the inquest, no doubt. A most unfortunate thing for you, Mr. Meyer."

"Most unfortunate," declared the proprietor of the restaurant, extending his thick hands pathetically. "Most ruinous to my business."

"We will go upstairs now," said Harley. "You will kindly lead the way, Mr. Meyer, and the whole thing will be quite clear to you, Knox."

As the proprietor walked out of the office and upstairs to the second floor Harley whispered in my ear:

"Where did she go?"

"No. — Hamilton Place," I replied in an undertone.

"Good God!" muttered my friend, and clutched my arm so tightly that I winced. "Good God! The master touch, Knox! This crime was the work of a genius—of a genius with slightly, very slightly, oblique eyes."

Opening a door on the second landing, Mr. Meyer admitted us to a small supper-room. Its furniture consisted of a round dining table, several chairs, a couch, and very little else. I observed, however, that the furniture, carpet, and a few other appointments were of a character much more elegant than those of the public room below. A window which overlooked the street was open, so that the plush curtains which had been drawn aside moved slightly to and fro in the draught.

"The window of the tragedy, Knox," explained Harley.

He crossed the room.

"If you will stand here beside me you will see the gap in the railing caused by the breaking away of the fragment which now lies on Mr. Meyer's desk. Some few yards to the left in the street below is where the assault took place, of which we have heard, and the unfortunate Mr. De Lana, who was dining here alone—an eccentric custom of his—naturally ran to the window upon hearing the disturbance and leaned out, supporting his weight upon the railing. The rail collapsed, and—we know the rest."

"It will ruin me," groaned Meyer; "it will give bad repute to my establishment."

"I fear it will," agreed Harley sympathetically, "unless we can manage to clear up one or two little difficulties which I have observed. For instance"—he tapped the proprietor on the shoulder confidentially—"have you any idea, any hazy idea, of the identity of the woman who was dining here with Mr. De Lana on Wednesday night?"

The effect of this simple inquiry upon the proprietor was phenomenal. His fat yellow face assumed a sort of leaden hue, and his already prominent eyes protruded abnormally. He licked his lips.

"I tell you—already I tell you," he muttered, "that Mr. De Lana he engage this room every Wednesday and sometimes also Friday, and dine here by himself."

"And I tell you," said Harley sweetly, "that you are an inspired liar. You smuggled her out by the side entrance after the accident."

"The side entrance?" muttered Meyer. "The side entrance?"

"Exactly; the side entrance. There is something else which I must ask you to tell me. Who had engaged this room on Tuesday night, the night before the accident?"

The proprietor's expression remained uncomprehending, and:

"A gentleman," he said. "I never see him before."

"Another solitary diner?" suggested Harley.

"Yes, he is alone all the evening waiting for a friend who does not arrive."

"Ah," mused Harley—"alone all the evening, was he? And his friend disappointed him. May I suggest that he was a dark man? Gray at the temples, having a dark beard and moustache, and a very tanned face? His eyes slanted slightly upward?"

"Yes! yes!" cried Meyer, and his astonishment was patently unfeigned. "It is a friend of yours?"

"A friend of mine, yes," said Harley absently, but his expression was very grim. "What time did he finally leave?"

"He waited until after eleven o'clock. The dinner is spoilt. He pays, but does not complain."

"No," said Harley musingly, "he had nothing to complain about. One more question, my friend. When the lady escaped hurriedly on Wednesday night, what was it that she left behind and what price are you trying to extort from her for returning it?"

At that the man collapsed entirely.

"Ah, Gott!" he cried, and raised his hand to his clammy forehead. "You will ruin me. I am a ruined man. I don't try to extort anything. I run an honest business—"

"And one of the most profitable in the world," added Harley, "since the days of Thais to our own. Even at Bond Street rentals I assume that a house of assignation is a golden enterprise."

"Ah!" groaned Meyer, "I am ruined, so what does it matter? I tell you everything. I know Mr. De Lana who engages my room regularly, but I don't know who the lady is who meets him here. No! 1 swear it! But always it is the same lady. When he falls I am downstairs in my office, and I hear him cry out. The lady comes running from the room and begs of me to get her away without being seen and to keep all mention of her out of the matter."

"What did she pay you?" asked Harley.

"Pay me?" muttered Meyer, pulled up thus shortly in the midst of his statement.

"Pay you. Exactly. Don't argue; answer."

The man delivered himself of a guttural, choking sound, and finally:

"She promised one hundred pounds," he confessed hoarsely.

"But you surely did not accept a mere promise? Out with it. What did she give you?"

"A ring," came the confession at last.

"A ring. I see. I will take it with me if you don't mind. And now, finally, what was it that she left behind?"

"Ah, Gott!" moaned the man, dropping into a chair and resting his arms upon the table. "It is all a great panic, you see. I hurry her out by the back stair from this landing and she forgets her bag."

"Her bag? Good."

"Then I clear away the remains of dinner so I can say Mr. De Lana is dining alone. It is as much my interest as the lady's."

"Of course! I quite understand. I will trouble you no more, Mr. Meyer, except to step into your office and to relieve you of that incriminating evidence, the lady's bag and her ring."

IV

THE SLANTING EYES

"Do you understand, Knox?" said Harley as the cab bore us toward Hamilton Place. "Do you grasp the details of this cunning scheme?"

"On the contrary," I replied, "I am hopelessly at sea."

Nevertheless, I had forgotten that I was hungry in the excitement which now claimed me. For although the thread upon which these seemingly disconnected things hung was invisible to me, I recognized that Bampton, the city clerk, the bearded stranger who had made so singular a proposition to him, the white-hatted major, the dead stockbroker, and the mysterious woman whose presence in the case the clear sight of Harley had promptly detected, all were linked together by some subtle chain. I was convinced, too, that my friend held at least one end of that chain in his grip.

"In order to prepare your mind for the interview which I hope to obtain this evening," continued Harley, "let me enlighten you upon one or two points which may seem obscure. In the first place you recognize that anyone leaning out of the window on the second floor would almost automatically rest his weight upon the iron bar which was placed there for that very purpose, since the ledge is unusually low?"

"Quite," I replied, "and it also follows that if the bar gave way anyone thus leaning on it would be pitched into the street."

"Your reasoning is correct."

"But, my dear fellow," said I, "how could such an accident have been foreseen?"

"You speak of an accident. This was no accident! One end of the bar had been filed completely through, although the file marks had been carefully concealed with rust and dirt; and the other end had been wrenched out from its socket and then replaced in such a way that anyone leaning upon the bar could not fail to be precipitated into the street!"

"Good heavens! Then you mean—"

"I mean, Knox, that the man who occupied the supper room on the night before the tragedy—the dark man, tanned and bearded, with slightly oblique eyes—spent his time in filing through that bar—in short, in preparing a death trap!"

I was almost dumbfounded.

"But, Harley," I said, "assuming that he knew his victim would be the next occupant of the room, how could he know—?"

I stopped. Suddenly, as if a curtain had been raised, the details of what I now perceived to be a fiendishly cunning murder were revealed to me.

"According to his own account, Knox," resumed Harley, "Major Ragstaff regularly passed along that street with military punctuality at the same hour every night. You may take it for granted that the murderer was well aware of this. As a matter of fact, I happen to know that he was. We must also take it for granted that the murderer knew of these little dinners for two which took place in the private room above the Café Dame every Wednesday—and sometimes on Friday. Around the figure of the methodical major—with his conspicuous white hat as a sort of focus—was built up one of the most ingenious schemes of murder with which I have ever come in contact. The victim literally killed himself."

"But, Harley, the victim might have ignored the disturbance."

"That is where I first detected the touch of genius, Knox. He recognized the voice of one of the combatants—or his companion did. Here we are."

The cab drew up before the house in Hamilton Place. We alighted, and Harley pressed the bell. The same footman whom I had seen admit the woman opened the door.

"Is Lady Ireton at home?" asked Harley.

As he uttered the name I literally held my breath. We had come to the house of Major Ragstaff's daughter, the Marchioness of Ireton, one of society's most celebrated and beautiful hostesses!—the wife of a peer famed alike as sportsman, soldier, and scholar.

"I believe she is dining at home, sir," said the man. "Shall I inquire?"

"Be good enough to do so," replied Harley, and gave him a card. "Inform her that I wish to return to her a handbag which she lost a few days ago."

The man ushered us into an anteroom opening off the lofty and rather gloomy hall, and as the door closed:

"Harley," I said in a stage whisper, "am I to believe—"

"Can you doubt it?" returned Harley with a grim smile.

A few moments later we were shown into a charmingly intimate little boudoir in which Lady Ireton was waiting to receive us. She was a strikingly handsome brunette, but to-night her face, which normally, I think, possessed rich colouring, was almost pallid, and there was a hunted look in her dark eyes which made me wish to be anywhere rather than where I found myself. Without preamble she rose and addressed Harley:

"I fail to understand your message, sir," she said, and I admired the imperious courage with which she faced him. "You say you have recovered a handbag which 1 had lost?"

Harley bowed, and from the pocket of his greatcoat took out a silken-tasselled bag.

"The one which you left in the Café Dame, Lady Ireton," he replied. "Here also I have"—from another pocket he drew out a diamond ring—"something which was extorted from you by the fellow Meyer."

Without touching her recovered property, Lady Ireton sank slowly down into the chair from which she had arisen, her gaze fixed as if hypnotically upon the speaker.

"My friend, Mr. Knox, is aware of all the circumstances," continued the latter, "but he is as anxious as I am to terminate this painful interview. I surmise that what occurred on Wednesday night was this—

(correct me if I am wrong): While dining with Mr. De Lana you heard sounds of altercation in the street below. May I suggest that you recognized one of the voices?"

Lady Ireton, still staring straight before her at Harley, inclined her head in assent.

"I heard my father's voice," she said hoarsely.

"Quite so," he continued. "I am aware that Major Ragstaff is your father." He turned to me: "Do you recognize the touch of genius at last?" Then, again addressing Lady Ireton: "You naturally suggested to your companion that he should look out of the window in order to learn what was taking place. The next thing you knew was that he had fallen into the street below?"

Lady Ireton shuddered and raised her hands to her face.

"It is retribution," she whispered. "I have brought this ruin upon myself. But he does not deserve—"

Her voice faded into silence, and:

"You refer to your husband, Lord Ireton?" said Harley.

Lady Ireton nodded, and again recovering power of speech:

"It was to have been our last meeting," she said, looking up at Harley.

She shuddered, and her eyes blazed into sudden fierceness. Then, clenching her hands, she looked aside.

"Oh, God, the shame of this hour!" she whispered.

And I would have given much to have been spared the spectacle of this proud, erring woman's humiliation. But Paul Harley was scientifically remorseless. I could detect no pity in his glance.

"I would give my life willingly to spare my husband the knowledge of what has been," said Lady Ireton in a low, monotonous voice. "Three times I sent my maid to Meyer to recover my bag, but he demanded a price which even I could not pay. Now it is all discovered, and Harry will know."

"That, I fear, is unavoidable, Lady Ireton," declared Harley. "May I ask where Lord Ireton is at present?"

"He is in Africa after big game."

"H'm," said Harley, "in Africa, and after big game? I can offer you one consolation, Lady Ireton. In his own interests Meyer will stick to his first assertion that Mr. De Lana was dining alone."

A strange, horribly pathetic look came into the woman's haunted eyes.

"You—you—are not acting for—?" she began.

"I am acting for no one," replied Harley tersely. "Upon my friend's discretion you may rely as upon my own."

"Then why should he ever know?" she whispered.

"Why, indeed," murmured Harley, "since he is in Africa?"

As we descended the stair to the hall my friend paused and pointed to a life-sized oil painting by London's most fashionable portrait painter. It was that of a man in the uniform of a Guards officer, a dark man, slightly gray at the temples, his face very tanned as if by exposure to the sun.

"Having had no occasion for disguise when the portrait was painted," said Harley, "Lord Ireton appears here without the beard; and as he is not represented smiling one cannot see the gold tooth. But the painter, if anything, has accentuated the slanting eyes. You see, the fourth marquis—the present Lord Ireton's father—married one of the world-famous Yen Sun girls, daughters of the mandarin of that name by an Irish wife. Hence, the eyes. And hence—"

"But, Harley—it was murder!"

"Not within the meaning of the law, Knox. It was a recrudescence of Chinese humour! Lord Ireton is officially in Africa (and he went actually after 'big game'). The counsel is not born who could secure a conviction. We are somewhat late, but shall therefore have less difficulty in finding a table at Prince's."

Tchériapin

THE ROSE

Examine it closely," said the man in the unusual caped overcoat. "It will repay examination."

I held the little object in the palm of my hand, bending forward over the marble-topped table and looking down at it with deep curiosity. The babel of tongues so characteristic of Malay Jack's, and that mingled odour of stale spirits, greasy humanity, tobacco, cheap perfume, and opium, which distinguish the establishment faded from my ken. A sense of loneliness came to me.

Perhaps I should say that it became complete. I had grown conscious of its approach at the very moment that the cadaverous white-haired man had addressed me. There was a quality in his steadfast gaze and in his oddly pitched deep voice which from the first had wrapped me about—as though he were cloaking me in his queer personality and withdrawing me from the common plane.

Having stared for some moments at the object in my palm, I touched it gingerly; whereupon my acquaintance laughed—a short bass laugh.

"It looks fragile," he said. "But have no fear. It is nearly as hard as a diamond."

Thus encouraged, I took the thing up between finger and thumb, and held it before my eyes. For long enough I looked at it, and looking, my wonder grew. I thought that here was the most wonderful example of the lapidary's art which I had ever met with, east or west.

It was a tiny pink rose, no larger than the nail of my little finger. Stalk and leaves were there, and golden pollen lay in its delicate heart.

Each fairy-petal blushed with June fire; the frail leaves were exquisitely green. Withal it, was as hard and unbendable as a thing of steel.

"Allow me," said the masterful voice,

A powerful lens was passed by my acquaintance. I regarded the rose through the glass, and thereupon I knew, beyond doubt, that there was something phenomenal about the gem—if gem it were. I could plainly trace the veins and texture of every petal.

I suppose I looked somewhat startled. Although, baldly stated, the fact may not seem calculated to affright, in reality there was something so weird about this unnatural bloom that I dropped it on the table. As I did so I uttered an exclamation; for in spite of the stranger's assurances on the point, I had by no means overcome my idea of the thing's fragility.

"Don't be alarmed," he said, meeting my startled gaze. "It would need a steam-hammer to do any serious damage."

He replaced the jewel in his pocket, and when I returned the lens to him he acknowledged it with a grave inclination of the head. As I looked into his sunken eyes, in which I thought lay a sort of sardonic merriment, the fantastic idea flashed through my mind that I had fallen into the clutches of an expert hypnotist who was amusing himself at my expense, that the miniature rose was a mere hallucination produced by the same means as the notorious Indian rope trick.

Then, looking around me at the cosmopolitan groups surrounding the many tables, and catching snatches of conversations dealing with subjects so diverse as the quality of whisky in Singapore, the frail beauty of Chinese maidens, and the ways of "bloody greasers," common sense reasserted itself.

I looked into the gray face of my acquaintance.

"I cannot believe," I said slowly, "that human ingenuity could so closely duplicate the handiwork of nature. Surely the gem is unique?— possibly one of those magical talismans of which we read in Eastern stories?"

My companion smiled.

"It is not a gem," he replied, "and while in a sense it is a product of human ingenuity, it is also the handiwork of nature."

I was badly puzzled, and doubtless revealed the fact, for the stranger laughed in his short fashion, and:

"I am not trying to mystify you," he assured me. "But the truth is so hard to believe sometimes that in the present case I hesitate to divulge it. Did you ever meet Tchériapin?"

This abrupt change of topic somewhat startled me, but nevertheless:

"I once heard him play," I replied. "Why do you ask the question?"

"For this reason: Tchériapin possessed the only other example of this art which so far as I am aware ever left the laboratory of the inventor. He occasionally wore it in his buttonhole."

"It is then a manufactured product of some sort?"

"As I have said, in a sense it is; but"—he drew the tiny exquisite ornament from his pocket again and held it up before me—"It is a natural bloom."

"What!"

"It is a natural bloom," replied my acquaintance, fixing his penetrating gaze upon me. "By a perfectly simple process invented by the cleverest chemist of his age it had been reduced to this gem-like state while retaining unimpaired every one of its natural beauties, every shade of its natural colour. You are incredulous?"

"On the contrary," I replied, "having examined it through a magnifying glass I had already assured myself that no human hand had fashioned it. You arouse my curiosity intensely. Such a process, with its endless possibilities, should be worth a fortune to the inventor."

The stranger nodded grimly and again concealed the rose in his pocket.

"You are right," he said; "and the secret died with the man who discovered it—in the great explosion at the Vortex Works in 1917. You recall it? The T.N.T. factory? It shook all London, and fragments were cast into three counties."

"I recall it perfectly well."

"You remember also the death of Dr. Kreener, the chief chemist? He died in an endeavour to save some of the workpeople."

"I remember."

"He was the inventor of the process, but it was never put upon the market. He was a singular man, sir; as was once said of him—'A Don Juan of science.' Dame Nature gave him her heart unwooed. He trifled with science as some men trifle with love, tossing aside with a smile discoveries which would have made another famous. This"—tapping his breast pocket—"was one of them."

"You astound me. Do I understand you to mean that Dr. Kreener had invented a process for reducing any form of plant life to this condition?"

"Almost any form," was the guarded reply. "And some forms of animal life."

"What!"

"If you like"—the stranger leaned forward and grasped my arm—"I will tell you the story of Dr. Kreener's last experiment."

I was now intensely interested. I had not forgotten the heroic death of the man concerning whose work this chance acquaintance of mine seemed to know so much. And in the cadaverous face of the stranger as he sat there regarding me fixedly there was a promise and an allurement. I stood on the verge of strange things; so that, looking into the deep-set eyes, once again I felt the cloak being drawn about me, and I resigned myself willingly to the illusion.

From the moment when he began to speak again until that when I rose and followed him from Malay Jack's, as 1 shall presently relate, I became oblivious of my surroundings. I lived and moved through those last fevered hours in the lives of Dr. Kreener, Tchériapin, the violinist, and that other tragic figure around whom the story centred. I append:

THE STRANGER'S STORY

I asked you (said the man in the caped coat) if you had ever seen Tchériapin, and you replied that you had once heard him play. Having once heard him play you will not have forgotten him. At that time, although war still raged, all musical London was asking where he had come from and to what nation he belonged. Then when he disappeared it was variously reported, you will recall, that he had been shot as a spy and that he had escaped from England and was serving with the Austrian army. As to his parentage I can enlighten you in a measure. He was a Eurasian. His father was an aristocratic Chinaman, and his mother a Polish ballet-dancer—that was his parentage; but I would scarcely hesitate to affirm that he came from Hell; and I shall presently show you that he has certainly returned there.

You remember the strange stories current about him. The cunning ones said that he had a clever press agent. This was true enough. One of the most prominent agents in London discovered him playing in a Paris cabaret. Two months later he was playing at the Queen's Hall, and musical London lay at his feet.

He had something of the personality of Paganini, as you remember, except that he was a smaller man; long, gaunt, yellowish hands and the face of a haggard Mephistopheles. The critics quarrelled about him, as critics only quarrel about real genius, and while one school proclaimed that Tchériapin had discovered an entirely new technique, a revolutionary system of violin playing, another school was equally positive in declaring that he could not play at all, that he was a mountebank, a trickster, whose proper place was in it variety theatre.

There were stories, too, that were never published—not only about Tchériapin, but concerning the Strad, upon which he played. If all this atmosphere of mystery which surrounded the man had truly been the work of a press agent, then the agent must have been as great a genius as his client. But I can assure you that the stories concerning Tchériapin, true and absurd alike, were not inspired for business purposes; they grew up around him like fungi.

I can see him now, a lean, almost emaciated figure with slow, sinuous movements and a trick of glancing sideways with those dark, unfathomable, slightly oblique eyes. He could take up his bow in such a way as to create an atmosphere of electrical suspense. He was loathsome, yet fascinating. One's mental attitude toward him was one of defence, of being tensely on guard. Then he would play.

You have heard him play, and it is therefore unnecessary for me to attempt to describe the effect of that music. The only composition which ever bore his name—I refer to "The Black Mass"—affected me on every occasion when I heard it, as no other composition has ever done.

Perhaps it was Tchériapin's playing rather than the music itself which reached down into hitherto unplumbed depths within me and awakened dark things which, unsuspected, lay there sleeping. I never heard "The Black Mass" played by anyone else; indeed, I am not aware that it was ever published. But had it been we should rarely hear it. Like Locke's music to "Macbeth" it bears an unpleasant reputation; to include it in any concert programme would be to court disaster. An idle superstition, perhaps, but there is much naïveté in the artistic temperament.

Men detested Tchériapin, yet when he chose he could win over his bitterest enemies. Women followed him as children followed the Pied Piper; he courted none, but was courted by all. He would glance aside with those black, slanting eyes, shrug in his insolent fashion, and turn away. And they would follow. God knows how many of them followed— whether through the dens of Limehouse or the more fashionable salons of vice in the West End—they followed—perhaps down to Hell. So much for Tchériapin.

At the time when the episode occurred to which I have referred, Dr. Kreener occupied a house in Regent's Park, to which, when his duties at the munition works allowed, he would sometimes retire at weekends. He was a man of complex personality. I think no one ever knew him thoroughly; indeed, I doubt if he knew himself.

He was hail-fellow-well-met with the painters, sculptors, poets, and social reformers who have made of Soho a new Mecca. No movement in art was so modern that Dr. Kreener was not conversant with it; no development in Bolshevism so violent or so secret that Dr. Kreener could not speak of it complacently and with inside knowledge.

These were his Bohemian friends, these dreamers and schemers. Of this side of his life his scientific colleagues knew little or nothing, but in his hours of leisure at Regent's Park it was with these dreamers that he loved to surround himself rather than with his brethren of the laboratory. I think if Dr. Kreener had not been a great chemist he would have been a great painter, or perhaps a politician, or even a poet. Triumph was his birthright, and the fruits for which lesser men reached out in vain fell ripe into his hands.

The favourite meeting-place for these oddly assorted boon companions was the doctor's laboratory, which was divided from the house by a moderately large garden. Here on a Sunday evening one might meet the very "latest" composer, the sculptor bringing a new "message," or the man destined to supplant with the ballet the time-worn operatic tradition.

But while some of these would come and go, so that one could never count with certainty upon meeting them, there was one who never failed to be present when such an informal reception was held. Of him I must speak at greater length, for a reason which will shortly appear.

Andrews was the name by which he was known to the circles in which he moved. No one, from Sir John Tennier, the fashionable portrait painter, to Kruski, of the Russian ballet, disputed Andrews's right to be counted one of the elect. Yet it was known, nor did he trouble to hide the fact, that Andrews was employed at a large printing works in South London, designing advertisements. He was a great, red-bearded, unkempt Scotsman, and only once can I remember to have seen him strictly sober; but to hear him talk about painters and painting in his thick Caledonian accent was to look into the soul of an artist.

He was as sour as an unripe grape-fruit, cynical, embittered, a man savagely disappointed with life and the world; and tragedy was written all over him. If anyone knew the secret of his wasted life it was Dr. Kreener, and Dr. Kreener was a reliquary of so many secrets that this one was safe as if the grave had swallowed it.

One Sunday Tchériapin joined the party. That he would gravitate there sooner or later was inevitable, for the laboratory in the garden was a *Kaaba* to which all such spirits made at least one pilgrimage. He had just set musical London on fire with his barbaric playing, and already those stories to which I have referred were creeping into circulation.

Although Dr. Kreener never expected anything of his guests beyond an interchange of ideas, it was a fact that the laboratory contained an almost unique collection of pencil and charcoal studies by famous artists, done upon the spot; of statuettes in wax, putty, soap and other extemporized materials, by the newest sculptors. While often enough from the drawing room which opened upon the other end of the garden had issued the strains of masterly piano-playing, and it was no uncommon thing for little groups to gather in the neighbouring road to listen, gratis, to the voice of some great vocalist.

From the first moment of their meeting an intense antagonism sprang up between Tchériapin and Andrews. Neither troubled very much to veil it. In Tchériapin it found expression in covert sneers and sidelong glances, while the big, lion-maned Scotsman snorted open contempt of the Eurasian violinist. However, what I was about to say was that Tchériapin on the occasion of his first visit brought his violin.

It was there, amid these incongruous surroundings, that I first had my spirit tortured by the strains of "The Black Mass."

There were five of us present, including Tchériapin, and not one of the four listeners was unaffected by the music. But the influence which it exercised upon Andrews was so extraordinary as almost to reach the phenomenal. He literally writhed in his chair, and finally interrupted the performance by staggering rather than walking out of the laboratory.

I remember that he upset a jar of acid in his stumbling exit. It flowed across the floor almost to the feet of Tchériapin, and the way in which the little black-haired man skipped, squealing, out of the path of the corroding fluid was curiously like that of a startled rabbit. Order was restored in due course, but we could not induce Tchériapin to play again, nor did Andrews return until the violinist had taken his departure. We found him in the dining room, a nearly empty whisky-bottle beside him.

"I had to gang awa'," he explained thickly; "he was temptin' me to murder him. I should ha' had to do it if I had stayed. Damn his hell-music."

Tchériapin revisited Dr. Kreener on many occasions afterward, although for a long time he did not bring his violin again. The doctor had prevailed upon Andrews to tolerate the Euxasian's company, and I could not help noticing how Tchériapin skilfully and deliberately goaded the Scotsman, seeming to take a fiendish delight in disagreeing with his pet theories and in discussing any topic which he had found to be distasteful to Andrews.

Chief among these was that sort or irreverent criticism of women in which male parties so often indulge. Bitter cynic though he was, women were sacred to Andrews. To speak disrespectfully of a woman in his presence was like uttering blasphemy in the study of a cardinal. Tchériapin very quickly detected the Scotsman's weakness, and one night he launched out into a series of amorous adventures which set Andrews writhing as he had writhed under the torture of "The Black Mass."

On this occasion the party was only a small one, comprising myself, Dr. Kreener, Andrews and Tchériapin. I could feel the storm brewing, but was powerless to check it. How presently it was to break in tragic violence I could not foresee. Fate had not meant that I should foresee it.

Allowing for the free play of an extravagant artistic mind, Tchériapin's career on his own showing had been that of a callous blackguard. I began by being disgusted and ended by being fascinated, not by the man's scandalous adventures, but by the scarcely human psychology of the narrator.

From Warsaw to Budapesth, Shanghai to Paris, and Cairo to London he passed, leaving ruin behind him with a smile—airily flicking cigarette ash upon the floor to indicate the termination of each "episode."

Andrews watched him in a lowering way which I did not like at all. He had ceased to snort his scorn; indeed, for ten minutes or so he had uttered no word or sound; but there was something in the pose of his ungainly body which strangely suggested that of a great dog preparing to spring. Presently the violinist recalled what he termed a "charming idyll of Normandy."

"There is one poor fool in the world," he said, shrugging his slight shoulders, "who never knew how badly he should hate me. Ha! ha! of him I shall tell you. Do you remember, my friends, some few years ago, a picture that was published in Paris and London? Everybody bought it; everybody said: 'He is a made man, this fellow who can paint so fine.'"

"To what picture do you refer?" asked Dr. Kreener.

"It was called 'A Dream at Dawn.'"

As he spoke the words I saw Andrews start forward, and Dr. Kreener exchanged a swift glance with him. But the Scotsman, unseen by the vainglorious half-caste, shook his head fiercely.

The picture to which Tchériapin referred will, of course, be perfectly familiar to you. It had phenomenal popularity some eight years ago. Nothing was known of the painter—whose name was Colquhoun—and nothing has been seen of his work since. The original painting was never sold, and after a time this promising new artist was, of course, forgotten.

Presently Tchériapin continued:

"It is the figure of a slender girl—ah! angels of grace!—what a girl!" He kissed his hand rapturously. "She is posed bending gracefully forward, and looking down at her own lovely reflection in the water. It is a seashore, you remember, and the little ripples play about her ankles. The first blush of the dawn robes her white body in a transparent mantle of light. Ah! God's mercy! it was as she stood so, in a little cove of Normandy, that I saw her!"

He paused, rolling his dark eyes; and I could hear Andrews's heavy breathing; then:

"It was the 'new art'—the posing of the model not in a lighted studio, but in the scene to be depicted. And the fellow who painted her!—the man with the barbarous name! Bah! he was big—as big as our Mr. Andrews—and ugly—pooh! uglier than he! A moon-face, with cropped skull like a prize-fighter and no soul. But, yes, he could paint. 'A Dream at Dawn' was genius—yes, some soul he must have had.

"He could paint, dear friends, but he could not love. Him I counted as—puff!"

He blew imaginary down into space.

"Her I sought out, and presently found. She told me, in those sweet stolen rambles along the shore, when the moonlight made her look like a Madonna, that she was his inspiration—his art—his life. And she wept; she wept, and I kissed her tears away.

"To please her I waited until 'A Dream at Dawn' was finished. With the finish of the picture, finished also *his* dream of dawn—the moon-faced one's."

Tchériapin laughed, and lighted a fresh cigarette.

"Can you believe that a man could be so stupid? He never knew of my existence, this big, red booby. He never knew that I existed until—until his 'dream' had fled—with me! In a week we were in Paris, that dream-girl and I—in a month we had quarrelled. I always end these matters with a quarrel; it makes the complete finish. She struck me in the face—and I laughed. She turned and went away. We were tired of one another.

"Ah!" Again he airily kissed his hand. "There were others after I had gone. I heard for a time. But her memory is like a rose, fresh and fair and sweet. I am glad I can remember her so, and not as she afterward became. That is the art of love. She killed herself with absinthe, my friends. She died in Marseilles in the first year of the great war."

Thus far Tchériapin had proceeded, and was in the act of airily flicking ash upon the floor, when, uttering a sound which I can only describe as a roar, Andrews hurled himself upon the smiling violinist.

His great red hands clutching Tchériapin's throat, the insane Scotsman, for insane he was at that moment, forced the other back upon the settee from which he had half arisen. In vain I sought to drag him away from the writhing body, but I doubt that any man could have relaxed that deadly grip. Tchériapin's eyes protruded hideously and his tongue lolled forth from his mouth. One could hear the breath whistling through his nostrils as Andrews silently, deliberately, squeezed the life out of him.

It all occupied only a few minutes, and then Andrews, slowly opening his rigidly crooked fingers, stood panting and looking down at the distorted face of the dead man.

For once in his life the Scotsman was sober, and turning to Dr. Kreener:

"I have waited seven long years for this," he said, "and I'll hang wi' contentment."

I can never forget the ensuing moments, in which, amid a horrible silence broken only by the ticking of a clock and the heavy breathing of Colquhoun (so long known to us as Andrews) we stood watching the contorted body on the settee.

And as we watched, slowly the rigid limbs began to relax, and Tchériapin slid gently on to the floor, collapsing there with a soft thud, where he squatted like some hideous Buddha, resting back against the cushions, one spectral yellow hand upraised, the fingers still clutching a big gold tassel.

Andrews (for so I always think of him) was seized with a violent fit of trembling, and he dropped into the chair, muttering to himself and looking down wild-eyed at his twitching fingers. Then he began to laugh, high-pitched laughter, in little short peals.

"Here!" cried the doctor sharply. "Drop that!"

Crossing to Andrews, he grasped him by the shoulders and shook him roughly.

The laughter ceased, and:

"Send for the police," said Andrews in a queer, shaky voice. "Dinna fear but I'm ready. I'm only sorry it happened here."

"You ought to be glad," said Dr. Kreener.

There was a covert meaning in the words—a fact which penetrated even to the dulled intelligence of the Scotsman, for he glanced up haggardly at his friend.

"You ought to be glad," repeated Dr. Kreener.

Turning, he walked to the laboratory door and locked it. He next lowered all the blinds.

"I pray that we have not been observed," he said, "but we must chance it."

He mixed a drink for Andrews and himself. His quiet, decisive manner had had its effect, and Andrews was now more composed. Indeed, he seemed to be in a half-dazed condition; but he persistently kept his back turned to the crouching figure propped up against the settee.

"If you think you can follow me," said Dr. Kreener abruptly, "I will show you the result of a recent experiment."

Unlocking a cupboard, he took out a tiny figure some two inches long by one inch high, mounted upon a polished wooden pedestal. It was that of a guinea-pig. The flaky fur gleamed like the finest silk, and one felt that the coat of the minute creature would be as floss to the touch; whereas in reality it possessed the rigidity of steel. Literally one could have done it little damage with a hammer. Its weight was extraordinary.

"I am learning new things about this process every day," continued Dr. Kreener, placing the little figure upon a table. "For instance, while it seems to operate uniformly upon vegetable matter, there are curious modifications when one applies it to animal and mineral substances. I have now definitely decided that the result of this particular inquiry must never be published. You, Colquhoun, I believe, possess an example of the process, a tiger lily, I think? I must ask you to return it to me. Our late friend, Tchériapin, wears a pink rose in his coat which I have treated in the same way. I am going to take the liberty of removing it."

He spoke in the hard, incisive manner which I had heard him use in the lecture theatre, and it was evident enough that his design was to prepare Andrews for something which he contemplated. Facing the Scotsman where he sat hunched up in the big armchair, dully watching the speaker:

"There is one experiment," said Dr. Kreener, speaking very deliberately, "which I have never before had a suitable opportunity of attempting. Of its result I am personally confident, but science always demands proof."

His voice rang now with a note of repressed excitement. He paused for a moment, and then:

"If you were to examine this little specimen very closely," he said, and rested his finger upon the tiny figure of the guinea-pig, "you would find that in one particular it is imperfect. Although a diamond drill would have to be employed to demonstrate the fact, the animal's organs, despite their having undergone a chemical change quite new to science, are intact, perfect down to the smallest detail. One part of the creature's structure alone defied my process. In short, *dental enamel* is impervious to it. This little animal, otherwise as complete as when it lived and breathed, has no teeth. I found it necessary to extract them before submitting the body to the reductionary process."

He paused.

"Shall I go on?" he asked.

Andrews, to whose mind, I think, no conception of the doctor's project had yet penetrated, shuddered, but slowly nodded his head.

Dr. Kreener glanced across the laboratory at the crouching figure of Tchériapin, then, resting his hands upon Andrews's shoulders, he pushed him back in the chair and stared into his dull eyes.

"Brace yourself, Colquhoun," he said tersely.

Turning, he crossed to a small mahogany cabinet at the farther end of the room. Pulling out a glass tray he judicially selected a pair of dental forceps.

II
"THE BLACK MASS"

Thus far the stranger's appalling story had progressed when that singular cloak in which hypnotically he had enwrapped me seemed to drop, and I found myself clutching the edge of the table and staring into the gray face of the speaker.

I became suddenly aware of the babel of voices about me, of the noisome smell of Malay Jack's, and of the presence of Jack in person, who was inquiring if there were any further orders. I was conscious of .nausea.

"Excuse me," I said, rising unsteadily, "but I fear the oppressive atmosphere is affecting me."

"If you prefer to go out," said my acquaintance, in that deep voice which throughout the dreadful story had rendered me oblivious of my surroundings, "I should be much favoured if you would accompany me to a spot not five hundred yards from here."

Seeing me hesitate:

"I have a particular reason for asking," he added.

"Very well," I replied, inclining my head, "if you wish it. But certainly I must seek the fresh air."

Going up the steps and out through the door above which the blue lantern burned, we came to the street, turned to the left, to the left again, and soon were threading that maze of narrow ways which complicates the map of Pennyfields.

I felt somewhat recovered. Here, in the narrow but familiar highways the spell of my singular acquaintance lost much of its potency, and already I found myself doubting the story of Dr. Kreener and Tchériapin. Indeed, I began to laugh at myself, conceiving that I had fallen into the hands of some comedian who was making sport of me; although why such a person should visit Malay Jack's was not apparent.

I was about to give expression to these new and saner ideas when my companion paused before a door half hidden in a little alley which divided the back of a Chinese restaurant from the tawdry-looking establishment of a cigar merchant. He apparently held the key, for although I did not actually hear the turning of the lock I saw that he had opened the door.

"May I request you to follow me?" came his deep voice out of the darkness. "I will show you something which will repay your trouble."

Again the cloak touched me, but it was without entirely resigning myself to the compelling influence that I followed my mysterious acquaintance up an uncarpeted and nearly dark stair. On the landing above a gas lamp was burning, and opening a door immediately facing the stair the stranger conducted me into a barely furnished and untidy room.

The atmosphere smelled like that of a pot-house, the odours of stale spirits and of tobacco mingling unpleasantly. As my guide removed his hat and stood there, a square, gaunt figure in his queer, caped over-coat, I secured for the first time a view of his face in profile; and found it to be startlingly unfamiliar. Seen thus, my acquaintance was another man. I realized that there was something unnatural about the long, white hair, the gray face; that the sharp outline of brow, nose, and chin was that of a much younger man than I had supposed him to be.

All this came to me in a momentary flash of perception, for imme-diately my attention was riveted upon a figure hunched up on a dilapi-dated sofa on the opposite side of the room. It was that of a big man, bearded and very heavily built, but whose face was scarred as by years of suffering, and whose eyes confirmed the story indicated by the smell of stale spirits with which the air of the room was laden. A nearly empty bottle stood on a table at his elbow, a glass beside it, and a pipe lay in a saucer full of ashes near the glass.

As we entered, the glazed eyes of the man opened widely and he clutched at the table with big red hands, leaning forward and staring horribly.

Save for this derelict figure and some few dirty utensils and scattered garments which indicated that the apartment was used both as sleeping and living room, there was so little of interest in the place that automati-cally my wandering gaze strayed from the figure on the sofa to a large oil painting, unframed, which rested upon the mantelpiece above the dirty grate, in which the fire had become extinguished.

I uttered a stifled exclamation. It was "A Dream at Dawn"— evidently the original painting!

On the left of it, from a nail in the wall, hung a violin and bow, and on the right stood a sort of cylindrical glass case or closed jar, upon a wooden base.

From the moment that I perceived the contents of this glass case a sense of fantasy claimed me, and I ceased to know where reality ended and mirage began.

It contained a tiny and perfect figure of a man. He was arrayed in a beautifully fitting dress-suit such as a doll might have worn, and he was posed as if in the act of playing a violin, although no violin was present. At the elfin black hair and Mephistophelian face of this horrible, won-derful image, I stared fascinatedly.

I looked and looked at the dwarfed figure of . . . Tchériapin!

All these impressions came to me in the space of a few hectic moments, when in upon my mental tumult intruded a husky whisper from the man on the sofa.

"Kreener!" he said. *"Kreener!"*

At the sound of that name, and because of the way in which it was pronounced, I felt my blood running cold. The speaker was staring straight at my companion.

I clutched at the open door. I felt that there was still some crowning horror to come. I wanted to escape from that reeking room, but my muscles refused to obey me, and there I stood while:

"Kreener!" repeated the husky voice, and I saw that the speaker was rising unsteadily to his feet. "You have brought him again. Why have you brought him again? He will play. He will play me a step nearer to Hell."

"Brace yourself, Colquhoun," said the voice of my companion. "Brace yourself."

"Take him awa'!" came in a sudden frenzied shriek. "Take him awa'! He's there at your elbow, Kreener, mockin' me, and pointing to that damned violin."

"Here!" said the stranger, a high note of command in his voice. "Drop that! Sit down at once."

Even as the other obeyed him, the cloaked stranger, stepping to the mantelpiece, opened a small box which lay there beside the glass case. He turned to me; and I tried to shrink away from him. For I knew—I knew—yet I loathed to look upon—what was in the box. Muffled as though reaching me through fog, I heard the words:

"A perfect human body . . . in miniature . . . every organ intact by means of . . . process . . . rendered indestructible. Tchériapin as he was in life may be seen by the curious ten thousand years hence. Incomplete . . . one respect . . . here in this box . . ."

The spell was broken by a horrifying shriek from the man whom my companion had addressed as Colquhoun, and whom I could only suppose to be the painter of the celebrated picture which rested upon the mantelshelf.

"Take him awa', Kreener! He is reaching for the violin!"

Animation returned to me, and I fell rather than ran down the darkened stair. How I opened the street door I know not, but even as I stepped out into the squalid alleys of Pennyfields the cloaked figure was beside me. A hand was laid upon my shoulder.

"Listen!" commanded a deep voice.

Clearly, with an eerie sweetness, an evil, hellish beauty indescribable, the wailing of a Stradivarius violin crept to my ears from the room above. Slowly—slowly the music began, and my soul rose up in revolt.

"Listen!" repeated the voice. "Listen! It is 'The Black Mass'!"

The Hand of the Mandarin Quong

I

THE SHADOW ON THE CURTAIN

Singapore is by no means herself again," declared Jennings, looking about the lounge of the Hôtel de l'Europe. "Don't you agree, Knox?"

Burton fixed his lazy stare upon the speaker.

"Don't blame poor old Singapore," he said. "There is no spot in this battered world that I have succeeded in discovering which is not changed for the worse."

Dr. Matheson flicked ash from his cigar and smiled in that peculiarly happy manner which characterizes a certain American type and which lent a boyish charm to his personality.

"You are a pair of pessimists," he pronounced. "For some reason best known to themselves Jennings and Knox have decided upon a Busman's Holiday. Very well. Why grumble?"

"You are quite right, Doctor," Jennings admitted. "When I was on service here in the Straits Settlements I declared heaven knows how often that the country would never see me again once I was demobbed. Yet here you see I am; Burton belongs here; but here's Knox, and we are all as fed up as we can be!"

"Yes," said Burton slowly. "I may be a bit tired of Singapore. It's a queer thing, though, that you fellows have drifted back here again. The call of the East is no fable. It's a call that one hears for ever."

The conversation drifted into another channel, and all sorts of topics were discussed, from racing to the latest feminine fashions, from ballroom dances to the merits and demerits of coalition government. Then suddenly:

"What became of Adderley?" asked Jennings.

There were several men in the party who had been cronies of ours during the time that we were stationed in Singapore, and at Jennings's words a sort of hush seemed to fall on those who had known Adderley. I cannot say if Jennings noticed this, but it was perfectly evident to me that Dr. Matheson had perceived it, for he glanced swiftly across in my direction in an oddly significant way.

"I don't know," replied Burton, who was an engineer. "He was rather an unsavoury sort of character in some ways, but I heard that he came to a sticky end."

"What do you mean?" I asked with curiosity, for I myself had often wondered what had become of Adderley.

"Well, he was reported to his C. O., or something, wasn't he, just before the time for his demobilization? I don't know the particulars; I thought perhaps you did, as he was in your regiment."

"I have heard nothing whatever about it," I replied.

"You mean Sidney Adderley, the man who was so indecently rich?" someone interjected. "Had a place at Katong, and was always talking about his father's millions?"

"That's the fellow."

"Yes," said Jennings, "there was some scandal, I know, but it was after my time here."

"Something about an old mandarin out Johore Bahru way, was it not?" asked Burton. "The last thing I heard about Adderley was that he had disappeared."

"Nobody would have cared much if he had," declared Jennings. "I know of several who would have been jolly glad. There was a lot of the brute about Adderley, apart from the fact that he had more money than was good for him. His culture was a veneer. It was his check-book that spoke all the time."

"Everybody would have forgiven Adderley his vulgarity," said Dr. Matheson, quietly, "if the man's heart had been in the right place."

"Surely an instance of trying to make a silk purse out of a sow's ear," someone murmured.

Burton gazed rather hard at the last speaker.

"So far as I am aware," he said, "the poor devil is dead, so go easy."

"Are you sure he is dead?" asked Dr. Matheson, glancing at Burton in that quizzical, amused way of his.

"No, I am not sure; I am merely speaking from hearsay. And now I come to think of it, the information was rather vague. But 1 gathered that he had vanished, at any rate, and remembering certain earlier episodes in his career, I was led to suppose that this vanishing meant—"

He shrugged his shoulders significantly.

"You mean the old mandarin?" suggested Dr. Matheson.

"Yes."

"Was there really anything in that story, or was it suggested by the unpleasant reputation of Adderley?" Jennings asked.

"I can settle any doubts upon that point," said I; whereupon I immediately became a focus of general attention.

"What I were you ever at that place of Adderley's at Katong?" asked Jennings with intense curiosity.

I nodded, lighting a fresh cigarette in a manner that may have been unduly leisurely.

"Did you see her?"

Again I nodded.

"Really!"

"I must have been peculiarly favoured, but certainly I had that pleasure."

"You speak of seeing *her*," said one of the party, now entering the conversation for the first time. "To whom do you refer?"

"Well," replied Burton, "it's really a sort of fairy tale—unless Knox"—glancing across in my direction—"can confirm it. But there was a story current during the latter part of Adderley's stay in Singapore to the effect that he had made the acquaintance of the wife, or some member of the household, of an old gentleman out Johore Bahru way—sort of mandarin or big pot among the Chinks."

"It was rumoured that he had bolted with her," added another speaker.

"I think it was more than a rumour."

"Why do you say so?"

"Well, representations were made to the authorities, I know for an absolute certainty, and I have an idea that Adderley was kicked out of the Service as a consequence of the scandal which resulted."

"How is it one never heard of this?"

"Money speaks, my dear fellow," cried Burton, "even when it is possessed by such a peculiar outsider as Adderley. The thing was hushed up. It was a very nasty business. But Knox was telling us that he had actually seen the lady. Please carry on, Knox, for I must admit that I am intensely curious."

"I can only say that I saw her on one occasion."

"With Adderley?"

"Undoubtedly."

"Where?"

"At his place at Katong."

"I even thought his place at that resort was something of a myth," declared Jennings. "He never asked *me* to go there, but, then, I took that as a compliment. Pardon the apparent innuendo, Knox," he added, laughing. "But you say you actually visited the establishment?"

"Yes," I replied slowly, "I met him here in this very hotel one evening in the winter of '15, after the natives' attempt to mutiny. He had been drinking rather heavily, a fact which he was quite unable to disguise. He was never by any means a real friend of mine; in fact, I doubt that he had a true friend in the world. Anyhow, I could see that he was lonely, and as I chanced to be at a loose end I accepted an invitation to go over to what he termed his 'little place at Katong.'

"His little place proved to be a veritable palace. The man privately, or rather, secretly, to be exact, kept up a sort of pagan state. He had any number of servants. Of course he became practically a millionaire after the death of his father, as you will remember; and given more congenial company, I must confess that I might have spent a most enjoyable evening there.

"Adderley insisted upon priming me with champagne, and after a while I may as well admit that I lost something of my former reserve, and began in a fashion to feel that I was having a fairly good time. By the way, my host was not quite frankly drunk. He got into that objectionable and dangerous mood which some of you will recall, and I could see by the light in his eyes that there was mischief brewing, although at the time I did not know its nature.

"I should explain that we were amusing ourselves in a room which was nearly as large as the lounge of this hotel, and furnished in a somewhat similar manner. There were carved pillars and stained glass domes, a little fountain, and all those other peculiarities of an Eastern household.

"Presently, Adderley gave an order to one of his servants, and glanced at me with that sort of mocking, dare-devil look in his eyes which I loathed, which everybody loathed who ever met the man. Of course I had no idea what all this portended, but I was very shortly to learn.

"While he was still looking at me, but stealing side-glances at a doorway before which was draped a most wonderful curtain of a sort of flamingo colour, this curtain was suddenly pulled aside, and a girl came in.

"Of course, you must remember that at the time of which I am speaking the scandal respecting the mandarin had not yet come to light. Consequently I had no idea who the girl could be. I saw she was a Eurasian. But of her striking beauty there could be no doubt whatever. She was dressed in magnificent robes, and she literally glittered with jewels. She even wore jewels upon the toes of her little bare feet. But the first thing that struck me at the moment of her appearance was that her presence there was contrary to her wishes and inclinations. I have never seen a similar expression in any woman's eyes. She looked at Adderley as though she would gladly have slain him!

"Seeing this look, his mocking smile in which there was something of triumph—of the joy of possession—turned to a scowl of positive brutality. He clenched his fists in a way that set me bristling. He advanced toward the girl—and although the width of the room divided them, she recoiled—and the significance of expression and gesture was unmistakable. Adderley paused.

"'So you have made up your mind to dance after all?' he shouted.

"The look in the girl's dark eyes was pitiful, and she turned to me with a glance of dumb entreaty.

"'No, no!' she cried. 'No, no! Why do you bring me here?'

"'Dance!' roared Adderley. 'Dance! That's what I want you to do.'

"Rebellion leapt again to the wonderful eyes, and she started back with a perfectly splendid gesture of defiance. At that my brutal and drunken host leapt in her direction. I was on my feet now, but before I could act the girl said a thing which checked him, sobered him, which pulled him up short, as though he had encountered a stone wall.

"'Ah, God!' she said. (She was speaking, of course, in her native tongue.) 'His hand! His hand! Look! *His hand!*'

"To me her words were meaningless, naturally, but following the direction of her positively agonized glance I saw that she was watching what seemed to me to be the shadow of someone moving behind the flame-like curtain which produced an effect not unlike that of a huge, outstretched hand, the fingers crooked, claw-fashion.

"'Knox, Knox!' whispered Adderley, grasping me by the shoulder.

"He pointed with a quivering finger toward this indistinct shadow upon the curtain, and:

"'Do you see it—do you see it?' he said huskily. 'It is his hand—it is his hand!'

"Of the pair, I think, the man was the more frightened. But the girl, uttering a frightful shriek, ran out of the room as though pursued by a demon. As she did so whoever had been moving behind the curtain evidently went away. The shadow disappeared, and Adderley, still staring as if hypnotized at the spot where it had been, continued to hold my shoulder as in a vise. Then, sinking down upon a heap of cushions beside me, he loudly and shakily ordered more champagne.

"Utterly mystified by the incident, I finally left him in a state of stupor, and returned to my quarters, wondering whether I had dreamed half of the episode or the whole of it, whether he did really possess that wonderful palace, or whether he had borrowed it to impress me."

I ceased speaking, and my story was received in absolute silence, until:

"And that is all you know?" said Burton.

"Absolutely all. I had to leave about that time, you remember, and afterward went to France."

"Yes, I remember. It was while you were away that the scandal arose respecting the mandarin. Extraordinary story, Knox. I should like to know what it all meant, and what the end of it was."

Dr. Matheson broke his long silence.

"Although I am afraid I cannot enlighten you respecting the end of the story," he said quietly, "perhaps I can carry it a step further."

"Really, Doctor? What do you know about the matter?"

"I accidentally became implicated as follows," replied the American: "I was, as you know, doing voluntary surgical work near Singapore at the time, and one evening, presumably about the same period of which Knox is speaking, I was returning from the hospital at Katong, at which I acted sometimes as anæsthetist, to my quarters in Singapore; just drifting along, leisurely by the edge of the gardens admiring the beauty of the mangroves and the deceitful peace of the Eastern night.

"The hour was fairly late and not a soul was about. Nothing disturbed the silence except those vague sibilant sounds which are so characteristic of the country. Presently, as I rambled on with my thoughts wandering back to the dim ages, I literally fell over a man who lay in the road.

"I was naturally startled, but I carried an electric pocket torch, and by its light I discovered that the person over whom I had fallen was a dignified-looking Chinaman, somewhat past middle age. His clothes, which were of good quality, were covered with dirt and blood, and he bore all the appearance of having recently been engaged in a very tough struggle. His face was notable only for its possession of an unusually long jet-black moustache. He had swooned from loss of blood."

"Why, was he wounded?" exclaimed Jennings.

"His hand had been nearly severed from his wrist!"

"Merciful heavens!"

"I realized the impossibility of carrying him so far as the hospital, and accordingly I extemporized a rough tourniquet and left him under a palm tree by the road until I obtained assistance. Later, at the hospital, following a consultation, we found it necessary to amputate."

"I should say he objected fiercely?"

"He was past objecting to anything, otherwise I have no doubt he would have objected furiously. The index finger of the injured hand had one of those preternaturally long nails, protected by an engraved golden case. However, at least I gave him a chance of life. He was under my care for some time, but I doubt if ever he was properly grateful. He had an iron constitution, though, and I finally allowed him to depart. One queer stipulation he had made—that the severed hand, with its golden nail-case, should be given to him when he left hospital. And this bargain I faithfully carried out."

"Most extraordinary," I said. "Did you ever learn the identity of the old gentleman?"

"He was very reticent, but I made a number of inquiries, and finally learned with absolute certainty, I think, that he was the Mandarin Quong Mi Su from Johore Bahru, a person of great repute among the Chinese there, and rather a big man in China. He was known locally as the Mandarin Quong."

"Did you learn anything respecting how he had come by his injury, Doctor?"

Matheson smiled in his quiet fashion, and selected a fresh cigar with great deliberation. Then:

"I suppose it is scarcely a case of betraying a professional secret," he said, "but during the time that my patient was recovering from the effects of the anæsthetic he unconsciously gave me several clues to the nature of the episode. Putting two and two together I gathered that someone, although the name of this person never once passed the lips of the mandarin, had abducted his favourite wife."

"Good heavens I truly amazing," I exclaimed.

"Is it not? How small a place the world is. My old mandarin had traced the abductor and presumably the girl to some house which I gathered to be in the neighbourhood of Katong. In an attempt to force an entrance—doubtless with the amiable purpose of slaying them both— he had been detected by the prime object of his hatred. In hurriedly descending from a window he had been attacked by some weapon, possibly a sword, and had only made good his escape in the condition in which I found him. How far he had proceeded I cannot say, but I should imagine that the house to which he had been was no great distance from the spot where I found him."

"Comment is really superfluous," remarked Burton. "He was looking for Adderley."

"I agree," said Jennings.

"And," I added, "it was evidently after this episode that I had the privilege of visiting that interesting establishment."

There was a short interval of silence; then:

"You probably retain no very clear impression of the shadow which you saw," said Dr. Matheson, with great deliberation. "At the time perhaps you had less occasion particularly to study it. But are you satisfied that it was really caused by someone moving behind the curtain?"

I considered his question for a few moments.

"I am not," I confessed. "Your story, Doctor, makes me wonder whether it may not have been due to something else."

"What else can it have been due to?" exclaimed Jennings contemptuously—"unless to the champagne?"

"I won't quote Shakespeare," said Dr. Matheson, smiling in his odd way. "The famous lines, though appropriate, are somewhat overworked. But I will quote Kipling: 'East is East, and West is West.'"

II

THE LADY OF KATONG

Fully six months had elapsed, and on returning from Singapore I had forgotten all about Adderley and the unsavoury stories connected with his reputation. Then, one evening as I was strolling aimlessly along St. James's Street, wondering how I was going to kill time—for almost everyone I knew was out of town, including Paul Harley, and London can be infinitely more lonely under such conditions than any desert—I saw a thick-set figure approaching along the other side of the street.

The swing of the shoulders, the aggressive turn of the head, were vaguely familiar, and while I was searching my memory and endeavouring to obtain a view of the man's face, he stared across in my direction.

It was Adderley.

He looked even more debauched than I remembered him, for whereas in Singapore he had had a tanned skin, now he looked unhealthily pallid and blotchy. He raised his hand, and:

"Knox!" he cried, and ran across to greet me.

His boisterous manner and a sort of coarse geniality which he possessed had made him popular with a certain set in former days, but I, who knew that this geniality was forced, and assumed to conceal a sort of appalling animalism, had never been deceived by it. Most people found Adderley out sooner or later, but I had detected the man's true nature from the very beginning. His eyes alone were danger signals for any amateur psychologist. However, I greeted him civilly enough:

"Bless my soul, you are looking as fit as a fiddle!" he cried. "Where have you been, and what have you been doing since I saw you last?"

"Nothing much," I replied, "beyond trying to settle down in a reformed world."

"Reformed world!" echoed Adderley. "More like a ruined world it has seemed to me."

He laughed loudly. That he had already explored several bottles was palpable.

We were silent for a while, mentally weighing one another up, as it were. Then:

"Are you living in town?" asked Adderley.

"I am staying at the Carlton at the moment," I replied. "My chambers are in the hands of the decorators. It's awkward. Interferes with my work."

"Work!" cried Adderley. "Work! It's a nasty word, Knox. Are you doing anything now?"

"Nothing, until eight o'clock, when I have an appointment."

"Come along to my place," he suggested, "and have a cup of tea, or a whisky and soda if you prefer it."

Probably I should have refused, but even as he spoke I was mentally translated to the Hôtel de l'Europe, and prompted by a very human curiosity I determined to accept his invitation. I wondered if Fate had thrown an opportunity in my way of learning the end of the peculiar story which had been related on that occasion.

I accompanied Adderley to his chambers, which were within a stone's throw of the spot where I had met him. That this gift for making himself unpopular with all and sundry, high and low, had not deserted him, was illustrated by the attitude of the liftman as we entered the hall of the chambers. He was barely civil to Adderley and even regarded myself with marked disfavour.

We were admitted by Adderley's man, whom I had not seen before, but who was some kind of foreigner, I think a Portuguese. It was characteristic of Adderley. No Englishman would ever serve him for long, and there had been more than one man in his old Company who had openly avowed his intention of dealing with Adderley on the first available occasion.

His chambers were ornately furnished; indeed, the room in which we sat more closely resembled a scene from an Oscar Asche production than a normal man's study. There was something unreal about it all. I have since thought that this unreality extended to the person of the man himself. Grossly material, he yet possessed an aura of mystery, mystery of an unsavoury sort. There was something furtive, secretive, about Adderley's entire mode of life.

I had never felt at ease in his company, and now as I sat staring wonderingly at the strange and costly ornaments with which the room was overladen I bethought me of the object of my visit. How I should have brought the conversation back to our Singapore days I know not, but a suitable opening was presently offered by Adderley himself.

"Do you ever see any of the old gang?" he inquired.

"I was in Singapore about six months ago," I replied, "and I met some of them again."

"What! Had they drifted back to the East after all?"

"Two or three of them were taking what Dr. Matheson described as a Busman's Holiday."

At mention of Dr. Matheson's name Adderley visibly started.

"So you know Matheson," he murmured. "I didn't know you had ever met him."

Plainly to hide his confusion he stood up and crossing the room drew my attention to a rather fine silver bowl of early Persian ware. He was displaying its peculiar virtues and showing a certain acquaintance with his subject when he was interrupted. A door opened suddenly and a girl came in. Adderley put down the bowl and turned rapidly as I rose from my seat.

It was the lady of Katong!

I recognized her at once, although she wore a very up-to-date gown. While it did not suit her dark good looks so well as the native dress which she had worn at Singapore, yet it could not conceal the fact that in a barbaric way she was a very beautiful woman. On finding a visitor in the room she became covered with confusion.

"Oh," she said, speaking in Hindustani. "Why did you not tell me there was someone here?"

Adderley's reply was characteristically brutal.

"Get out," he said. "You fool."

I turned to go, for I was conscious of an intense desire to attack my host. But:

"Don't go, Knox, don't go!" he cried. "I am sorry, I am damned sorry, I—"

He paused, and looked at me in a queer sort of appealing way. The girl, her big eyes widely open, retreated again to the door, with curious lithe steps, characteristically Oriental. The door regained, she paused for a moment and extended one small hand in Adderley's direction.

"I hate you," she said slowly, "hate you! Hate you!"

She went out, quietly closing the door behind her. Adderley turned to me with an embarrassed laugh.

"I know you think I am a brute and an outsider," he said, "and perhaps I am. Everybody says I am, so I suppose there must be something in it. But if ever a man paid for his mistakes I have paid for mine, Knox. Good God, I haven't a friend in the world."

"You probably don't deserve one," I retorted.

"I know I don't, and that's the tragedy of it," he replied. "You may not believe it, Knox; I don't expect anybody to believe me; but for more than a year I have been walking on the edge of Hell. Do you know where I have been since I saw you last?"

I shook my head in answer.

"I have been half round the world, Knox, trying to find peace."

"You don't know where to look for it," I said.

"If only you knew," he whispered. "If only you knew," and sank down upon the settee, ruffling his hair with his hands and looking the picture of haggard misery. Seeing that I was still set upon departure:

"Hold on a bit, Knox," he implored. "Don't go yet. There is something I want to ask you, something very important."

He crossed to a sideboard and mixed himself a stiff whisky-and-soda. He asked me to join him, but I refused.

"Won't you sit down again?"

I shook my head.

"You came to my place at Katong once," he began abruptly. "I was damned drunk, I admit it. But something happened, do you remember?"

I nodded.

"This is what I want to ask you: Did you, or did you not, see that *shadow?*"

I stared him hard in the face.

"I remember the episode to which you refer," I replied. "I certainly saw a shadow."

"But what sort of shadow?"

"To me it seemed an indefinite, shapeless thing, as though caused by someone moving behind the curtain."

"It didn't look to you like—the shadow of a *hand?*"

"It might have been, but I could not be positive."

Adderley groaned.

"Knox," he said, "money is a curse. It has been a curse to me. If I have had my fun God knows I have paid for it."

"Your idea of fun is probably a peculiar one," I said dryly.

Let me confess that I was only suffering the man's society because of an intense curiosity which now possessed me on learning that the lady of Katong was still in Adderley's company.

Whether my repugnance for his society would have enabled me to remain any longer I cannot say. But as if Fate had deliberately planned that I should become a witness of the concluding phases of this secret drama, we were now interrupted a second time, and again in a dramatic fashion.

Adderley's nondescript valet came in with letters and a rather large brown paper parcel sealed and fastened with great care.

As the man went out:

"Surely that is from Singapore," muttered Adderley, taking up the parcel.

He seemed to become temporarily oblivious of my presence, and his face grew even more haggard as he studied the writing upon the wrapper. With unsteady fingers he untied it, and I lingered, watching curiously. Presently out from the wrappings he took a very beautiful casket of ebony and ivory, cunningly carved and standing upon four claw-like ivory legs.

"What the devil's this?" he muttered.

He opened the box, which was lined with sandalwood, and thereupon started back with a great cry, recoiling from the casket as though it had contained an adder. My former sentiments forgotten, I stepped forward and peered into the interior. Then I, in turn, recoiled.

In the box lay a shrivelled yellow hand—with long tapering and well-manicured nails—neatly severed at the wrist!

The nail of the index finger was enclosed in a tiny, delicately fashioned case of gold, upon which were engraved a number of Chinese characters.

Adderley sank down again upon the settee.

"My God!" he whispered, "his hand! His hand! *He has sent me his hand!*"

He began laughing. Whereupon, since I could see that the man was practically hysterical because of his mysterious fears:

"Stop that," I said sharply. "Pull yourself together, Adderley. What the deuce is the matter with you?"

"Take it away!" he moaned, "take it away. Take the accursed thing away!"

"I admit it is an unpleasant gift to send to anybody," I said, "but probably you know more about it than I do."

"Take it away," he repeated. "Take it away, for God's sake, take it away, Knox!"

He was quite beyond reason, and therefore:

"Very well," I said, and wrapped the casket in the brown paper in which it had come. "What do you want me to do with it?"

"Throw it in the river," he answered. "Burn it. Do anything you like with it, but take it out of my sight!"

III

THE GOLD-CASED NAIL

As I descended to the street the liftman regarded me in a curious and rather significant way. Finally, just as I was about to step out into the hall:

"Excuse me, sir," he said, having evidently decided that I was a fit person to converse with, "but are you a friend of Mr. Adderley's?"

"Why do you ask?"

"Well, sir, I hope you will excuse me, but at times I have thought the gentleman was just a little bit queer, like."

"You mean insane?" I asked sharply.

"Well, sir, I don't know, but he is always asking me if I can see shadows and things in the lift, and sometimes when he comes in late of a night he absolutely gives me the cold shivers, he does."

I lingered, the box under my arm, reluctant to obtain confidences from a servant, but at the same time keenly interested. Thus encouraged:

"Then there's that lady friend of his who is always coming here," the man continued. "*She's* haunted by shadows, too." He paused, watching me narrowly. "There's nothing better in this world than a clean conscience, sir," he concluded.

Having returned to my room at the hotel, I set down the mysterious parcel, surveying it with much disfavour. That it contained the hand of the Mandarin Quong I could not doubt, the hand which had been amputated by Dr. Matheson. Its appearance in that dramatic fashion confirmed Matheson's idea that the mandarin's injury had been received at the hands of Adderley. What did all this portend, unless that the Mandarin Quong was dead? And if he were dead why was Adderley more afraid of him dead than he had been of him living?

I thought of the haunting shadow, I thought of the night at Katong, and I thought of Dr. Matheson's words when he had told us of his discovery of the Chinaman lying in the road that night outside Singapore.

I felt strangely disinclined to touch the relic, and it was only after some moments' hesitation that I undid the wrappings and raised the lid of the casket. Dusk was very near and I had not yet lighted the lamps; therefore at first I doubted the evidence of my senses. But having lighted up and peered long and anxiously into, the sandal-wood lining of the casket I could doubt no longer.

The casket was empty!

It was like a conjuring trick. That the hand had been in the box when I had taken it up from Adderley's table I could have sworn before any jury. When and by whom it had been removed was a puzzle beyond my powers of unravelling. I stepped toward the telephone—and then remembered that Paul Harley was out of London. Vaguely wondering if Adderley had played me a particularly gruesome practical joke, I put the box on a sideboard and again contemplated the telephone doubtfully for a moment. It was in my mind to ring him up. Finally, taking all things into consideration, I determined that I would have nothing further to do with the man's unsavoury and mysterious affairs.

It was in vain, however, that I endeavoured to dismiss the matter from my mind; and throughout the evening, which I spent at a theatre with some American friends, I found myself constantly thinking of Adderley and the ivory casket, of the mandarin of Johore Bahru, and of the mystery of the shrivelled yellow hand.

I had been back in my room about half an hour, I suppose, and it was long past midnight, when I was startled by a ringing of my telephone bell. I took up the receiver, and:

"Knox! Knox!" came a choking cry.

"Yes, who is speaking?"

"It is I, Adderley. For God's sake come round to my place at once!"

His words were scarcely intelligible. Undoubtedly he was in the grip of intense emotion.

"What do you mean? What is the matter?"

"It is here, Knox, it is here! It is knocking on the door! Knocking! Knocking!"

"You have been drinking," I said sternly. "Where is your man?"

"The cur has bolted. He bolted the moment he heard that damned knocking. I am all alone; I have no one else to appeal to." There came a choking sound, then: "My God, Knox, it is getting in! I can see . . . the shadow on the blind . . ."

Convinced that Adderley's secret fears had driven him mad, I nevertheless felt called upon to attend to his urgent call, and without a moment's delay I hurried around to St. James's Street. The liftman was not on duty, the lower hall was in darkness, but I raced up the stairs and found to my astonishment that Adderley's door was wide open.

"Adderley!" I cried. "Adderley!"

There was no reply, and without further ceremony I entered and searched the chambers. They were empty. Deeply mystified, I was about to go out again when there came a ring at the door-bell. I walked to the door and a policeman was standing upon the landing.

"Good evening, sir," he said, and then paused, staring at me curiously.

"You are not the gentleman who ran out awhile ago," he said, a note of suspicion coming into his voice.

"Good evening, constable," I replied.

I handed him my card and explained what had occurred, then:

"It must have been Mr. Adderley I saw," muttered the constable.

"You saw—when?"

"Just before you arrived, sir. He came racing out into St. James's Street and dashed off like a madman."

"In which direction was he going?"

"Toward Pall Mall."

The neighbourhood was practically deserted at that hour. But from the guard on duty before the palace we obtained our first evidence of Adderley's movements. He had raced by some five minutes before, frantically looking back over his shoulder and behaving like a man flying for his life. No one else had seen him. No one else ever did see him alive. At two o'clock there was no news, but I had informed Scotland Yard and official inquiries had been set afoot.

Nothing further came to light that night, but as all readers of the daily press will remember, Adderley's body was taken out of the pond in St. James's Park on the following day. Death was due to drowning, but his throat was greatly discoloured as though it had been clutched in a fierce grip.

It was I who identified the body, and as many people will know, in spite of the closest inquiries, the mystery of Adderley's death has not been properly cleared up to this day. The identity of the lady who visited him at his chambers was never discovered. She completely disappeared.

The ebony and ivory casket lies on my table at this present moment, visible evidence of an invisible menace from which Adderley had fled around the world. Doubtless the truth will never be known now. A significant discovery, however, was made some days after the recovery of Adderley's body.

From the bottom of the pond in St. James's Park a patient Scotland Yard official brought up the gold nail-case with its mysterious engravings—and it contained, torn at the root, the incredibly long finger-nail of the Mandarin Quong!

The Key of the Temple of Heaven

I

THE KEEPER OF THE KEY

The note of a silver bell quivered musically through the scented air of the ante-room. Madame de Medici stirred slightly upon the divan with its many silken cushions, turning her head toward the closed door with the languorous, almost insolent, indifference which one perceives in the movements of a tigress. Below, in the lobby, where the pillars of Mokattam alabaster upheld the painted roof, the little yellow man from Pekin shivered slightly, although the air was warm for Limehouse, and always turned his mysterious eyes toward a corner of the great staircase which was visible from where he sat, coiled up, a lonely figure in the *mushrabiyeh* chair.

Madame blew a wreath of smoke from her lips, and, through half-closed eyes, watched it ascend, unbroken, toward the canopy of cloth-of-gold which masked the ceiling. A Madonna by Leonardo da Vinci faced her across the apartment, the painted figure seeming to watch the living one upon the divan. Madame smiled into the eyes of the Madonna. Surely even the great Leonardo must have failed to reproduce that smile—the great Leonardo whose supreme art has captured the smile of Mona Lisa. Madame had the smile of Cleopatra, which, it is said, made Cæsar mad, though in repose the beauty of Egypt's queen left him cold. A robe of Kashmiri silk, fine with a phantom fineness, draped her exquisite shape as the art of Cellini draped the classic figures which he wrought in gold and silver; it seemed incorporate with her beauty.

A second wreath of smoke curled upward to the canopy, and Madame watched this one also through the veil of her curved black lashes, as the Eastern woman watches the world through her veil. Those eyes were notable even in so lovely a setting, for they were of a hue rarely seen in

human eyes, being like the eyes of a tigress; yet they could seem voluptuously soft, twin pools of liquid amber, in whose depths a man might
lose his soul.

Again the silver bell sounded in the ante-room, and, below, the little
yellow man shivered sympathetically. Again Madame stirred with that
high disdain that so became her, who had the eyes of a tigress. Her
carmine lips possessed the antique curve which we are told distinguished the lips of the Comtesse de Cagliostro; her cheeks had the
freshness of flowers, and her hair the blackness of ebony, enhancing the
miracle of her skin, which had the whiteness of ivory—not of African
ivory, but of that fossil ivory which has lain for untold ages beneath the
snows of Siberia.

She dropped the cigarette from her tapered fingers into a little silver
bowl upon a table at her side, then lightly touched the bell which stood
there also. Its soft note answered to the bell in the ante-room; a white-
robed Chinese servant silently descended the great staircase, his soft red
slippers sinking into the rich pile of the carpet; and the little yellow man
from the great temple in Pekin followed him back up the stair-way and
was ushered into the presence of Madame de Medici.

The servant closed the door silently and the little yellow man, fixing
his eyes upon the beautiful woman before him, fell upon his knees and
bowed his forehead to the carpet.

Madame's lovely lips curved again in the disdainful smile, and she
extended one bare ivory arm toward the visitor who knelt as a suppliant
at her feet.

"Rise, my friend!" she said, in purest Chinese, which fell from her
lips with the music of a crystal spring. "How may I serve you?"

The yellow man rose and advanced a step nearer to the divan, but
the strange beauty of Madame had spoken straight to his Eastern heart,
had awakened his soul to a new life. His glance travelled over the vision
before him, from the little Persian slipper that peeped below the dra-
pery of Kashmiri silk to the small classic head with its crown of ebon
locks; yet he dared not meet the glance of the amber eyes.

"Sit here beside me," directed Madame, and she slightly changed
her position with that languorous and lithe grace suggestive of a creature
of the jungle.

Breathing rapidly betwixt the importance of his mission and a new, intoxicating emotion which had come upon him at the moment of entering the perfumed room, the yellow man obeyed, but always with glance averted from the taunting face of Madame. A golden incense-burner stood upon the floor, over between the high, draped windows, and a faint pencil from its dying fires stole grayly upward. Upon the scented smoke the Buddhist priest fixed his eyes, and began, with a rapidity that grew as he proceeded, to pour out his tale. Seated beside him, one round arm resting upon the cushions so as almost to touch him, Madame listened, watching the averted yellow face, and always smiling—smiling.

The tale was done at last; the incense-burner was cold, and breathlessly the Buddhist clutched his knees with lean, clawish fingers and swayed to and fro, striving to conquer the emotions that whirled and fought within him. Selecting another cigarette from the box beside her, and lighting it deliberately, Madame de Medici spoke.

"My friend of old," she said, and of the language of China she made strange music, "you come to me from your home in the secret city, because you know that I can serve you. It is enough."

She touched the bell upon the table, and the white-robed servant reëntered, and, bowing low, held open the door. The little yellow man, first kneeling upon the carpet before the divan as before an altar, hurried from the apartment. As the door was reclosed, and Madame, found herself alone again, she laughed lightly, as Calypso laughed when Ulysses' ship appeared off the shores of her isle.

God fashions few such women. It is well.

II
THE TIGER LADY

"By heavens, Annesley!" whispered René Deacon, "what eyes that woman has!"

His companion, following the direction of Deacon's glance, nodded rather grimly.

"The eyes of a Circe, or at times the eyes of a tigress."

"She is magnificent!" murmured Deacon rapturously. "I have never seen so beautiful a woman."

His glance followed the tall figure as it passed into a smaller salon on the left; nor was he alone in his regard. Fashionable society was well represented in the gallery—where a collection of pictures by a celebrated artist was being shown; and prior to the entrance of the lady in the strangely fashioned tiger-skin cloak, the somewhat extraordinary works of art had engaged the interest even of the most fickle, but, from the moment the tiger-lady made her appearance, even the most daring canvases were forgotten.

"She wears tiger-skin shoes!" whispered one.

"She is like a design for a poster!" laughed another.

"I have never seen anything so flashy in my life," was the acrid comment of a third.

"What a dazzlingly beautiful woman!" remarked another—this one a man. While:

"Who is she?" arose upon all sides.

Judging from the isolation of the barbaric figure, it would seem that society did not know the tiger-lady, but Deacon, seizing his companion by the arm and almost dragging him into the small salon which the lady had entered, turned in the doorway and looked into Annesley's eyes. Annesley palpably sought to evade the glance.

"You know *everybody*," whispered Deacon. "You must be acquainted with her."

A great number of people were now thronging into the room, not so much because of the pictures it contained, but rather out of curiosity respecting the beautiful unknown. Annesley tried to withdraw; his uneasiness grew momentarily greater.

"I scarcely know her well enough," he protested, "to present you. Moreover—"

"But she's smiling at you!" interrupted Deacon eagerly.

His handsome but rather weak face was flushed; he was, as an old clubman had recently said of him, "so very young." He lacked the restraint usual in cultured Englishmen, and had the frankly passionate manner which one associates with the South. His uncle, Colonel Deacon, a mordant wit, would say apologetically:

"Reggie" (Deacon's father) "married a Gascon woman. She was delightfully pretty. Poor Reggie!"

Certainly René was impetuous to an embarrassing degree, nor lightly to be thwarted. Boldly meeting the glance of the woman of the amber eyes, he pushed Annesley forward, not troubling to disguise his anxiety to be presented to the tiger-lady. She turned her head languidly, with that wild-animal grace of hers, and unsmiling now, regarded Annesley.

"So you forget me so soon, Mr. Annesley," she murmured, "or is it that you play the good shepherd?"

"My dear Madame," said Annesley, recovering with an effort his wonted sang-froid, "I was merely endeavouring to calm the rhapsodies of my friend, who seemed disposed to throw himself at your feet in knight-errant fashion."

"He is a very handsome boy," murmured Madame; and as the great eyes were turned upon Deacon the carmine lips curved again in the Cleopatrian smile.

She was indeed wonderful, for while she spoke as the woman of the world to the boy, there was nothing maternal in her patronage, and her eyes were twin flambeaux, luring—luring, and her sweet voice was a siren's song.

"May I beg leave to present my friend, Mr. René Deacon, Madame de Medici?" said Annesley; and as the two exchanged glances—the boy's a glance of undisguised passionate admiration, the woman's a glance unfathomable—he slightly shrugged his shoulders and stood aside.

There were others in the salon, who, perceiving that the unknown beauty was acquainted with Annesley, began to move from canvas to canvas toward that end of the room where the trio stood. But Madame did not appear anxious to make new acquaintances.

"I have seen quite enough of this very entertaining exhibition," she said languidly, toying with a great unset emerald which swung by a thin gold chain about her neck. "Might I entreat you to take pity upon a very lonely woman and return with me to tea?"

Annesley seemed on the point of refusing, when:

"I have acquired a reputed Leonardo," continued Madame, "and I wish you to see it."

There was something so like a command in the words that Deacon stared at his companion in frank surprise. The latter avoided his glance, and:

"Come!" said Madame de Medici.

As of old the great Catherine of her name might have withdrawn with her suite, so now the lady of the tiger skins withdrew from the gallery, the two men following obediently, and one of them at least a happy courtier.

III

TWIN POOLS OF AMBER

The white-robed Chinese servant entered and placed fresh perfume upon the burning charcoal of the silver incense-burner. As the scented smoke began to rise he withdrew, and a second servant entered, who facially, in dress, in figure and bearing, was a duplicate of the first. This one carried a large tray upon which was set an exquisite porcelain tea-service. He placed the tray upon a low table beside the divan, and in turn withdrew.

Deacon, seated in a great ebony chair, smoked rapidly and nervous-ly—looking about the strangely appointed room with its huge picture of the Madonna, its jade Buddha surmounting a gilded Burmese cabinet, its Persian canopy and Egyptian divan, at the thousand and one costly curiosities which it displayed, at this mingling of East and West, of Christianity and paganism, with a growing wonder.

To one of his blood there was delight, intoxication, in that room; but something of apprehension, too, now grew up within him.

Madame de Medici entered. The garish motorcoat was discarded now, and her supple figure was seen to best advantage in one of those dark silken gowns which she affected, and which had a seeming of the ultra-fashionable because they defied fashion. She held in her hand an orchid, its structure that of an odontoglossum, but of a delicate green colour heavily splashed with scarlet—a weird and unnatural-looking bloom.

Just within the doorway she paused, as Deacon leaped up, and looked at him through the veil of the curved lashes.

"For you," she said, twirling the blossom between her fingers and gliding, toward him with her tigerish step.

He spoke no word, but, face flushed, sought to look into her eyes as she pinned the orchid in the buttonhole of his coat. Her hands were flawless in shape and colouring, being beautiful as the sculptured hands preserved in the works of Phidias.

The slight draught occasioned by the opening of the door caused the smoke from the incense-burner to be wafted toward the centre of the room. Like a blue-gray phantom it coiled about the two standing there upon a red and gold Bedouin rug, and the heavy perfume, or the close proximity of this singularly lovely woman, wrought upon the high-strung sensibilities of Deacon to such an extent that he was conscious of a growing faintness.

"Ah! You are not well!" exclaimed Madame with deep concern. "It is the perfume which that foolish Ah Li has lighted. He forgets that we are in England."

"Not at all," protested Deacon faintly, and conscious that he was making a fool of himself. "I think I have perhaps been overdoing it rather of late. Forgive me if I sit down."

He sank on the cushioned divan, his heart beating furiously, while Madame touched the little bell, whereupon one of the servants entered.

She spoke in Chinese, pointing to the incense-burner.

Ah Li bowed and removed the censer. As the door softly reclosed:

"You are better?" she whispered, sweetly solicitous, and, seating herself beside Deacon, she laid her hand lightly upon his arm.

"Quite," he replied hoarsely; "please do not worry about me: I am wondering what has become of Annesley."

"Ah, the poor man!" exclaimed Madame, with a silver laugh, and began to busy herself with the teacups. "He remembered, as he was looking at my new Leonardo, an appointment which he had quite forgotten."

"I can understand his forgetting anything under the circumstances."

Madame de Medici raised a tiny cup and bent slightly toward him. He felt that he was losing control of himself, and, averting his eyes, he stooped and smelled the orchid in his buttonhole. Then, accepting the cup, he was about to utter some light commonplace when the faintness returned overwhelmingly, and, hurriedly replacing the cup upon the tray, he fell back among the cushions. The stifling perfume of the place seemed to be choking him.

"Ah, poor boy! You are really not at all well. How sorry I am!"

The sweet tones reached him as from a great distance; but as one dying in the desert turns his face toward the distant oasis, Deacon turned weakly to the speaker. She placed one fair arm behind his head, pillowing him, and with a peacock fan which had lain amid the cushions fanned his face. The strange scene became wholly unreal to him; he thought himself some dying barbaric chief.

"Rest there," murmured the sweet voice.

The great eyes, unveiled now by the black lashes, were two twin lakes of fairest amber. They seemed to merge together, so that he stood upon the brink of an unfathomable amber pool—which swallowed him up—which swallowed him up. . . .

He awoke to an instantaneous consciousness of the fact that he had been guilty of inexcusably bad form. He could not account for his faintness, and reclining there amid the silken cushions, with Madame de Medici watching him anxiously, he felt a hot flush stealing over his face.

"What is the matter with me!" he exclaimed, and sprang to his feet. "I feel quite well now."

She watched him, smiling, but did not speak. He was a "very young man" again, and badly embarrassed. He glanced at his wrist-watch.

"Gracious heavens!" he cried, and noted that the tea-tray had been removed, "there must be something radically wrong with my health. It is nearly seven o'clock!"

The note of the silver bell sounded in the ante-room.

"Can you forgive me?" he said.

But Madame, rising to her feet, leaned lightly upon his shoulder, toying with the petals of the orchid in his buttonhole.

"I think it was the perfume which that foolish Ah Li lighted," she whispered, looking intently into his eyes, "and it is you who have to forgive me. But you will, I know!" The silver bell rang again. "When you have come to see me again—many, many times, you will grow to love it—because I love it."

She touched the bell upon the table, and Ah Li entered silently. When Madame de Medici held out her hand to him Deacon raised the white fingers to his lips and kissed them rapturously; then he turned, the Gascon within him uppermost again, and ran from the room.

A purple curtain was drawn across the lobby, screening the caller newly arrived from the one so hurriedly departing.

IV
THE LIVING BUDDHA

It was past midnight when Colonel Deacon returned to the house. René was waiting for him, pacing up and down the big library. Their relationship was curious, as subsisting between ward and guardian, for these two, despite the disparity of their ages, had few secrets from one another. René burned to pour out his story of the wonderful Madame de Medici, of the secret house in Chinatown with its deceptively mean exterior and its gorgeous interior, to the shrewd and worldly elder man. That was his way. But Fate had an oddly bitter moment in store for him.

"Hallo, boy!" cried the Colonel, looking into the library; "glad you're home. I might not see you in the morning, and I want to tell you about—er—a lady who will be coming here in the afternoon."

The words died upon René's lips unspoken, and he stared blankly at the Colonel.

"I thought I knew all there was to know about pictures, antiques, and all that sort of lumber," continued Colonel Deacon in his rapid and off-hand manner. "Thought there weren't many men in London could teach me anything; certainly never suspected a woman could. But I've met one, boy! Gad! What a splendid creature! You know there isn't much in the world I haven't seen—north, south, east and west. I know all the advertised beauties of Europe and Asia—stage, opera, and ballet, and all the rest of them. But this one—Gad!"

He dropped into an arm-chair, clapping both his hands upon his knees. René stood at the farther end of the library, in the shadow, watching him.

"She's coming here to-morrow, boy—coming *here*. Gad! you dog! You'll fall in love with her the moment you see her—sure to, sure to! I did, and I'm three times your age!"

"Who is this lady, sir?" asked René, very quietly.

"God knows, boy! Everybody's mad to meet her, but nobody knows who she is. But wait till you see her. Lady Dascot seems to be acquainted with her, but you will see when they come to-morrow—see for your-self. Gad, boy! . . . what did you say?"

"I did not speak."

"Thought you did. Have a whisky-and-soda?"

"No, thank you, sir—good night."

"Good night, boy!" cried the Colonel. "Good night. Don't forget to be in to-morrow afternoon or you'll miss meeting the loveliest woman in London, and the most brilliant."

"What is her name?"

"Eh? She calls herself Madame de Medici. She's a mystery, but what a splendid creature!"

René Deacon walked slowly upstairs, entered his bedroom, and for fully an hour sat in the darkness, thinking—thinking.

"Am I going mad?" he murmured. "Or is this witch driving all London mad?"

He strove to recover something of the glamour which had mastered him when in the presence of Madame de Medici, but failed. Yet he knew that, once near her again, it would all return. His reflections were bitter, and when at last wearily he undressed and went to bed it was to toss restlessly far into the small hours ere sleep came to soothe his troubled mind.

But his sleep was disturbed: a series of dreadfully realistic dreams danced through his brain. First he seemed to be standing upon a high mountain peak with eternal snows stretched all about him. He looked down, past the snow line, past the fir woods, into the depths of a lovely lake, far down in the valley below. It was a lake of liquid amber, and as be looked it seemed to become two lakes, and they were like two great eyes looking up at him and summoning him to leap. He thought that he leaped, a prodigious leap, far out into space; then fell—fell—fell. When he splashed into the amber deeps they became churned up in a milky foam, and this closed about him with a strangle grip. But it was no longer foam, but the clinging arms of Madame de Medici! . . .

Then he stood upon a fragile bridge of bamboo spanning a raging torrent. Right and left of the torrent below were jungles in which moved tigerish shapes. Upon the farther side of the bridge Madame de Medici, clad in a single garment of flame-coloured silk, beckoned to him. He sought to cross the bridge, but it collapsed, and he fell near the edge of the torrent. Below were the raging waters, and ever nearing him the tigerish shapes, which now Madame was calling to as to a, pack of hounds. They were about to devour him, when—

He was crouching upon a ledge, high above a street which seemed to be vaguely familiar. He could not see very well, because of a silk mask tied upon his face, and the eyeholes of which were badly cut. From the ledge he stepped to another, perilously. He gained it, and crouching there, where there was scarce foothold for a cat, he managed fully to raise a window which already was raised some six inches. Then softly and silently—for he was bare-footed—he entered the room.

Someone slept in a bed facing the window by which he had entered, and upon a table at the side of the sleeper lay a purse, a bunch of keys, an electric torch, and a Service revolver. Gliding to the table René took the keys and the electric torch, unlocked the door of the room, and crept down a thickly carpeted stair to a room below. The door of this also he opened with one of the keys in the bunch, and by the light of the torch found his way through a quantity of antique furniture and piled up curiosities to a safe set in the farther wall.

He seemed, in his dream, to be familiar with the lock combination, and, selecting the correct key from the bunch, he soon had the safe open. The shelves within were laden principally with antique jewelery, statuettes, medals, scarabs; and a number of little leather-covered boxes were there also. One of these he abstracted, relocked the safe, and stepped out of the room, locking the door behind him. Up the stairs he mounted to the bedroom wherein he had left the sleeper. Having entered, he locked the door from within, placed the keys and the torch upon the table, and crept out again upon the dizzy ledge.

Poised there, high above the thoroughfare below, a great nausea attacked him. Glancing to the right, in the direction of the window through which he had come, he perceived Madame de Medici leaning out and beckoning to him. Her arm gleamed whitely in the faint light. A new courage came to him. He succeeded, crouched there upon the narrow ledge, in relowering the window, and leaving it in the state in which he had found it, he stood up and essayed that sickly stride to the adjoining. ledge. He accomplished it, knelt, and crept back into the room from which he had started. . . .

The head of an ivory image of Buddha loomed up out of the utter darkness, growing and growing until it seemed like a great mountain. He could not believe that there was so much ivory in the world, and he felt it with his fingers, wonderingly. As he did so it began to shrink, and shrink, and shrink, and shrink, until it was no larger that a seated human figure. Then beneath his trembling hands it became animate; it moved, extended ivory arms, and wrapped them about his neck. Its lips became carmine—perfumed; they bent to him . . . and he was looking into the bewitching face of Madame de Medici!

He awoke, gasping for air and bathed in cold perspiration. The dawn was just breaking over London and stealing grayly from object to object in his bedroom.

V

THE IVORY GOD

The great car, with its fittings of gold and ivory, drew up at the door of Colonel Deacon's house. The interior was ablaze with tiger lilies, and out from their midst stepped the fairest of them all—Madame de Medici, and swept queenly up the steps upon the arm of the cavalierly soldier.

All connoisseurs esteemed it a privilege to view the Deacon collection, and this afternoon there was a goodly gathering. Chairs and little white tables were dotted about the lawn in shady spots, and the majority of the company were already assembled; but when, in a wonderful golden robe, Madame de Medici glided across the lawn, the babel ceased abruptly as if by magic. She pulled off one glove and began twirling a great emerald between her slim fingers. It was suspended from a thin gold chain. Presently, descrying Annesley seated at a table with Lady Dascot, she raised the jewel languidly and peered through it at the two.

"Why!" exclaimed René Deacon, who stood close beside her, "that was a trick of Nero's!"

Madame laughed musically.

"One might take a worse model," she said softly; "at least he enjoyed life."

Colonel Deacon, who listened to her every word as to the utterance of a Cumæan oracle, laughed with extraordinary approbation.

There was scarce a woman present who regarded Madame with a friendly eye, nor a man who did not aspire to become her devoted slave. She brought an atmosphere of unreality with her, dominating old and young alike by virtue of her splendid pagan beauty. The lawn, with its very modern appointments, became as some garden of the Golden House, a pleasure ground of an emperor.

But later, when the company entered the house, and Colonel Deacon sought to monopolize the society of Madame, an unhealthy spirit of jealousy arose between René and his guardian. It was strange, grotesque, horrible almost. Annesley watched from afar, and there was something very like anger in his glance.

"And this," said the Colonel presently, taking up an exquisitely carved ivory Buddha, "has a strange history. In some way a legend has grown up around it—it is of very great age—to the effect that it must always, cause its owner to lose his most cherished possession."

"I wonder," said the silvern voice, "that you, who possess so many beautiful things, should consent to have so ill-omened a curiosity in your house."

"I do not fear the evil charm of this little ivory image," said Colonel Deacon, "although its history goes far to bear out the truth of the legend. Its last possessor lost his most cherished possession a month after the Buddha came into his hands. He fell down his own stairs—and lost his life!"

Madame de Medici languidly surveyed the figure through the upraised emerald.

"Really!" she murmured. "And the one from whom he procured it?"

"A Hindu usurer of Simla," replied the Colonel. "His daughter stole it from her father together with many other things, and took them to her lover, with whom she fled!"

Madame de Medici seemed to be slightly interested.

"I should love to possess so weird a thing," she said softly.

"It is yours!" exclaimed the Colonel, and placed it in her hands.

"Oh, but really," she protested.

"But really I insist—in order that you may not forget your first visit to my house!"

She shrugged her shoulders.

"How very kind you are, Colonel Deacon," she said, "to—a rival collector!"

"Now that the menace is removed," said Colonel Deacon with laboured humour, "I will show you my most treasured possession."

"So! I am greatly interested."

"Not even this rascal René," said the Colonel, stopping before a safe set in the wall, "has seen what I am about to show you!"

René started slightly and watched with intense interest the unlocking of the safe.

"If I am not superstitious about the ivory Buddha," continued the Colonel, "I must plead guilty in the case of the Key of the Temple of Heaven!"

"The Key of the Temple of Heaven!" murmured a lady standing immediately behind Madame de Medici. "And what is the Key of the Temple of Heaven?"

The Colonel, having unlocked the safe, straightened himself, and while everyone was waiting to see what he had to show, began to speak again pompously:

"The Temple of Heaven stands in the outer or Chinese City of Pekin, and is fabulously wealthy. No European, I can swear, had ever entered its secret chambers until last year. One of its most famous treasures was this Key. It was used only to open the special entrance reserved for the Emperor when he came to worship after his succession to the throne—that was, of course, before China became a Republic. The Key is studded almost all over with precious stones. Last year a certain naval man—I'll not mention his name—discovered the secret of its hiding-place. How he came by that knowledge does not matter at present. One very dark night he crept up to the temple. He found the Keeper of the Key—a Buddhist priest—to be sleeping, and he succeeded, therefore, in gaining access and becoming possessed of the Key."

A chorus of excited exclamations greeted this dramatic point of the story.

"The object of this outrage," continued the Colonel, "for an outrage I cannot deny it to have been, was not a romantic one. The poor chap wanted money, and he thought he could sell the Key to one of the native jewellers. But he was mistaken. He got back safely, and secretly offered it in various directions. No one would touch the thing; moreover, although of great value, the stones were very far from flawless, and not really worth the risks which he had run to secure them. Don't misunderstand me; the Key would fetch a big sum, but not a fortune."

"Yes?" said Madame de Medici, smiling, for the Colonel paused.

"He packed it up and addressed it to me, together with a letter. The price that he asked was quite a moderate one, and when the Key arrived in England I dispatched a check immediately. It never reached him."

"Why?" cried many whom this strange story had profoundly interested.

"He was found dead at the back of the native cantonments, with a knife in his heart!"

"Oh!" exclaimed Lady Dascot. "How positively ghastly! I don't think I want to see the dreadful thing!"

"Really!" murmured Madame de Medici, turning languidly to the speaker. "*I* do."

The Colonel stooped and reached into the safe. Then he began to take out object after object, box after box. Finally, he straightened himself again, and all saw that his face was oddly blanched.

"It's gone!" he whispered hoarsely. "The Key of the Temple of Heaven has been stolen!"

VI

MADAME SMILES

René entered his bedroom, locked the door, and seated himself on the bed; then he lowered his head into his hands and clutched at his hair distractedly. Since, on his uncle's own showing, no one knew that the Key of the Temple of Heaven had been in the safe, since, excepting himself (René) and the Colonel, no one else knew the lock combination, how the Key had been stolen was a mystery which defied conjecture. No one but the Colonel had approached within several yards of the safe at the time it was opened; so that clearly the theft had been committed prior to that time.

Now René sought to recall the details of a strange dream which he had dreamed immediately before awakening on the previous night; but he sought in vain. His memory could supply only blurred images. There had been a safe in his dream, and he—was it he or another?—had unlocked it. Also there had been an enormous ivory Buddha. . . . Yet, stay! it had not been enormous; it had been . . .

He groaned at his own impotency to recall the circumstances of that mysterious, perhaps prophetic dream; then in despair he gave it up, and stooping to a little secretaire, unlocked it with the idea of sending a note round to Annesley's chambers. As he did so he uttered a loud cry.

Lying in one of the pigeon-holes was a long piece of black silk, apparently torn from the lining of an opera hat. In it two holes were cut as if it were intended to be used as a mask. Beside it lay a little leather-covered box. He snatched it out and opened it. It was empty!

"Am I going mad?" he groaned. "Or—"

"You are wanted on the 'phone, sir."

It was the butler who had interrupted him. René descended to the telephone, dazedly, but, recognizing the voice of Annesley, roused himself.

"I'm leaving town to-night, Deacon," said Annesley, "for—well, many reasons. But before I go I must give you a warning, though I rely on you never to mention my name in the matter. Avoid the woman who calls herself Madame de Medici; she'll break you. She's an adventuress, and has a dangerous acquaintance with Eastern cults, and I can't explain properly. . . ."

"Annesley! the Key!"

"It's the theft of the Key that has prompted me to speak, Deacon. Madame has some sort of power—hypnotic power. She employed it on me once, to my cost! Paul Harley, of Chancery Lane, can tell you more about her. The house she's living in temporarily used to belong to a notorious Eurasian, Zani Chada. To make a clean breast of it I daren't thwart her openly; but I felt it up to me to tell you that she possesses the secret of post-hypnotic suggestion. I may be wrong, but I think *you* stole that Key!"

"I!"

"She hypnotized you at some time, and, by means of this uncanny power of hers, ordered you to steal the Key of the Temple of Heaven in such and such a fashion at a certain hour in the night . . ."

"I had a strange seizure while I was at her house. . ."

"Exactly! During that time you were receiving your-hypnotic orders. You would remember nothing of them until the time to execute them— which would probably be during sleep. In a state of artificial somnambulism, and under the direction of Madame's will, you became a burglar!"

As Madame de Medici's car drove off from the house of Colonel Deacon, and Madame seated herself in the cushioned corner, up from amid the furs upon the floor, where, dog-like, he had lain concealed, rose the little yellow man from the Temple of Heaven. He extended eager hands toward her, kneeling there, and spoke:

"Quick! quick!" he breathed. "You have it? The Key of the Temple."

Madame held in her hand an ivory Buddha. Inverting it she unscrewed the pedestal, and out from the hollow inside the image dropped a gleaming Key.

"Ah!" breathed the yellow man, and would have clutched it; but Madame disdainfully raised her right hand which held the treasure, and with her left hand thrust down the clutching yellow fingers.

She dropped the Key between her white skin and the bodice of her gown, tossing the ivory figure contemptuously amid the fur.

"Ah!" repeated the yellow man in a different tone, and his eyes gleamed with the flame of fanaticism. He slowly uprose, a sinister figure, and with distended fingers prepared to seize Madame by the throat. His eyes were bloodshot, his nostrils were dilated, and his teeth were exposed like the fangs of a wolf.

But she pulled off her glove and stretched out her bare white hand to him as a queen to a subject; she raised the long curved lashes, and the great amber eyes looked into the angry bloodshot eyes.

The little yellow man began to breathe more and more rapidly; soon he was panting like one in a fight to the death who is all but conquered. At last he dropped on his knees amid the fur . . . and the curling lashes were lowered again over the blazing amber eyes that had conquered.

Madame de Medici lowered her beautiful white hand, and the little yellow man seized it in both his own and showered rapturous kisses upon it.

Madame smiled slightly.

"Poor little yellow man!" she murmured in sibilant Chinese, "you shall never return to the Temple of Heaven!"

ABOUT S. T. JOSHI

S. T. JOSHI is the author of *The Weird Tale* (1990), *H. P. Lovecraft: The Decline of the West* (1990), and *Unutterable Horror: A History of Supernatural Fiction* (2012). He has prepared corrected editions of H. P. Lovecraft's work for Arkham House and annotated editions of Lovecraft's stories for Penguin Classics. He has also prepared editions of Lovecraft's collected essays and poetry. His exhaustive biography, *H. P. Lovecraft: A Life* (1996), was expanded as *I Am Providence: The Life and Times of H. P. Lovecraft* (2010). He is the editor of the anthologies *American Supernatural Tales* (Penguin, 2007), *Black Wings* I–VI (PS Publishing, 2010, 2012, 2013), *A Mountain Walked: Great Tales of the Cthulhu Mythos* (Centipede Press, 2014), *The Madness of Cthulhu* (Titan Books, 2014–15), and *Searchers After Horror: New Tales of the Weird and Fantastic* (Fedogan & Bremer, 2014). He is the editor of the *Lovecraft Annual, Spectral Realms,* and *Penumbra* (all published by Hippocampus Press). Among his works of fiction are *The Recurring Doom: Tales of Mystery and Horror* (Sarnath Press, 2019) and *Something from Below* (PS Publishing, 2019).

www.ingramcontent.com/pod-product-compliance
Lightning Source LLC
Chambersburg PA
CBHW070445030726
47503CB00004B/901